Read all of the adventures in the Ari Ara Series!
The Way Between, The Lost Heir, and Desert Song

The Way Between

Between flight and fight lies a mysterious third path called *The Way Between,* and young shepherdess and orphan Ari Ara must master it . . . before war destroys everything she loves! She begins training as the apprentice of the great warrior Shulen, and enters a world of warriors and secrets, swords and magic, friendship and mystery.

The Lost Heir

Going beyond dragon-slayers and sword-swingers, *The Lost Heir* blends fantasy and adventure with social justice issues in an unstoppable story that will make you cheer! Mariana Capital is in an uproar. The splendor of the city dazzles Ari Ara until she makes a shocking discovery . . . the luxury of the nobles is built by the forced labor of the desert people.

Desert Song

Exiled to the desert, Ari Ara is thrust between the warriors trying to grab power . . . and the women rising up to stop them! Every step she takes propels her deeper into trouble: her trickster horse bolts, her friend is left for dead, and Ari Ara has to run away to save him. But time is running out - can she find him before it's too late?

Praise for the Ari Ara Series:
The Way Between & The Lost Heir
by Rivera Sun

"Ms. Sun has created a world filled with all the adventure and fun of mystics, martial arts, and magic contained in *The Hobbit, The Ring Trilogy*, and the *Harry Potter* series but with deeper messages. There are not enough superlatives to describe this series!" - **Brenda Duffy, Retired Teacher**

"In this book Rivera Sun pulls off an impressive feat, creating an original exciting story that deftly teaches ways to create a world that works for all. Thank you, Rivera Sun, for another outstanding contribution to the field of nonviolence through this series!" - **Kit Miller, Executive Director, M.K. Gandhi Institute for Nonviolence**

"I highly recommend gathering the children around you and reading *The Way Between* and *The Lost Heir* so everyone can enjoy and embrace these masterfully-told, exciting adventures." - **Scotty Bruer, Founder of PeaceNow**

"I highly recommend this novel to adults and children alike. You will be inspired by Ari Ara!" - **Angela Parker, Mother and Board Member of the Social Justice Center of Marin**

"Rivera Sun is an amazing author. The way she threads the principles of nonviolence into the fabric of her novels is a beautiful experience. It is an education that everyone in the world needs - now more than ever." - **Heart Phoenix, River Phoenix Center for Peacebuilding**

"During times when so many of us, especially the young, are still figuring out how to make this planet more just and livable, this book couldn't have come at a better time." - **Patrick Hiller, War Prevention Initiative**

Desert Song

-a Trickster Horse, a Girl in Exile, and the Women Rising Up-

with love,

Desert Song

Copyright © 2020 by Rivera Sun

Rising Sun Press Works
P.O. Box 1751, El Prado, NM 87529
www.riverasun.com

Library of Congress Control Number:
2019910539

ISBN (paperback) 978-1-948016-04-9
(hardback) 978-1-948016-07-0
(ebook) 978-1-948016-08-7
Sun, Rivera 1982-
Desert Song

For my mother, Kathryn Simonds

Other Works
by Rivera Sun

Novels, Books & Poetry
The Way Between
The Lost Heir
Desert Song
The Adventures of Alaren
The Dandelion Insurrection
The Roots of Resistance
The Dandelion Insurrection Study Guide
Rise & Resist
Billionaire Buddha
Steam Drills, Treadmills, and Shooting Stars
Rebel Song
Skylandia: Farm Poetry From Maine
Freedom Stories: volume one
The Imagine-a-nation of Lala Child

RISING SUN PRESS WORKS

A Community Published Book Supported By:

Karen Lane
Bruce Nygren
Maja Bengtson
DeLores H. Cook
Sid Sibo
Cody Riechers
Jayanne Sindt
The Learning Council
Brian Cummings
Shelagh Bocoum
CV Harquail
Sofian & Shefer Family
Gerry Henkel
Barbara Gerten
Caitlin Waddick and Ursula, Anika, Rustum, and Asim Zia
Darien & Glenn Cratty
Johnny Mazzola
Marirose NightSong
Daniel Podgurski
Jeralita Costa
Elizabeth Cooper
Leslie A. Donovan
Dolly, Xyler, and Adam Vogal
Ken and Gail Kailing
Manny Hotchkiss and Mary Ryan-Hotchkiss
Rosa Zubizarreta
Kristi Branstetter
JoAnn Fuller
Joe and Bella Schenk
Annie Kelley, Multifaith Peaceweaver
Ka'imi Nicholson, Wayne Bow & Ari Bow
Andrew S. Oliver
David Spofford

Jaige, Adam and Aubrey
Deborah Cooper
Scott Springer, Class Teacher, The Bay School
Beverly Campbell
Leah Boyd
Beth Remmes

. . . and many more!

Thank you.

Desert Song

by

Rivera Sun

Table of Contents

Table of Contents, cont.

CHAPTER ONE

. . . . .

The Ancestor Wind

The Ancestor Wind played across the mountains. It leapt the peaks and tickled the bellies of the valleys. It was the breath of the world, from a newborn's first gasp to an elder's last sigh. The Ancestor Wind filled the lungs of the living and lifted the weightless souls from the old husks of their bodies. Carried by the wind, the spirits of the ancestors roamed across the sky that stretched endlessly above the desert. Unseen, they slid on the soft hiss of the breeze into villages to whisper advice in the ears of their descendants. They howled warnings in the edges of storms. They slipped into dreams and guided the fates of the people.

The Ancestor Wind carried the spirits like an invisible, unruly horse leaping for the sheer joy of motion, diving for the thrill of plummeting, laughing for the delight of existing. The wind knocked the treetops dizzy and tried - in vain - to topple the eternal stones. It ran unseen fingers through long pine needles and chuckled over craggy boulders clinging to steep slopes. It dove through the pass and skidded to an astonished halt.

A hundred ... a thousand ... two thousand ... three thousand or more people marched steadily along the worn dirt road. The scent of the distant riverlands clung to them, but their features marked them as sons and daughters of the desert. The wind swirled in delighted recognition: the water workers were returning at last.

For too many years, the Ancestor Wind had watched these people leave, sorrow riding their backs as they sold their labor to their enemies in exchange for the precious water needed by their families in the desert. Just weeks ago, the river that once trickled in miserly grumbles had suddenly swelled into full-bodied laughter. Set free from the dam in the riverlands of Mariana, water surged into the dry fields of the desert. In the silt-laden mouth of the mountain pass, astonished farmers sang to welcome the water's return before channeling it into irrigation ditches. The spring would burst green this year, lifting that sacred color across the valleys and plains.

Delighted at the return of all things living and green, the Ancestor Wind sprang aloft, charging toward the high white plumes of the towering clouds, dancing in the realm of light and air. Then it dove back down to the people who walked in a long snake through the Middle Pass. The wind rippled gleefully and wound through their heads and shoulders, purring like a cat.

"The Ancestor Wind comes to greet us!" a man cried.

A cheer rose at the words of Tahkan Shirar, the man the Marianans called the Desert King. In his own people's eyes, he was not a king; he was their Harrak-Mettahl, their honor-keeper, a role the Marianans had no words to describe. Tahkan Shirar was craggy, like the mountains; bronzed by sun and experience. His grey-green eyes shone like twin springs in the dry lines of his weathered face. His comment echoed through the long line of walkers, bringing tears to eyes and smiles to

2

faces. Heads lifted. Hearts surged in chests. Three thousand people raised their fingers to the wind to catch its blessing. The scent of heat and bitter herbs flooded their nostrils. Memories of their beloved desert swelled in their hearts as the wind touched their heads in benediction. It rippled the copper hair of a young girl and paused.

This one was different.

The scent of water and distant lands clung to her, along with hints of a childhood in the shadows of the massive trees on the High Mountain slopes. The girl was formed by rain, moss, dark pines, and black stones. The Ancestor Wind studied her. She must be the one the black hawk had spoken about, the girl raised by the Fanten women, but not a Fanten; trained among warriors, but not a warrior; child of the river queen, but not accepted as their royal heir; daughter of the desert who had never seen the sands; the one whose name meant *not this, not that, but everything possible in between*: Ari Ara de Marin en Shirar, the Lost Heir to Two Thrones.

A mass of copper curls flung out wildly from her head. Wiry muscles ran tight to bones. The girl was strongly built, lean rather than willowy. At twelve-and-a-half, her features had the look of stretched canvas. It was the mark of growth. Caught between ages, Ari Ara still laughed with her child's honest peal of delight, but also tripped over feet that had grown longer than her experience. When she thought no one was watching, her blue-grey eyes tracked the motions of the older girls, surveying the terrain she would soon trek across.

The Ancestor Wind saw all of this in a swift sweep of scrutiny. Before the girl's curls had settled from its ruffling touch, the wind moved on to her companions. A riverlands warrior with night-dark hair chatted companionably with the youngest sister of the Desert King. She had been gone six long years. The scents of fog and moss clung to the dry iron of her desert blood. Beside her walked an old warrior. The wind swirled in surprise. Years ago, this scarred, grey-haired man had come to these lands bearing peace and love. Years later, he returned, heralding war and death. Now, Shulen walked beside Tahkan Shirar like a friend. The desert dwellers smiled at him, welcoming him instead of fighting him, celebrating him instead of fearing him.

Confused, the wind swept up to the high crosscurrents to ask the messenger hawks for news. While the wind raced the clouds, it carried the tidings to the mountains peaks: the Desert King was returning with his people and his daughter . . . and he brought the water and an old enemy with him.

Further west along the snake-bends of the pass, a woman built of rage and muscle, bitterness and blood, tilted her head to the wind. Strands of auburn-dark hair whipped her cheeks and clung to the hard facets of Moragh Shirar's face. The wind whispered its secrets in her ear: water, her sister, her brother the Desert King, her long-lost niece . . . and *him*, the enemy.

Her lips pulled back from her teeth in a snarl. Under her, a roan horse stilled, hide rippling with tension, preparing for the battle cry he sensed building in the storm of the woman's fury.

Shulen the Butcher had returned, the man whose heart was hard enough to bash in heads, whose very skin protected him like stone armor, whose hands were stained with the blood of her people . . . including her beloved's.

She would die before she let his feet touch her lands. Let others sing his praises for finding her brother's daughter. That did not excuse him from losing her in the first place. Let fools forgive and forget how he had led the War of Retribution, charging into battles based on lies. The death of his wife and child along with the riverlands queen was no excuse for the murder of her people.

Moragh Shirar wheeled her horse in the direction of the wind's whispers. She was a taut arrow of sinew and strength, green eyes narrowed under her mane of hair, muscles clenched with long-held hate, throat roughened with battle cries. When she rode, the warrior women followed, leather tunics supple and tough, skin weathered by the elements, lives armed with ferocity and courage. These were the Black Ravens, sisters cloaked in mourning black, harbingers of war, talon and beak ready for vengeance, the emblem of two wings emblazoned on their backs.

Moragh and her riders galloped onward. Shulen the Butcher would pay for his crimes.

Above them, the ravens wheeled. Their caws sent a shiver through the wind.

CHAPTER TWO

. . . . .

The Way Station

The pass filled with the swell of song. Thousands of voices reverberated off the slopes and thundered like a flood through the curving mountains. Song flowed like the wind through the desert people. It accompanied their morning prayers and lulled small children into sleep at dusk. It was the link from the past to the future. It was how the living threaded the wisdom of the ancestors into the world they would leave to their descendants. The melody they sang was an old one, known to every person since childhood - except for the girl who hummed along and tried to learn the words in a language that still felt strange on her tongue.

Ari Ara let the verses wash over her. Later, by the evening fire, she would ask someone to teach her the words. For now, she simply let the eddies and currents of the song flood through her until the music rippled out her limbs into dance. Enthralled in the song, her banishment did not matter. Her exile from the lush riverlands of her mother's people did not bother her. Her difference from her father's desert people did not worry her. The otherness of her amber skin next to their deeper bronze tones, the strangeness of their language on her tongue, the pounding of her heart as they neared the foreign land that was to be her home-in-exile . . . all of this dropped away like a shed snake skin as she danced. She drew her focus inside her limbs, and shut out everything but the narrow world of motion and momentum, rhythmic heartbeats and pounding blood.

"Look out!"

Her father's cry broke her reverie. His strong hands shot out and snatched her back from the path of her next leap. A snake slithered out from under the white sand that lined the edges of the road. The serpent stared balefully at them, coiling against a large stone, hissing and defensive. Its forked tongue flicked out.

"Just a little sand serpent," Tahkan Shirar told his daughter with a sigh of relief, naming the non-poisonous species, "but you never know what's under the sand."

The desert was an unforgiving land; its punishments for inattention and ignorance were swift and absolute. Desert children her age knew better than to leap without looking. They stepped with caution and awareness. Tahkan Shirar did not want his daughter to lose the wild abandon and bold courage of her upbringing in the High Mountains, but it must be tempered if she were to survive in these lands.

"The sands are always speaking to you, daughter," he told her gently as she stared back at the harmless snake. He showed her the parallel furrows she had blithely danced over. "These lines were a warning that our serpent friend slept peacefully beneath the sun-warmed sand. It's best not to wake a sleeping snake. Like any of us, he doesn't enjoy a rude awakening. If it had been a blue adder, you would have been dead upon minutes of your meeting."

A shudder ran through them both. To ease the shock still clenching her muscles, Tahkan steered her down the path, showing her other messages in the sand. Here, a grouse hid her eggs. There, a cluster of jagged, grey shale revealed the possibility of finding flint stones to strike life into fire.

"And here," Tahkan said, pointing to a darker circle in the light sand, "is a great blessing in our dry desert. Can you guess what this is? I will give you a hint: your aunt is named after this."

"A hidden spring!" Ari Ara exclaimed, glancing at the younger of her father's two sisters. Mirrin Shirar had lived in hiding during the War of Retribution, preserving the Shirar family lineage in case her siblings, Tahkan and Moragh, had died in battle. Afterwards, she had changed her name to Mahteni to enter Mariana - the homelands of their enemies - as a water worker ... and a spy for her brother, seeking his missing daughter.

Ari Ara helped her father dig the moist sand into a shallow bowl. They crouched on their heels as the water pooled and the sand settled. People walked past them, nodding respectfully to their Harrak-Mettahl, the honor-keeper whom the Marianans mistakenly called the Desert King. The desert culture had no equivalent to the Marianan royals. They called no man "king". No woman could command them as queen. When Tahkan had married Alinore, the Queen of Mariana, the official documents denying her and all her descendants and relatives any control, ownership, or dominion over the desert could have filled a book. The descendants of King Shirar had long ago renounced the ways of monarchy. Instead, the Shirars passed on the role of honor-keeper as a family lineage, generation after generation. They *earned* their people's respect by showing them how to uphold and restore *harrak* - the honor, integrity, and dignity of the people. Among the desert people, Ari Ara was heir only to the potential of following in the Shirar family lineage of honor-keeping.

Tahkan snorted softly under his breath. To a Marianan, that would be a paltry inheritance compared to the vast wealth of their royal family. But, to a Harraken, fortunes were shameful. Only one's honor mattered. Harrak was the greatest treasure of the desert, so much so that they called themselves the Harraken: the People of Honor, Dignity, and Integrity.

Ari Ara shifted impatiently. Tahkan hid his smile. The girl was twelve-and-a-half, but she had yet to learn the patience that marked desert girls of her age. The lives of her peers were shaped by slow-moving time, wide-open spaces, endless skies, and the vast quiet that served as the backdrop to the beauty of the desert songs. It was a far cry from the hustle and bustle of the raucous Mariana Capital. The desert girls absorbed patience from the pace of their daily lives. Even her High Mountain childhood hadn't taught Ari Ara that quality.

"Is it ready yet?" she asked, cupping her hand to the surface of the water.

But the sinewy man did not answer her. He gestured for her to be quiet and lifted his head to the wind. He stilled. A sense of power radiated from him like summer heat off a black stone. As people passed, their eyes glanced to see what made him pause. He offered a flash of a smile to reassure them and gestured for them to continue walking down the dusty road.

"What's wrong?" Ari Ara asked.

"Shhh," Tahkan hushed her. "Let me listen to the wind."

He rose to standing. Strands of hair the color of burnished copper slid loose from the tie at the nape of his neck. Calloused hands brushed them back. He shaded his eyes. In the hard blue of the sky, a raven wheeled overhead.

"Trouble?" Shulen murmured, pausing by the other man's side. The Marianan warrior bore his history in his scars. His build ran in bands of muscles hardened by a lifetime of training. His iron-grey hair was tied back at the base of his skull. The blue eyes of his youth had faded into slate. Deep grooves furrowed the planes in his face. An air of quiet clung to him along with the qualities of time-weathered stone.

"Moragh," Tahkan said, pointing to the bird overhead. The two exchanged a long, silent look. Tahkan Shirar gripped his friend's shoulder.

"We are nearly at the old Way Station ruins," he said to the older man. "Take the girl - and Emir Miresh, who knows what she'd do at the sight of a young Marianan warrior like him - and wait for my message. The rest of us will make camp by the river and await my sister. I will talk sense into her, somehow."

Both men wore identical, grim expressions. Matching prayers swift and silent appealed to the ancestors for protection. Moragh Shirar could dance the death dance of divine warriors. She could call lightning to heel like a dog. When she was clear-eyed, she was sheer magic. But when madness lay upon her like a second skin, Moragh was a devil-wind, a demon-monster, unstoppable and unpredictable.

To the side of the road, a footpath broke away, zigzagging up the slopes of scree and boulders. Shulen collected the two youths and left the bustle of the water workers behind. Low shrubs dotted the mountainside. Scraggly grasses grew close to slanted rocks, drinking the sparse moisture gathered by the leaning slabs of stone.

"Where are we going?" Ari Ara asked Shulen, leaping from one boulder to the next as they picked their way up the steep slope.

Emir Miresh trailed silently behind Shulen, his dark eyes observant and alert. The eighteen-year-old read the tension in the old warrior's shoulders. He signaled to the younger girl to leave their teacher alone. She glared back at the black-haired youth for a moment then ignored him. Emir Miresh, quiet and self-contained, the finest warrior in Mariana, had chosen to follow his mentor into exile. He stood as tall as grey-haired Shulen, slight and lithe as a cat, but strong, armed with the watchfulness of his warrior training, still and calm from his lessons in the Way Between. That ancient practice was neither fight nor flight, violence nor avoidance, but everything else possible in between. He and Ari Ara were Shulen's first apprentices in the practice. It had been founded thousands of years ago by Alaren, the younger brother of the two kings who ruled the ever-feuding nations on either side of the Border Mountains.

"We are going to Alaren's Way Station," Shulen replied, as Ari Ara hopped down onto the path and skipped backwards in front of him, impatient for his answer. "Or rather, the ruins of it."

He did not tell them about the dangers that neared on the road below.

A yelp of delight shot out of the girl. She darted ahead in excitement, red hair bobbing behind her like a torch. Emir cupped his hands to his mouth to call her back, but Shulen shook his head.

"Let her go," he requested, studying the muscled youth pensively. Emir Miresh was the son he never had: disciplined, deeply loyal, and fiercely protective. Since childhood, he had trained for and served as a royal bodyguard, first to Ari Ara's cousin, then to her. Shulen gripped his shoulder.

"Trouble nears," he told Emir. "An old blood debt must be settled."

The youth's face grew grave.

"If anything happens to me - " Shulen began.

"It won't," Emir protested.

"Regardless," the older man continued in a steady tone, "you must watch over Ari Ara. She is the Marianan heir in spite of the nobles' banishment."

"I can't imagine the Harraken wish her ill," Emir argued.

Shulen's slate-grey eyes swept up the towering slopes of boulders and pines.

"Her greatest danger is her youth," he answered. "Promise me you will try to steady her."

Again, Emir protested. Shulen cut him off.

"Promise me."

"I will."

Shulen clapped him on the back and gestured for him to go on ahead. He wanted to pick his way up the trail more slowly. He was not an old man, but the weight of his years pressed on him this afternoon. Guilt and grief, loss and loneliness wore him down like the eroded stones on the high peaks, whipped by sun and sleet, wind and lightning strikes. He wished his two apprentices had another handful of years between them. They needed more experience, maturity, and wisdom in case anything happened to him.

Enough of that, he chided himself, cutting off his dark musings. He was not likely to fall to Moragh Shirar's wrath. Even if he'd long passed his youth, he was still more than a match for any warrior. He straightened his shoulders. Moragh claimed a blood debt upon him and sought to duel to the death. He would not grant her such satisfaction - neither his life nor hers would be forfeited. He was not just an ordinary warrior, after all. Shulen was also the lineage holder of the Way Between. He would use its skills to face Moragh Shirar. There was no need to fight to the death.

Ahead, he heard the laughter of the youths as Ari Ara

pounced on Emir's back like a mountain lion. They were his pride and joy, those two, as dissimilar as oil and water, and yet each equally strong and determined. When they reached the outcropping that held the ruins, their excitement burst out in awed gasps. Thousands of years ago, when the world was young, Alaren had built a home along the East-West Road through the Middle Pass. Here, Alaren's Way Station had forged peace in difficult times. Now, all that remained were crumbling ruins.

An apt metaphor for the state of peace in our world, Shulen reflected wryly.

Alaren's practices had been abandoned. The Way Between had been forgotten. As people ignored the lessons of the middle path between fight and flight, the world plunged into unending wars and violence. The Way Between survived only in secrecy. For generations, Shulen's family had taught it only to their children. Then, the childless, grey-haired warrior had chosen Emir and Ari Ara as his apprentices. When the girl was discovered to be the long-lost heir, the Way Between had revived after the centuries of hiding.

This Way Station loomed legendary in the imaginations of the two youths. They had heard many stories of this place: here was the mountainside upon which Alaren had once walked; there was his turnip patch, now an eroded pile of rubble. Had his hand touched this rock? Had his footsteps tread beneath theirs? Ari Ara and Emir wandered, awestruck, exploring and speaking in hushed tones. They reverently touched the stones of the foundation, edges softened and rounded by the weathering of millenniums. Once, the Way Station had sat closer to the road and river. Time had traced its finger through the furrow of the pass. Over thousands of years, the bottom of the canyon had lowered. Now, the ruins overlooked the valley floor.

Shulen sat down on a flat slab that had once been Alaren's hearthstone. He had visited this site many times. As a boy, he had helped rebuild the retaining walls that struggled to preserve this place against the onslaught of erosion. A major earthquake or landslide would sever the ruins from the mountainside one day, but Shulen's lineage had prolonged the coming of that catastrophe, honoring the founder of their path by planting trees above the ancient site to hold the slope, and channeling water diversions around the sides. Shulen took a loaf of bread, a rind of cheese, a handful of dried apples, and some nuts out of his bag. He placed his waterskin beside the small meal. He closed his eyes to the warm, insistent press of sunlight, and pondered what to say to the youths when they returned from exploring the ruins, hungry for food and stories.

Centuries ago, during the Great Persecution, the followers of the Way Between had fled from Mariana into these Border Mountains. One by one, village after village, they were hunted down and executed. Shulen's family survived by hiding, by blending in with the nomadic shepherds that wandered these ranges. In secret, they preserved the teachings and trainings, but unlike their ancestors, they also trained in the Warrior's Way. Death snapped at their heels. Survival seemed to require sacrificing their beliefs. He stared out at the plume of dust rising from the road below. If his ancestors' fear, long ago, had not driven them to train their children in violence and warfare, that madwoman Moragh Shirar would not be seeking vengeance from him today.

"There may come a time in your life," he told his apprentices when the pair came to join him, "when you feel like violence is your only option. With every breath in your body, try to find and follow the Way Between instead."

He said this more for Emir's benefit than for Ari Ara. She

had been raised by the Fanten women in the High Mountains; their abhorrence of violence had been instilled in her. Emir had been trained in the ways of violence *and* in the Way Between. His path followed in Shulen's footsteps, and the old warrior did not want to see the youth's eyes shadowed with memories of battlefields.

"Is it better to die, then?" Emir asked, his dark eyebrows drawn together.

Shulen's shoulders lifted then fell.

"I cannot make that judgment for you," Shulen answered slowly. "I can only say that there have been many times when I faced a choice between killing or being killed, and you see the decision I made."

He spread his calloused hands. He was here. The other person was not.

"But long before those moments," he confessed, "my path was littered with choices - not easier ones, but choices that could have kept me out of that final deadly decision - and I chose to keep walking toward the need for violence."

The consequences haunted him still. One rode toward him even now, demanding payment in blood for her beloved wife's death. He cast a worried glance toward the ravine floor then abruptly changed subjects, allowing the youths to pepper him with questions about the Way Station. In the ruins, the old warrior told stories of peace to the youths, wishing he had listened more closely all those years ago.

Down below, Tahkan Shirar shaded his eyes and stared up at the mountainside. Shulen and the two youths were hidden behind the sightlines of the ridge. Relieved, he turned back to where the dust of the approaching riders rounded the last bend of the pass. The Black Ravens burst into view, a force of momentum and dust, creaking leather and pounding hoof beats.

A ripple of curiosity rose up from the encampment. Heads lifted. People turned. Eyes squinted into the cloud of dust. The riders halted. The plume parted. A cheer rose up at the sight of the fierce and proud women astride their tall, long-legged horses. Among her enemies, Moragh Shirar was a demon. Among her people, she was legendary.

"Sister," Tahkan called out, stepping forward.

"Where is he?"

Her words fell like stones, hard and uncompromising, stopping him in his tracks. The crowd of former water workers fell silent, shifting uneasily at the sudden tension between the siblings.

Tahkan Shirar clucked his tongue.

"What's this? No words of welcome? No proper greeting to your family?"

His voice echoed off the steep slopes, sharp with disapproval. His face smiled, but his eyes warned her to tread carefully. He reached his fingers out to her horse. The roan nuzzled his hand. Moragh stiffened. Her lips drew down in a horseshoe across her chin. A ritual greeting tumbled out of her, tossed down at his feet like a sack of grain. The words rang hollow; her mind was fixed on vengeance. Her blazing, half-wild eyes scanned the crowd.

"Shulen the Butcher, killer of our people, is not welcome in our land," she spat.

Her brother spoke swiftly, countering her view. The water workers had saved the warrior from execution by the Marianans; he had aided their return, taught them his skills, protected them . . . and found the missing child of the Shirar lineage.

"He cannot hide behind the girl, using her as a shield for the wrongs he has done," Moragh stated in her gravelly voice.

Tahkan gripped her knee, shaking it slightly. He could see the gleam of fury in her eyes. He sensed her magic scouring the crowd, searching for the warrior. He jostled her to break her focus. His sister fell into battle trances as swiftly as others dozed off in the noonday sun. He needed her clarity now.

"None of us are saints, sister. Leave it be. Shulen's recent deeds outweigh the others, good for bad and bad for good."

"How can you ignore the past? My wife is dead. Your wife is dead. Your daughter was only recently regained - "

"Silence."

Moragh's mouth moved. No sound came out. Quick as an attacking sand lioness, her glare raked its claws across his face. The people gasped, disturbed to see him use the power of Desert Speech to stop the words from coming out of his sister's mouth. Harrak-Tala was more than just a language; it bound and shaped reality. Tahkan Shirar could make visions dance upon his songs. He could call the ancestors down from the wind. He could stop an army in its tracks. But Moragh Shirar descended from the same lineage, wielded a similar power through the magic and incantation of her words. People edged away, nervously retreating from the sense of an impending fight.

"Do not use my losses to justify your hate," Tahkan growled. "And remember, the war left dead on all sides. We have all suffered. Let us not cause more pain."

The lioness of a warrior shook herself from top to bottom. Her jaw ground. Her eyes flashed. A guttural growl rumbled in her throat. Her horse danced sideways, whinnying as her rider struggled to break free of her brother's binding.

At last, Tahkan released her. She lifted her chin defiantly, but when she spoke, her words were measured.

"He cannot enter our lands. If he does, I will call upon our laws . . . he owes me a blood debt."

"I will not lose either of you to a death duel," her brother argued back. "Moragh, put away your sword, get off your horse, and let us talk this through."

"I will not break bread with that monster!"

"I did not say you had to," Tahkan replied evenly. "We shall talk, you and I . . . and Mahteni-Mirrin, unless your rage has clouded your eyes to the presence of our younger sister?"

The scold in his tone broke Moragh's heat like a thunderstorm on a summer day. Moragh testily dropped the subject. Her brother had always been able to dance verbal circles around her; his words were his strongest magic, rippling like water and clear as a spring. With an irate sigh, she swung her leg over the horse and leapt to the ground. Moragh strode forward to clasp hands with the younger sister she remembered as a laughing child, then a somber teenager, then a lonely young woman in hiding during the war. The years had stretched long since Mirrin went into the riverlands as the water worker Mahteni. She returned to the desert as a woman strong in her own counsel and confident in her abilities. The three Shirars walked down to the river where the chatter of water over stone concealed their words even from the prying ears of the wind.

They spoke until dusk, their words heated and intense, but at last, Tahkan left his sisters by the river and hiked up the footpath to the ruins of the Way Station. The light dwindled swiftly and he crossed the final rise guided only by the flickering light of the small fire the old warrior and the two youths had built. Hearing his footsteps crunching on the gravel of the path, Emir leapt up. He darted forward, silent as a shadow, to see who approached.

"It's the Desert King," he reported back.

Tahkan Shirar raised a hand in greeting as he hopped over

the low stone wall into the bowl of the ruins. They had set up a humble campsite, expecting to spend the night. If they were fortunate, Shulen had told the youths, they might receive a dream from Alaren's spirit. Tahkan and Emir settled down by the warmth of the fire. At this mountainous altitude, the stars brushed the peaks. Even this late in the spring, the heat of the day surrendered swiftly to the night.

"What did she say?" Shulen asked.

"Who?" Ari Ara demanded, curious as ever.

"Moragh," Tahkan and Shulen answered together.

"My *aunt* is here?" the girl yelped, astonished, craning her head down to the darkness-cloaked slope. Below, the campfires flickered like lightning bugs.

Tahkan tweaked her inquisitive nose to remind her that she was sticking it into a story that had not yet been told . . . but the girl had not grown up in the desert, so the meaning of the gesture was lost on her. She crossed her arms over her chest and lifted her eyebrows expectantly.

"Yes, your aunt," Tahkan answered with a sigh. "Your fierce, brave, magical, and absolutely mad Aunt Moragh came with her women warriors to demand our old friend here settle his blood debts."

"What?!" she cried.

Emir elbowed her to stop interrupting or the full story would never be told. He knew the debts Shulen owed the widows and grieving mothers of the desert. All warriors racked up such debts to the ones they robbed of a sibling, child, parent, friend, or lover.

"And?" Shulen queried.

"Moragh neither forgives nor forgets," Tahkan reported, poking the logs in the fire.

A shower of sparks rose and vanished. An uneasy quiet

grew.

"But," Tahkan finished, "she agrees to hold her hand until a village sing can decide if your role in returning the water and freeing our people outweighs your role in the war."

"What's a village sing?" Ari Ara asked, looking from one man to the other in confusion.

"It is how we decide things, in groups," Tahkan answered.

"Like the Nobles' Assembly?" she questioned, a shiver running up her spine. She hadn't enjoyed her encounters with that group of powerful figures in Mariana. They'd nearly started a war, rejected her claim of royal blood, exiled her along with Shulen, and thrown out her bid for the Marianan throne. Half of them still hoped she'd meet an early demise in the hot desert lands.

"No, our ways are different. Here, we believe that everyone is part of the Harraken Song - the collective music of all our voices, the song of all of our lives - and thus, everyone's voice must be heard in the village sings," Tahkan replied. "Though, in this case, it will be a city sing with the inhabitants of Turim City."

Ari Ara's eyes widened. She'd never heard of such a thing.

"And you sing?" she asked, frowning as she tried to imagine how that worked.

Tahkan smiled.

"Eventually," he replied with a chuckle. "After endless talking, we sing to see if we are in accord - *to sense if we're all on the same note*, as the saying goes. If some disagree, they raise a discordant sound and we go back to talking."

"What if they just can't sing?"

Tahkan laughed heartily.

"All Harraken can sing."

Then, quick as the mercurial mountain weather, the desert

man's bronze skin stretched taut over his cheekbones. The corners of his mouth drew downward in a frown.

"What is it?" Shulen pressed, a flurry of concern rising over his initial relief.

Tahkan's grey-green eyes lifted.

"My sister insists that you cannot set foot in the desert," Tahkan explained carefully. He held up his hand to halt the outbursts of the youths. "Until the city sing makes its decision, she reserves the right to collect your blood debt."

"She reserves only her right to try," Shulen remarked, implacable as always. He was not likely to be cut down by Moragh Shirar in a duel - not unless she called upon magic beyond his reckoning. Such tactics were forbidden in collecting blood debts, but when battle madness set in, the Desert King's sister did not constrain herself to mere mortal's rules. Shulen stared at the flames for a long moment then lifted his burning eyes to the cool ink of night. He waited until the white diamonds of stars returned to his sight. The moment he had been exiled along with Ari Ara, he had worried that this problem would arise.

"When does the city sing next meet?" he asked Tahkan.

"The city's sing is usually held when the light of the full moon floods the sands."

Shulen spread his hands toward the fire. He nodded. It was just over a week away.

"I will await word of their decision, then," he answered. "Though, I would ask you to remind everyone that I am not easily killed, even by Moragh Shirar."

He ignored the protests of his apprentices.

"I also warn you that if any harm comes to her," Shulen pointed at Ari Ara, "not even the ancestors will protect Moragh from my wrath."

Tahkan nodded grimly, tipping his head toward Emir Miresh.

"Moragh did not wish to grant him entry," he mentioned, "but I insisted that Emir Miresh be allowed to accompany us."

Tahkan stretched out a hand and laid it on Ari Ara's head. He did not expect any danger to his daughter from his people . . . but they could not know what might unfold. Someone, after all, had hunted down his wife all those years ago. Only last year, an assassin had tried to kill his daughter in the riverlands. Emir Miresh was the most highly trained member of the Marianan royal guard - after Shulen - and while he hoped the youth's abilities would not be needed, he also would not spurn the protection the young man offered. The desert was a land of harsh beauty and wild skies, evocative songs and proud people. It was a land of magic and legend . . . and a place of many dangers.

CHAPTER THREE

. . . . .

The City That Guards The Mountains

The first sight of the city halted Ari Ara in her tracks. A stone skittered over the edge of the road, knocking and clacking as it hit the boulders below. She shivered, struck silent by the sight of her new home. The expanse of sky above the wide plateau staggered her. Turim, the City That Guards the Mountains, crouched like a great beast readied to leap. The city bristled with defenses, all tooth and claw. Archers and guards patrolled the high wall that encircled the clustered buildings. Dwellings, storehouses, and work halls pressed close together, sharing walls of dun bricks and pale stone. Armed riders rode in sweeps around the fields that spread like a quilt beyond the city's gates. Irrigation ditches meandered in serpentine ribbons through the green sprouting crops. The river curled like a blue snake, down from the mountains, under a grated archway in the defensive wall, through the city, then down over the high cliffs at the back edge of the buildings. Beyond, white sand and chartreuse grasses rose and fell in sculpted waves until the distant horizon swallowed everything from view.

Looking out at the shining light and sweep of sands, Ari Ara felt the weight of her exile. A lump choked in her throat, one part thrilled excitement at the strangeness of this land, another part nervousness at the thought of making her home among her father's people. What if they didn't like her? What if they banished her, too? What if she disappointed Tahkan? A pang of loss for her old home - *homes,* she corrected - ripped through her. She clamped down on her sudden longing for the clear streams and black rocks of the High Mountains, or even the tiled roofs and tangled alleys of Mariana Capital.

Stop that, she told herself firmly. *You're being ridiculous.*

She wrinkled her nose, remembering what it was really like; she'd never truly belonged in any of the places she'd lived. The Fanten girls made fun of her bumbling lowlander ways. The monastery orphans had been leery of her High Mountain wildness. The capital's noble youths had mocked her for being a Fanten shepherdess. The street urchins had treated her with the aloof yet awestruck attitude appropriate for a legendary royal heir. Ari Ara straightened her spine. Strange as this place was, she couldn't go back to Mariana . . . she had to make her home here. She'd studied Harrak-Tala, the Desert Speech, on the long journey over the mountains. She'd memorized every song she heard around the evening campfires. She'd scrutinized the mannerisms and cultural quirks of the former water workers. For once, she was determined to fit in. She'd prove to her father that she belonged here with him.

A thud of hoof beats startled her. Moragh rode past, scowling. The black feathers tied to the ends of her hair fluttered like wings. A shadow flew overhead. Ari Ara glanced up. Where the Black Ravens rode, their cawing, beady-eyed birds followed. On the journey down the western slope of the Middle Pass, Ari Ara had seen the women warriors training the ravens to understand Desert Speech. The intelligent creatures could be used as scouts, spies, and messengers. They also attacked upon command, as ferocious as the warhorses of the Black Ravens. One swooped close, forcing Ari Ara to duck. Moragh laughed mockingly.

Ari Ara sighed. From the moment she had met her fierce warrior aunt, they'd been circling each other like a pair of alley cats, hackles up, hissing in distrust. Moragh and her Black Ravens had decided to escort the returning former water to Turim City. Throughout the journey, Ari Ara had often caught Moragh staring at her with brooding dislike, her eyes narrowed with suspicion. The warrior woman treated Emir Miresh with even harsher disdain, calling him the Butcher's Dog and refusing to speak to the youth directly. Emir stuck close as a shadow to Ari Ara when the woman was around. Worried that Moragh might use her battle magic on her niece in a fit of temper, Tahkan taught Ari Ara the Harrak-Tala word that warded off the binding effects of the desert language.

"If her madness veils her eyes," Tahkan told Ari Ara, "you must know how to counter her."

Ari Ara thought of this as Moragh kicked her roan into a canter and left Ari Ara coughing on her dust. Ahead of them, the water workers rounded the last bend of the long switchback road that led to the city. They lifted a song of exaltation at the sight of their homelands, the city heights, and the brimming green fields.

> *Green,* they sang, *the color of the sacred,*
> *the sign of life and living*
> *the burst of joy in living plants*
> *as the blue serpent coils*
> *through the fields.*

The song swelled around Ari Ara like a wave. Hands touched her head in gratitude as people passed. Fingers flicked from foreheads to the wind in blessing. Her father had warned her that her first glimpse of his lands might invoke sorrow: crumbling walls, tired goats chewing dry twigs, dusty fields lying fallow, a sea of sand slowly swallowing the land . . . but she saw none of that as they approached Turim City.

Instead, hope flickered like a spark catching the kindling's edge. People had flocked from all over the desert lands to help plant the fields this spring. Walls of buildings were being repaired. Fresh mud plaster had been applied over stacked stones. The sands had been thrust back from the marginal farmland. The shy green of fresh sprouts burst out everywhere. The mountains bloomed in an exuberant chartreuse. The lowlands shrubs gleamed silver green. Rows of fruit trees shimmered in alternating varieties, some fluttering with pale pink or shocking rose flowers, others showering white petals. The earliest blooming varieties were adorned with young leaves and tiny, hard fruits. Everywhere she looked, she saw green . . . and suddenly understood why, to the desert-dwelling people, green was the color of joy.

They entered Turim in the late afternoon. A row of flowering apricot trees stretched their boughs over the road into the city, welcoming the travellers with delicious shade. The townspeople tossed showers of fallen petals over their returning friends. Cries of delight and surprise punctuated the chanting song of welcome as families recognized kin. Former water workers leapt from the procession to embrace their relatives. The Harraken erupted in grins and joyful tears as they reunited.

At the center of the city, Tahkan waved away the cheers and curious stares, telling his people to go bathe, rest, and prepare for the feast that evening. He threw his arm over Ari Ara's shoulders and steered her past the throng. They slipped into a courtyard through a pair of intricately carved wooden doors. The ring of buildings bordered a luscious garden of flowering plants, ancient trees, and lichen-covered stones. A branch of the river curved through the space, singing its trickle-song sweetly. Despite the clamor of voices in the square, an aura of quiet sanctuary hovered in this calm courtyard.

"Is this your home?" she whispered to Tahkan.

"No," he laughed, "I'm afraid the Harrak-Mettahl does not dwell in such elegance. My bed is often nothing more than my cloak . . . though the canopy of stars outshines any man-made dwelling. This is a shared garden and gathering place, tended and used by all inhabitants of Turim City. It is an honor that they share it with you."

The upper story rooms served as guest quarters for visitors without family homes. The lower floor held a common kitchen, a gathering room, and a healers' hall. Everything was simply and lovingly tended. The Harraken prided themselves not on ornate treasures, but on inner riches of honor, community, culture, and connection.

The aroma of spices for the evening feast made Ari Ara's stomach growl. Tahkan chuckled and sent her off with Mahteni to the women's bathhouse. The pools of hot water seemed a wild luxury after six weeks of traveling over the mountains. She tugged the tangles out of her curls and scrubbed the grime out from under her nails. Out of her pack came her mother's dress of rare white silk. Mahteni eyed the creases and asked one of the women if she would freshen it up. A smile bloomed on the woman's face. She lifted the dress with reverence; it was famous in their lands. Later, when it returned shining and unwrinkled, Ari Ara put on the gown made with desert silk in a Marianan weave. The dress was cut in an open-backed Fanten style that showed the black lines of the Mark of Peace that had been inked between her shoulder blades at birth and proved she truly was her father's daughter.

"You've grown," Mahteni remarked in a tone of surprise. "That hem is three finger widths higher than it used to be."

Ari Ara stared at her ankles as they peeked out from under the skirt of the dress.

"Hold still," Mahteni insisted. "I'm going to braid this wild mane into a desert crown."

Ari Ara half-wished she could wear something else. This white dress made her stand out as a foreigner. The other girls wore dazzling layers of fine silks with billowing sleeves and flowing skirts. Long, sleeveless over-robes with intricate embroidered patterns belted above the other layers. Scarves wrapped in bands around pinned-up hair. For most of the year, the desert dwellers dressed in the shades of tan, fawn, and dun. Their daywear was made of simple, sturdy fabrics that blended humbly with the sand of their arid lands. But, on special occasions, such as celebrations and rituals, festivals and feast days, they brought out their famed silks and burst into bloom like the tiny, brilliant flowers of spring. For this evening's feast, every last Harraken shook the wrinkles out of their prized silk robes and drew brightly-colored dresses out from cedar trunks. They unrolled their ancestors' song sashes and tied them around their waists. They wrapped embroidered silk bracelets from wrists to elbows.

Even Emir Miresh had been offered fine robes, for all that he was an enemy warrior. When they returned to the courtyard at dusk, he drew stares as he took up his position at Ari Ara's side. His classic Marianan features - dark hair, light skin, and fine bones - proclaimed him every inch the foreigner. Emir took it all in stride, his face a trained mask of inscrutability, his eyes indicating no unease or discomfort.

Ari Ara envied him. A flutter of nerves clawed her stomach. Her eyes darted from one Harraken girl to the next, picking up visual cues on proper manners and behavior. She'd disregarded all those in Mariana Capital and wound up exiled. Here, she didn't have the luxury. There was nowhere left to go.

As she greeted people with her father, she felt fingers darting out to touch the Mark of Peace inked into her back, seeing if it - and she - were real. Throughout it all, Ari Ara tried to behave as a proper desert girl should. She mimicked the postures of the other girls. She cast her eyes downward and smiled bashfully at compliments.

"What's the matter with you?" Emir hissed in her ear with a worried look. "You're not getting sick, are you?"

Ari Ara groaned and gave up. She met eyes honestly - *boldly*, people whispered. She answered questions in her faltering Harrak-Tala - *such an accent*, they murmured. She laughed - *brash and loud*, they muttered. She shrugged her bare shoulders - *scandalously bare*, some grumbled. She stuck close to Tahkan; Emir stuck close to her - *what's that river dog boy doing here, anyway?* they complained. Her father beamed at her with unmistakable pride - *she's bewitched him just like her mother did*, they gossiped.

She saw contortions of emotion twisting their expressions. Fingers flicked from forehead to the wind in respect . . . or to ward away malevolent spirits. Her father had warned her of these reactions. She was his daughter, but she was also the daughter of their enemies. She bore his shock of copper hair and her mother's river-water eyes. The Harraken did not set her on an imagined pedestal, as the Marianans had once done to their Lost Heir - her desert father was not a king in his people's

31

eyes; her blood was not royal in that regard - but a war had been fought to find her and many people's loved ones had died because of her. On the other hand, she had won the Harraken water workers their freedom and returned the sweet singing water to the desert. Like Shulen, her reputation among these people was mixed. Ari Ara could feel their eyes measuring her up, wondering if she was worth the terrible sacrifice of the war.

Her cheeks burned with guilt and shame at this - she didn't think anything was worth the cost of war. There were always other ways to address a conflict; there was always a Way Between. A treaty could have allowed the Marianans to search the desert and the Harraken to search the riverlands. Or they could have formed joint teams to conduct searches together. Or they could have simply waited. A missing royal heir would not remain in hiding forever; at some point, the Lost Heir had to reappear to claim her birthright.

When the garden courtyard was crammed to the rafters and people lined the rooftops, Tahkan raised his hands for silence. He spoke the ritual words of welcome and celebration. He praised the blessing of reunions and returning hope.

"Let us feast and sing, together, as one people, past, present, and future . . . a future that looks bright and green, thanks to the water returned by my daughter's courage." He gestured for Ari Ara to stand next to him as the water workers lifted the piercing Honor Cry for her. "My daughter may be new to the desert, but the blood of a true Shirar runs in her veins. She may have much to learn of our songs, language, and ways, but she already understands harrak."

A smattering of incredulous murmurs rose at that bold statement. How could a foreigner understand harrak?

"Give her one year," Tahkan boasted, a smile bursting proudly from cheek to cheek, "and you will see that she will follow in her father's footsteps as our next harrak-mettahl!"

An explosion of sound erupted: cheers, whistles, clapping, but also uneasy rumbles, shocked gasps, hissed asides. Ari Ara could see the discord in the shadowed and glowing faces around the common fire. She shifted awkwardly from foot to foot, feeling nervous. Her cheeks burned with the high praise, but she also wished her father hadn't put such high expectations on her. Not yet. Not with the feel of Desert Speech still strange on her tongue.

Ari Ara sought Mahteni's reassurance, but was startled to see glowering disapproval scowling on her aunt's features. Her green eyes flashed angrily at Tahkan. Her throat worked over the words she swallowed. For a fleeting moment, she stabbed her niece with a glare of jealous resentment. Then, she saw the girl's startled expression and Mahteni dropped her anger.

"Not your fault," she murmured in Marianan to the girl. "He should not have said that."

She could see the questions building up in Ari Ara's face. Mahteni shook her head and mouthed: *later*. Her brother, oblivious to the tension, was passing the ritual cup of water around. The feast would soon be brought out. This was neither the time nor the place to start a quarrel about the succession of the role of harrak-mettahl; nor about whether or not Ari Ara could take up those duties. By Shirar tradition, both she and Ari Ara had equal rights to take up the role next. Mahteni agreed with her brother that the girl had the integrity and courage required by the position, but her niece was far from ready. Unlike Mahteni, she did not know the ways of the Harraken people. She was just learning their songs and language. She still spoke with a thick accent. Most of all, she couldn't sing like a Shirar; she couldn't pull visions out of thin air. Mahteni had seen her do it once, but Ari Ara needed more practice. She had to be able to sing the stars down from the sky, breathe life into the stories of the past, and call the ancestors down from the wind. Perhaps, one day, after years of training, she would be ready, but Tahkan should not have put pressure on her tonight. Mahteni could sense the girl squirming under the intensity of so many stares.

When the feast was carried out and the gazes shifted from Ari Ara to the food, a sigh of relief slipped from her. The welcoming feast, she happily discovered, was nothing at all like the stuffy royal receptions in Mariana. People mingled, shared dishes, licked fingers, laughed, sang, and swapped stories. After the feast, a hush fell. A sense of anticipation hung on the night air. The crackles and hiss of the common fire sounded loud against the sudden quiet. The press of the crowd grew as more figures squeezed into the courtyard. People lined the balconies and the rooftops. Mothers sat on the ground close to the fire and pulled children onto their laps. Men crouched on their heels behind them. Eyes swung to Tahkan Shirar. When the last whispers fell silent, the Ancestor Wind spoke, murmuring across the ink-and-diamond sky.

Tahkan Shirar began to sing.

Ari Ara had seen him evoke images on air, but each time, it raised the hair on her arms and sent tingles down her spine. The power of Desert Speech lifted in song brought the story to life, fashioning visions out of firelight and swirling smoke, shining darkness and ancient magic. Her father's voice did not have the flashy range and cultivated tones of a Marianan stage singer, but Tahkan Shirar expressed the heart and soul of his people. His singing rasped and cracked. It laughed at its edges and wept in its core. He captured the beauty and pain of living in an exquisite and embattled world. His wry grin sparked smiles on listeners' faces. His troubled eyes brought tears to others' gazes. Tahkan Shirar was a master of his profession: to keep the honor, dignity, and integrity of his people, to restore harrak if it was lost, and to remind them of who they truly were.

The songs rose around the common fire for hours. Hot tea was poured and sipped. The front rows near the fire changed places with the back. Children nestled in their parents' arms. In a world of light, heat, wind, and wide expanses of sky and plain, songs wove the Ancestor Wind into the lungs of the living and out into the future that unfolded in each step. There were songs to greet the rising sun and bid the setting sun farewell. There were songs to welcome the growing grass and to encourage the grain to cook. There were work songs for spinning and weaving. There were play-songs for children's games. Wherever Harraken gathered, song rose up.

As the stars swung overhead, Tahkan noticed Ari Ara's head drooping. He nudged her to her feet, murmuring that she and Emir could steal away to sleep.

"But I want to hear the songs," she protested.

"You will," he promised. "You have your whole life to hear the songs."

He walked her to her room, kissed the top of her head, then returned to his duties as Harrak-Mettahl. Ari Ara lingered a moment longer by the doorway, then crossed to the balcony rail to peer down. Her father slipped back in among his people and threaded his voice in with the chorus. Ari Ara tilted her head up to the cool night air. Even the stars looked different here; the familiar constellations mixed with tiny stars that blazed like a field of mountain wildflowers.

Emir settled against the roof pillar next to her. The bond of their foreignness tied them together. Ari Ara let the songs of the Harraken wash over her. Stars trembled in the inky darkness overhead. One fell like a drop of dew across the black sky and vanished.

"Same stars up there as at home," Emir remarked, "there's just more of them than you can see over the Mariana Capital streetlights."

"I miss Shulen," Ari Ara confessed.

He nodded. He did, too. He promised her that they'd stick together in this strange land . . . and that he'd still beat her in trainings for the Way Between.

"You can *try*," she scoffed, laughing, grateful for the familiarity of their friendship.

Below, the desert song shifted into a slow lullaby for the children, the words speaking of gentle rains and warm night winds. Half-veiled images rose in the edges of the fire's embers: mothers rocking children, and in turn being rocked by their mothers, back and back through the generations all the way to Shirar and his mother, reminding them that the long chain of love that cradled humanity over thousands of years would also carry them through this night to the dawn of tomorrow's future.

Ari Ara nudged Emir.

That's Alaren and Marin's mother, too, she mouthed, naming Shirar's brothers: Marin who had founded Mariana, and Alaren who took no country, but traveled the world teaching the Way Between to all.

Emir's smile shone. No matter how strange their cultures had become, they were all descended from the same mothers somewhere back in the time beyond remembering.

CHAPTER FOUR

. . . . .

The Warriors Meet

Tahkan woke Ari Ara as the first wistful birdcalls sang out from the branches of the blossoming trees. Dawn light crept over the mountains and tiptoed into the city. Murmurs of awakening filtered through the slatted shutters in the inner windows. Ari Ara's limbs curled into a ball. She didn't want to get out of the comfortable tangle of blankets. Tahkan whispered and gently shook her shoulder, a smile creasing the weathered lines by his eyes. He hadn't slept; he'd sung through the night with his people.

"You can rest later at the sun's peak," he told her, "when the heat drives everyone into the shade. Now, you should rise and greet the dawn in your new home.

Leaving Emir asleep, Tahkan brought her to the garden. Quiet and barefoot, people gathered, hands cupped around mugs of dark bitter *makh* to wake them. No one spoke; the silence rested companionably among them. Eyes avoided meeting, tracing the patterns of the tiles or the sliver of light beaming on the rooftops. A clunk and clatter of small noises emerged from the swinging doors of the kitchen. The scent of morning porridge traveled with the wafting steam and smoke.

37

The people stood in a wide circle. One by one, they added their voices to the low hum of prayer that the Harraken used to clear their minds and unify their hearts before beginning the day. Ari Ara wove her higher pitch in with her father's deeper tone as she had since the first morning of the long walk from Mariana to the desert. She heard Mahteni's clear voice slide into harmony with her family. As the hum of existence splintered into the many pitches of the clans, Ari Ara heard Moragh's rough growl merge with the family thread. The warrior woman's voice had startled Ari Ara the first time she'd heard it, a cross between a guttural croak and a rumble of thunder. Moragh rarely sang casually with her people. Even as a small child, she knew her path: her voice chanted the war chants and to call fury and courage into warriors before battle. Her younger brother, Tahkan, had been trained to sing the thousands of songs in the Harraken repertoire. Mahteni, a full decade younger than her siblings, had also been trained in the duties of the harrak-mettahl, ready to carry on the tradition if Tahkan had died.

Light poured into the courtyard garden. The song settled into silence again, but this time, the quiet smiled, alive with energy. This was the way of the desert, that they sang the day into existence together. Without their voices, they believed, the unfolding pattern of the world would alter. The song that was lost would leave the day orphaned from the love and wisdom of the past.

As Ari Ara and Tahkan tried to cross the courtyard for breakfast, they were stopped every two steps by people greeting the Harrak-Mettahl. He had been gone for nearly a year; his people had a thousand questions for him. Ari Ara's stomach rumbled. Spotting Emir standing under the eaves of the roof, Tahkan gestured for her to go ahead and join him.

She and Emir collected bowls of warm porridge with gratitude and retreated to a quiet corner of the garden. They had just finished the last spoonful when a shadow fell across them. A pack of young Harraken warriors gathered in a half-ring, broad-shouldered and muscular. Wariness marked their expressions. Hands tarried at belt knives and sword hilts. Ari Ara could feel Emir's casual posture masking his taut alertness as he set his bowl aside. She glanced beyond the knot of bodies; Tahkan's head was barely visible among the families. She spotted Mahteni at the far end of the courtyard, immersed in conversation. The warriors were young, the oldest only a handful of years older than Emir. Most would have earned their warriors' mark after the War of Retribution ended. They eyed Emir Miresh as if they would like to try their swords against his.

Bad idea, Ari Ara warned them silently, a scowl crossing her features.

Emir, noting her look, kicked her calf. She replaced her frown with a strained smile.

"Care to join us?" Emir offered cordially.

"It is not our tradition to share breakfast with our enemies," one stated coolly.

"Too bad," Ari Ara retorted.

Emir kicked her again.

"Uh, I mean, shared meals are good for building peace," she added, finishing with a lame flash of a grin.

"I am Emir Miresh," the tall youth told them.

He stretched his hand out, palm up in greeting toward the nearest warrior. The desert youth's rigorous training had bulked up his muscles, but his jawline battled his baby cheeks, giving him a puffy and glowering countenance. He eyed Emir for a long, tense moment, carefully noting the other young man's lean intensity and the cool confidence that comes with strength and ability. Emir was not as bulkily muscled as the Harraken warrior, but Ari Ara knew that her friend's strength lay hidden under his quiet surface. She half-hoped the bristling young warrior would have the idiocy to challenge Emir; he looked like a good trouncing would deflate his arrogance.

The Harraken youth passed his hand over Emir's outstretched fingers so swiftly it was almost a dismissal. Breaths drew in at the implied insult. Emir's dark eyes glinted.

"I see our ways are different," he remarked. "In my country, such a gesture would be rude. Show me how to greet a warrior in your customs."

He narrowed his eyes, continuing to hold out his hand palm up.

"Or did you mishear my name?" he asked pointedly.

Ari Ara blinked. In his subtle way, Emir had just challenged the youth. The others stiffened. She glanced from one face to the next. The black-haired Marianan could beat them, undoubtedly, but at what cost? A scuffle would mar the morning, as well as cast a long shadow over the efforts to build good relations between the two countries. Ari Ara shifted slightly, preparing to use the Way Between to break up the fight, but another youth spoke up.

"Gorlion was, uh, distracted," this youth explained, hastily holding his palm over Emir's for the properly respectful length. "We came to meet the daughter of our Harrak-Mettahl. We have heard unbelievable things about you."

A sigh of tension ran out of the group. The heat of their curiosity shifted from Emir to Ari Ara. They appraised her openly, clearly skeptical that so small and slight a girl as she could have beaten Shulen the Butcher in the Champion's Challenge that won back the water for the desert. The conversation turned to the usual questions about her years as a Fanten shepherdess, the Way Between, and the Mark of Peace on her back. Then Gorlion cut in with an unexpected query.

"Is it true that Marianan warriors have no say in things? That they just follow orders like a pack of dogs?"

Ari Ara opened her mouth to fling back a hot, proud retort, but Emir jumped in before her.

"In my country, a warrior earns rank by demonstrating discipline and loyalty. He is promoted to higher positions when his valor and courage are matched by wisdom and respect."

Though Emir's tone was cool, it was clear he thought the other youth lacked those qualities. Ari Ara chewed her lower lip . . . Emir's ideals didn't always play out in reality. Many of the nobles were warriors and commanders; few matched Emir's description.

"But when the Stout Lady - "

Ari Ara winced at the deliberate mistranslation of the Great Lady Brinelle's title.

"- says *jump,* you just ask, *how high?"* Gorlion needled, sneering at Emir.

Tahkan suddenly appeared behind the young warriors. Mahteni stood at his heels.

"If I told you that shoving your head in the sand," the Harrak-Mettahl said with an icy-edged tone of disapproval, "would increase your harrak more than your current words, would you stop talking like a fool?"

Mahteni frowned at the sharpness of the rebuke.

"The ways of Marianans and Harraken are different," the man told the young warriors, "and until you understand and respect those differences, there is no honor in criticizing them. There is much you could learn from Emir Miresh, young Gorlion. Better sword technique . . . if not better manners."

Mahteni stiffened. Her quiet in-drawn breath paused in her chest. Tahkan held the young warrior's eyes for a long, stern moment. Then he waved his hand and told the youths to go attend to their business. This was a day for celebration, not quarrel.

As the youths tromped off with dark looks and muttered undertones, Mahteni rounded on her brother.

"And you call yourself the Harrak-Mettahl?" she hissed. "That was a petty blow to the young man's pride. You will regret those words."

"He started this fight," Tahkan said with a shrug.

Ari Ara and Emir exchanged wide-eyed glances and then studied their toes. It was impossible not to hear the siblings' argument, however.

"A harrak-mettahl lifts up the honor of his people," Mahteni reminded him, "not slaps them down and shames them in front of an enemy warrior."

"Emir Miresh is not an enemy," Tahkan countered.

"No," Mahteni agreed, "but he is to those boys ... especially now that their Harrak-Mettahl has favored a Marianan over them."

"Gorlion was squandering his harrak by needling my daughter and her friend."

"And you squandered your honor in how you handled it!" Mahteni chastised him.

"Enough!" Tahkan snapped. "Who are you to tell your Harrak-Mettahl where honor lies?"

Mahteni stared at him with narrowed eyes.

"The next harrak-mettahl," she told him bluntly, "one who remembers that even the Harrak-Mettahl can lose harrak."

He drew breath to quarrel, but a man approached, clearing his throat, reluctant to intrude. He had a message for Tahkan, an urgent and uncomfortable one, judging by the strained expression on his face. The men's heads bent together. Suddenly, Tahkan snapped upright, lips pressed white with anger.

"What? What is it?" Mahteni asked.

"It seems the city sing will not be held," Tahkan said tightly. "A warriors meet has been convened this morning to decide on Moragh's claim of a blood debt against Shulen."

He cleared his throat in irritation.

"And it sounds like they do not intend to invite Moragh to attend."

Mahteni gasped in surprise - both at the cancellation of the city sing and the maneuvering to exclude her sister.

"You go find Moragh," he ordered Mahteni. "I'll go stall - or stop - them."

Mahteni nodded and darted off. Tahkan gestured for the two youths to follow him. At the far end of the garden, he led them down a flight of stone stairs into an underground wing. The air was deliciously cool; even this early in the morning, the burning heat rose. Storage rooms lined the narrow halls, filled with pressed oils, cured meats, grains, dried fruits, cases of nuts, jars of spices, and hanging herbs.

At the end of the corridor, Tahkan turned into a small room. Illuminated by candles, seven men sat along a battered wooden table. Deep furrows ran the length of the wood, scarred as the men's faces, cracked and dark with age. The flickering light carved the men into wooden statues, stern and scowling. Emir edged closer to Ari Ara. Tahkan broke the silence.

"Is this, then, what passes for justice since I left? A handful of bitter warriors hiding in darkness to sentence a man to death?"

Ari Ara's breath caught in her throat at the boldness of the words. Tahkan leaned his palms on the table's edge and swung his head from side to side. His expression shifted as he grasped the eyes of each man: a twitch of humor for one, a reproving frown for another, a glare, a question, an arched eyebrow. Tahkan Shirar was the Harrak-Mettahl; he knew each man like his own hand, their stories, their strengths, their weaknesses and desires. He was not surprised to see them here, but neither was he pleased.

"Where is the sun or moon to bear witness?" he asked softly. "Where is the wind to carry your song to the ancestors? Where are the women and children and elders to balance your views with their own?"

"Times change, Tahkan," one warrior said, shrugging his broad shoulders.

"Yes, but not to this. Why has a warriors meet been called instead of a city sing?"

"You bring our enemies among us, Shulen the Butcher and this boy," accused another man, pointing at Emir. His lips frowned under his beard. His shaggy eyebrows drew into a thick, solid line. "This warriors meet was the best way to deal with this, to avoid panic and hasty action, and to reach a wise decision among those who know this danger best."

Tahkan roared with laughter, his voice knocking around the stone walls and hitting heads hard enough to make two of the seven wince. Then he silenced abruptly, his humor gone.

"Can you not hear the joy in this city?" he asked them, pointing above. "We have traveled with the Marianan warriors for months with no panic or disaster. Times change, yes, and Shulen has changed, too. Thousands of our people owe their lives and freedom to him."

"How many lost their lives to his sword on the battlefield?" one of the warriors shot back.

"How many will live this year from the water singing in the river?" Tahkan answered.

"This girl was the one who won back the water," another warrior growled. "Not him."

"Who do you think suggested our strike in the mills? Who prepared the supplies for our exodus from Mariana? Who thought to have us gather in the enemy's capital city to save my daughter's life? Indeed, who was brave enough to spare and save my own life?" Tahkan's voice dropped quiet and serious. His eyes sought and held the other men's, willing them to listen to reason. "On the scales of right and wrong, Shulen is clearing his debt. Let him live and tip those scales in our favor. We can afford patience. We cannot know what the future holds. We may yet need him as our ally."

"We have chewed on this decision since the ravens brought word of the question," the oldest of the group stated.

From the look on his face, Ari Ara suspected the decision boded darkly for Shulen. Her father made a disparaging sound.

"You have not asked the people," he grumbled.

"We who have seen him on the battlefield know him best," a burly warrior insisted again.

"Any mother who lost her son to Shulen knows him as well as you," Tahkan answered, "and any father whose daughter returns today because of him deserves to help decide his fate."

He stared them down, one by one, until they dropped their eyes. Shulen's history entwined with Tahkan's too deeply to cut loose. Shulen had saved Tahkan's wife's life by giving her time to hide. At the cost of his own wife and child's lives, Shulen had fought off attackers long enough to allow the pregnant Queen Alinore to take refuge in the Fanten cave. It was Shulen who had found Ari Ara eleven years later, and Shulen who told Tahkan the news against the orders of the Marianans.

"You've chewed on this, you say," Tahkan stated, "now spit out your decision."

"We will not let Moragh claim blood debt," one answered, "but Shulen cannot enter these lands."

Tahkan's shoulders drooped.

"My sister will not be happy with your decision," he remarked.

"But will you abide by it?" the thick-bearded warrior challenged, lifting his chin.

A flash of understanding whipped through the Harrak-Mettahl. He hid it as swiftly as it appeared. He studied a scrape on his knuckles.

"What say the Tala-Rasa?" he asked.

A surge of disappointment, palpable as the wind, ran through the seven. Ari Ara caught sight of a knowing smile twitching in the corners of Tahkan's lips.

"The Tala-Rasa have refused to meet with us," the oldest warrior confessed.

"Then this is neither a warriors meet nor a city sing," Tahkan answered shortly, "just a handful of warriors trying to make decisions they have no right to make."

He rose and gestured to Ari Ara and Emir to follow as he left.

They ran into Mahteni at the top of the stone stairs. Moragh hovered behind her, a black shape backlit by blinding light. Ari Ara blinked and rubbed her eyes at the brightness. As they reached the landing, the muscular warrior woman grabbed her brother's arm, her expression fierce.

"What did they say?" Moragh croaked.

"They have no authority to make decisions," Tahkan spat in a flat tone, shaking his head. "The Tala-Rasa do not acknowledge their leadership."

Mahteni's eyes widened. Moragh's smirk grew.

"They must have decided against you," the warrior woman guessed.

Tahkan halted his stride. He sighed.

"Sister, they cannot make this decision, not by our customs, and it would be wrong for me to accept any verdict from them."

"I knew it!" Moragh crowed. "They took my side."

Tahkan whirled, his eyes blazing.

"No, sister. They decided against you. They agreed with me that Shulen deserves exemption from your blood feud. But without the Tala-Rasa's presence or support to legitimize them, why should either of us listen to them?"

"It was a warriors meet," Moragh answered testily, shrugging.

"Why weren't *you* there, then, oh warrior-sister-of-mine? Or some of your Black Ravens?" Tahkan needled her. "It was a men's meet . . . and such gatherings decide nothing. I will seek the Tala-Rasa and wait for a city sing."

Moragh stilled. Her jaw clenched. She spat into the plants, muttering about men and the games of men. She eyed Mahteni and nudged her.

"Tell him," she ordered her younger sister. "Tell him the stories you heard last night. Tell him what the Harraken women say."

Mahteni shifted uneasily.

"We heard some of these reports while we were in Mariana," she reminded her brother. "The warriors have been usurping power, refusing to end warriors-rule even though the threat of war is over. The problem has only gotten worse."

"Precisely," Moragh hissed, clutching Tahkan's arm. "These so-called warriors meets are listened to and obeyed, but there are no women at the meets. We have tried to join the warriors meets, my Ravens and I. They barred us from participating."

She snapped with outrage, dropping his arm and pacing in frustration.

"We were told to hold our own meet . . . which isn't the point. They are cutting out our voices; there hasn't been a full Harraken Sing since you left. Everything is decided by male warriors. In many places, the village sings haven't been held since before the war."

Moragh tossed her lion's mane irritably. Tahkan studied his sisters thoughtfully.

"How many village sings have been replaced by warriors meets?" he asked.

"Too many," Moragh answered darkly. "You were needed here, brother. There is no honor in the way they are ignoring our voices. Did you hear that they're holding a Meet of Meets at the Summer Solstice? They're trying to take over permanently."

Tahkan startled. Mahteni gasped.

"It's true," Moragh insisted. "I heard the news last night. The Black Ravens were not invited."

She pounded her fist against the stone wall in fury. The insult galled her to the core.

"They claim that my women are not true warriors," Moragh growled angrily, "and I told them I would spill their blood faster than the river dogs' if they said that again. Did we not walk the fire at the same initiation ceremonies? Did we not fight in the same war?"

"Are you thinking of going to the Meet of Meets and demanding your place at the table?" Mahteni interrupted, pressing her sister for information.

Moragh scowled. She hadn't decided yet.

"You shouldn't go," Mahteni urged her. "Your presence only legitimizes them."

"She's right," Tahkan added. "I shouldn't go, either."

Moragh blinked at him in surprise.

"But you're a warrior . . . "

"I am also the Harrak-Mettahl," he stated somberly, "and there is no honor, no harrak, in this. You should take a clear stand against the Meet of Meets, Moragh, not just because of the insult of being excluded, but because of the dishonor of how they are silencing the village sings."

"We shall see. I will discuss it with my Black Ravens when I return home."

With that, Moragh's face snapped shut like a book. She whirled and stalked away. At the gate of the building, she whistled through her fingers and her roan trotted into view. She leapt to the horse's back and wheeled about.

"Where is she going?" Ari Ara asked.

Tahkan sighed.

"North, to the Black Ravens Stronghold."

"She won't go after Shulen, will she?" Ari Ara asked anxiously.

"No."

Tahkan's voice was soft and certain. Moragh would lose harrak if she went back on her word to wait. He shaded his eyes and scanned the bright sky. His face scrunched against the glare. High above, a black speck wheeled in the cloudless blue. He whistled and the bird folded its wings and dove earthward. Recognizing Nightfast, the messenger hawk her father had given her last year, Ari Ara held out her arm for the bird to land. Tahkan borrowed writing tools from the nearby meeting room and scrawled a note to Shulen, urging him to stay put. He would find another way to stop the blood debt.

"How?" Mahteni pressured him, demanding answers as he tied the tight scroll of parchment to Nightfast's yellow leg. Ari Ara winced at the grip of the bird's talons, but didn't complain.

"We have to restart the city sing," Tahkan explained, cinching the knot, "and go to the Meet of Meets, and convince the warriors to give up this nonsense, and find the Tala-Rasa, and gain their support."

"You have more tasks than time to do them in," Mahteni remarked mildly as her brother gestured for Ari Ara to toss the hawk aloft.

Their eyes followed the shrinking bird as he winged west.

"Yes," Tahkan conceded with a sigh, "that's why one of us should stay here and the other should go to the Meet of Meets."

"You'll only legitimize them if you go," Mahteni warned.

"I know," Tahkan agreed. "That's why I think *you* should go."

Mahteni blinked at him. Surprise widened her eyes.

"Me?!"

"Are you not next in line to be harrak-mettahl?" he said, jibing at her. "You can search for the Tala-Rasa along the way."

Mahteni snorted and tossed a skeptical look at her brother.

"Everyone knows you can't *find* the Tala-Rasa," she reminded him. "You have to let them find you."

"Who are the Tala-Rasa?" Ari Ara interjected, curiosity welling up like boiling gold under her skin. "*What* are they?"

"Ah," Tahkan replied with a chuckle. "The Tala-Rasa are songholders. Without their approval, or presence, no decision is final and no rule holds fast."

He frowned. The Tala-Rasa loved historic events - anything that made a good song one day. For them to miss the water workers' return and Ari Ara's arrival indicated that something was terribly amiss. He'd never heard of them vanishing like this, refusing to lend their presence to Harraken daily life. With the Tala-Rasa in hiding, marriages couldn't be held, babies would be left unnamed, grave rites could not be performed, and spirit rituals would be left undone. The ghosts of the departed wouldn't be able to find their way to the Ancestor Wind, and - Tahkan's eyes narrowed in a flash of understanding - and no new warriors could be initiated. Without the Tala-Rasa, decisions - great and small - would not be woven into ballad and history.

The Harraken were guided by song and tradition. It was the foundation upon which their culture rested. Everyone stood as equals in the Harraken Song. Everyone participated in making decisions at the village sings . . . except in times of war. When the Marianans attacked or invaded, the people switched to warriors-rule. The smaller, swifter warriors meets made sense in times of chaos and danger, times when no one had time for long talks around fires, times when the common fires could not be lit for fear of attack. But in times of peace, the warriors should step down to let the people govern themselves once more. Only, they hadn't. Tahkan winced, thinking of the thousand things he had to do in order to change the situation.

"Mahteni," he remarked, turning to his sister. "How soon can you be ready to leave?"

"I have only to fetch my travel pack and some fresh supplies," she answered with a proud lift of her chin.

"Good. The solstice is only a few weeks away and there is much to accomplish on your way to the Meet of Meets."

If his sister wanted to be the next harrak-mettahl, he thought grimly, she would have to learn to bear the heavy weight of the role.

CHAPTER FIVE

. . . . .

Desert Horses

Two hours later, as they walked through the winding alleys of Turim City, Tahkan was still explaining to Mahteni which people she should stop and talk with, where she should travel, and what she should say. All through the city, as they collected fresh traveling supplies from the storehouses, he continued to add details. Ari Ara and Emir trailed after the siblings, ignoring the adults' conversation as they peered between corridors and under archways into courtyards. Every so often, Tahkan cast a backwards glance and called out a tidbit of Harraken history between his instructions to Mahteni. Finally, his sister lifted her hand.

"Enough," she stated. "I have only a few weeks. I cannot visit every Harraken in that time."

"And watch out for the warriors," he warned, rambling on despite her words. "When they realize what you're doing, some may try to stop you. And if you see the Tala-Rasa - "

"Tahkan!" she snapped. "I know."

He grumbled something about just trying to help. She muttered about fending for herself for the past six years. He sighed. She glared. Then they rounded the corner of the alley and the astonished cries of the two youths broke their tension.

A stunning view spread before them. The city's dwellings ended abruptly at a chest-high stone wall. Cliffs plummeted down a hundred feet to a narrow lake fed by the river that cascaded over the precipice in a thunderous waterfall. A strip of green meadow followed the lakeside. Beyond that, a sea of white sand dunes rose and fell to the western horizon. Ari Ara and Emir leaned over the stone wall that ran the length of the cliffs. At the bottom were the horses.

Chestnut, roan, dappled grey, shining blacks: they dotted the green meadow as far as the eye could see. Fillies and colts gamboled beside nursing mares. A pair of stallions raced along the edge of the white sands. Untethered, fenceless, they grazed on the grass and gathered by the edge of the lake, magnificent, tall, and proud.

"Do all these horses belong to people in the city?" Ari Ara stammered, awestruck by the sheer number of animals.

"There is a centuries-old debate on who belongs to whom: horse or rider?" Tahkan replied. "I would guess that a third of the horses down below look to someone in the city. Another third will travel with a human when they feel like it. The rest would never deign to carry a human about."

He led them to a hidden staircase carved into the cliff. The steps zigzagged down a chute, opening onto railed landings that overlooked the plain. Toward the bottom, narrow balconies served as viewing platforms during horse races - and defensive balustrades in times of siege. The staircase ended beside the lake. A line of storage rooms had been carved into the base of the cliffs to provide space for tack and grooming tools.

Ari Ara and Emir stared in awe at the horses. The creatures rose even taller than they had looked from atop the cliffs. These were not the shaggy ponies, placid and patient, that Ari Ara had seen the High Mountain villagers using to pull carts and plow fields. Long-legged and powerful, the desert horses rippled with strength. They crowded around the humans, curious and massive. The shortest one stood as high as Tahkan's shoulder - and he was not a small man. The rest towered over Ari Ara, bumping their flanks up against her and narrowly missing her feet with their stamping hooves. The horses' manes rippled with hints of fire and wind. Under the familiar grassy aroma, the scent of heat and dust clung to their hides. Their black eyes reflected the blue of the sky. Mahteni whistled through her fingers. A mare with a jet black mane and a misty coat shoved through the pack to reach her, head bobbing in delight.

"Good to see you, too, old friend," the desert woman murmured.

Mahteni's farewells were brief. She hung her saddlebags over the horse's back, slung her waterskin over her shoulders, urged her niece to avoid trouble, and repeated back Tahkan's last instructions. He sang a safe journeying song to bless her travels. Then she sprang to the back of the grey horse with a leap Ari Ara couldn't follow. As she rode away, she swiveled and called back to her brother.

"She needs a horse, you know."

Tahkan blinked in surprise.

"I thought it was too late," he murmured.

Mahteni's laugh rang out.

"It's tradition," she reminded him. Then she waved her arm in one last farewell and cantered off.

"What tradition?" Ari Ara asked.

Tahkan's slow smile grew.

"Harraken custom holds that a father chooses his daughter's first horse. I thought I had missed my chance, finding you so late in life, but Mahteni thinks you've never had a horse?"

Ari Ara tossed him a wild-eyed look and gulped, muttering under her breath as she flushed red as an apple.

"What was that?" Tahkan asked.

She shook her head and wouldn't answer.

Emir leaned close and murmured an explanation to Tahkan: she'd *never* ridden a horse - not once in her entire life. The older man threw an askance look back at the youth.

Well, she'll have to learn, Tahkan thought. The daughter of the Harrak-Mettahl *must* be able to ride. It was a matter of harrak, a point of honor and pride.

He whistled. A tall, black mare by the river lifted her head. Her ears flicked toward the figures by the high cliff. She shook her dark mane and paced over.

"She is annoyed at me for leaving her for so long," Tahkan chuckled.

Tahkan's mare sniffed Ari Ara from foot to head, sneezed twice, and turned her fine-boned head in Tahkan's direction with a long-suffering expression.

"Stop that," Tahkan chided. "This is my daughter - of course she's a rival for my affection. Go find a good friend for her among your four-legged relatives, would you? And this is Emir Miresh, a great young warrior from the riverlands. If Tekli is about, tell him I request a favor."

Ari Ara and Emir raised their eyebrows over the man's conversation with the horse . . . but when the mare trotted away and returned with two other horses in tow, their mouths fell open.

"She understood you?" Emir blurted out in disbelief. "What magic is this?"

"Only our language," Tahkan answered simply. "Or perhaps her intelligence."

He shrugged. It was difficult to interpret whether a

stubborn horse couldn't or *wouldn't* understand your requests. Who was he to judge? He welcomed a short, piebald horse with a black mane and tail, and introduced him to Emir.

"You are both from the riverlands. Tekli will know your Marianan words for stop and go, and respond to your style of riding. He has run with our horses for years since we rescued him from Marianan merchants."

He left Emir and Tekli to get acquainted and turned to the second horse with a skeptical look. The black mare had chosen a golden blonde stallion with a distinctive white mane.

"Are you mad? He'll kill her," he objected in a low hiss to his mare.

The mare stared steadily back at her human, nostrils puffing, lips curling back from her teeth in what Ari Ara suspected was a horse-laugh. Then the mare quieted and nudged Tahkan with her forehead.

"You're certain?" he asked her, eyeing the golden horse with a father's worried disapproval.

Desert children grew up on horses, riding behind or in front of their parents or older siblings, taking turns riding solo on the more tolerant horses. When they grew old enough, the mothers chose their sons' first horse and the fathers chose their daughters'. The friendship might last only a season or two, though insightful parents tried to find horses that would make lasting bonds with their humans. Tradition held to pairing complementary qualities: a headstrong boy was given a cautious horse; a shy girl was offered a confident one. The pair learned from one another and the two grew into balanced members of the desert society. Even so, Tahkan had known many protective fathers who selected the sweetest, most even-tempered old mares for their daughters.

This was not what the black mare had in mind for Tahkan

Shirar's daughter.

"What's his name?" Ari Ara asked.

"Zyrh," he answered, reluctant to pair his daughter with this horse.

Zyrh meant trickster. He was the pride and horror of the desert, infamous for his pranks. He would flirt with a dignified warrior until he had the proud man on his back. Then he'd fling him off. Zyrh would let vain young women climb up. Then he'd dump them in the mud. He'd do the opposite of whatever the young men ordered, turning them into the laughing stock of their village. On the other hand, Zyrh had carried village matriarchs with a gentleness that eased their old joints. He had pulled a drowning child from a river. He had freed a pen of horses rounded up by foreign merchants who wanted to sell them in Mariana. For all his faults, Zyrh had a sense of justice and an intelligence unmatched among the desert horses.

"I make no promises," Tahkan warned, "but we could give it a try."

Zyrh nickered and pointed his ears. Ari Ara ducked as he swatted his tail in her face. She grabbed it and held it still.

"Stop that!" she chided, shaking her finger at his nose.

Zyrh replied with a horse-laugh and yanked his tail - still gripped in her hand - hard enough to tug her off balance. The golden horse spun around and bit her shirtsleeve.

"That's gross," she told him. "Do you know how much you slobber?"

His rear flank bunched. His hoof lifted. Ari Ara darted backwards in case he kicked.

"This horse is trying to kill me," she hollered as Zyrh spun to face her, legs wide like a dog playing a game.

Tahkan broke into laughter. He looked at the mare. She bobbed her head.

"You're right," he answered. "They deserve each other."

"What?!" Ari Ara yelped.

Tahkan hid a smile. This might work, after all. The girl had gone from an orphan shepherdess to a royal heir in one short year. She needed someone to keep her humble, to stop the whirling dizziness of her life. She stood on the cusp of adolescence, exiled from one country, a stranger to the other. If Zyrh would let her ride him, he would keep her sane, even if she hated every minute of the horse's mischievous lessons.

"I'm not getting on this thing," Ari Ara protested.

"I will have a talk with him," Tahkan promised, stepping forward to hold his hand under the golden stallion's velvety nose. Zyrh fidgeted as the Harrak-Mettahl pinned him with a stern gaze. Tahkan began to sing in a low murmur of a chant. Zyrh's head dropped. He chuffed his breath through his nostrils. His long lashes blinked slowly. When Tahkan's song ended, the horse shook his mane as if breaking free of a spell.

"What did you tell him?" Ari Ara asked, impressed.

"I reminded our friend that he comes from an ancient desert lineage . . . as do you. I told him what we tell all our daughters' first horses: I expect him to save your life, brave all dangers, fly faster than the wind, alert you to approaching storms, and bite any uncouth boy who dares to insult you."

Ari Ara laughed. Tahkan grinned and spoke further.

"I told him that if a time comes when he must run like no other horse in the history of the world, he must do it even if it breaks his heart, even if his hooves turn to molten fire from the speed of his gallop, even if time parts and the wind gaspingly surrenders the race."

Tahkan's expression was severe. He meant every word.

"Well, that's not asking much," Ari Ara replied, rolling her eyes.

He beckoned her closer and laid a hand on the short bristles of the horse's hide.

"I had thought to begin with saddling your horse," Tahkan remarked with a grimace, "but there are two ways of riding in the desert, and Zyrh does not surrender to a saddle and bridle."

"You mean I have to ride bareback?!" Ari Ara exclaimed, eyes wide.

"Zyrh will keep you on . . . or not," Tahkan added. "No reins or saddle will change that."

"Can't you give me another horse?" Ari Ara questioned as Zyrh stamped his hoof and eyed her with devilish anticipation. "A dull Marianan horse?"

"I could," he replied, reluctantly.

"But what?" Ari Ara wondered, sensing his hesitation. "Will you lose harrak if I won't ride Zyrh?"

"Er, yes," Tahkan confessed with an uncomfortable sigh, "though, it's nothing a Harrak-mettahl cannot spare."

She caught the unspoken truth, however: a true daughter of the desert would not ride like the river dogs.

"Alright," she groaned, her pride spurring her into action, "show me how to get on him."

Tahkan's grin lit up, delighted at her courage. He eyed her height and pointed to a large boulder. He suggested she climb on top of it until she could leap into the saddle like Mahteni had done.

"Show me," Ari Ara said. "I bet I can do it."

He whistled for his mare and demonstrated the three leaping mounts: one from a standing position with hands on the horse's back, one with no hands, and one from a running start. His horse stood proud and still, showing off her excellent manners. Then he dismounted and held Zyrh by the sides of his head so the horse wouldn't dodge away as she practiced.

"Be good," he muttered to the creature. "Let her gain some confidence, at least."

Ari Ara's head barely reached Zyrh's withers, so she stepped back several paces, bolted into pounding strides, and took a hurtling leap. Her hands pushed off his back to give her enough height to swing her leg around and over.

"Like that?" she asked, clutching Zyrh's neck as he jolted at her sudden weight.

"That will do," Tahkan answered with a smile.

"Now what?"

The two sides of the horse had names, he told her: *alshun* and *saak,* courage and trust, the two virtues that guided desert riders. He showed her how to use her legs to signal to Zyrh.

"Excellent," he encouraged her as the horse began to move like rippling water under her. He could see her knuckles turning white as they clutched the horse's mane, but a smile broke out on her face.

"We'll make a desert rider out of you, yet," he boasted.

Zyrh snorted and sidestepped. She slid off his back with a shocked 'o' of consternation hanging on her lips. Tahkan helped her up from the dust.

"Perhaps I spoke too hastily. Let's try again."

"Wouldn't it be easier with reins?" she asked.

"No doubt, but in battle, you'd need to hold a sword in one hand and a shield in the other."

Ari Ara swiveled to face her father.

"No, I won't," she retorted hotly. "I'm not ever fighting in war. Who would I fight for or against? My father's people or my mother's? I'm going to use the Way Between to stop wars."

"Lakash en kelay," Tahkan vowed softly under his breath, "may it be so."

He gestured to her to get back on the horse. This time,

however, Zyrh bolted away as she leapt, whinnying and shaking his head.

"He's laughing at me!" Ari Ara protested, landing in the dust.

She tried again. Zyrh dodged her. She stuck her tongue out at Emir as he laughed. The third time, her father held the horse still. Then he put her through her paces, showing her how to ride at a walk, a canter, and a trot. Zyrh taught her how to fall. Fortunately, her training in the Way Between had already taught her how to protect herself from hard landings.

By late afternoon, her temper was as sharp as her hunger. Tahkan was pulled away by a huddle of anxious-faced men requesting his intervention in a brewing conflict. He told Ari Ara and Emir to brush their horses down and then come up for dinner. At the first balcony, he leaned over the rail, cupped his hands around his mouth, and called back to them.

"Stay out of trouble!"

They waved to show they'd heard. He nodded and trudged up the steps behind the men. At first, Zyrh stood still and let her brush him down with a currycomb. Then the devilish beast shot a stream of piss at her feet. She jumped back and threw the brush at his flank. He raced away and promptly rolled in the dust.

"Fine!" she hollered. "See if I ever brush you again!"

"He's just doing it because he knows you'll react," Emir told her, picking up the brush.

Ari Ara made a face and let him use the brush on Tekli.

"I should use it on you," he teased, picking bits of dried grass out of her hair. "You look like you spent the day rolling in the dust like Zyrh."

"I did," she reminded him grumpily, slapping his hand away.

A burst of laughter rang out from behind them. They whirled. A group of desert youths drew close, led by the young warrior Gorlion.

"A *real* Harraken would know how to ride that horse."

The sneering comment struck her like an arrow. She tensed, trying to hide the hurt his words caused her. Her face flushed red. She knew she wasn't a true Harraken, but he didn't have to rub it in! She glared back at Gorlion as he leaned against the rough-cracked trunk of a nearby tree, his arms crossed over his chest. Beside him, a handful of young warriors and skinny younger brothers imitated his posture.

"Ignore him," Emir advised her in an undertone.

"I bet you can't even make it down to the end of the lake without falling off," he scoffed.

"I can, too," she shot back, indignant. "I'd even beat you there."

"Ari Ara," Emir began in a warning tone.

"What's the matter, river dog? Worried she'll lose harrak?" another youth jibed. He flung his head back and woofed like a dog, mocking Emir and setting off a chorus of howls from the others.

Zyrh came dancing over, skin quivering and nostrils flaring. He snapped at the warrior youths and hung his head over Ari Ara's shoulder in a surprising show of solidarity.

"Let's race then, riverlands girl," Gorlion challenged. "Harrak to the winner."

The others repeated the last phrase in a chant. Ari Ara set her chin. She may not be a skilled rider, but she'd seen Zyrh galloping. He was fast. She waved aside Emir's protests and took a running leap to the golden horse's back. He let her land - which she took as a sign that he wanted to race as much as she did.

Gorlion's stallion pranced and paced, pawing the ground impatiently. Zyrh held stark still, except for the twitching ripple of tension that shivered in his flank. One of the youths drew a line in the sand. Another held up his scarf. A third counted down.

"Three . . . two . . . one . . . go!"

The two horses burst into motion. Ari Ara clutched fistfuls of Zyrh's ivory mane. The horse morphed into a mass of muscle and thundering energy. He moved in long, leaping strides. The ground beneath her blurred. Gorlion's stallion sprinted, lithe and swift. The desert youth rode well, tucked low to his horse's back. As they pulled ahead and left her in the dust, he ducked his head under his elbow and laughed mockingly.

"Go," Ari Ara urged her horse, refusing to give up.

Zyrh bolted forward, doubling the length of his stride. Ari Ara clutched the band of muscle at the arch of his neck and clenched her legs tight around the horse's torso. His legs stretched forever as they flew across the sand. The shore of the lake sped past. Despite her white-knuckled grip, a surge of thrilled excitement whipped through her. She let out a whoop of exhilaration. Zyrh sensed her enthusiasm, lengthened his neck, and exploded. Ari Ara's eyes widened. The golden horse galloped as if he was made of wind. They gained on Gorlion. They caught up to the stallion. Then they passed the other horse and pulled ahead. The sound of the competing racer's hoof beats fell back. Ari Ara cheered as Zyrh reached the end of the lake yards ahead of the other horse.

And then he kept on running.

CHAPTER SIX

· · · · ·

Moonlight Pursuit

The night pooled around Mahteni, magnificent in its depth. Moonlight silvered the wide plain. The wind rippled the grasses like marsh reeds quivering in the currents' flow. Piles of rock and a few twisted old trees dotted the flat expanse, scattered like giant's crumbs across the floor. They crouched, dark with shadows, unknowable in their hidden mysteries.

Mahteni rode quietly through the shine of silver, letting the horse pick her way through the grasses. The light wind lifted the curls from her face. The cool air quieted her worried heart. The expanse of night made room for her thoughts as she mulled on all she had seen and heard. She had detoured up a foothill trail to visit a village and speak with the elders. Their hesitant comments and murmured asides confirmed what she had noticed in Turim. The winds had shifted since she had left six years ago.

She did not like the direction they blew.

Once and always, until now, men and women stood as equals in Harraken culture. A boy could spin and weave; a girl could hunt and ride. A man could tend the hearth fire and children; a woman could work the forges or ride to war. Decisions were made by everyone, all together, at the village sings. At least, that's what Mahteni's memory insisted. But, she reluctantly admitted, that was over a decade ago. During the five years of war, the warriors had commanded absolute authority. At the end of those terrifying times, she had gone into Mariana disguised as a water worker. She had heard reports that the warriors had been reluctant to give up control, even after the first tenuous years of ceasefire had ended. Three years ago, her brother had written about his relief that the first village sing had started up again . . . but his hope for peace was short-lived. Just before Ari Ara was found, the Marianans had threatened to invade again, convinced the desert people had taken their heir. The Harraken shifted back to warriors-rule, worried about the possibility of attack. But the war had been averted, and a time of peace had arrived. The village sings ought to have been restored; the Harrak-Mettahl should have insisted on it, but Tahkan had neglected his duties in order to sneak into Mariana to meet his daughter. She did not blame him for that choice, but she also saw the mess he had left behind. With the warriors barring women from the meets, the decisions slanted toward their priorities . . . and that shift was reflected in the changes in their culture.

During the welcoming feast in Turim, and again at this village, she had sat among one family and then the next, offering the Shirar family's greetings, listening to the news and gossip . . . and noticing the things left unsaid. She silently watched the women rise and serve the men. Her green eyes followed the shushing of girls and the pampering of boys. She kept track of who did the talking and whose sentences were trampled by another. She watched to see who lent a hand with the dishwashing, and who sat with feet up on the tables, picking their teeth with a belt-knife. She joined the women in peeling fruit and chopping vegetables, asking after this woman or that friend, carefully tracking whose fathers or brothers were now named as leaders where once mothers and sisters had earned that praise. She questioned the old women about the frequency of the village sings and watched the heads shake. In many places, there hadn't been a village sing - a real one with everyone involved - for months, sometimes years.

The grandmothers who had grown up before the war yearned for the fairness of the village sings. Their lined faces crinkled with distaste as they complained about warriors-rule. It was one thing for the warriors to assume the mantle of authority when the Harraken were under attack, but in times of peace, warriors should not be settling disputes over wandering chickens and broken hearts and which fields to plant with what crops. How would they understand why one grandmother couldn't share a house with another, but must be respectfully accommodated at the other end of the village? How could they know that the rocky field would support *kerat* grain, but would need twice as much water? How would the warriors know the importance of negotiating clay rights evenly among the potters? How would they understand the need to allocate timber harvests for new looms instead of spears and shields?

When voices are silenced from the Harraken Song, Mahteni thought darkly, *the music is not complete.* The decisions weakened and faltered. The harmony became unclear. Discord was sown between people. Resentments built into hatred.

Mahteni sighed. Shifting her weight on the horse's back, her muscles screamed in protest. She hadn't ridden this long since she departed for Mariana, but her duties required her to travel far and ride hard. She would journey by moonlight and rest through the midday heat; such was the way of the desert.

67

As much as she worried about the political tensions, Mahteni also reveled in returning - at long last - to her home. The scents of bitter herbs and dust, the silken touch of the wind, the burnish of heat and light . . . she'd missed them all.

Suddenly, her horse froze. Her ears swiveled, listening. Mahteni peered into the silver shadows, hair rising on her arms. A pair of voices clamored from beyond the next pile of boulders, arguing.

"I don't care if I have to walk all the way back to Turim, I am *not* getting on that horse!"

Mahteni frowned and nudged her mare forward, recognizing that indignant tone of voice.

"What in the name of Shirar are you two doing here?" she called out as she rounded into sight and spotted Ari Ara's unruly hair and Emir's muscled form.

The story launched from the youths' lips at the same time, full of contradictions and quarrels. From what she could gather, Ari Ara had been foolish enough to be goaded into racing a boy, her trickster horse hadn't stopped, and Emir had torn after her as fast as the short little riverlands horse could carry him. As soon as Zyrh slowed to a walk, Ari Ara threw herself off his back. Emir had caught up to her hours later as she stomped back south.

"You're at least two hours' journey from Turim," Mahteni warned them, "longer on foot."

"That's what I keep telling her," Emir pointed out in an aggrieved tone.

"I don't trust that beast as far as I can throw him," she muttered, glaring at the trickster horse and rubbing her rear end, "and that's nowhere."

"Come," her aunt urged, holding out her hand and leaning toward the girl. "You can ride with me. I'll take you back."

She tried to mask her dismay. She didn't have time for this, but she had no choice. The youths could not be left wandering the desert alone. Mahteni hauled the girl up in front of her and turned them back toward Turim, resenting every footstep. Ari Ara sensed her storm of emotions and hunched her shoulders.

"It wasn't my fault the idiot horse kept going," she muttered.

"What on earth possessed you to accept Gorlion's challenge?" Mahteni questioned her, eyeing the long-legged Zyrh as the golden horse picked his way beside them. "You could have broken your neck."

"It was a matter of harrak," Ari Ara replied stiffly.

Mahteni stifled a sigh. The girl was a Shirar, through and through.

Emir stiffened beside them and flung up a hand in warning. His head swiveled as he scanned the shadows of a pair of looming rock mounds on either side of their path. Mahteni caught his alarm and cast her senses along the wind. She heard its secrets of hidden horses and creaking leather.

"Trouble?" the youth asked the desert woman.

"I don't know. Stay alert," Mahteni warned him.

She called out to the hidden riders and nudged her horse ahead. A gruff voice answered with a greeting. A band of riders emerged from the silver-and-black shadows. Thirty armed horsemen spread into a circle around them.

"Mirrin Shirar, well met," said their leader, a stocky man with broad, muscled shoulders who rode with casual ease.

"Greetings. I go by Mahteni now," she answered with a relieved sound, recognizing the man. She gestured to the ring of riders. "Is this your idea of a welcome?"

"Ah, well," the other answered, shaking his head. "We've

been tracking you. We've orders to escort you back to Turim."

"Me?" Mahteni exclaimed, surprised. "It was the children who had a mishap with a horse. I have other tasks to attend to."

He waved his hand.

"We know nothing about these two. Our orders are specifically to bring you back."

"Why?" she asked sharply.

"The warriors meet will answer those questions when we return."

Mahteni tensed at the hard tone in the man's voice. The riders said they were following orders - whose? Someone didn't want her to try to persuade people to abandon warriors-rule. They would undoubtedly try to keep her in Turim City until after the Meet of Meets at Summer Solstice. She glanced at the two youths and bit back a groan. She had to get away, but she couldn't leave them. They'd use Ari Ara to pressure her father. Tahkan could resist all the warriors in the world for the sake of harrak, but he would fling his harrak to the wind for the sake of his daughter. If he thought - even for a moment - that she might be harmed, he would give his support to warriors-rule. As for Emir, she couldn't trust the warriors not to harm him. Even in desert clothes, his features and pale skin marked him as Marianan. She let her horse stamp back an irritated pace, bringing her close to Emir.

"At my command, follow me as fast as you can," she murmured to him in Marianan.

"What are you saying?" the leader barked, suspicious.

"I am just easing my companion's concern over your armed . . . escort," she told him. "You do not want him to fight you, believe me."

The warriors nodded, reassured. They kicked their horses around and started back toward Turim.

"What - ?" Ari Ara began to ask.

Mahteni hissed at her to be silent. She pulled the girl closer to her on the mare.

"We are about to ride hard and fast," her aunt murmured to her, "and we cannot have you falling off."

As the company of riders moved forward, an opening broke to the north.

"Now."

Mahteni's word rang with the force of command. She and Emir spun their horses about and charged through the opening. Mahteni held Ari Ara tight as the girl gripped the mare's mane. Zyrh wheeled and raced at their heels. Behind them, shouts and cries rose up. A thunder of hoof beats pounded after them. Ari Ara felt Mahteni chant in a long stream of words, invoking a ritual that blessed their horses with sure footing and speed.

The ground blurred. The pounding hoof beats drummed. They raced desperately through the darkness. Ari Ara's knuckles turned white in the grey mare's black mane. Emir rode low to his horse's back. Mahteni chanted to counter the curses flung at their heels by the riders behind them. Ari Ara wondered how long Tekli, the stocky little Marianan horse, could keep up with the staggering pace of the long-legged desert runners. Mahteni's mare galloped as easily as she walked, Zyrh hadn't even broken a sweat, but perspiration darkened the flanks of the riverlands horse. His mouth lathered. He grew wild-eyed. He stumbled once, but caught his footing on the next stride. Emir scanned the darkness ahead, looking for a place to hide . . . or fight.

Suddenly, Zyrh whinnied a fierce challenge to the riders behind them. Emir called out as the horse spun away.

"Leave him!" Mahteni shouted, tightening her one-armed hold on Ari Ara as the girl twisted to look.

The golden horse dropped back and wheeled around, sleek-boned in the moonlight. He charged one of the riders and brought him up short. He sprang after the second, outstripping the stallion in an incredible burst of speed. He shoved the pursuers off course around a mound of rocks. Ari Ara craned over her shoulder and caught a glimpse of the golden horse rearing in front of another rider. Zyrh harried the riders' horses, nipping and striking. He drove the pursuers away like a sheep dog steering a flock. Against their riders' will, Zyrh herded the horses up a canyon, away from his people.

Mahteni veered east, calling for Emir to follow. It was a desperate night. They rode, then walked, then rode again, not daring to halt. At dawn, they stumbled into a slot canyon, staggering with exhaustion. There, they dismounted and walked with the horses, allowing them to rest.

"If it rains, we will be trapped," Emir cautioned, glancing at the grey clouds pressing against the distant mountainsides.

Mahteni eyed the storm. Deep circles hung under her eyes and her skin shivered with weariness. A late spring storm like this might be thinned from the first hints of summer heat. It might merely come down as a sprinkle.

"If we can make it past the Needle's Eye," she told Emir, "there is a place to hide and rest. The rain, if it falls, will likely only fall on the upper mountains. If it releases on the lower mountains, it will at least cover our tracks. We can continue out the other side of the canyon tomorrow."

Ari Ara trudged up the sandy path of the dry riverbed. Any plan was better than no plan.

Emir gripped Mahteni's elbow.

"You said *if . . .* "

"It will be fine," she told him, though she glanced warily at the gathering clouds. If the rains fell too hard, too low, or too early, they could be trapped in the slot, swallowed by the flash of water pouring into the narrow space. If this were late summer, when the pounding daily thunderstorms came, she wouldn't risk it. But today, they just might make it.

Even in her exhaustion, Ari Ara stared in awe at the canyon. The walls rose vertically, curved and carved by a long-extinct river, a memory of older times. The passage narrowed until the crumbling sandstone scraped the horses' flanks. They whinnied uneasily. The sound hit flat against the press of rock. The sky tightened into a winding ribbon of grey overhead. A few times, it vanished behind an overhang. Gnarled old pines clung stubbornly to the crumbling white slopes, perched precariously on nothing but the tenacity of their roots.

A tiny drop hit Ari Ara's arm. Then another. High above them, the wind thrashed. Bits of dust and grass and dry pine needles tumbled down onto their heads.

"Hurry," Mahteni murmured, though their legs felt leaden and their feet heavy as stone.

The Needle's Eye was not far, but the sand underfoot was turning dark and bruise-colored. The invisible trickle of an underground stream was rising. They quickened their steps. Small puddles pooled in the horses' footprints. As they squeezed through a tight bend, the choke of the canyon's curving sides sent a knot of fear down Ari Ara's spine. If the passageway tightened any further, the horses wouldn't fit.

"Quickly," Mahteni urged as the sand turned to sodden mud.

The thread of water grew into a tiny stream. Mahteni splashed up a small cascade of falls that swelled by the second. Emir's horse balked as the spout of water thickened. Tekli refused to leap, slamming Emir hard against the canyon wall in panic. A shower of pebbles broke loose. One stung the horse's flank and Tekli lunged forward, landing on the other side with shivering skin and flaring nostrils. Emir hauled Ari Ara up against the weight of the current. The canyon widened here, curling in a bend around a massive and determined old tree. The water rose to their shins as they sloshed onward. Ari Ara cried out as she stepped into a hidden hollow and fell to her thighs. She flailed. The current swept her feet out from under her. Emir lunged, grabbed her tunic, and hauled her back to standing.

The water deepened, coming up to their knees and rising further still. Soon, they slogged through thigh-deep water. Emir and Mahteni staggered against the current. Ari Ara clung to the horse's neck. The water had reached her chest. When Emir realized her feet were no longer anchored to the sand, he hoisted her on top of Tekli.

"We're almost there!" Mahteni hollered over the roaring grumble of the water.

Ari Ara sighed in relief, but then gasped. The Needle's Eye had turned into a monster, a growling serpent of water, twisting and falling through the tight, oval opening. The force of the river pounded the canyon sides, flinging pebbles and sand into the muddy waters.

"The bottom is flat," Mahteni told Emir. "The horses can make it if we guide them past their fear."

"It's too deep for us, though," Emir cried. "We'll never wade through it."

"We'll climb," Mahteni told him grimly, pointing to the narrow gap of the canyon walls. Ari Ara was too short; she would have to try to ride the horse through the slot.

There was no time to argue. Emir and Mahteni braced their hands and feet against the two sides of the canyon walls and inched over the falls. On the other side, a shoulder opened. An old bend of the river had carved a high cave and deposited a flat bank of sand and stone beneath it. A thick tree rose between boulders. Mahteni called to the horses and urged them forward.

"Please," Ari Ara whispered to Tekli, shuddering with fear and exhaustion. Mahteni's mare heard the woman's calls and surged forward. Tekli followed his friend. The tall mare's wake carved an easier path for the smaller Marianan horse. The water pounded against the horses' chests. Ari Ara prayed their hooves wouldn't slip out from under them. Mahteni and Emir called and whistled, urging the horses to fight the pounding current.

At last, they made it through the Needle's Eye. The mare staggered up the bank to the cheers of the humans. Released from her bulk, the surging water slammed into Tekli. The smaller horse jolted. His hooves scrambled against the sandy bank. He braced against the tug of the water. Ari Ara hung on with white-knuckled fists, her legs shaking from clenching the round barrel of the horse's girth. The flashflood surged up in waves and tried to shove her off Tekli's back. Emir and Mahteni's shouting thundered dimly in her ears.

"Try," she urged in Desert Speech, invoking the magic and power of the language.

The horse turned into the current and staggered toward the bank. Tekli heaved his bulk up onto solid ground. Ari Ara's eyelids lowered in relief.

"Thank you," she whispered, sliding off.

She didn't even remember touching the ground.

CHAPTER SEVEN

. . . . .

Mirrin's Hideaway

She woke, warm, dry, and famished. The embers of a fire crackled. The scent of damp earth and soaked desert shrubs mingled with the wood smoke. She sat up in a nest of blankets. A long, soft robe folded about her. The ends of the sleeves flapped over her hands. Her wet tunic and trousers had been hung up to dry. Golden afternoon light snuck through canvas-covered windows. A wall of clay mud bricks enclosed the mouth of the tall cave, forming a dwelling. The single room was simple, yet sufficient. Rows of shelves had been carved into one wall; a sleeping pallet fitted into a niche in another. The hearth vented into the canyon. Judging from the cobwebs in the upper corners and the thick layer of dust, it had not been occupied for years. Emir was rolled up in a blanket, sound asleep. Mahteni entered through the wooden door with an armload of branches from the foot of the massive tree outside.

"Awake then?" she murmured softly, seeing Ari Ara's curious gaze. "Come, you must be hungry."

She fed another branch into the coals and stirred a pot of porridge, urging the girl to eat heartily. Their supply of oats had been soaked, so she'd cooked the lot, setting aside a small pot and forming small hearthstone-baked cakes with the rest.

"Why did those riders chase us?" Ari Ara asked.

"They wanted to stop me from persuading the warriors to give up warriors-rule," Mahteni answered. Her tone held steady and even, but a sliver of her inner worry showed in the way she chewed her lower lip.

"What about my father?" Ari Ara wondered, eyes anxious. "Do you think he's alright?"

Mahteni nodded.

"They won't hurt him?"

"Tahkan?" the woman laughed dryly. "No. They'll probably spoil him rotten, trying to corrupt his integrity and convince him to support them. He'll argue until he's blue in the face, and he'll either win them over or they'll give up on him, eventually."

Ari Ara sighed with relief.

"What is this place?" she asked curiously as her aunt handed her a bowl of steaming porridge.

"My old home," Mahteni answered with a wry glance at the cobwebs.

She had spent her teenage years here, hidden away during the war, kept safe from assassination and kidnapping. If her brother had died in battle, she would have taken up the duties of the harrak-mettahl. It had been desperately lonely. She had only the songs to keep her company. She eyed Ari Ara as the girl shoved the long sleeves of the robe back to her elbows. Mahteni had been only a few years older than the twelve-year-old; mature enough to know the importance of her lineage, but young enough to resent giving up songs with the villagers, flirtations with boys, and a life in the heart of her culture. The time alone had tempered her. When she emerged from the hidden cave at the end of the war, she called herself Mahteni, not Mirrin, and carried silence like a sword and secrecy as her armor. It gave her strengths neither of her siblings possessed and served her well as a spy in Mariana. In her own way, she was as much a leader of her people as her siblings.

Ari Ara ran her finger around the bowl and licked it clean. Mahteni passed her a comb and told her to work the tangles out of her hair. Then she rose.

"Where are you going?" the girl asked.

"To see what awaits us at the canyon top," the desert woman answered, slinging a waterskin over her shoulder. "We will leave tonight at moonrise so long as the clouds and rain hold off."

Ari Ara groaned. Every muscle in her body screamed in protest at the mere thought of getting back on a horse. Mahteni chuckled. From the expression she'd seen on her mare's face, the feeling was mutual. Mahteni gave Ari Ara strict instructions to tend the fire, turn the oatcakes, stay inside, and feed Emir when he woke. She pointed to an old jar of salve on the shelf. Time had mellowed some of its healing properties, but it should still ease sore muscles. Mahteni intended to leave the horses here and hike on foot. She could scale a goat path up the canyon side to scout, rather than ride up the obvious path out of the top of the slot canyon. As she opened the wooden door, she paused and turned back to Ari Ara.

"If I don't return - "

"Don't say that!" Ari Ara squawked. Words had strange power in the desert.

" - leave at moonrise and head north along the mountains' feet to Moragh's Stronghold," Mahteni continued. "Fill your waterskins at every stream and spring . . . the last leg is deathly dry."

"How will I know - "

"As soon as you get within a day's ride, her ravens will spot you."

Mahteni shouldered her waterskin. She moved to depart, then paused in the sunlight-flooded doorway. She cleared her throat uneasily and glanced at Emir's black hair and fine-boned Marianan features.

"When you get to Moragh's," she warned, "don't let her kill the boy."

Ari Ara's blue-grey eyes rounded into wide circles. A dozen questions bloomed on her tongue, but Mahteni strode swiftly down the canyon. By the time, Ari Ara shook off her surprise, her aunt had vanished around the bend.

*   *   *

"She should be back," Ari Ara worried, pacing the length of the cave, rubbing her elbows against the encroaching chill of night.

The dwindling embers of the fire flickered against the walls, orange and shadowed. Emir poked the coals with a stick and sent a shower of sparks leaping up. He glanced out the window. A flood of silver poured down the white walls of the canyon. He had packed their belongings, readied the horses, made Ari Ara eat again, bundled up the cooked oatcakes, and put the hidden dwelling back to rights. For the last hour, he had forced Ari Ara to work the soreness out of her limbs with training exercises in the Way Between. The black fall of darkness had given way to the faint glimmers of moonlight.

Still, Mahteni did not return.

"Put these on," he told her, passing her a pair of breeches he had found in the cedar trunk.

"They're too big."

"Wear yours then," he answered shortly.

"They're still wet," she complained.

Emir shot her an exasperated look.

"Quit stalling, get dressed, and get on the horse."

She made a face.

"We should wait for Mahteni," Ari Ara grumbled.

"What did she tell you?" Emir pressed again.

"I told you already," Ari Ara muttered.

She had repeated Mahteni's instructions and directions a dozen times already.

"Nowhere in there did she tell us to stay here," Emir pointed out, his training as a warrior urging him to obey orders. "We can keep an eye out for her as we go up the canyon."

The girl cast a doubtful look at him, but she pulled on the breeches under her long robe and rolled up the cuffs. Emir passed her a pair of belts - one for the pants that she hitched up and one to throw around the outside of the robe. He took out his knife and gestured for her to come over so he could cut the extra length off the ends of her garments.

"These are Mahteni's old clothes," she objected, pulling away.

"Ari Ara," Emir said slowly, biting back the surge of his impatience and annoyance, "we are going to be traveling hard and far across unknown terrain in a region where we just rode away from pursuing horsemen. Tripping on your hem is a danger we cannot risk. Mahteni will understand."

He sliced off the bottom of the robe and started to work on the cuffs of her pants. She stared sullenly at the top of his head, knowing he was right and resenting it.

Honestly, she grumbled silently, *just because he's five years older than me doesn't give him the right to order me around.*

Ari Ara tossed her hair back and lifted her chin. Then she

marched out into the moonlight and clucked to the mare, stomping up the canyon before Emir could tell her where to go. He ignored her temper, dowsed the fire, and barred the door shut with a heavy stone before jogging after her.

The night loomed with shadows and dangers. The crunch of hoof steps in the damp sand bounced strangely off the steep sides. Boulders shape-shifted into lurking creatures. Nocturnal animals rustled just out of sight. The horses flinched at the noises, skittish. Emir followed a step behind Ari Ara, letting her lead, but watching the shadows warily. His eyes traced the canyon top for signs of motion.

"There's no one up there," Ari Ara told him when he made them pause and draw back under an overhang.

Emir motioned her to keep silent, staring at a dark shape clinging to the edge of the cliff above them.

"It's a rock," she stated, scooping up a pebble and hurling it at the spot.

The clatter of stone on stone confirmed her words.

"You can see that clearly?" Emir asked her in surprise.

"Yes. Right down to the speckles in the stone," she boasted.

Emir's eyebrows rose, but he gestured for her to lead onward. The Fanten women who had raised Ari Ara were rumored to see in the dark as clearly as in the day. It must be the effects of their wild herbs, Emir mused, since Ari Ara wasn't related to them by blood and birth. He put her on lookout duty, which at least kept her focused on something other than her complaints.

As they emerged from the canyon onto the slopes of the foothills, they paused to scan the area. The mountains loomed above them, flooded with moonlight. Twisted shrubs cast long shadow-stripes across the loose scrabble of the hills. Below them, the plain spread like a silver-blue lake. Grasses rippled in the gentle wind. The orb of the moon stared at them from the cloudless satin sky. They saw no tracks or signs of people. Mahteni had vanished.

Reluctantly, they headed north, riding along the foothills until the sliding shale forced them down onto the edges of the plain. They made slow progress. Eroded dry streams formed gullies between the hills. Mounds of boulders offered cover from spying eyes, but also hid dangers in their hulking shadows. When Ari Ara fell asleep and slid off in a thud, Emir eyed the moon. They had a few more hours of light before the gleaming circle sank beneath the western horizon. He told her to get back on the horse.

The command touched a lit matchstick to the dry tinder of her temper. Her anger burned off her drowsiness. She lifted her chin stubbornly and refused to talk to Emir as they continued riding. He gritted his teeth and tried to remember if he'd been this prickly at her age. He gave up with a sigh. At her age, he'd been in warrior training under Shulen; copping attitudes was not permitted.

Just as the moon dropped onto the horizon's edge, the sound of trickling water leapt up like clear music in the night. Between the crumbling edges of an eroded gully, a tiny stream ran down the foothills into the plain. Uphill, Emir spotted a tumble of boulders that would hide them from sight. He called a stop. Ari Ara dropped to the ground, pulled her cloak tight around her, and sank into sleep. Emir rubbed down the horses, let them drink, and tied them loosely to a twisted juniper tree. Then he sprawled on the earth, back pressed against the cool boulders. He tried to stay awake, uneasily realizing that they should keep watch. His eyes shut before his exhausted mind even finished the sentence.

Emir woke her before dawn. She grumbled and tugged her

cloak over her head, burrowing her face into the crook of her arm. The youth bit back a flare of annoyance. *A warrior* would be up on her feet already, but Ari Ara had never had that kind of discipline. Stubbornness, yes; determination, yes. Those qualities made her push herself hard, but she only followed orders when she wanted to, and ignored them when she didn't. Like right now.

"Get up," he hissed. "We need to move before the sun gets too hot."

She mumbled that it wouldn't get hot for hours. Emir grabbed the edge of her cloak and yanked upward. She shrieked as she tumbled out and lay sprawled across the rough ground.

"I would have dumped water on you, but that'd be wasteful in the desert," he snapped, stalking away.

She threw a handful of sand at his boots. Every bit of her body ached. Even her blisters had blisters. Ari Ara cupped her hands in the tiny stream and splashed her face. She refilled her waterskin carefully then climbed on Mahteni's horse. She let the mare follow Tekli as she tried to doze on the horse's back. Her father had told her that the Harraken could travel all night by sleeping while riding and changing horses at villages. She nearly slipped off twice before she twisted her hands into the mare's black mane.

"Don't do that," Emir scolded, waking her abruptly from a half-doze.

He untangled her wrists. The horsehair had cut into her flesh, leaving red welts. Her fingers tingled as the blood flooded back into them.

"I'm tired," she argued, rubbing her hands and wincing.

"We'll stop and rest during the midday heat," he promised. "Don't loop yourself up like that. If you fell and the mare bolted, you'd be dragged under her and trampled."

He nudged Tekli ahead so she wouldn't argue with him. The sun climbed higher. By midmorning, the beauty of the desert foothills at dawn had transformed into a blisteringly white-hot oven. Ari Ara stopped arguing as their thirst rose; even she knew better than to waste breath and water on pestering him.

As the sun pounded on them like a drum, Emir scoured the foothills for shade, shelter, and water. To the west, the flat plains glistened with heat. To the east, the sloping scree of rocks and shale offered little relief. The heat waves wavered into strange shapes. Twice, he startled with alarm as a shrub transformed into a rider then evaporated into nothing.

"Let's rest and ride at moonrise," Ari Ara begged, her voice rough and dry.

"We've got to keep going. If we miss the next water source in the dark, we'll be in trouble," Emir cautioned.

They rode onward. The horses plodded wearily, not even bothering to lip the mountain grasses. At dusk, as his heart sank in despair, Ari Ara called out that she heard water. The spring burbled against a tumble of rocks. They opened a small pool and channeled the trickle into a second wallow to let the horses slurp thirstily. Emir refilled their waterskins and dolled out a few oatcakes - less than they wanted, but more than they could spare during a journey of unknown length. He considered trying to catch some game - he'd seen rabbits along their path - but his exhaustion hit him like an avalanche and buried him under the weight of sleep.

They traveled like this for two more days, resting in bits and pieces in the worst of the heat or where water and shade offered small comforts. They saw no signs of people. Emir made her repeat Mahteni's instructions until she was sick of acting like a talking parrot. The open hillsides gave way to a conifer forest and the faint trail through the orange needles offered them hope that this was the way to Moragh's. They found no water though, and Emir rationed their sips until Ari Ara's head thudded dully and the edges of the world blurred. That evening, she could hardly chew the dry rock of the oatcake. Her temper grew shorter with every bite. Her waterskin was still half-full and she lifted it to her lips.

"Not so much," Emir warned her, seeing her throat gulp.

"Stop telling me what to do," she snapped back testily. She lowered the waterskin, though.

"Did you tie up the horses?" he asked her.

"You don't tie up desert horses," she grumbled. Her limbs felt heavy as rocks; she didn't want to get up and tie the horses.

"You do if you need them," Emir countered. "Did you - "

"Yes. Alright? I did it already," she spat back, rolling onto her side and turning her back to him, not caring if she lied.

In the morning, the horses were gone.

CHAPTER EIGHT

· · · · ·

Thirst

"You said you tied them!" Emir yelled at her.

The dawn burst with the sharp promise of sweltering heat. The dry pine needles scented the air with sweet resinous perfume. The insects whined in the forest branches. Ari Ara and Emir faced off nose-to-nose, glaring with equal ferocity.

"They're probably close," she muttered, cross and guilty, whirling to scan the trees for their flicking tails.

"We can't spend a day chasing them," Emir argued. "We have to find water. This is all your stupid fault."

She stuck her tongue out at him. He swallowed the urge to slap her . . . or punch a rock, neither of which would help this situation.

"Grow up," he muttered.

"You first," she shot back, kicking the carpet of pine needles at him.

She winced as she stubbed her toe on a buried stone.

"Serves you right," he spat out. "Give me that waterskin."

He stuck his hand out for the waterskin she clutched in one fist. She glowered back at him.

"Why should I?" she fumed.

"If you're going to act like a child, I'm not letting you carry something so important."

"Fine," she shouted back. "If you're going to act like a pompous donkey, you can carry it like the pack mule you are!"

She hurled the waterskin at his head. He ducked instinctively. It hit the boulder behind him and burst. The dark stain of water ran down the stone.

"You idiot!" Emir shouted. A horrified look dawned on his face. "You absolute fool."

Her anger melted into a shocked fear.

"Oh no, no," she moaned. "I didn't mean to - it was an accident - I thought you'd catch it."

"Shut up," Emir snapped heartlessly.

He picked up the broken waterskin and stalked off through the trees. He didn't look back. Ari Ara trailed behind him miserably. Emir refused to speak to her, quivering with so much tense fury that it shimmered off his back like heat waves.

All day, they stumbled through the pine forest without finding water. The trees shrunk to wizened sentinels mocking the pair. Unknown to them, beneath their feet, a seam of water slid down from the mountain peaks between the stone strata. The desert trees lapped up the subterranean streams and stored the water in their thick roots. The Harraken knew to dig down and tap the bulbous roots that served as hidden storage flasks for the trees. The two young foreigners didn't . . . and what they didn't know could kill them.

By the second afternoon, thirst overcame all thoughts of hope and despair. The orange needles crackled underfoot. The wind hissed like snakes in the branches above. When they were forced to rest, they found they could not rise. They sat together, backs against the same tree, delirious visions clouding their minds. A raven cackled from the bough overhead. Its voice sounded like dry stones knocked together. Emir threw a pebble at it, but missed. Ari Ara drifted into hallucinations and dreams. She saw her dream-body slip out of the sprawled shell of her parched life-body like the legends of the Fanten women who had raised her. She saw her second self walking on the wind. She strode up an invisible staircase of air until she reached the cackling raven in the branches above them. She gripped it by the beak.

"Naughty beast," she scolded. "Go get my Aunt Moragh or I'll tell the wind to abandon you and all your hatchlings."

The bird flapped and squawked in alarm, bound by her hold on his black beak. She released him and watched him wing southeast as she floated wearily back down into the hard bundle of bones that made up her all-too-mortal body. Her last thought was that they should walk in the southeast direction, the same path of the raven, if they ever rose from this spot.

She roused hours later to the strange sensation of talons and hard-skinned feet pacing along her ribs. Black wings swiped her sides. A cawing sound banged against her ears.

Go away, she thought, *I'm not dead yet.*

She opened her mouth to speak, but no sound came out of the dry riverbed of her throat. She felt hands lifting her up. Her head lolled. Her limbs drooped, useless. Her eyelids hung heavy, but she glimpsed images of oiled leather and women warriors. Moragh's auburn hair flashed at the edge of her sight. Ari Ara's lips split and bled over her relieved smile.

"Gather their things," she heard Moragh command in her rasping voice.

"And the boy?" someone asked, a note of concern tingeing the words.

A pause.

"Leave him," Moragh answered coldly. "One less Marianan river dog to grow into an enemy."

Ari Ara tried to cry out; her mouth screamed in a soundless rasp. She struggled, but her limbs refused to obey her commands. She tossed her dream-body out of the anchor of her pain like a trumpet's call bursting from a horn.

Help! she cried to the hills in a voice no ordinary mortal could hear. *Help him!*

Then the blackness took her. Her dream-body scrambled up and down the forested hills searching for someone - anyone - who would save Emir.

CHAPTER NINE

· · · · ·

The Black Ravens Stronghold

Ari Ara woke with the sensation that years had passed; that she'd been torn in half and slammed back together; that she'd lost some irreplaceable treasure without meaning to . . .

Emir!

She bolted up at the realization, a croaking sound bursting from her lips. The room spun. She flopped back against the pillow.

"Emir? Where is Emir?" she said, her voice as weak as a mewing kitten.

"That's all she says, poor dear," said a woman, pushing aside the curtain that covered the entry and approaching with another figure on her heels. "Over and over, all through the fever and exhaustion."

She was a plump woman worn thin by life. Her hands wrung a cloth with grim expertise and mopped Ari Ara's brow. Ari Ara shut her eyes as the cool water sent a shiver through her limbs.

"We could not have brought him here," a harsh rasp of a voice replied in a tone hinting of long arguments and debate.

Moragh.

"You should not have left him," the healer reproached the warrior.

"He's gone now," Moragh said with a creak of leather indicating a shrug.

Ari Ara shoved the cloth aside and pushed against the healer's surprisingly firm hold.

"Where is he? What did you - "

"Nothing," Moragh informed her harshly. "We did nothing - which is more than he would have done for us."

"That's not true!" Ari Ara blurted out, arguing to cover the rising panic in her chest.

"He is a warrior; he would slit our throats without flinching."

"You killed him!?" Ari Ara shouted, gripping her temples as the room spun again.

Moragh shook her head in a terse negation. A grim smile tugged her lips into a thin line.

"My patrol sweeps report that he is gone. They searched the area in case scavengers - "

Ari Ara threw her hands over her ears. If words wove truth in Desert Speech, she did not want to hear Moragh's words spell Emir's death.

"He could still be alive, then," Ari Ara insisted.

Moragh shrugged. She doubted it and didn't particularly care if the buzzards feasted on his bones.

"Why?" Ari Ara demanded. "Why didn't you bring him back with us?!"

"Sit up," Moragh ordered.

Her arms crossed over the blackened leather of her chest plate. She shook her auburn mane sharply to silence the healer's protests. If the girl was her niece by blood, she was as strong as the iron veins that ran through the bones of the mountain ranges. The two stared at each other for a long, fierce moment. Then Ari Ara gritted her teeth, ignored her spinning head, and shoved herself up to sitting, biting back a grimace at her soreness and weakness. Moragh nodded in satisfaction and paced to the far side of the alcove. She flung back the patched blanket curtain.

Ari Ara's mouth fell open. Women. Children. Makeshift sleeping rolls folded into stacks along one wall. Benches and tables pulled into place. Huge tureens of soup carried out of one side door. Hundreds of people packed the long hall. Women warriors wove among them, identifiable in their oiled leather with the distinctive raven wing emblem on the back. A row of ravens perched in the rafters, cackling and commentating on the bustle below.

"More women come to me each day," Moragh remarked, turning from the scene and drawing close to Ari Ara, her rasping voice dropping into a low tone as she sat on the edge of the cot. "We are their only refuge and I cannot - will not - compromise that by bringing in men ... especially young enemy warriors."

"Where . . . why are they here?" Ari Ara asked.

Moragh studied her calloused hands. For a moment, her face grew pained. Her eyes bore shadows of hurt and betrayal. Disappointment in her people laced her words as she spoke.

"Something is spreading among our clans. A blight? A plague? I do not know what to call it. My brother is the master of words, not me. The wars have done it, and the rise of warriors-rule through the warriors meets. One by one, day by day, the women's voices are being silenced, cut from the Harraken Song."

Ari Ara frowned and shifted to lean against the wall as she

listened. She studied the back of Moragh's bowed head. Her aunt's muscled shoulders clenched tense with worry. A hundred questions pressed against Ari Ara's throat, but she held them in, afraid that if she interrupted, the fiery-haired woman warrior would stop speaking.

The war ended years ago, Moragh explained, but still the warriors ruled. Decisions and judgments were sent to the warriors meets . . . but warriors-rule was not guided by the same wisdom as the village sings.

"There can be no justice for women when only men decide their fates," Moragh spat out bitterly. "More and more, when a man beats his wife, the warriors say he must have been justified. When a girl refuses to marry her father's choice, the warriors meets force her to marry the man. When a grandmother is ignored by her descendants and shoved to the margins of her own home, the warriors tell her to stop complaining so much. When two women quarrel over one man, the warriors just laugh and jest about how lucky he is."

Moragh spoke on, her eyes tracing from one woman to the next, telling the stories of why they had fled their clans and sought Moragh's protection. At first, it had only been a few. In the beginning, Moragh had simply asked her brother to intercede on the women's behalf.

"But the Harrak-Mettahl left abruptly last year, sneaking into Mariana to meet you," Moragh reminded Ari Ara, "and we were left without recourse. I tried a few times, but . . . "

Her shoulders hunched then dropped. She spread her hands apart to indicate the limits of her strength. She was a warrior, not a harrak-mettahl. She could challenge the offenders to honor duels, but she could not reconcile girls to their opinionated fathers nor make grown men remember why they should respect their frail grandmothers.

"So, I shelter the women and their children, at least until Tahkan can fix this mess."

Moragh leaned her elbows on her knees and hung her head, ashamed of her powerlessness. She was not afraid to stand against any man in battle, but she did not know how to stop the warriors from cutting the women's voices from the Harraken Song. She could not fight all the battles that needed to be fought. The women would have to stand up for themselves.

"I protect them, shelter them, and teach them to fight," she explained. "An army of women can defend their rights far better than a single champion."

A hand fell on her shoulder. Moragh flinched, but it was just the girl, her eyes wide with conflicting emotions of compassion for her aunt's challenges and anger at the abandonment of her friend.

"This is why I could not bring him here," she told the girl, her eyes speaking the apology her voice could not utter. Her life was made of difficult choices; this one had not been the worst, not even close to the worst. "He may have survived. I do not know."

She turned away from the worry welling up in the girl's eyes.

"Tell me how you came to be on your own in our woods," Moragh said, gesturing for the healer to fetch some soup for the girl. "It is a dangerous journey even for those of us who know this terrain."

Ari Ara swallowed the lump in her throat and explained. Moragh's face grew tight at the mention of the riders, and grave at the report of Mahteni's disappearance. She rose and paced the confines of the alcove, tiring Ari Ara with questions until the healer insisted she let the girl rest. Moragh muttered about sending out messenger hawks and stormed away. Ari Ara sank back against the pillow, almost too tired to eat, feeling like she had been squeezed through a clothes wringer.

"Is she always like that?" she sighed.

"Yes," the healer replied caustically, "except when she's worse."

As soon as she could rise, Moragh put her to work. Everyone worked; the tasks required to shelter hundreds of women and children began before dawn and slowed only in the evening when the main hall turned into a field of slumbering bodies. The smallest children shook out rugs and ported bundles from storage rooms to the kitchen. Their older siblings chopped vegetables for the cooks and pounded herbs under the watchful eyes of the healers. The younger women tended the fields just outside the high walls that enclosed the training yard. The older women worked the looms and sewed tunics and a hundred other tasks. Everyone rotated through trainings in self-defense.

"Even you," Moragh warned Ari Ara.

"I can defend myself with the Way Between," she retorted indignantly. She could hold her own against the best of warriors and told Moragh so.

The older woman lifted a dark auburn eyebrow.

"We will test that claim when you are fully recovered," she decided, choosing not to argue with the girl. "Until then, train by yourself in the Way Between. Regain your strength."

The next morning, before the sun wilted her like a lettuce leaf, Ari Ara found a relatively still corner of the dusty yard. At first, she felt limp and creaky. Steadily and methodically, she worked through the limbering exercises until her body felt fluid as the talkative stream that ran under the walls and through the edge of the yard. She sensed the eyes of the women and children flicking in her direction as she built up speed and momentum, shifting from foundational trainings into more difficult lunges, rolls, leaps, and dives. She ignored them; she was used to stares.

Ari Ara pushed her training harder. Sweat formed on her brow. Her legs ached. Dust covered her clothes. The exertion silenced her worries. She surrendered to the solidity of muscles and gravity, the loft of leaps and the hard impact of landings. She rolled across the dirt and sprang to her feet, whirling to face her imagined partner.

"What are you doing?" a young voice asked in a skeptical tone.

She spun. A small cluster of girls had gathered at a wary distance. Their wiry arms crossed over their faded work robes. Some hooked their thumbs into woven belts and met her gaze boldly. Others flushed and avoided meeting her eyes.

"Practicing the Way Between," Ari Ara told them, realizing with a jolt that they were barely younger than she had been when she first apprenticed to Shulen.

"What's that?" one asked.

"A way of stopping violence without causing further harm," Ari Ara answered, beginning to move again.

"You look silly," a black-haired girl scoffed.

"That's because I'm practicing alone," she answered, "dodging the wind and evading the invisible. If you saw me with Emir or Shulen - "

Shrieks erupted. The girls scattered in all directions - except for one who watched Ari Ara with a guarded expression.

"Why'd they run away?" Ari Ara asked her.

"You mentioned Shulen the Butcher," the girl muttered, turning her head and spitting into the dust. "They're afraid of him."

"Are you?" Ari Ara asked, a sick feeling in her stomach to

think of her mentor causing that kind of fear.

The girl shook her head.

"I'm only afraid of what I need to be. There's no war now . . . why should I fear a memory?"

"What are you afraid of, then?" Ari Ara asked, mostly to keep the conversation going.

"My stepfather," the girl answered in a tight tone. She glared at Ari Ara then stalked away across the dusty training yard.

It was only when she turned that Ari Ara saw the fading welts and bruises on the back of the girl's legs where she'd been brutally caned with a switch.

"He beat her," Ari Ara murmured to herself.

"Yes," Moragh's hard voice answered.

The warrior woman had noticed her guards' distraction on the upper wall and followed their gazes to the redheaded girl's leaps and whirls.

Like a cat darting at unseen threats, Moragh thought. She scolded the Black Ravens for neglecting their posts and headed down to the girl, arriving in time to overhear the last exchange.

"Now you know why we must be able to fight back," Moragh stated in an uncompromising tone. "Not just dance around shadows."

She scoffed at the girl. Ari Ara's ears burned red.

"The Way Between *is* fighting back," she argued. "It's fighting back *differently* . . . in a way where you can change, heal, and maybe even live together in the same village again."

Moragh looked affronted.

"Do *not* presume to know better than us how our lives must be handled, girl," she growled. "I stopped the invasion of your mother's people; I have left thousands dead at my feet. I have seen and done things beyond your wildest nightmares." She gestured to the women training in the yard. "This is not your problem to critique or challenge. Close your mouth. Do as you are told. Is that clear?"

"Perfectly," Ari Ara shot back furiously.

Then Moragh stormed away, leaving Ari Ara pierced by the stares of the others.

For the rest of the day, Ari Ara obeyed her aunt's instructions. She drank her soup. She ate her bread. She rested. Built strength. Did the tasks assigned to her. She also studied the Black Raven's guard rotations and eyed the gates, but when she tested her ability to leave, two strong-armed women blocked her path.

"Moragh's orders," they answered when she wanted to know why she wasn't allowed out.

Ari Ara backed away, inwardly seething. How dare her aunt keep her captive! No one held a follower of the Way Between against her will. She was determined to retrace her path to where they had abandoned Emir. She wanted to search the area with her own eyes. If she found his trail . . . she wouldn't finish that thought, but she did surreptitiously pocket dried fruits and nuts, oatcakes and a spare waterskin.

That evening, she collected the necessary tools for travel and hid them under her cot: a rucksack, a flint stone, anti-venom medicines to counter snakebites. After hours of furtive searching, she found her old travel gear and cloak in a storage room. She stored a second water skin alongside the first and scoured the Stronghold for a map. She didn't find one, but she ran across blank parchment, a quill, and a vial of black ink. She stowed them away, reasoning that if she left Moragh a note before she left, the warrior woman would at least know where she'd gone . . . just in case she did run into trouble. Also, her messenger hawk, Nightfast, was bound to catch up to her and she could send a note to her father so he wouldn't worry.

Ari Ara chewed her lip as she lay awake in her cot at night, planning. The important thing was to find Emir; he could be weakened or injured or desperate for water - Ari Ara cut off the thought abruptly. It was her fault he was in danger. She'd leave tomorrow before dawn. Everyone would assume she'd risen early to practice the Way Between in the cool semi-darkness. By the time they thought to look for her, she'd be far ahead of them.

CHAPTER TEN

· · · · ·

The Young Tala-Rasa

Slipping up and over the outer wall was simple. The drop jarred her, but she gritted her teeth and flattened against the cool stones with the hood of her dark cloak drawn up over her bright hair. When no shouts of warning rang out, she crossed the open space between the wall and forest, thanking the ancestors for the Fanten skills that allowed her to slip between shadows and walk with a silent tread. She'd never fool a Fanten, but the Black Ravens patrolling this section did not detect the small ripple in the semi-darkness as she darted through the trees.

She'd gleaned a rough idea of the region from the women who were sent to gather firewood. She pried the details of where they'd found her and Emir from two young Black Ravens who felt guilty about leaving the youth behind. He was a handsome youth even if he was a river dog, one had said, and perhaps it hadn't been right to leave him for the scavengers. Ari Ara fought the urge to roll her eyes. Even half-dead with cracked skin and bleeding lips, Emir Miresh could apparently charm the skin off a snake and the disdain off a Black Raven's heart. Too bad it hadn't worked on Moragh Shirar.

In their delirium, she and Emir had staggered past the Stronghold without realizing it. They'd collapsed in the pine forest slightly to the northwest. Ari Ara set off in that direction at a steady pace, keeping a careful eye out for the landmarks she'd learned from her inquiries.

By the time the rising sun burned the sweet coolness from the dawn, Ari Ara had found the spot where they'd sunk down against the tree trunk. Days had passed, but the lack of rain and the shelter of the pines had left the tracks clear enough in the dust. She had once tracked wandering lambs in her days as a High Mountain shepherdess tending the Fanten flock of black, long-legged sheep. Carefully pacing in a ring around the perimeter of the area, she drew upon those skills as she read the messages in the ground.

Ari Ara saw paw prints of predators - not the huge sand lions that were said to prowl the lower altitudes, but one of the striped dogs that usually ran in packs. Emir must have been long gone when the creature paused to sniff the spot; the clawed tracks trotted onward. A surge of hope rose in her chest . . . there were no signs of a scavengers' feast. At the far end of her cautious circle of inspection, she paused.

Two sets of human feet had halted here. They'd dismounted from horses, shuffling the ground, perhaps conferring. They were not Black Ravens; the women warriors wore leather boots. These tracks belonged to supple sandals woven from the fibers of a desert shrub. Something had made these two pause. Her eyes traced the footsteps, her heart rate increasing with every print. They could have approached the sprawled figure . . . hefted him . . . staggered under the weight . . . returned to the horses and set off northwest.

Ari Ara followed the trail. A flare of fury surged in her heart. The hoof prints remained clear; the Black Ravens on the patrol sweep hadn't even bothered to follow the trail. Her anger at her aunt's abandonment of Emir burned furiously in her; she struggled to keep it contained. Her father had often warned her to master her temper. She was a Shirar . . . her words could call lightning from the sky, or so the legends claimed.

She followed the tracks westward through the forest. At midday, she reached a rocky streambed and lost the trail. The riders could have gone up or down; she didn't know which. Frustrated, she sat down in the shade to rest and think. She tried listening to the wind, but she wasn't Harraken enough to understand its whispers the way her father did. She ate, napped for an hour, and then flipped a flat stone with white flecks on one side to determine which direction to search first.

"Downstream it is," she said.

Her words sounded loud and lonely against the soughing wind moving through the long pine needles overhead. Ari Ara clambered down the stacks of water-smoothed boulders. The trickling stream wound through a rocky watercourse, burbling and chuckling at secret jokes. Ari Ara followed it in a slow zigzag, hopping from one side to the other to search the edges for any muddy prints of travelers and horses. She kept a watchful eye on the high banks, in case the riders had walked further in among the shrubs.

An hour later, she'd seen nothing. She skidded on a patch of loose gravel, catching her fall with flailing arms. Irritated, she snatched up a stone and flung it along the boulders lining the streambed, listening to the clack, clunk, smack of stone hitting stone.

An affronted whinny burst out from behind the last boulder. A familiar gold head shook its ivory mane in protest.

"Zyrh?!" Ari Ara cried, astonished to see the horse.

She scrambled over the boulders until she drew closer.

Ari Ara froze.

Someone stood on top of the horse's back, casually, as relaxed as an acrobat. The person turned, slight and slender. A pair of blazing green eyes pinned Ari Ara.

"*There* you are," the youth stated with a mixture of exasperation and excitement. "I've been looking all over for you."

"Why?" Ari Ara questioned, squinting curiously at the stranger.

The figure on the horse's back could be either boy or girl, and was not much older than Ari Ara. A tight crown of coppery-black curls framed the youth's angular face. A simple tunic with a scarlet belt contrasted the stranger's deep umber skin.

"Professional curiosity," the youth answered, hopping from Zyrh's back to a grey boulder, lithe as a goat and just as bony. "I'm Tala."

A hand shot out, palm up in greeting. Ari Ara tentatively placed hers over it, palm down. The heat between their skin tingled. Ari Ara stared openly. A wry smile curled across the youth's lips. An echo of laughter leapt up, unexpected and inexplicable, in Ari Ara's heart.

"Confuses everyone at first," Tala said, cheerfully unperturbed by her frank gaze, "but a girl named Ari Ara ought to know something about being *neither this nor that*. I'm one of the Tala-Rasa; we walk the unknowns, the spaces between this and that, the margins of village and wild, mountain and valley, inside and out."

The words drummed rhythmically, an almost-incantation refusing to be a clear chant. Tala's bemused laughter underscored the sound.

"Where have you been?" Ari Ara blurted out. "My Aunt

Mahteni has been looking for you."

Tala gave a wry snort - everyone knew the best way to *find* the Tala-Rasa was to let them find you.

"We've been in the mountains," Tala replied, "avoiding the warriors."

"So, what are you doing here?" Ari Ara asked, suspiciously.

"Er, well," the bird-like youth avoided her eyes with a sheepish look. "The elders were just sitting around talking and talking, trying to figure out what to do. We sang *all* the old songs until our voices croaked like toads in dried up ponds. I told the others that what we needed was a *new* song, but no one ever listens to me."

Tala's thin shoulders lifted and fell.

"Finally, I got bored and left the elders to their endless songs and talk. We weren't going to find a new song just sitting around reciting the old ones." Tala's long fingers spread in an open-handed gesture of surrender.

"I see," Ari Ara said, though she didn't, not really. "What do I call you? Do you have a name?"

"No, no. Only my birth parents still use my once-name. Now I'm Tala, one of the thirteen all called Tala, or Tala-Rasa collectively, named for what we are. We're songholders, teachers, travelers, speakers, storytellers, witnesses, and arbitrators of fates," Tala recited, "all of these things and more."

The Tala-Rasa defied convention while standing at the center of Harraken culture. They flaunted expectations while being teachers of tradition. They broke custom while maintaining history in song and story.

"Our job is to know the rules in order to change them when the time is right," Tala said.

"Sounds like a tough job for so few people," Ari Ara commented.

Tala nodded vigorously. Once, Tala mentioned ruefully, there were hundreds of Tala-Rasa. Now there were only thirteen.

"Or twelve, if you ask my elders," Tala sighed, "but I know the songs and the singing of songs, so they can't keep the Ancestor Wind from stealing my birth-name and giving me the title of Tala-Rasa."

Ari Ara gave up trying to understand it all and asked the question at the forefront of her mind.

"Are all the Tala-Rasa, um, neither male nor female?" she asked.

"Oh, certainly, but we're not not-female or not-male. We simply are as we are - though even that changes."

"That's confusing," Ari Ara pointed out.

"Confusion is the start of a question," Tala answered with a cheeky wink.

"What - how does one describe a Tala?" Ari Ara asked. "He? She?"

"It's simple in Desert Speech. Use *ze, zir, zirs* instead of *he, him, his* or *she, her, hers.* I've heard the Marianan's language can't handle us as well, having only two genders, or lack of gender like *it, its,*" Tala explained while balancing on the thin edge of one of the boulders. "Maybe *they? Theirs?* Neutral plural? I rather like the idea of confusing everyone about whether I'm one or many."

"You already do that," Ari Ara muttered under her breath as Tala slowly circled, examining her from grubby knees to disheveled hair.

"Am I more or less what you expected?" Ari Ara asked irascibly, feeling like a goat under inspection at a market.

"Both," Tala pronounced. "More stubborn, less tall."

Ari Ara made a face at the description. Tala waggled a long

finger under her nose.

"Stubborn can be useful. So can being short. After all, tall people hit their heads on short doorways."

"You're crazy!" Ari Ara shot back, but she was laughing despite herself.

"Oh yes, sanity is for those who stay behind fences and follow rules."

Tala cocked zirs head at her.

"You don't look like that kind of sane . . . which is why I advise you to come with me to find the river dog boy."

"River dog boy?" Ari Ara cried, hope flaring in her chest like a blaze on dry kindling. "You mean Emir Miresh?"

"Yes," the youth said with a grin. "A naughty raven told me he was in the area."

Tala's wickedly delighted laughter leapt from boulder to boulder, clear as a bell, neither high nor low. Ari Ara wanted to shake him . . . her . . . zir, she corrected herself sternly as her mind stumbled a bit before reorienting to the new pronoun.

"Do you know where he is?" Ari Ara asked, rising to standing.

"No," Tala answered with a little shrug and a sly wink, "but I know who will."

CHAPTER ELEVEN

· · · · ·

Throw-the-Bones

They traveled swiftly, Ari Ara riding behind Tala on Zyrh. To her annoyance, the mischievous horse behaved perfectly for the odd songholder. Ari Ara had greeted the golden creature with wary respect; after all, Zyrh had shown great loyalty and courage by chasing off the riders. The unrepentant beast promptly swiveled to the side and whacked her in the face with his tail. Though Zyrh was cheerfully - disgustingly - obedient to Tala, any time Ari Ara was left on his back alone, he shimmied and shied and tried to dump her in the dust. Once, she swore Zyrh stepped right out from under her, leaving her hanging midair for an astonished second before she thudded to the earth, adding bruises on top of sore muscles.

Up a long, winding ravine, tucked into a pocket meadow, lived a seer named Throw-the-Bones. Her home - if you could call it that - was a hide-covered lean-to half dug into the earth. A sod roof of desert grass grew above it; a rangy, horned goat bleated at them from on top. A desert chicken scratched in the dirt out front, scraggly-feathered with a flopping ochre comb. A dry bone-and-branch fence ringed the hut, white and stark, bleached by the blazing blue sky. Tala nudged Zyrh through the listing gate then slid off to push it shut.

"Leave it open," a voice croaked out, dry as a spiny toad.

A hunched figure staggered toward them. Dangling locks of hair masked her face. Her grotesque cloak of rodent skulls, crows' beaks, birds' feet, and shed snakeskins lurched with every step.

"You'll be leaving quicker than you came," the woman rasped. "They all do."

"Not Tala, Throw-the-Bones, you know that," Tala called out soothingly.

"What's that?" the figure cried with surprise, pushing back her matted hair and shading the sun from her eyes. "Tala? Well, that changes things. Come in for tea!"

Ari Ara blinked as the bedraggled figure dropped the rasping voice and tossed off a tangled wig. The slender, middle-aged woman cast aside the cloak with a look of disgust. She patted the stray wisps of brown hair back into place and straightened her spine. She wore a clean tunic and a bright blue belt. The wrinkles around her eyes creased at Ari Ara's astonished expression and she burst out laughing merrily.

"The ole cloak-and-croak act is just to scare away unwanted visitors," she said, "but a friend of Tala's is a friend of mine."

She winked and squeezed Tala around the shoulders. Ari Ara dismounted and followed the other two toward the hut. The woman turned with a brisk, no-nonsense attitude and eyed Ari Ara.

"You must know I'm Throw-the-Bones, but who are you? Potential Tala-Rasa?"

Ari Ara shook her head.

"Ari Ara Shirar en Marin."

Throw-the-Bones' mouth dropped open. Her eyes rolled back in her sockets. A tremor shuddered through her. Tala calmly pinched the woman's nose, held her mouth shut, and counted to thirty. At thirty-three and a half, Throw-the-Bones threw Tala off, gasping.

"Thanks," Throw-the-Bones coughed out. "Ack. That was a strong one. Good thing she didn't come on her own."

Tala let the wheezing seer lean on zirs shoulders and lurch into the shade of the hut. Throw-the-Bones settled in a chair as the young songholder gathered a trio of small cups along with a little clay teapot. The youth opened the lid and sniffed cautiously.

"Just a bit of spring mint," Throw-the-Bones told the youth. "Nothing to worry about."

She threw back her first cup and gestured impatiently for another while Ari Ara stood frozen in the doorway with an appalled look on her face, wondering what had just happened.

"Visions, love," Throw-the-Bones explained, pointing to a three-legged stool and gesturing for the girl to sit. "Such a bother, really."

"Wh-what would have happened if Tala hadn't held your nose?" Ari Ara asked, tentatively sitting down.

Throw-the-Bones shrugged.

"Maybe I'd wake on my own a few hours later . . . or not."

She shivered despite the red flush on her skin and sweat beads on her brow.

"Given the strength of these visions, I might never have come out of them, though old Stew's trained to peck me back to life if I don't feed him his grain on time."

She pointed to the chicken, which stretched his neck and crowed before strutting out of sight. When Ari Ara turned back, Throw-the-Bones' sharp eyes were fixed on her face.

"What did you see?" Ari Ara asked, clutching the edge of the stool and steeling herself. There was already one prophecy about her and it wasn't pleasant. To her surprise, the middle-aged woman simply rolled her eyes and shoved her cup across the rough surface of her table for more mint tea.

"Oh no, it doesn't work like that. Not even for you, though I'm sorely tempted to make an exception." Throw-the-Bones leveled a stern look at Ari Ara. "No, no, if I risk death to see your future, you've got to pay prettily for that knowledge."

"But I didn't ask you to see my future!" Ari Ara objected.

"Precisely. Which is why I don't charge for seeing, only for telling. I'll be keeping my vision in my silence until you're ready to pay."

"You won't tell anyone else?"

"Certainly not!" Throw-the-Bones retorted, looking insulted. "That's unethical. Didn't you explain?"

The last was directed accusatorily at Tala, who simply shrugged. The woman blew an exasperated sigh and turned back to Ari Ara.

"The bone fence, the skull cape, the raspy voice; that's all for show. Idiots come to me to find their true loves or destinies. Most of them have lives so dull it pains me to wade through the visions."

She rubbed her temples. People lived. They tended goats. They met a girl. They married a boy. Children were born.

"Everyone dies," Throw-the-Bones sighed, "and I always see that. It's where I get most of my knowledge, though no one likes to hear that. I peek in at the funerals, count the wedding rings and scars, notice how many children have gathered, and look for any telltale callouses on people's hands. That's enough to hint at a life . . . though occasionally, I see more. Wars and famines. Bold lives and cowardly deaths. Simple existences and perfect happiness. Long-living elders and easy exits. Short flickers and sudden snuffing outs."

Throw-the-Bones' face grew shadowed. Her fingers clutched the clay cup hard enough to turn her knuckles white.

"I can see why you wouldn't want too much company," Ari Ara said gently. "I'm sorry if hearing my name caused you distress."

The brown-haired woman looked up. Her eyebrows lifted.

"In all my years," she murmured, "no one has ever said that."

She held out her hand and squeezed Ari Ara's palm in gratitude.

"When the day comes that you face a crossroad of no clear choices, come to me, and I will tell you which way you went."

"You could tell her now," Tala pointed out, "and spare her the trip."

Throw-the-Bones snatched the teapot away and sloshed some more in her cup.

"You are both too young to know the wisdom of anything," she grumbled. "Especially you, cheeky Tala. Such impertinence! Do I tell you how to sing the old songs? No. You do your job and trust me to do mine."

Tala looked sufficiently chastened . . . at least until the youth tossed Ari Ara a hidden wink behind the seer's back.

"But none of this is the question you came to ask, is it?" Throw-the-Bones asked suddenly with a sharp astuteness, looking from one to the other.

"I need to find my friend Emir Miresh," Ari Ara explained.

"The Marianan warrior?" Throw-the-Bones asked in surprise.

Ari Ara nodded and related the tale of how she lost him.

The woman listened with a troubled expression. She tapped

her fingers on the wooden table in agitation. She grimaced.

"Oh, I hate this," she groaned to Tala. "Take the cups and fetch the bones."

Tala cleaned everything off the battered table. Ari Ara stared at the surface . . . the blackened gouges looked like a map . . . ah! She tilted her head; it was the desert. There were the mountains, the foothills, the winding streams and rivers. Thin red lines wove in intricate patterns through it all, perplexing her. She reached out to touch the web. Throw-the-Bones slapped her hand away.

"Don't meddle. I'm going to find your friend's bones, living or dead."

Ari Ara blanched.

Tala returned with a basket of old bones, large and small, some shiningly clean, others with bits of gristle still attached. Throw-the-Bones began to ask her a series of questions about Emir.

"Short or tall?"

"Tall."

She picked out the tiny fish and bird bones and discarded them to the side.

"Old or young?"

"Young," Ari Ara answered, watching the woman's hands fly as she tossed out the cracked and yellowed old bones.

"Color of eyes?"

"Uh, blue, I think," Ari Ara stammered. She hadn't really thought about it.

"Hmm, not clear enough," the seer answered. "Stout or slender?"

"Slender."

"Water or fire?"

"Water. He's like a river when he moves."

Each time she answered, Throw-the-Bones sorted out more bones until the choice was down to two. She weighed them in her palms, thinking, then set aside one.

"Here, hold this," the older woman ordered, tossing the other vertebra to Ari Ara.

"Ew!" she screeched, dropping it with a disgusted grimace. There were still red tendons attached to it.

Throw-the-Bones eyed her, shook her head, and picked the bone up.

"Hmm, how about this, then?" the woman asked, turning suddenly and snatching something off the high shelf behind her.

It was a strange stone, smooth with time and a river's touch, black as ink, and warm against Ari Ara's palm.

"What is it?" Ari Ara asked, holding it up to the light.

"An old thing from long ago," Throw-the-Bones answered. "A tree's heart turned to stone by lightning. A bone that is not a bone."

She stretched out her hand. Ari Ara gave it back. Throw-the-Bones nodded approvingly as she rolled back her sleeves and weighed the lightning stone in her palm.

"Your friend has a very old soul and a truly good heart. If we find him, don't lose him again," the seer advised her. "You do not find friends like him every day."

Ari Ara nodded silently, suddenly hot with embarrassment over the way she'd treated Emir. Throw-the-Bones began to chant in a low voice, cupping her hands around the lightning stone. She shook her hands, slowly at first, then rhythmically, chanting faster and faster until she opened her palms above the table. Her eyes traced the arc of the fall to where the stone landed squarely with a single thump, no bounce, no spin.

"This is Moragh's Stronghold," Throw-the-Bones stated,

pointing to a black mark slightly east of the stone. "You last saw Emir here, just to the northwest."

Ari Ara nodded. Throw-the-Bones picked up the lightning stone. She repeated the chanting and shaking, though the words changed slightly. A crackle of energy snapped through the hut. Her hands split open. The stone fell. It hit the mark northwest of the Stronghold then spun and spun and spun along the red lines, wavering from one side of the table to the other, traveling the length from north to south. Finally, it came to rest in the Middle Pass of the Border Mountains.

Throw-the-Bones scowled and harrumphed in surprise. Ari Ara opened her mouth to ask, but the woman lifted her hand for silence.

"Tala, sing the Truth-Telling Song."

"But - "

"Do it!"

All the hairs on Ari Ara's arms rose up as the two voices joined, one singing, one chanting. The air tightened as if bound by an invisible noose. Throw-the-Bones shook the stone between her palms. Her whole body rattled with the gesture, quicker and quicker. Then, the woman's hands flew open. The lightning stone hit the table and spun in place for a long moment. It fell at the exact same spot as before in the middle of the Border Mountains.

Tala squinted at the table. Throw-the-Bones scowled and folded her arms over her chest.

"That," she stated flatly, "was not what I was expecting."

Ari Ara couldn't stay silent any longer.

"What? What does it mean?" she blurted out.

Throw-the-Bones' fingers stretched out.

"There is where you left him." She pointed to the first spot then moved, tracing the wandering pathway of the second toss.

"This is where he has been . . . or will be," she said. "It's never exactly clear."

"So, he's alive!" Ari Ara cried in relief.

"Maybe," the woman answered with a scowl. "Maybe not. A spinning bone indicates that someone is on the edge of life and death, spirit and mortal life. I have never seen a bone dance the threshold line as long as that. It is strange."

Throw-the-Bones tapped her chin.

"The third toss is where you will meet again. Here in the Border Mountains. But your friend still spun the spirit-mortal dance. Why would anyone move him over all that distance if he were sick or injured or near death? That, I cannot understand."

She had thought the bones hid the truth on the second toss; that's why she had Tala sing the Truth-Telling Song. The melody made the bones fall honestly.

"Whatever that was, it's speaking the truth."

"When should I meet him there?" Ari Ara asked, pointing to the mountains.

Throw-the-Bones looked up, eyes clouded and distant.

"Do not seek him. Your paths will find each other."

Then she shivered out of her reverie, stoked the fire, and refilled the teapot. She bustled about the hut, ignoring Ari Ara's pestering questions, packing away the bones, replacing the odds-and-ends on the table, tossing a handful of grain to Stew the Chicken. Tala quietly rose and gestured to Ari Ara to follow; they'd get no more out of Throw-the-Bones.

"Wait."

The woman's voice stopped them as they left. She snatched the lightning stone off the table.

"Take this."

"I couldn't," Ari Ara protested.

Throw-the-Bones shook her head.

"It is tied to him now. I can't use it again."

She grabbed Ari Ara's wrist, turned her hand over, and placed the black stone in the girl's palm.

"There is the matter of payment, too," Throw-the-Bones said sternly.

"I have little - " Ari Ara began.

The woman held a finger up to her lips and tilted her head as if listening . . . or remembering.

"You will travel the dragon ranges, the desert ridges, the marshlands, the desert sands," she chanted in an odd, distant tone. "Your paths will crisscross past the Crossroads, but your eyes will not meet until after the women and warriors collide, and the exile is exiled from exile."

Throw-the-Bones' eyes rolled back in her head. She shivered. The woman's limbs shook from head to toe. She gasped as if she was resurfacing from a deep dive into a cold lake. She braced her trembling palms on the table.

"For payment," she croaked, "you will promise me something."

"What?" Ari Ara asked warily.

"When the young warrior returns, the old warrior will ask for your help. You will give it," Throw-the-Bones stated firmly.

A shiver and tingle ran through Ari Ara's spine. She nodded.

"No more questions now," the seer insisted. "I have no more answers for you."

She hustled them out the door, onto Zyrh, and beyond her gate. As the latch clicked into place, she eyed the redheaded girl riding away. She had no more answers for Ari Ara Shirar en Marin, not until they next met on the long road called life.

CHAPTER TWELVE

· · · · ·

Orryn's Tale

"Now what?" Ari Ara groaned as they rode away from the bone fence.

In front of her, Tala's slender shoulders lifted then fell. The heat of the afternoon sun soaked into them. The dry gravel crunched under the horse's steps. Hidden in the low shrubs and spindly grasses, insects struck up a high-pitched whine. The sound surrounded them like a band of tiny, unseen warriors, sharp and piercing, buzzing at the edges. Ari Ara's shoulders twitched uneasily. Every fiber in her body resisted returning to the Stronghold - Moragh's wrath undoubtedly awaited - but she didn't know where else to go. She'd failed to find Emir . . . and she couldn't just set off for the Middle Pass on her own. She groaned and laid her forehead on Tala's thin shoulder.

"Don't worry," Tala told her, craning around, "we'll find this warrior friend of yours. Throw-the-Bones promised."

"But what if he's dead?" Ari Ara objected. "What if there's nothing left but his spirit, wandering in the Ancestor River?"

"Wind," Tala corrected her. "We call it the Ancestor Wind here. It's too dry for spirit rivers."

Ari Ara kicked the air in frustration. Zyrh swiveled his head and snapped his teeth at her. She made a face back, knowing the beast wouldn't throw her off with Tala sitting in front of her. They rode quietly after that, backtracking, re-tracing the path toward the Black Ravens Stronghold. The sun crept lower on the western horizon, infusing the landscape with lingering gold light. Suddenly, Zyrh stilled under them, ears flicking back and forth, listening. In the spill of boulders and short twisted trees ahead of them, a figure ducked out of sight.

"Show yourself!" Tala called out in a ringing tone of command. "I am Tala-Rasa! No truth or person hides from me."

A sound of relief leapt out, followed by a woman. The traveler wore the simple garb of the desert: a long tunic over pants made from pale cloth that reflected the sun's glare, accented by the bright band of a vermillion belt and wrist ties to keep the dust out. The woman's face was haggard and she approached wearily as if she had ridden hard for days. She was tall; her limbs seemed to stretch forever. Sunlight crowned her dark brown hair. Ari Ara's mouth flew open in surprise as she recognized the woman.

"Orryn?"

Orryn had crossed the Border Mountains with Ari Ara, one of the thousands of water workers released from servitude by the end of the Water Exchange. She was capable and self-contained, a woman who knew her business and took care of it. She quarreled with no one and tolerated no one's nonsense. Her almond-shaped eyes rounded into walnuts at the sight of the red-haired girl.

"Ari Ara Shirar?!" Orryn exclaimed, running forward to clasp the girl's outstretched hand.

"What are you doing here?" the question sprang from their

lips at the same time.

"It's a long story," Ari Ara answered with a short laugh.

"Come, share my meal and your story," Orryn offered, gesturing to the cluster of boulders where she had made camp.

Tala eyed the sun as it sank down toward the low edge of the distant western horizon and nodded. The daylight stretched long this time of year; they could talk for a while before continuing on to the Black Ravens Stronghold. Zyrh strode forward, calling out in a whinny. A horse answered from behind the boulders then stepped into view. The two horses sniffed each other and exchanged secrets in their silent, unfathomable horse language. The people settled down by a brushwood fire crackling in a dug pit. A small pot with a meager stew bubbled. Tala added substance to the broth from zirs pouch of powdered stores of dried beans and vegetables.

"Sounds like we both leapt out of the frying pan into the fire," Orryn mentioned as Ari Ara told her tale. "I haven't heard anything about Emir Miresh, but I've been avoiding those who might know."

At their curious looks the woman recounted her story.

"The welcome back home wasn't what I expected," Orryn confessed, a bitter note cracking her voice. When they had arrived in Turim, she had been dismayed to find her family house in the city boarded up and empty. Usually her grandmother stayed through the hot season, maintaining the clan's participation in the shared fields, hosting those from other families who stayed to work. Orryn worried that the elderly woman had died while she had been working in the Marianan factories. Eager to see her family, Orryn had asked her horse to carry her to the far north where vast plains of grass provided grazing for horses, goats, and cattle. Her family spent the spring through harvest there. She rode hard over the plains and up the canyons to the hills. When she found the grazing camp, she had breathed a sigh of relief to see the silver hair of her grandmother.

"But there was trouble," Orryn recounted with an ominous tone.

All had seemed normal at first: a celebratory meal, singing, the family's joy at seeing her. But that night, while the men snored and the children murmured in dreams under the star-strewn sky, her grandmother crept close to her sleeping roll, woke her with a finger to her lips, and beckoned for her to follow.

"You must take Nalia and flee tonight," the old woman begged her tall granddaughter.

"I laughed at first," Orryn told the two youths. "Nalia was to be married soon. I had just arrived. Where did the old woman think we would go?"

The grandmother told her to go to the Black Ravens, or back to Turim City. She insisted that anywhere was better than staying - the would-be husband was a cruel man, the girl had barely crossed into womanhood, this was no love match; her little sister was being traded for cattle.

"*And you will be, too,* my grandmother warned me," Orryn related, her eyes flashing at the indignity of such an insult. "I told my grandmother that I had just stopped the mills of Mariana, ridden the river dragon to the capital, defied the enemy in the heart of their homeland, and rescued the descendant of Shirar! No man would marry me against my will. It goes against our traditions!"

Orryn's chin tilted up in pride and fury.

"I confronted my father that very night," Orryn related with a rueful shake of her head. "I told him he had less honor than the river dogs, who, for all their idiocies, at least let their women marry as they choose. We are not cattle to be traded, I told him."

Nalia had been tearfully tugging on one of her arms, her grandmother clutching the other, begging her to stop

"He struck me," Orryn said quietly, "and ordered me to be silent or he would haul me in front of the warriors meet to be flogged for forgetting the honor of serving one's family."

Her voice choked on the irony of the words. She had sacrificed years of her life to secure the water for the families of the desert . . . and *this* was what she came home to? Orryn broke free and ran, whistling for her horse. She called for Nalia to come, but her father and brothers seized her. So, Orryn rode away into the night, following her grandmother's instructions to seek out Moragh.

"And here I am," Orryn sighed, tossing a branch onto the fire, "headed to the Black Ravens to ask for their aid. No Harraken woman is married against her will! We cannot stand for this."

Ari Ara stirred uneasily.

"What do you think Moragh will do?" she asked. "Force the men to back down at sword point? Honor challenge your father? Moragh's looking for an excuse to start a fight. She's training women to become warriors - "

Orryn cut her off with a sharp look.

"If it is a choice between fighting or being flogged, the women should fight."

"It's not," Ari Ara shot back, lifting her chin. Dusk light gleamed in her hair. "There's always a Way Between. We could train the girls and women the way Shulen trained the water workers."

"What about Nalia?" Orryn asked anxiously. "She'll be married by the week's end. The former water workers like me have some training in the Way Between, but the rest don't. They won't have time to train - "

"They don't have time to train as warriors, either," Ari Ara pointed out. "Maybe Moragh's Black Ravens can best a Harraken warrior, but most of the women sheltering at the Stronghold couldn't. If you pick a fight with the men right now, you'll probably lose."

Orryn's face grew stony and frustrated.

Tala tossed a stick in the fire.

"Ari Ara's right. If you're called to an honor challenge, you get to pick the weapons. And everyone knows it's stupid to choose the weapon your opponent is better at using."

"The Way Between served us well in Mariana," Orryn acknowledged. "If it offers an alternative, I'd be glad to hear it. I just don't see what can be done."

"How soon is the wedding?" Ari Ara asked.

"In a few days," Orryn reported. Her grandmother had told her that Nalia was to be escorted to the marriage by her father and uncle. They would meet the groom at the Meet of Meets at Summer Solstice.

"From the sound of it, the marriage could happen right there," Orryn spat out bitterly, "with no proper ceremony, no songs, no feast, no family."

"Without a Tala?!" the songholder youth exclaimed, shocked. "It will have no weight. Even a hand-fasted love match must be brought before the Tala-Rasa to be formally recognized."

Orryn shook her head worriedly.

"The warriors intend to change those rules at the Meet of Meets," she reported. "My brother told me that the warriors are trying to change things so that they are the only authorities. A warriors meet of seven warriors present at a wedding ceremony would count as being more official than even the Tala-Rasa."

Tala made a spluttering sound, outraged. The youth jumped up and began kicking the dust into plumes, threatening to strip every last warrior's name from the Ancestor Song.

"Something has to be done!" Tala exploded. "We can't let them do this."

"Moragh will know what to do," Orryn said.

"Yeah, she'll cut their heads off," Ari Ara muttered.

Orryn started to argue, but Tala intervened.

" Ari Ara and I can go to the Meet of Meets and see what can be done," ze offered to Orryn, "and you can ride to the Black Ravens Stronghold and ask Moragh to come. Perhaps we will succeed before she arrives."

Orryn squeezed Tala's shoulder, grateful for the compromise. Ari Ara reluctantly agreed to the plan after the songholder pointed out that they could search for Emir along the way; the Meet of Meets was in the same direction as Throw-the-Bones' spinning stone prophecy. As the lavender greys of dusk surrendered to the deep night, they banked the fire. They agreed to depart at dawn; the waning moon wouldn't offer much light to guide them. Ari Ara and Tala would ride west. Orryn would travel east to fetch the women warriors.

"Do you have any idea what we're going to do?" Ari Ara whispered to Tala as they rolled into their cloaks on the opposite side of the embers from Orryn.

Tala's head shook.

"Well, we better think of something before Moragh arrives," Ari Ara grumbled.

She sent a silent appeal to Alaren's ancestor spirit. They had to find a Way Between before Moragh brought violence down upon her own people.

CHAPTER THIRTEEN

. . . . .

The Meet of Meets

The Meet of Meets turned the basin of the wide, shallow valley into seething mass of tents and horses, gear and supply wagons, leather and metal. The clang and thud of men sparring in friendly competition interspersed with the clamor of the cooks' kitchen. The rumble of thousands of men's voices rose like a river, low and loud. The severity of armed warriors was accompanied by the unruly air of men merging games and business, jovial festivities and serious discussions. Sentries patrolled the perimeter on horseback. The main entrances to the tangle of tents were guarded. Getting in would be difficult. Getting out might be impossible.

Ari Ara and Tala lay flat on their bellies between the standing stones of an eroded escarpment that overlooked the valley from the north. The lowering sun cast long shadows, striping the terrain in black and gold bands. Ari Ara cupped the light out from her eyes with her palms and peered southward. Zyrh stood stock still behind them, hidden from view by the curve of the ridgeline, ears pricked in the direction of a field of horses on the western outskirts. Tala had given him firm instructions to stay put.

They had no plan ... or rather, they had a dozen plans, each more harebrained than the last. Ari Ara had suggested that she distract the warriors and make them chase her. Meanwhile, Tala could locate Nalia, got her out of the encampment, and ride to Moragh's.

"But why would the warriors chase you?" Tala retorted with a pragmatic frown. "You're the daughter of the Harrak-Mettahl. They're more likely to invite you to the wedding."

Ari Ara made a face and conceded the point. Tala suggested that they put a sleep-song on the men, the kind Harraken mothers used on babies.

"But then Nalia would be asleep, and maybe me, too," Ari Ara argued. "How are you going to get us both on Zyrh and keep singing?"

She suggested that she honor challenge the bridegroom, but Tala nixed the idea.

"They can't fight you, you're just a child," Tala scoffed.

"I stood against Shulen!" she protested, indignantly.

"It's a matter of harrak," Tala answered with a shrug. "Warriors don't beat children."

Ari Ara scowled, thinking of the bruises she'd seen on the girls at Moragh's.

"What about a Champion's Challenge, like I used in Mariana?" she countered. "It's an older law."

Tala's nose wrinkled. Ze frowned.

"The loser is put to death," ze reminded Ari Ara in a worried tone.

"I won't lose!" she exclaimed. "I beat Shulen."

" - if even one drop of your precious Shirar blood hits the sand, Tahkan Shirar will dismember me for encouraging you."

So, that was out.

"Maybe we could talk them into not marrying her off," Ari Ara sighed.

"Maybe," Tala answered dubiously.

On and on they went, swapping schemes.

"I say we just charge in there, grab her, and explain it all later," Ari Ara stated as they stared down at the mass of tents and warriors.

"That's the dumbest thing I've heard yet," Tala groaned. "One or both or all three of us will end up with daggers in our backs. We don't even know where she is. Even if we did manage to find her and get away, we wouldn't get far. Zyrh's fast, but with three people on his back, even he can't outrun the warriors' horses."

"Oh, right."

Below them, a dusty track led into the camp. The two youths ducked out of sight as a band of riders passed. Behind them, a supply wagon slowly drove along. The youths pulled their shirts over their mouths and noses against the dust, eyes watering with the effort to choke down coughs. The voices of the driver and his assistant carried, booming in half-shouted words over the rumble of the wheels.

" . . . those Marianans are sending spies in . . . it'll be armies next . . . "

"That was a warrior, mark my words. Did you see his build under that pale fish skin?"

"Emir!" Ari Ara gasped.

Tala flung a hand over her mouth and choked off her words, hissing at her to be quiet.

"Seemed a bit young - " the driver argued.

"They breed 'em like that, raise 'em up to kill us," the assistant insisted.

Ari Ara pushed up on her elbows to eye the supply wagon.

Tala shoved her head down.

"They know about Emir!" Ari Ara whispered.

"Throw-the-Bones said you wouldn't see him until - "

"Stay here," Ari Ara cut Tala off and darted down the ridge in a half-crouch.

When she reached the edge of the trail, she flung herself behind a boulder. Ignoring Tala's frantic hissing, she peeked around the edge. The driver and his assistant were still immersed in their conversation. The end of the wagon kicked up a cloud of dust as it passed. The sunset threw lances of light through the plumes. Ari Ara sprinted from the rock to the wagon and hopped silently onto the tail of the cart. She leaned against the heavy ale barrels and swung her legs off the back. Ari Ara calculated that she could eavesdrop for five minutes - no more - before the wagon got too close to the checkpoint. One old tree and a stack of boulders would provide her last, risky cover. She'd have to stay hidden there until nightfall then cautiously evade the patrols to rejoin Tala. She eyed the setting sun. Dusk was minutes away. She decided it was worth the risk to find out more about Emir.

To her frustration, the two men nattered on about crops and brews and how much to charge the warriors in barter for the ale. The brewers were from an eastern village that sat in a mountainous nook just south of Moragh's territory. They always needed protection from their fears of Marianan invasion, but lately, the Black Ravens had refused to patrol their area, citing the number of women who had run off from their village.

"Moragh's mad as a wet cat and crazy to boot," the driver scoffed. "She's stealing all our women, hoarding them up there with the Black Ravens."

"Some say she's building an army."

"Hah. I'd like to see her take on those warriors. That's a real army. Takes a real man to be a real warrior. Those girls are just fooling themselves."

Ari Ara bet he wouldn't dare say that to Moragh's face. She readied to leap off the wagon, disappointed they hadn't said more about Emir. The men's next words stopped her.

"The warriors have the right idea, taking charge. They'll be holding the first wedding-by-warriors-rule tomorrow, I hear."

"Yes, they've got the girl and her father here, camped out, waiting."

Nalia!

Ari Ara vacillated briefly, then decided to stay on the wagon. If she could find out where Nalia was being held, they could help her escape! The old tree passed by. A swirl of dust hung in the air by its trunk. She couldn't jump off now, anyway. Ari Ara craned around the barrels then ducked her head down to look at the underside of the wagon bed. Perfect!

As they neared the sentry checkpoint, the driver slowed to a halt. The dust swirled up. The guards squinted. Ari Ara dropped off. She rolled underneath the wagon, pressed her back to the wooden slats of the bed's underbelly, and lifted her hands and feet to brace against the trusses. It was an uncomfortable, muscle-straining position, but she was hidden from view. Ari Ara gritted her teeth over every second of banter between the sentries and the driver. Sweat beaded on her face and dripped silently onto the ground beneath her. Her hands grew slick. She pressed her arms harder against the timbers to keep from slipping. At last, the wagon driver climbed back up to his perch and flicked the reins at the horses to move along. She almost lost her grip when the wheels rocked jarringly over a series of ruts, but managed to hold on.

The ale wagon's arrival was met with cheers from the warriors. For a nerve-wracking moment, Ari Ara thought she'd never be able to roll out unseen. Then the wagon pulled up beside a tent and the press of bodies on one side obscured the view underneath. She dropped and rolled alongside the bottom of the tent. Ari Ara shimmied backwards on her belly and elbows until she could worm into the shadows. A stack of boxes hid her from one side; the cart blocked the view from the other. She rubbed her aching wrists, pondering her next move. The growing dusk offered her best protection, but rows of torches were being lit throughout the roads and pathways between the tents.

She watched the warriors milling around the ale cart. Spirits ran high, boisterous and jovial, but she could also see anxious worry and glimmers of uncertainty in their faces. Beyond the wagon, a huddle of warriors sat somber and grim, refusing to drink and celebrate. Ari Ara thought of what Tahkan had told her about lost harrak. It was as if she could hear him in her ears - she startled. That wasn't memory! That *was* her father's voice.

Ari Ara rose cautiously to a crouch, one hand on the warm, dusty earth. She had to be careful if she didn't want to get caught. She took a deep breath and grounded herself in the Way Between. Shulen had taught her how to slip between the wind and the currents of a rushing river. She studied the gaps between the tents and the bands of light and shadow. When she darted forward, she slipped among the tents no more visible than an errant breeze. She sensed the tromp of booted footsteps and froze, holding her breath. When they passed, she slid across the open space and ducked behind a stack of crates. She peered out. From here, she could see a pack of warriors drinking and singing in a wide circle around a common fire pit. The crowd sang loudly and lustily, laughing through a courting song that sounded strange without the women's counterpart. She spotted Tahkan's lean and craggy features on the far side of the ring of warriors. His clear and familiar voice spoke, breaking through the warriors' rough tones.

"That song is sweeter with the women's chorus."

His words fell like stones into the pond of the men's singing. A silence spread. Feet shuffled. Hands rose to scratch the backs of necks. Eyes darted away from the Harrak-Mettahl and his gentle, but starkly clear rebuke. Then a man rose, stocky and hairy, a warrior who might once have been handsome before the years dragged his body one way and his hopes the other. He slung an arm over Tahkan's shoulders with familiarity and held up a jug of ale, pressing it upon the thin man's lips.

"Drink with us, Tahkan," the man guffawed, "for the good women are all dead and even the bad ones are mad at us."

"I cannot," Tahkan chided, pushing the jug away. "If I drink the grain that should feed the children, the women will be mad at me, too . . . and I don't have your good looks to woo them back."

He lightened his tone at the end, pulling his words just shy of insult. The men chuckled. The drunken man laid his head against Tahkan's.

"You get them to sing then, Harrak-Mettahl-hic!" the man urged, slurring his words.

"I've told you," Tahkan reminded him. "You can't expect them to lift their voices to your song."

Several of the men grumbled. Others nodded in agreement. Small spats of arguments broke out. Tahkan held up a hand.

"The women are unhappy with you for good reason," he told the warriors, "and they will be even angrier when they hear you forced that young woman into marriage against her will."

A roar of protest erupted. The warriors leapt to their feet. The man shoved away from Tahkan. He fumbled for his sword - only to realize that the Harrak-Mettahl had unhooked the belt sheath and taken it from him while the man leaned drunkenly on his shoulder.

"She's just headstrong," someone called out.

"They're all ungrateful fools!" another person shouted. "All those women!"

"Stubborn old nags!" another cried in agreement.

"Such sentiments will hardly restore their affections," Tahkan warned them. He toyed with the hilt of the man's sword as if to remind them that he knew his way around such weapons. Then he tossed it to the ground with a disgusted look. He strode off, shaking his head.

Ari Ara drew back behind the crates and followed him, creeping through the tangled alleys between the tents. She lost him at a large, square tent, circled back to crane around the corner, and then checked the far side. She frowned. She could hear her father's voice speaking, but she couldn't see him anywhere.

Ah! She realized with a start that his words rumbled through the tent's woven wall. He must have gone inside. She pressed her cheek to the earth and peered under the bottom edge. A low cot stood on the other side. Ari Ara lifted the fabric cautiously to get a broader view. A sconce of candles cast flickering light. An old carpet, worn with use and travel, kept down the dust. A wood chest doubled as a table and a storage box. A pair of tin cups sat on top of it along with a loaf of bread and a rind of cheese. Ari Ara willed her stomach not to rumble.

Tahkan slouched in a chair, feet kicked out in front of him. Another man paced the length of the tent, his boots striding back and forth in agitation. He was a solid barrel of a man, thick with muscle and broad-shouldered. A beard bristled over his chin. Above it sat a wide nose broken several times over. Deep canyons of worry lines surrounded his eyes. His gaze was unexpectedly gentle, unguarded. He had the look of someone who was fearless in battle, but fair-minded with his men.

He lumbered across the tent and threw his bear-like limbs onto the cot. Ari Ara winced as it groaned and sagged. He slid his elbows onto his knees and let his calloused hands hang limp. Tahkan's gaze followed him. For a moment, she suspected that he saw her peering under tent. She held her breath. His face remained immobile. Then he looked away as a burst of raucous laughter rose up outside. His face contorted in a grimace.

"They will rue this celebration . . . and not just for their hangovers tomorrow. Warriors-rule will cast a long shadow over the Harraken," Tahkan predicted darkly.

"They only want to protect their people," the bear of a man argued. "You should support them."

"How can I, Kirkan?" Tahkan replied. "I have sisters and a daughter who will be silenced by warriors-rule. I could never look them in the eyes again."

Ari Ara grinned, proud of his stance.

"The Meet of Meets decided to offer the Black Ravens a place among the warriors," Kirkan reminded him. "Any warrior - woman or man - may now sit at the warriors meets."

"Moragh will be pleased," Tahkan remarked with a sour tone, "but Ari Ara will never be a warrior. She follows the Way Between."

"You love her dearly," Kirkan remarked.

"My daughter brings me harrak along with joy," he admitted with a proud smile.

"We must guard her well," Kirkan urged, his jaw set. "The Marianans will want her back. They will come with armies to collect her."

Tahkan's coppery hair glinted in candlelight as he shook his head in disagreement.

"Not for years," he said, chuckling, remembering how much controversy she had caused. "She turned the nobles on their heads far better than I have ever done."

"They will appoint her second cousin king, then," Kirkan speculated with a frown.

"Let them. We will have *her*." Tahkan's green eyes blazed, glowing with pride and hope. He spoke in a fervent hush, too low for her to hear except for the words: *courage . . . fire . . . a true Shirar*. A slow flush burned in Ari Ara's cheeks at the praise. She wondered if he'd say these things if he knew about her fight with Emir and her arguments with Moragh.

"That's why we must be vigilant," Kirkan interrupted, stirring impatiently. "Now is not the time to relax our defenses. I don't like it any more than you do, but perhaps it is wise to keep warriors-rule in place. At least until we are certain the river dogs will not attack."

Tahkan rubbed his face with his palms. Weariness dripped from his features. His eyes hung with shadows of late nights, early risings, and endless arguments. He had talked circles around the issues, but made little progress. Tahkan slouched lower in the chair with his ankles crossed at the boots, thin fingers forming a steeple. He sighed.

"I cannot support the warriors meets," Tahkan said firmly. "So long as they maintain warriors-rule in a time of peace, the Harrak-Mettahl must be silent among them."

"Come, be reasonable," Kirkan urged.

"Mahteni fasted for ten days to show that she will not eat at a table where she is not an equal," Tahkan burst out, his voice ragged with worry. "And even that did not remind them of where harrak lies!"

He scowled. The warriors had caught her scouting above the slot canyon and held her captive to force Tahkan to attend the Meet of Meets. He came, but refused to give his support. His younger sister had resisted them by fasting, living on harrak alone, trying to sway the warriors to shift their votes. She had not succeeded.

"She ate this afternoon," Tahkan reported bitterly, "after the vote approving warriors-rule. I convinced her that there was wisdom in retreating so she could fight again."

"What will you do, now?" Kirkan asked.

The Harrak-Mettahl shook his head and shrugged. He didn't know, not yet.

"I must do something, though," he said, "for my sisters' sake . . . for my daughter's . . . for all the women . . . indeed, for all of our people. I wish I could stand with the warriors, but it is not possible."

"Then you leave them no choice but to move against the will of the Harrak-Mettahl," the warrior stated unhappily.

"Yes." Tahkan rose with that and crossed to the dark-haired man. He clasped the warrior's shoulder. "We go separate ways but with the same love of our people and country. I beg you to keep a strong grip on the warriors. Power goes to the head quicker than ale."

"And the girl - Nalia - will you honor challenge on her behalf?" Kirkan asked him.

A troubled look clouded Tahkan's face. Slowly, reluctantly, he shook his head.

"I cannot act on this. It is a risk to my harrak that I cannot wager. If no one else intercedes, I will challenge the marriage's validity once we find the Tala-Rasa."

Ari Ara's jaw dropped in shock. How could he? How dare he? She opened her mouth to protest, but before she could speak, a hand clamped over her mouth.

"Shhh," breathed a figure in a warrior's tunic, pulling her

back from the tent. "It's me."

"Tala?" Ari Ara hissed into the other's palm, twisting and squinting into the darkness.

Ze was dressed in borrowed warrior's gear. A too-long, crimson tunic bunched up under a leather chest plate. A broad-brimmed leather hat was shoved down tightly over zirs curls. Urging Ari Ara to silence, Tala tugged her away from the tent into the darker alleyways.

"What are you doing here?" Ari Ara whispered.

"Keeping you out of trouble," Tala muttered back. "*I*, at least, have every right to be here. I'm Tala-Rasa."

"Then why the disguise?" Ari Ara scoffed, plucking at the shoulder of the crimson tunic and knocking the brim of the hat slantwise.

"Whether or not I'm *supposed* to be here has nothing to do with my *right* to be here," Tala retorted. The other Tala-Rasa would be furious if ze got caught while they were all boycotting the Meet of Meets to deny it legitimacy. "Plus, as a young warrior, I can always claim I caught you snooping and pretend to escort you to the authorities while actually dragging you out of here."

"I found Tahkan," Ari Ara said, filling Tala in on what she'd overheard. "Why won't he honor challenge for Nalia?"

"Because he might lose," Tala answered with a snort. "If he waits until after the wedding, he can appeal to the Tala-Rasa and prevent it from ever happening to anyone else." Tala shrugged. "Not that it matters much, since we're going to rescue her. She's over by the horse field. Come on."

Ari Ara trotted behind the thin songholder as they wove through the warren of tent alleys. They stopped cautiously at the edges of the roads and darted across when no one was watching. Tala didn't have Fanten skills, but zirs dark skin hid well in the night. One time, a warrior nearly spotted them, but Ari Ara dove behind a tent while Tala whipped out a salute. The man strode onwards.

At last, they reached the edge of the horse field. Crouched by a stack of hay bales, Ari Ara and Tala studied the scene. The shadows of the horses' bulky bodies shifted in the darkness, a sense of mass and muscle lurking beyond the torchlight. A pair of herders had made camp beside the watering troughs. A small, round tent, compact and sturdy, sat under a lone, old pine. Beyond, the rocky slope rose to the northern escarpment where Zyrh was hidden. Near the flickering light of the fire, a girl slightly older than Tala scrubbed a battered traveling cook pot out with sand. A pair of men - Nalia's father and uncle - lounged against a stray boulder, backs to stone, legs drawn up, hands hanging over knees.

"What's the plan?" Ari Ara whispered, hardly daring to make a sound.

Tala took a breath to answer, but one of the men spoke.

"Where are you going?" the father asked as Nalia rose and stepped toward the rising slope.

"To relieve myself," came the quavering reply.

"Be quick about it."

Tala nudged Ari Ara. They slid toward the sound of Nalia's footsteps as the young woman walked into the night. She did not stop to relieve herself. With a nervous glance over her shoulder, she darted behind a bush and kept climbing up the slope, hidden by the darkness.

"What's she doing?" Ari Ara hissed.

"Running away," Tala guessed, surprised.

They ran after her, cutting across the hillside. At the first crest, Nalia dropped into a crouch, listening to see if the two men had followed. She was tall like her sister, long of limb and sinewy where her sister stood muscular. Long black hair fanned around her face. When she stilled, the darkness swallowed her whole. Only the faint rasp of her breath and a thin shine of starlight revealed her.

"Running away?" Tala said in her ear, speaking a swift silencing word to cut off the young woman's startled scream. "You won't get far without water and a horse."

"Good thing we have both," Ari Ara added, holding up a hand with a gesture of greeting. "Orryn sent us."

The young woman's frightened tension collapsed in a slump of relief. Tala released her from the silencing word.

"Thank the ancestors," Nalia breathed. "I'd rather die trying to get to the Black Ravens than marry some rotten warrior against my will."

They didn't have much time. The men below were already casting suspicious glances into the night.

"Take Zyrh," Ari Ara urged, guiding her up the slope and pointing to where the horse was hidden behind a ridge. "Ride northeast and you'll probably run smack into the Black Ravens."

"What will you two do?" Nalia whispered.

"Distract them," Tala answered, eyes glowing with mischief.

Nalia didn't hesitate. She clasped their hands and slipped off without a further word. Tala tossed off zirs hat and shucked the warrior's garb, revealing the simple tunic of zirs profession. Ze explained the plan to Ari Ara.

"You'll be doing all the running," Tala stated.

Ari Ara didn't like the sound of that, but didn't argue. Below, the father spoke to the uncle.

"She should be back by now."

Ari Ara pulled her dark cloak tighter around her and ran off into the night. Tala strode purposefully forward, crunching the gravel and rocks underfoot.

"Here she comes," the uncle replied soothingly.

"That's not - "

Tala began to sing, stepping into the feeble edges of firelight. The men blinked at the sudden appearance of a Tala-Rasa, and offered surprised gestures of respect. Tala's verses spoke about an upcoming wedding and the men began to smile, thinking the songholder had come to witness the ceremony. Ari Ara caught only fragments of the words as she crept closer to the horse field. On the shadowy edge of the campsite, the warriors' horses - hundreds of them - lifted their heads, ears swiveled toward Tala's song.

The ancestress gathered up her harrak, Tala sang,
and ran into the night
away from unwanted marriage
into the arms of her destiny.

Ari Ara had just reached the boulders closest to the horses when the two men registered the song's meaning. They roared in objection and scrambled into action, guessing the young woman had run away. Ari Ara sprang out among the nearest cluster of horses, startling them. One bolted. Another reared. The father and uncle whirled and spotted her. The herd bunched and slammed up against each other. Fear triggered the horses into a massive stampede. Some panicked and bolted into the Meet of Meets, falling into tents and knocking over torches. A flare burst up. Flame caught canvas. Shouts rang out.

Ari Ara gulped, but didn't have time to worry about the mayhem. She lunged as a pair of horses charged toward her, flapping her arms and shouting to force them to veer aside. She sprinted off as Nalia's father and uncle chased after her. She bolted the other direction as warriors poured out of the Meet of

Meets. While Tala stood implacably on one foot, singing about women's honor and the right of women to choose their partners, Ari Ara scrambled like a mad hare, chasing horses and avoiding men. She cursed Tala's crazy plan on one breath and yelled at the horses on the next. She dove under the uncle's grasp and skidded past the father. She darted between a group of warriors and leapt over a low pile of rocks. She sprinted into the darkness and hoped they wouldn't follow her. She heard hoof beats and dove to the side, but it was just Tala.

The songholder rode up on one of the horses, stretched out a hand, and hauled her up. They charged off onto the plain, leaving the chaos far behind. When they were certain they weren't being followed, they turned toward Moragh's territory. It was dawn before they halted. They reached the southern edges of the pine forest that marked the boundary of Black Raven lands. Relieved, they rolled up in their cloaks and fell asleep. They slumbered restlessly, flooded with wild dreams of chases and horses and songs about young girls running away to find their destinies.

They woke to the sound of creaking leather.

CHAPTER FOURTEEN

. . . . .

The Druach

The sparse trees of the pine forest towered like a cathedral, tense with the stillness of silenced birdsong. The high sun shot shafts of light down through the scabbed-bark trunks. Pools of black shadows encircled the bases. Moragh's Black Ravens surrounded them, grim-faced and glowering. Nalia and Orryn stood among them, faces anxious and troubled. Moragh Shirar frowned down at her niece, her skin rippling with electric tension. The fierce warrior woman's brows darted to a point in concentration. She spoke the command of rising. Ari Ara scrambled to her feet. Next to her, Tala stilled with the wariness of a deer confronted by a sand lioness.

"What were you thinking?" Moragh growled dangerously. "Running off from the Stronghold? Sneaking into the Meet of Meets? Causing trouble at every turn?"

Nalia shifted uneasily, murmuring an inaudible defense of the two youths. Moragh cut her off with an impatient gesture. She had heard the news of last night's escapade. Orryn had explained why Ari Ara had run off. Nalia had told her about being rescued by the two youths at the Meet of Meets. Just after dawn, her brother's messenger hawk had found her, urging her to protect Nalia and keep an eye out for Ari Ara. He added a hastily scrawled plea: *if you see my daughter, tell her to go to Tuloon Ravine with Tala and stay out of sight. The warriors' anger burns hotter than the fire she set. I will meet her there.*

"I didn't mean to burn down the tents," Ari Ara protested, "but I had to do something."

"And when the warriors come to my gate accusing me of kidnapping Nalia?" Moragh demanded, her eyes narrowed. "What should I tell them, then?"

"The truth," Ari Ara answered hotly. "She ran away. According to desert traditions, no woman can be married against her will."

Moragh's face turned hard.

"I told you before and I tell you again," she warned the girl. "Do not pretend to know our ways better than us."

"Oh?" Ari Ara snapped back. "You think Nalia should have stayed to get married off?"

"I did not say that," Moragh fumed, pointing a gloved finger at the girl. "My Black Ravens and I were already on our way to deal with this."

"With a bloodbath!"

"With a necessary show of force," Moragh retorted. "We have to teach these brutes not to trifle with us."

"Violence is never necessary," Ari Ara said stubbornly. "There's always another way."

"Ah yes," Moragh scoffed. "Your precious Way Between. One day, little girl, you are going to get caught by someone bigger and stronger than you, and find your nonsense won't keep you alive."

"Someone like Shulen the Butcher?" Ari Ara shot back, lifting her chin. "Because I stood against him and lived to tell the tale."

"The Butcher is losing his edge," Moragh sneered. "Unlike some of us."

"Is that a challenge?" Ari Ara flung back.

Gasps broke out, but she was too angry to care. Someone softly warned Moragh to leave the girl alone. Tala called out to Ari Ara not to fight with her aunt. The rest of the warrior women fell silent. Ari Ara eyed her aunt warily. Flecks of white flashed in the woman's dark eyes. Her muscles tensed into cords of hard rope. Ari Ara sensed the air tighten around her like the moment before a lightning strike.

"*Argha!*" Ari Ara cried, throwing herself backward instinctively as she used the word her father had taught her to neutralize the binding force of her aunt's magic.

Moragh's face contorted.

"Who taught you that?" she choked out.

"My father," Ari Ara answered.

Few knew the word; even fewer could use it effectively. Ari Ara could see her aunt's fury rising at the spilled secret. Any of her enemies could learn it now. The thick-tongued Marianans might not be able to work the power of the word, but her fellow Harraken could, including any warriors she confronted.

"How dare he!" Moragh growled, striding closer.

Ari Ara backed away. She bumped up against a pine tree. Moragh's fist slammed the trunk above Ari Ara's head. Bits of bark showered down on her.

"You reek of drowned rats and river dogs," Moragh growled. "Like a snake, you crawl into my brother's heart and hiss in his ears. What right have you to know our secrets? You pretend to be a daughter of the desert, but you're nothing but a riverlands upstart."

Ari Ara's patience snapped. She wouldn't stand around

being insulted and bullied by her aunt. She dropped to the ground and sprang away like a cat, sprinting out of reach. Moragh was after her in a flash. The warrior lunged and nearly caught her, but Ari Ara dodged at the last second.

"Why are you doing this?" Ari Ara cried. "I'm your niece. Your blood is in my veins. Your name is in my Woman's Song!"

That caught Moragh by surprise. The grip of her temper loosened slightly. Ari Ara spoke swiftly, using her words like a crowbar to pry the door of reason back open. The Woman's Song was a ritual of the desert, a traditional song for a young girl who has just received her first moon blood and is envisioning what kind of woman she wishes to grow into. With Mahteni's guidance, Ari Ara had added verses about her mother's peacebuilding, her Aunt Brinelle's leadership, and the Fanten Grandmother's strength. Mahteni had suggested including Moragh's fierceness, a trait the girl already shared with her aunt.

Moragh's expression shifted, disdain replacing anger's heat.

"Bah, you are still a child," she spat out, straightening, dropping her fighting stance, and walking away. She did not fight children; there was no harrak in it. "Someday, we will match, you and I, and we will see if your Weakling's Way lives up to your claims."

"It does," Ari Ara proclaimed.

"Hah," Moragh scoffed. "You are young and foolish. I'd like to see you honor challenge hundreds of warriors, fathers, and husbands using your Way Between. One of them will slice your foolish head from your shoulders."

"The Way Between is more than a bunch of fancy fighting moves," Ari Ara protested. "In Mariana, Mahteni and others organized thousands of water workers with the Way Between. They used strikes to shut down the factories. They marched on the capital to demand their water rights. They used their unarmed bodies to protect Shulen from execution. If they can use the Way Between to end the Water Exchange, we can use it here to end warriors-rule."

"It won't work," Moragh predicted coldly.

"How do you know if you don't try?" Ari Ara insisted.

Moragh clenched her jaw. Her hands balled into fists. Her face turned red.

"Let her try," Tala's voice rang out, clear and strong. The slender youth stepped forward, lifting zir hands between the quarrelling pair.

"You say she is young," Tala told Moragh. "Then help her grow. Do your duty as her eldest aunt. Set her to her woman's task, her *druach*."

A flurry of gasps broke out around the circle. Moragh scowled. Tala took a deep breath and continued.

"She bleeds her moon blood, sings her Woman's Song, but as you said, she is a child still. By our customs, she must complete a *druach* set by her oldest relative," Tala paused, pinning Moragh's eyes, "and that is you."

A gleam entered Moragh's gaze. A thin smile spread across her lips.

"Very well," she agreed. "Her druach is to return the women's voices to the Harraken Song. That will give her a chance to prove that her Weakling's Way works."

She scoffed at her niece.

"And if it doesn't," she vowed, "I will ride upon those men and make them pay for their injustices with pain."

A hush fell over the women. Anxious glances leapt from face to face.

"Moragh, are you sure this is wise?" one of the warriors asked. "It could be dangerous for her."

"Life is dangerous," Moragh retorted with a callous shrug, eyeing the defiant girl, "and if she runs off from my safekeeping ... well, you can't protect someone who refuses to be protected."

She said the last with a twisted little smile over an old memory.

"She's just a child," someone protested.

Moragh shook her head firmly.

"If my fierceness is in her Woman's Song, then she bleeds like all of us and must begin to make her way in our desert ... unless she's too afraid."

Moragh smirked, already anticipating the girl's failure. Ari Ara lifted her chin, stubborn and determined. She wasn't afraid.

"I'll do it."

Moragh gave her an appraising glance.

"You don't lack for pride, girl," she stated approvingly, baring her teeth in a snarl of a smile. "I give you that."

She curtly ordered them to go to Tuloon Ravine and wait for Tahkan. Then she snapped her fingers, spun on her heel, and called her Black Ravens to follow. They took Nalia and Orryn with them, leaving the two youths alone.

CHAPTER FIFTEEN

. . . . .

Travel Songs

"Arrrgh!" Ari Ara screeched, kicking up a cloud of dust. "She makes me so mad!"

Tala coughed and waved the plume away. Zyrh sneezed and shook his head as he paced behind Ari Ara's stalking stride. Moragh had left him with them and taken the horse they had ridden off with from the Meet of Meets. Ari Ara missed the reasonable creature already. Zyrh nudged her between the shoulder blades with his head, annoyed at the dust she kicked up. Ari Ara shoved him away, yelping as she tripped over the spines of a dusky purple cactus huddling low to the ground. A stream of curses poured out of her in Marianan.

"Welcome to the joys of family," Tala commented wryly from zirs perch on the horse's back. "You love them; you hate them. You'd ride into danger to help them, and you still want to shake them until their bones rattle."

The youth whistled the melody of a humorous tune recounting the antics of a notoriously quarrelsome Harraken family long ago. In every verse, one of them fought with another and wound up getting into some pickle that only their family could help them sort out. The Tala-Rasa taught it to each generation of children, occasionally adding a new verse based on a true story. Tala eyed the furious girl whacking the silken seed pollen off the shrubs and suspected a new verse was in the making.

Or verses, Tala amended with a wide grin. The life of Ari Ara Shirar en Marin would likely inspire a hundred songs.

"I ought to be looking for Emir," Ari Ara grumbled.

"There's no point," Tala answered. "Throw-the-Bones said not to. And you can't, anyway. Moragh's given you a *druach.*"

"What is that, exactly?" Ari Ara asked, frowning over the unfamiliar word. Whatever it was, it rang with power, hinting at serious endeavors and strict rules of ritual.

"A druach," Tala explained, "is a rite of passage . . . a quest . . . or a task."

The youth spoke the definitions reluctantly, as if the word *quest* was too grandiose and the term *task* was too mundane. Tala toyed with Zyrh's ivory mane.

"After a girl's monthly blood comes in - or after a boy's voice cracks - their oldest relative chooses a druach for the youth, a proving task or test."

Usually, it was a responsibility paired with an opportunity, such as driving the clan's flocks to new pastures or fetching an elder from one village to another.

"But you," Tala pointed out with a small laugh, "aren't an ordinary case. What is crossing great distances to you, a girl from the High Mountains in exile from your mother's land? What is fetching an elder for someone who brought thousands of our people - and the water - back to the desert?"

"But I didn't do that alone," Ari Ara protested. "Everyone helped with that."

Tala gave her a strange look.

"So much the better," Tala answered. "You Marianans think heroes shoulder burdens alone; we Harraken scoff at such arrogance. A heroine, to us, is someone who shows she can inspire others to work together to do what's right."

The cultural differences between her mother and father's peoples startled Ari Ara, spinning her frame of reference around. She felt alien to this arid landscape with a sky so wide it made her dizzy with its boundlessness. She stared at the aching, endless blue and the slow spill of the pine-studded hills onto the plain. To the east, the Border Mountains rose like hulking giants, stark peaks barring her path back to the riverlands. Like it or not, she was here to stay.

"How am I supposed to fix the problems between the warriors and the women?" she grumbled. "Where do we even start?"

"We start by going to Tuloon," Tala answered pragmatically.

Tuloon Ravine lay several days of riding to the northwest on the edge of the vast plain. They traveled in the cool hours, stopping at noon as the sun's heat scorched down. Tala knew the land intimately and had a song for every rock and rise. The songholder greeted the forked-tongued snakes and darting lizards like old friends. Ze teased the sour-faced toads as they squatted, spiny as cacti and still as stones in the dust. Ze serenaded the packs of sleek-footed, two-horned deer that sprang out of the drying grasses and sped off. Once, a herd of huge, shaggy, hump-backed wild oxen the color of Zyrh thundered across their path, stopping them for an hour as the massive herd pounded past.

Tala walked or rode with a constant song of songs, one flowing into the next. To say the desert was made of song, Ari Ara swiftly realized, was an understatement. Tala's memory contained thousands of tunes, including ballad-songs from millenniums of Harraken history.

"How do you remember all that?" Ari Ara gaped.

Tala shrugged.

"It's not as hard as you might think. The land is a map of our songs. Every rock has a story, every mountain has a song, every field has at least a little ditty, each village has over a dozen songs associated with it by the time it's a generation old. I sing them as I travel, that's how I was taught. It's why the Tala-Rasa always wander: to sing the songs of the people and places back to them and remind them of who they are."

At midday, the youth guided Zyrh to a spring and dug out a watering trough. A pair of trees arched over the cool water and offered shade. They shared oatcakes, refilled their waterskins and dozed with cool rags draped over their eyes. When the first touch of lengthening shadow broke the afternoon heat, Ari Ara forced herself through a set of training exercises in the Way Between. She missed Emir and Shulen so strongly that the world blurred, but she blinked her tears back and kept going. She couldn't risk losing her edge; her encounter with Moragh had demonstrated that. She finished the exercise and paused to catch her breath. She reached for the waterskin and noticed Tala watching her with a blend of awe, mystification, and wistful yearning.

"The exercise makes more sense with two people," Ari Ara explained, "but you can practice with the wind or the sunlight or anything, really."

"Could I learn?" Tala asked, eyes alight with curiosity.

"Oh, yes!" Ari Ara cried, thrilled that the youth had asked.

Thus began a routine that shaped their days: rise before dawn, ride to the next water source, rest through the midday heat, practice the Way Between, and travel at dusk for a few hours. They crossed a crumbling salt flat of blinding white dust. They tread through an eerie dead forest of charred and burned branches. They climbed winding switchback paths over an obsidian ridge of shining black stone. The desert unfolded, step by step, strange and magnificent, no two places alike. Ari Ara had always imagined her father's land as flat and dry, but the reality filled her with wonder. She had thought there would be no water, but, in truth, water shaped the culture of the desert, sparse and sacred. Villages clustered along the handful of rivers - streams, really - that snaked through the land. She enjoyed traveling with Tala, who knew hundreds of tales. The days flew by swiftly. The young songholder was fascinated by the riverlands and plied Ari Ara with questions. The Fanten intrigued Tala, who referred to the elusive forest-dwelling people as distant cousins of the Tala-Rasa ... at least, that's what Ari Ara thought the Harrak-Tala words meant. Her vocabulary was growing daily, but Tala's speech was the most poetic and complex she'd encountered. It was a mark of the Tala-Rasa's calling, her friend explained.

"We never forget a word, and we keep them alive for others," Tala explained, building a small, grass-fed fire to cook a powdered stew for dinner.

"Has it always been like this?" Ari Ara asked, flopping onto the grass with relief, splaying her limbs into the soft greenness of the pasturelands. Tomorrow, they would reach Tuloon. "With the warriors meets cancelling the village sings and making all the decisions? And is it like this everywhere in the desert?"

"No, and no," Tala answered, voice rough with bitterness. "The War of Retribution changed everything. I will sing the ballad for you."

Tala's clear voice rang out like a reed pipe, high and bright.

The youth's range was startling, soaring high like silver bells and bird's whistles, then dropping low as a man's all the way down to the rumble of shaking mountains. The words Tala evoked shivered with time and history. It was believed that when the Tala-Rasa sang, the ancestors spoke through them.

From the time beyond memory, men and women had always been equals in Harraken culture. This was the world that Ari Ara's mother, Queen Alinore, had encountered when she first visited. This was the way of life upon which the peacebuilding young queen had forged the basis of trust between the two populaces of long-time enemies. Queen Alinore's marriage to Tahkan Shirar opened a golden era of exchange and peace. Trade flourished. Youth programs initiated host exchanges and built friendships across borders. Tala's song illuminated the hope of these times, almost unfathomable to those born during or after the bitter War of Retribution. The clouds of darkness closed in from both sides of the border. Shadows cast by fear, hatred, and violence dashed the hopes of a generation.

The Harraken swore they *were not* like the riverlands people. Fathers forbade daughters from acting like the "uncouth Alinore, so forward and manipulative". Husbands told wives to stay home with the children - unlike Alinore's monstrous cousin Brinelle who left her young son at home to ride into battle against them.

But it was more than hatred of the Marianans that fueled the current tensions. As the war dragged on, the strong men were called to fight. The women were sent to hide and flee with the children. The warriors meets made emergency decisions, quick choices to save lives and protect their people.

"It was necessary for survival, but the balance of our culture was tipped," Tala added on a worried note. "The warriors did not let go of power after the war ended. Not all the village sings were started again. Because most warriors were men, the women's voices were slowly silenced."

The power of Desert Speech brought the scenes to life as Tala sang the story in a long ballad. Swirling in the smoke of their grass-fed fire, Ari Ara saw visions of the vicious cycle of warriors making choices to support young men's trainings and war preparations. She saw people - mostly women - objecting and being silenced and pushed to the sidelines. She saw the warriors meets growing in strength and authority as the sullen and resentful glares of women spread from face to face. She saw women fleeing to Moragh's Stronghold and women weeping in the dark, fists to mouths to keep silent sobs from waking those around them. Then, abruptly, as if waking from a nightmare, the vision halted. Tala's face came back into focus. The fire had burned down to embers.

"Why'd you stop?" Ari Ara asked, a plaintive note creeping into her voice.

"The Tala-Rasa tell the past, not the future. We are not soothsayers. What comes next is up to the people."

Ari Ara's eyes narrowed as she caught a faint sense of rote phrases in her friend's words.

"Is that what you truly believe? Or is that just what you're supposed to say?" she challenged, crossing her arms over her chest.

Tala threw her a startled and uncomfortable look.

"I have been warned - repeatedly - to listen and recite, not speak and meddle," Tala answered with a grimace. Ze picked up a stick and stoked the coals back to life, tossing a few twigs in with angry strength. "But, what is a voice if not to sing? Every story is woven out of many strands of possible stories. History is not neutral. Many of the thirteen Tala-Rasa would have sung a different song than I did tonight. If the Tala-Rasa can create new songs out of the present, why not sing warnings of the future, too?"

The youth's bright eyes gleamed across the fire.

"If warriors-rule or Moragh's violence are the only answers, what is someone like me to do? Neither seem like good songs!"

Tala shuddered. Neither male nor female, what place would ze have in this new culture? Would Tala be the dominator? Or the dominated?

"Is that why you came looking for me?" Ari Ara asked. "Seeking the girl who is neither this nor that?"

Tala nodded vigorously, a grin spreading wide.

"I came looking for the daughter of our Harrak-Mettahl, the one who restored our water, honor, and people, the follower of the Way Between."

Tala's laughter rang out. From the lopsided grin, Ari Ara suspected that her life sounded like a legend to most people. Suddenly, her father's words came back to her from a letter he had written her last year.

You will find, Ari Ara Shirar en Marin, that your legends grow far taller than you. You will catch up to them in time.

A silence fell. Tala's sharp gaze stayed fixed on Ari Ara. The fire danced. A night bird hooted in the distance. The breeze carried a slip of cooler air across the pastures.

"If you were allowed to sing a future song," Ari Ara said quietly, "what story would it tell?"

A shimmering intensity burned in the youth's eyes as if the music pressed suddenly against the confines of zir chest.

"It would tell," Tala began, speaking the story instead of singing it, swallowing back emotion, "of two youths who did not fit into the world as it was . . . and so set out to change it, together. It would tell of a girl who knew little of her father's culture, but recognized wrong when she saw it. It would sing of the Way Between, a legend among us, returning like the water and nourishing our harrak, our honor, until it grew green and strong again."

Tala's face flushed, neck burning red like a boy's, long eyelashes fluttering like a girl's, teeth biting lips like all nervous young ones who reveal their fierce vulnerabilities like first crushes then wait for disaster or euphoria to strike. Ari Ara said nothing for a long time, thinking about the words. Tala turned redder and redder. At last, the youth drew the cloak hood over zes tight crop of black curls with their iron-ore edges, hiding zirs face.

"Just think it over and tell me in the morning," came the muffled comment.

"I don't need until morning," Ari Ara answered, blinking as she realized her friend was waiting in agony for her reply.

The hooded figure stilled.

"And?"

So much weighed on that one word.

Ari Ara smiled and curled on her side.

"I like the sound of your song," she said.

A muted squeal of excitement leapt out of the youth. Ari Ara's grin gleamed in the darkness. Then the two closed their eyes without speaking further, letting sleep pull their thundering hearts and racing minds into visions and dreams.

CHAPTER SIXTEEN

· · · · ·

Tuloon Ravine

The ravine ran east to west, a deep gorge carved by an old river thousands of years ago. A tiny trickle of a stream sang memories of those thunderous currents. The stones of the ravine walls amplified its voice. In the center of the deep, shaded gorge, a town had been carved into the tall cliffs. A latticework of ladders, stairs, and porches connected the apartment levels. Ari Ara counted six stories stacked one above the next. People ran, light-footed, across the rope bridges strung high overhead from one side of the ravine to the other. As Tala led Zyrh carefully through the crowded, wooden walkways at the base of the cliffs. Ari Ara twisted and gaped, trying not to fall off as she looked at everything all at once.

At the common house, Tahkan and Mahteni waited. They rose from the shade of the stone porch, stepping down the stairs, faces bearing a mixture of relief and disapproval. Ari Ara slid off Zyrh's back slowly, seeing her father's stern scowl. Tala greeted the Harrak-Mettahl with a cheeky wink and bombarded him with questions: what exactly had the Meet of Meets decided? What were the warriors planning now? What could be done to stop warriors-rule?

159

"Let me greet my daughter," Tahkan countered, holding up his hands to ward off the assault of questions, "and then I'll give you some answers, young Tala."

Tahkan held Ari Ara's face in his palms for a long moment, reading the time and distances that had passed, noting the changes in her eyes. For days, as he put out the fires she had inflamed in tents and angry warriors, he had debated what to say to his daughter. From one source and another, he had patched together a rough idea of her wanderings and mishaps over the past weeks. One part of him - the reckless, wild spirit he shared with her - wanted to laugh and cheer at her bold rescue of Nalia. Another part of him - the somber, calculating side - groaned at her disruption of his carefully laid plans. He had intended to use Nalia's forced marriage to haul the very notion of warriors-rule in a time of peace before the judgment of the thirteen Tala-Rasa. With such a clear offense of Harraken law, they could disband warriors-rule. Nalia's marriage would be dissolved and the whole problem would be resolved.

Tahkan rubbed his temples. So much for that idea. Ari Ara had wrecked it - along with a third of the encampment. The warriors resented - even detested - his daughter now, not just for the fire and scattered horses, but for the challenge to their authority and the shaming of their harrak. Not only had she snuck into the Meet of Meets right under their noses to rescue Nalia, she had also taken the honorable course of action no one else had dared to take. Every last one of those warriors - including him - should have risen to Nalia's defense. The young woman had protested the marriage bitterly; Harraken law was clear.

As he held his daughter's face in his hands, Tahkan Shirar found he could not weigh her actions on the scales of right and wrong. She had raced off from Turim, but only because the trickster horse had bolted. She had disobeyed Moragh by leaving without permission, but she had done it to help Emir. She had snuck into the Meet of Meets, but only to rescue a young woman from a forced marriage.

"What am I going to do with you?" he murmured, seeing anxiety and defiance written in equal measures across her young face. "Come, you'd best tell me all that has transpired."

He slung the youths' travel packs over his shoulder, and gestured for them to come into the shade of the stone balcony. Ari Ara flung her wiry arms around Mahteni. The woman's fast-whittled features curved into a smile. She stroked the dust from the girl's red hair and murmured that she was proud of her rescue of Nalia.

"Really?" Ari Ara whispered back, eyes wide.

"I would have done the same, had I been able," Mahteni assured her. A flash of outrage sparked in her eyes. She had never supported Tahkan's strategy - women were not pawns to be played for political goals - and was thrilled that the youths had taken bold action. She hoped it would spark more defiance among the Harraken women and girls.

She settled onto the cushion of a wooden bench and drew Ari Ara down next to her. Tahkan leaned against the carved rail, arms folded over his chest. Tala hopped up beside him, swinging zirs legs. Ze wasn't going to get in trouble. Only the Tala-Rasa could censure the umber-skinned youth.

Ari Ara told her tale, starting with Gorlion's challenge to race. Tahkan listened without interruption, his face and reactions inscrutable. At the end, he stood quietly, chin to chest, for a long, taut moment. Ari Ara tried not to squirm. Finally, he lifted his gaze and startled her with an unexpected question.

"One thing I do not understand," he murmured. "How did

you and Emir run out of water? You both know to ration your supply."

Ari Ara swallowed nervously. She'd glossed over her temper tantrum with Emir, leaving out the part where she pitched the waterskin at his head. A flush heated her cheekbones. She confessed that she'd neglected to tie the horses.

"And they ran off with your waterskins?" her father guessed.

"Er, not exactly," she admitted reluctantly. "One broke."

Her father raised an eyebrow. "It just broke?"

Her face reddened further.

"No," she sighed, spitting out the whole truth at last. "I lost my temper and threw the waterskin at Emir. I thought he would catch it, but it hit a boulder and split."

Her voice dropped off. She sensed Tahkan's eyes grow stern.

"I was wrong," she admitted in a small voice. "Whatever the punishment is, I accept it."

She stared at her hands, unable to lift her head. Her father was silent for so long, she thought he'd somehow stalked away without a sound. She risked a quick glance. He sat still, looking sadly at her. His gaze was gentle, not wrathful; sorrowful, not scornful.

"I do not need to punish you," he answered. "You are stinging yourself hard enough. I will say this: you have lost harrak in my eyes."

Ari Ara's face turned stony. That was a harsh phrase in a culture that prized their honor over rubies and their integrity over gold. She could hear the pain in Tahkan's voice. He was deeply disappointed in her.

"You also hid the truth," he remarked in an aching tone, "and by not telling the whole truth, your harrak sinks even lower. Always tell the truth, Ari Ara, even if it is hard."

"I'm sorry," she murmured, her throat choking over the words.

"I know," Tahkan sighed, "and this remorse is what shows me that you still have enough honor left to begin to rebuild your harrak."

He studied her thoughtfully, hoping she understood. He - of all people - should know: restoring honor when you have lost it is one of the most difficult tasks, painful and slow. Many people feared to walk through the fire of that process, choosing paths that further squandered their harrak. Ari Ara had the strength to admit her wrongs and seek to make them right. No father wanted to see his child go through this, but neither would he abandon her in this moment - or any moment - until she restored her honor.

"We will find Emir," Tahkan promised. A swift flash of concern crossed his face. "And you will send a message to Shulen, telling him the whole truth of what happened."

The thought sent a shudder through her. Her mentor had lost so much - a wife, a small child - she couldn't imagine his pain at losing Emir, who was more than an apprentice to Shulen. The youth was practically a son; Shulen had raised him from childhood to become the greatest warrior in the world. Ari Ara trembled at the thought of telling Shulen that Emir Miresh might have been killed not by an army of enemies, but through her childish temper tantrum.

She swallowed hard and nodded. Tahkan released his breath in a silent sigh that only Mahteni noticed. He rubbed the tension from his brow, pinching the bridge of his nose. He did not like disciplining Ari Ara any more than she enjoyed being disciplined . . . but that, he knew, was the responsibility of being a parent.

"Now, young Tala," he said, shifting the subject to give

Ari Ara time to sort through her storm of emotions, "you had questions for me?"

Tala blurted out half a dozen questions in one long rattle of a sentence. Tahkan's chuckle rumbled loose from his chest. He held up a hand to stem the outburst of the youth's curiosity. Swiftly, he outlined what had occurred at the Meet of Meets: the warriors voted to assert their right to rule in a time of peace. They justified the decision by the vague threat of Marianan attack. They had hoped to use Nalia's wedding as a celebratory exercise of their newfound authority, but the young woman's resistance and rescue had thwarted that attempt. Now, they rode out in all directions to set up warriors meets in villages and towns, establishing their rule. The one concession to Tahkan's concerns and Mahteni's fast was to include women warriors in making the decisions at the warriors meets. They promised to open a path toward joining the warriors' ranks and planned to implement mandatory battle training for all Harraken.

"All male Harraken," Mahteni cut in sharply.

"And any women who choose to join them," Tahkan clarified. The warriors training would be mandatory for men, voluntary for women.

"After all," Mahteni muttered under her breath. "It'd be such a bother to their glorious, heroic image to have to halt a drill to change diapers."

Ari Ara smothered a laugh at the sight of her father's scowl.

"That's not the intention - "

"Oh?" Mahteni flung back, her bony features taut with skepticism. "Beyond the common fire, Tahkan, the warriors' noble sentiments fell off like false smiles. Kirkan may be sincere in his concern for the women and children, but many warriors lust for control. In their view, the women should be silenced from the Harraken Song and made to shoulder the mundane and onerous work of providing food and shelter for our people."

"You think their protection worthless, then?" Tahkan barked sharply.

"I did not say that," she replied, holding up a hand firmly to stop his quick retort. "Each task is equally worthy, and each task should be shared equally by all Harraken, not divided by men and women."

"Men are more suited for war - "

"Hah! I dare you to say that to our sister," Mahteni lifted an eyebrow and pursed her lips.

Tahkan's eyes darted away from her unblinking stare.

"Can anything be done to stop warriors-rule?" Ari Ara asked, eyes wide with worry. Her training in the Way Between had taught her that when war culture dominated a society, war inevitably erupted.

Mahteni wrapped a reassuring arm around her shoulders.

"Yes. Much can be done," she remarked. "The vote for warriors-rule held only a slight majority. Many of the warriors objected."

"How many?" Tala asked.

"Too many on the warriors' side, too few on ours," Tahkan answered with a sigh.

"But," Mahteni interjected fiercely, "most Harraken have not yet been consulted. The women. The non-warriors. The elders."

"Are we are going to ask them?" Tala asked with a sly smile and a raised eyebrow. "After all, *Farrah sang the Outcry to the women, not the warriors.*"

Mahteni laughed at the old saying.

"That is exactly what we should do," she stated determinedly, lifting her chin.

Seeing Ari Ara's mystified expression, Tahkan explained:

long ago, in ancient times, a young woman named Farrah resisted her father's choice of a husband for her. She fled her home, but refused to hide. Instead, she lifted a sharp and piercing song of protest - the Outcry - at the gates of every village, calling the women to her side, demanding that they had a right to choose whom they would marry. After that, tradition maintained that no Harraken woman would be forced to marry against her will. It was this belief that sparked the outrage in Orryn over her sister's marriage and inspired Nalia to resist by running away.

"So," Ari Ara exclaimed, "there are *songs* about times like this?"

"Sure, *old* songs," Tala groaned. "There's a bunch of Outcry Ballads."

The songholder rattled off a list of names: Farrah, Annoush, Mirka, Tala-Oon, Karinne, Shireen, women of legendary times who cried out for justice and rose up for change. People still recognized the names, though the songs weren't as popular as they once were.

"No one wants to hear about rebellious women in times of war," Tala confessed with a little shrug. "We're asked to sing of warriors and great battles."

"So, these women weren't fighters?" Ari Ara asked.

"Oh, they were fighters, alright," Tahkan chuckled, "just not with swords. They fought with words and courage . . . kind of like the Way Between. Actually, there might be a connection."

His face pinched in thought. He hummed a little bit of tune, eyebrows drawn together, remembering. Tala caught the melody and sang a verse as the song resurfaced in zirs memory.

"Yes, that's it," Tahkan confirmed. "The women are known as *The Women of the Outcry*, after a song of protest they each lifted, each calling on the tradition established by the women who came before. But the first Outcry was lifted by the women who worked with Alaren as they tried to stop King Shirar's war."

"You see, after Farrah," Tala told Ari Ara, relating the story in breathless rush, "the Outcry became a ritual . . . a timeless variation of a song with new words for every occasion. Shireen cried out against the rule of kings. Mirka sang for the hungry children. Karrine Shirar, your ancestor, demanded her place as harrak-mettahl."

"So, you're saying?" Ari Ara asked, slowly seeing the spark of an idea leap from one pair of Harraken eyes to the next.

"It's time to lift the Outcry again," Mahteni said with a determined look.

Ari Ara gasped at the boldness of the idea!

"We must call the women into action," Mahteni declared. "They must stand up for their rights as their ancestors did before them. We will ride across the desert and raise the Outcry in every village, one-by-one, like lighting signal fires across the mountain ridges until the desert shines with light and harrak."

Sparks leapt from her words when she spoke, invoking the deepest meanings of harrak. Tala gasped, danced in a circle, and clapped in laughing appreciation.

"You must be the one to lift the Outcry," Tala urged, clasping Mahteni's hand. "You are a woman, a Shirar, and the next-in-line to be harrak-mettahl. As the representative of the Tala-Rasa, I will hear your song."

The words rang with ritual meaning.

"She will not lift it alone," Tahkan added. He would sing the Outcry with her . . . and the way things stood, Mahteni-Mirrin's song would be the only voice with support of both the Harrak-Mettahl and the Tala-Rasa. Mountains would crumble before the strength of the song. Stars would fall in prophecies from the sky. Legends would grow in their footsteps. Songs would tell their story for centuries to come.

At least, Tahkan amended wryly, *if they succeeded.*

CHAPTER SEVENTEEN

· · · · ·

The Outcry

Dawn broke. The people of Tuloon Ravine stirred at the thinning of the grey light. In the tiers of dwellings carved into the cliffs, murmurs and rustles from the slowly-awakening town rose up. In a ground-level home, an old woman rubbed the chill of the night from her bones. She lit the morning fire, murmuring a quiet song to welcome the day. Around her, the family slept. The grandmother's thin and wrinkled fingers cast a pinch of herbs into the flames. The incense carried her prayers aloft, up to the Ancestor Wind.

Let the wrongs be righted, she sang, *let the balance be restored.*

A man's voice grumbled for quiet, telling her to stop yammering and start the water boiling for *mahk*. The look she threw at his prone figure could have soured milk, but she left to fetch water for the kettle. Sighing over the injustices of the world, she stepped out the door with the water bucket. From her, so many lives had come. Yet, still she rose before first light - before the men - and started working before the proper songs had been sung to wake the day.

No good comes of letting the sun rise unsung, she thought fiercely.

On the edge of the stream, she halted. A slight breath of mist lifted from the water's surface. Four figures stood on the other side. Two were tall and strong. Two were small and slender. Of the pair caught between childhood and adulthood, one was dark as the *churruk* tree, the other was pale as a cactus spine with hair as red as a Shirar's. The old woman squinted - her eyes weren't as sharp as they used to be - and blinked owlishly.

Ancestors! she gaped. There was the youngest Tala-Rasa, standing on one foot, staring back at her, chanting in a breath of song. Beside the youth stood the Harrak-Mettahl and his younger sister. *The red-haired girl must be his daughter,* the old woman thought, dropping her bucket in astonishment.

Above her, the Ancestor Wind stilled, listening.

In the cliffs, heads appeared in windows, rubbing sleep from eyes and turning their ears in the direction of the singer. One by one, the old woman's family sat up, wondering at the sound. They lumbered out the door, scratching their bellies and yawning. One boy scanned the slope toward the stream and saw his grandmother frozen still as a statue watching the chanting songholder. He tugged his father's arm. Then he ran to rouse his uncles. His cousins followed their parents out onto the balconies. Their friends gathered in clusters on the bridges. At last, the entire town had been roused.

Tala sang to the dust, stepping in a small, rhythmic circle, head bowed, face half-hidden by the dawn shadows, hair blazing in a crown of light. A groove wore into the earth from zirs footsteps. Tala stepped inside its protective ring. A ripple of gasps rose up from the watchers ... old legends tickled the edges of their memories, ballads of ancient stories sung by the Tala-Rasa around the common fires.

The thin-boned youth paused. The dust swirled around zirs

legs. The planes of the youth's face tilted up to the sky. The sun touched Tala's brow, setting the hard blue sheen of its blessing on the songholder's umber skin. For one breath, two, three, ze inhaled deeply, connecting to the ancestors who lived in the wind. Tala called to them, gathered the legends of those who come before, the women who had once lifted the Outcry against their people, whose names were once known to all Harraken. A shiver ran through the townspeople. The spirits drew close, shimmering in the air. Where the ancestors touched the earth, swirls of dust rose up.

The young Tala invoked their presences through the song.

Farrah, the daughter married against her will, who ran off into the night to find her true love, whose life and death gave birth to the law that Harraken women marry as they will.

Shireen, who ended the reign of kings and started the village sings.

Annoush, who threw herself between her husband's blows and her child, and first lifted the Outcry against such abuse.

Tala-Oon, whose Outcry against the constraints of men and women made space for those who were both, neither, and something else altogether.

Mirka, whose song denounced greed and won back the grain to feed the starving children, and wove harrak into their culture forever.

Karrine, who took her rightful place after her father's death, the next Shirar to shoulder the burdens of the harrak-mettahl.

Tala summoned them from their endless journeying in the wind. It took time. The shadows yawned and stretched as the sun poured into the ravine. From time to time, the red-haired girl brought water to the singing Tala, carefully avoiding the ring of footsteps lest the ancestors curse her for interfering. The villagers crouched down on their heels, watched and waited in foreboding suspense as the young Tala invoked the Outcry. The zenith sun compressed their shadows into stepping-stones and the flat harsh light stripped away untruths. The heat intensified. The words of the song chanted onward. The drone of insects suspended.

The sun shifted overhead and touched the fingertips of its golden streaks to the youth's western cheek. Ze's shadow lengthened to twice as long as ze was tall. So, too, would words spoken at sunset cast long shadows into the future. The ancestor spirits rustled. Tala's offering of endurance and patience was accepted. The moment to speak current truths arrived.

Mahteni-Mirrin stepped forward, drawing her spine tall, lifting her head proudly. The breath of the Ancestor Wind filled her lungs. The Outcry rose up, harsh and metallic, scraping the ears and grinding the melody with the grit and dust of life. She sang the whispers that ran across the desert winds: the injustices she had seen, the rumors she had heard, the flight of Nalia and Orryn. She sang of the women who sought shelter from the Black Ravens. She sang of warriors and men who would not listen to their people.

These are wrongs, Mahteni sang,
wrongs that must be righted,
wrongs that shame us
and steal our harrak like thieves.
We are being robbed
of that which makes us Harraken.
We are losing our way,
stumbling in dust storms
stirred up by all these wrongs.

The last verse cried out that the stories were more numerous than the stars that would soon appear. Then the Harrak-Mettahl joined his voice to his sister's song. Together, they called for a village sing around the common fire. With Farrah as their witness, they demanded the right to let the unheard truths be spoken. The Ancestor Wind would listen. The Harrak Mettahl would hear the song. A Tala-Rasa would bear witness. The people would have a chance to restore their harrak.

Tala sang the last chorus, a ritual line that asked the people for their support. The youth sang with a cracking voice, hoarse from the long hours of chanting and singing. The songholder stepped to the edge of the ritual circle. The youth called out the Outcry's invitation once more.

Silence.

A breath.

A stir of wind.

Then the answer came.

One lone voice, an old woman's crackled tone, sang out the ritual greeting that invited guests to gather around the common fire. Tala called out again. As the woman responded, her daughter's voice joined in. Tala took another step, breaking the line of the circle worn by ritual footsteps at dawn. The dusk light veiled the weariness in the youth's face, but they saw the red-haired girl catch the songholder as ze staggered. Once more, the ragged call issued forth. This time, the whole town sang out the reply.

When the people gathered and heard the sound of their voices - the sound of every person, young and old, man and woman, warrior and not - the choice was clear: Tuloon Ravine could not support warriors-rule. They would hold their village sing and listen to the wisdom of every person who dwelled in the cliffs.

From one place to the next, the four travelers rode. At the gates of each village, the Outcry rang out, startling, strong, harsh, and clear as the light of the desert. Where their voices wove, visions walked. Where their words spoke, lies toppled. Where their song roared, silence broke. Where their Outcry lifted, the Ancestor Wind swept down from the sky. Where their stories were heard, harrak was restored.

It was to Tahkan and Mahteni's credit that so many village sings were willingly held. The two Shirars voiced not only the shame and loss of honor, but also the pride that comes from doing what was right in order to restore the honor of the village. Mahteni and Tahkan made it possible for people to change. They made it possible for people to forgive. They worked a great healing among their people. As in any healing, there was pain and discomfort, but also relief and the rebuilding of strength. Hurts and angers were spoken and heard. Men and warriors swallowed hard at the stories the women told. A few openly wept. Tahkan quieted the outspoken. Mahteni drew out the comments of the shy and afraid. Tala murmured silent songs, lips moving, memorizing the events. Each story they heard added to the next Outcry. Each village's sufferings were heard in the next. They never sang the same Outcry twice . . . there were too many true stories to tell. The full list would take days to sing.

Ari Ara watched and listened. A peculiar ache grew in her heart, a longing to have been raised among the Harraken, to speak without accent and be greeted without stares, and to fully understand the significance of the Outcry. She could sense the shiver of magic in the air. She could hear the murmurs of old legends and myths. She caught wind of new songs emerging from their actions. At each village they visited, she learned one more nuance of the deep meaning of the rituals . . . but it was like lifting a lantern along a night journey filled with looming dark shapes she couldn't quite see. It made her lonely.

She longed to find Emir, who would understand exactly how she felt. She scanned the horizons and searched the villages as they traveled, but no one had heard anything about a wandering Marianan warrior.

Tahkan, sensing her loneliness, set out to teach her the Outcry. He began one night as the four travelers ringed the embers of their cook fire, camped under the stars as they journeyed between villages. The night brimmed with starlight and fireflies. A serenade of hidden crickets chanted in the darkness.

"Let's hear your voice, daughter," he remarked unexpectedly, startling everyone. "If you're going to learn the Outcry, then we need to hear the strength of your lungs."

"Now?" Ari Ara squeaked, put on the spot. She sang all the time - but with others, blending her voice in with her aunt's or Tala's, piping along when the villagers sang folk tunes. She squirmed uncomfortably at the idea of singing on her own.

"Yes," her father answered, a slight frown pulling a chasm of shadow across his face, "sing Shireen's Song."

Mahteni let the robe she was repairing fall forgotten to her lap. Her green eyes shifted uneasily from Tahkan to the girl. Tala sat still as a round-eyed owl, watching the exchange.

"Come," he encouraged. "I know you love that song."

It was true, it was one of her favorite ballads, telling of how courageous Shireen, a descendant of Shirar, gave up her ancestor's throne to empower the Harraken to rule together in the village sings. Ari Ara adored all of the stories of the Women of the Outcry and the way they defied their culture to do what was right. She begged to hear them over and over. Tahkan's ballads came alive with visions so strong, she once reached out to touch them. When Mahteni sang the songs, her wry humor brought nuances to the legends: Farrah's fire and passion burned in a surprisingly short frame; Annoush's motherly curves jiggled with honesty as she protected her child; Karinne's knees knocked together with nervousness as she demanded her rightful place as the next harrak-mettahl.

"Come on," he urged his daughter. "Sing for me."

He needed to know if her voice was strong enough to lift the Outcry. That melody was harsh, ripping, powerful. It required the strength of charging warriors and the ferocity of battle cries - which was not what he heard in her voice when she finally began to sing.

Ari Ara's tone was tentative and wavering. She fumbled the words and lost the chord. The weak sound shriveled against the vastness of the night. Hearing uncertainty and off-key notes in her voice, Ari Ara faltered. A flush rose on her cheeks. Tahkan stopped her on the third verse, muttering about mewing kittens.

Ari Ara slammed up her anger like a shield over her hurt.

"Tahkan!" Mahteni snapped, appalled at his comment. "She didn't grow up with song the way we did; you have to teach her what we learned at our parents' knees."

He tried. That night and many others, he tried to instruct his daughter in how to pull the Ancestor Wind down into her living lungs, how to stretch and open her vocal chords, how to sustain the notes with power and grace. It was painful for everyone. Tahkan, a man born with a natural voice, had no idea how to teach her to sing. He rejected Tala's suggestions, resented Mahteni's interventions, and snapped at Ari Ara's stammering attempts. The more he criticized her, the more nervous she got. The more mistakes she made from nervousness, the more critical he grew in a vicious cycle that left both of them furious and sulky.

Ari Ara's matching temper didn't help the situation. She covered her nerves with belligerence and her embarrassment with anger. The two sparked and snapped and stung each other through each lesson. Tala bit back laughter - the girl in a temper was the spitting image of her father in a fury: jutting chin, proud tilt of head, hands balled into fists - but no one else found it funny. The sessions invariably ended with one of the pair storming off in frustration.

"If she sings like that at the Finding Ceremony, everyone will laugh at her," Tahkan bellowed as Mahteni hissed at him to hush. Ari Ara had stomped off into the desert; her tight-clenched muscles stood outlined against the deeper blues of the night sky.

"Oh nonsense," Mahteni snorted. "No one expects perfection at the Finding Ceremony."

She shot him an indulgent grin. Before they participated in the Harraken Sing, the youth were required to sing solos in front of everyone. The "Finding Your Voice" Ceremony was a rite of passage, another step in becoming an adult in Harraken society. She and Tahkan had watched plenty of youth with shaking knees and quaking voices stumble through the test. It didn't matter how good or bad they were, Mahteni reminded her brother.

"They're not the descendent of Shirar!" Tahkan burst out. "How can she be the next harrak-mettahl if she can't sing?"

"Maybe she won't be a harrak-mettahl," Mahteni answered evenly. "She has her own path to walk."

"She's my daughter!"

"Daughters do not belong to their fathers," Mahteni snapped back. "We are not possessions."

"She can lift the Outcry, I know she can," Tahkan insisted, returning to that challenging song. "She's just not trying."

"She can't do it, Tahkan," her aunt retorted flatly. "She has neither the strength nor the confidence. Not on her own. Not yet. Let her sing with us, but don't make her sing alone."

Tahkan paced around the fire. Mahteni folded her arms over her chest.

"If you keep pushing her," she warned her brother, "she'll snap shut like a lock and refuse to sing at all. Let her be."

Tahkan grumbled, but eventually agreed. He looked at his sister with an anguished expression.

"What if she never learns?" he asked. "What if she's never able to make song-visions walk on the air like a true Shirar?"

"I saw her do it, once," Mahteni replied gently. "Back in Mariana, during her Woman's Song, she made them dance - light, pale things, but she did it. Just give her time."

The days blistered into furnaces. Beyond the patches of irrigated fields, the green withered and dried. Tans and dusty golds spread from horizon to horizon, broken only by the tired lizard-skinned cacti and the startling chartreuse of the waist-high *gurse* bush. Tala sang the Lovers' Farewell to the green, promising to meet again when the late summer rains reunited them. Mahteni told Ari Ara that the quickening of spring and the planting festivals brought many lovers - young and old - together. Then the dry winds blew them apart as traders departed on routes and herders sought the mountain pastures and farmers tarried by their crops. The summer rains drew herders down from the high meadows onto the wide plain, but many lovers would not break bread together as a whole community until the harvest, or even the Harraken Sing in the years it was held.

"Tell me more about the Harraken Sing," Ari Ara requested as they wound through a dry gully toward a western village near the mountain foothills.

"We haven't held one in years," Tala grumbled.

"Perhaps that will soon change," Tahkan soothed.

"It better," Tala retorted and the young songholder burst into an old teaching tune:

In the south, beneath the Deep Sands Valley,
the Harraken journey to the Old Ones' shadows,
where we tell the year's telling
speak the secrets of passing time,
and sing the future as we dare to see it.

Mahteni saw Ari Ara's perplexed expression and explained.

"The Harraken Sing is a months-long gathering in the south. We spend the whole winter working through our disputes. It's like Mariana's Nobles Assembly, but for everyone," the desert woman explained.

Ari Ara nodded with sudden comprehension. Tala lifted an eyebrow.

"Does Mariana cut the women out of the song, too?"

Ari Ara laughed at the thought and shook her head. No one would dare silence the Great Lady Brinelle. Marianans knew better than to try to dominate their women, she thought, and said so proudly to the others. Mahteni, however, made a strangled sound of disbelief.

"When thirteen people make all the decisions for everyone else, it does not matter if they are men or women," she choked out.

"Thirteen?" Tala exclaimed in a shocked tone, horrified at the thought. "That's like the Tala-Rasa singing for everyone."

A surge of stubborn loyalty flared in Ari Ara's chest. She didn't like the Nobles Assembly very much, but she loved her mother's people for all their flaws. She wouldn't let her father's people pretend superiority over them. Her objections set off a long debate that ran in circles around who should be able to speak for whom, and if anyone could ever replace another voice in the song. Just when the arguments grew as heated as the day, Tala cut through with the final word.

"The Marianans can do as they like. As for the Harraken, we know that everyone's voice strengthens the Harraken Song - from the baby's first wail to the elder's last exhale, as the saying goes. If two heads are better than one, all of our heads are better than some."

Ari Ara surrendered. She couldn't argue with that!

CHAPTER EIGHTEEN

. . . . .

River Dog Ghost

Ari Ara asked after Emir everywhere they traveled, but heard worse than nothing. Many people reacted with hostility to the idea of the Mariana Champion wandering in their desert. Faces grew dark with distrust and hate. Several warned that if he wasn't dead, he soon would be. Ari Ara fought her impatience, worry, and a sense that their slow circuit of the northwestern quadrant of the desert was drawing her further and further from her friend.

Then, one day, a young goatherd raced into a silk weaving town at the foot of the Shushti Dunes, face white with fright, stammering that he had seen the ghost of a Marianan warrior. Tahkan and Mahteni were in the middle of a contentious village sing, full of hot tempers and arguments. Ari Ara had drifted off, seeking shade. She and Tahkan had been striking sparks all week. His lingering resentment over the aborted singing lessons rubbed her like grit in the eyes, making her tear up at the slightest sharp tone. His disappointment in her cut her to the bone. She couldn't stomach sitting next to him in the village sing, bored and silent, listening to the impassioned and headstrong Harraken argue for hours while he hid his disappointment in her from them. In Turim City, he had boasted to everyone that she would follow in his footsteps. Now, he could barely stand the sight of her, stabbed by the sharp edges of his broken dreams.

At least, that was what Ari Ara suspected. When she whispered her suspicions to Tala, her friend told her she was overreacting. Ari Ara didn't believe it. She was stretched like a taut bowstring, tiptoeing around her father and avoiding meeting his eyes.

As the village sing erupted into shouts - one faction leaping to their feet; the other gesticulating wildly - Ari Ara leaned against the support beam of the weaving hall's porch, glad she wasn't in the middle of that storm. A motion caught the corner of her eye. She turned. Near the well, a skinny goatherd had just run into the village. His skin glistened with sweat. He fanned his tunic desperately as he panted. Between gasps, he blurted out a strange tale to the cluster of wide-eyed small children that surrounded him.

"It must have been a ghost," the boy stammered. "Why else would a Marianan be wandering this far west?"

"Could have been a spy," another lad blurted out.

"Hah, he couldn't get this far - the warriors would kill him," someone scoffed.

The goatherd insisted that it was an unhappy spirit that had stepped out of the Ancestor Wind to plague them.

"What did he look like?" Ari Ara called out, interrupting the heated argument.

"Horrible," the boy claimed with a dramatic shudder. "Dark hair, long the way the river dogs wear it; pale as a fish."

It *had* to be Emir! Who else could it be?

"When did you see him? Where?" she pressed the goatherd.

The boy pointed north to the golden hills of dust and light, an hour's journey on foot. He'd raced his goats back with him; they bleated and clustered around the youths as he drew up water from the well for them. In the village sing, a few people looked up at the commotion. They gestured for quiet and turned back to the meeting. Ari Ara thanked the boy and ran to get Tahkan. She wove through the people until she reached his side. She tapped his shoulder.

"Affa?" she whispered, using the Harraken word for father.

He frowned and shook his head slightly, hushing her. This silk weaving town held great power and esteem among the Harraken. If they could restart the village sing here, many others would follow suit. It was famous for its silks, but while the family clans taught their daughters the secrets of the silk trade, they trained their sons as warriors. The family clans were proud of their generations of fighters. Many of them saw warriors-rule as a chance for the men to take charge. For the past hour, the men had dominated the village sing, shouting and interjecting. They were trying to intimidate the women - and it seemed to be working.

"Not now," he murmured back, face strained with the difficulty of following all the disagreements.

"It's important," she hissed. "Emir is close by."

That caught his attention. She whispered what the goatherd had said. Tahkan's brow furrowed. He nodded.

"When this is done - "

"But he might be gone by then!" Ari Ara objected.

Eyes turned toward her at her outburst.

"Wait until I can go with you," Tahkan ordered her in a stern undertone.

Then he waved her away and turned back to the discussion.

Ari Ara stormed out. The village sings lasted for hours,

sometimes days! By the time this one finished, Emir could have moved in any direction!

I have to find him! Ari Ara thought desperately. If no one could go with her, she'd take Zyrh. Her father always said the horse was as smart as any person. She scowled. Tahkan especially liked to say that with a laugh when the beast ran around in circles ignoring her commands.

Well, for once, that horse was going to do what she said! Ari Ara grabbed her travel sack - she knew better than to go anywhere without supplies - and headed toward the herd. Zyrh was easy to spot among the darker blacks and browns and roans. He even trotted over when she whistled softly. So far so good. She managed to get up on his back, but as soon as she turned him north, he dug his hooves into the ground and refused to move.

"Oh, for ancestors' sake," she cursed. "I'll go on foot."

She swung off and grabbed her rucksack. Zyrh spun around and blocked her path. She hit his flank with her palm and ducked under his neck to the other side. He bit her shirt. She yanked it out and heard it rip.

"You . . . you . . . beast!" she shouted, trying to dart around him again.

He gave up after a few minutes, staring at her with lowered head and an expression of annoyance, blowing snorts through his nostrils. Ari Ara ignored him and marched off.

The terrain rose and fell in gentle swells. There wasn't much shade, but the walking was easy. She cut a wandering path through the dips between the dunes. The further she walked, the higher the ridges climbed until they grew into low hills dotted with shrubs. She watched the ground, keeping her eye out for snakes under the sand. She smirked, feeling rather proud of herself for spotting an underground spring. She was congratulating herself on her knowledge of the desert when the drift edge she'd been walking along collapsed. She slithered sideways. The sand poured on top of her feet and buried her ankles as she skidded down the slope.

"Wha-at?!" she yelped, dropping her pack and flailing in surprise.

In startled panic, she used the Way Between to roll onto the top of the avalanching sand and slide to the bottom of the dune. She scrambled away from the collapsing rise, backing up until she felt the edge of the next dune on her spine. She froze, fearing it would shift and bury her.

My father was right, I should have waited for him, Ari Ara admitted silently, trembling from head to toe. She'd have to avoid those sinking edges. She rolled to her hands and knees, about to push to standing.

She stilled.

A pair of hot yellow eyes stared back.

CHAPTER NINETEEN

. . . . .

Sand Lioness

Dagger-length teeth bared at the edge of her sight. The rip-rumble of the sand lioness' snarl rattled in her bones. Boiling gold eyes pinned her into place. The tawny fur of the cat's shoulders twitched with tension. The silver undercoat rippled. The massive tail flicked.

Terror flashed through Ari Ara. The predator was big as a horse, built of solid muscle. The powerful cat could run faster than her, pounce twenty feet in a single leap, and shred shale with claws the length of Ari Ara's forearm.

The cat roared.

The wind of her breath blew Ari Ara's copper hair back from her wide-eyed face. The crouched lioness tightened to spring - then a black shape leapt in front of her.

A man roared back in a low, powerful bellow, throat-ripping, loud, and fierce.

Tahkan, she gasped, recognizing her father.

The lioness flinched in surprise then snarled. Tahkan roared again, a primal, outraged holler of protectiveness as he stood over his daughter. The lioness backed up a pace. A third roar burst from the Harrak-Mettahl, cracking at the end, human vocal chords faltering, but it was enough. The lioness backed down, slunk out of range, and then padded away swiftly between two dunes.

Ari Ara was swept up in strong, wiry arms. She was stunned speechless.

"Are you hurt? Are you alright?" Tahkan spluttered, his hands trembling.

He held her close then pushed her away to check for injuries then pulled her close again. Ari Ara saw Zyrh sniffing the sand lioness' tracks suspiciously. Tahkan followed her gaze and mumbled an explanation: the horse had galloped into the middle of the village sing and pulled him by the shirt until he had obeyed Zyrh's demand to get on his back.

"You ... you roared back at a sand lioness," Ari Ara murmured weakly. "I didn't know you could do that."

"Neither did I," Tahkan admitted, ducking his head sheepishly. He wasn't thinking straight. He hadn't even drawn his dagger. From yards away, he'd spotted her sprawled figure and leapt from the horse's back. He dove between his daughter and the sand lioness, ready to tear the beast apart with his bare hands. Tremors of emotion ran like earthquakes through his spine: fear, loss, fury. Shudders of aftershocks rumbled through him. Tahkan Shirar loved his daughter - his beautiful, young, immature, headstrong daughter - with a ferocity that frightened him. All of the pain of Alinore's death, the horrors of the war, the decade of longing and searching for Ari Ara: it all boiled down to an unflinching, ferocious urge to keep her alive. He would have ripped that sand lioness apart with his bare hands. He would slaughter armies to protect her. But when the greatest danger to his daughter was her? He spun. His glare pierced like arrows.

"How dare you disobey me!" he thundered. "I told you to wait. You could have been killed!"

"By the time you were done, Emir could have been long gone!" she objected, blue-grey eyes wide in her shock-paled face.

"From now on, you will stay by my side," he ordered, stern and uncompromising. "No more running off on your own."

Ari Ara flinched at his tone. Her muscles clenched. She hated being ordered around.

"You can't tell me what to do," she protested.

"I'm your father," he reminded her. "I have every right - even a duty - to tell you what to do. You're too young to take care of yourself!"

"No, I'm not!" she retorted. She balled her hands into fists at her sides and glared at him. How dare he say that! "I grew up fending for myself in the High Mountains. I took care of myself. You weren't *there*."

Tahkan flinched. He turned his head to the side to hide the flash of pain that ripped through him. His fear-driven anger evaporated like dew on sun-scorched dunes. When he spoke, it was in a low, sorrow-laden tone.

"There are many things I regret, Ari Ara. Things I cannot change. Alinore's death. Missing eleven years of your life. The fact that my daughter is practically a stranger to me. I look at you and see my family's hair, your mother's eyes; but who are you beyond that? I do not know. I am just trying to protect you long enough to get to know you."

"Huh," she snorted, unconvinced. She mimicked Moragh's rasping croak and quoted her aunt's words. "You can't protect someone who refuses protection."

Tahkan's face turned paled, recognizing the phrase. Years ago, he had laughed at Moragh's worry and used that phrase to brush aside her objections to her wife, Sorrin, joining the battle against the invading Marianans. *She is inexperienced*, Moragh had protested, *I'm just trying to protect her.*

You can't protect someone who refuses to be protected, he had argued, pointing to Sorrin's eagerness to fight, to show her strength, to defend her country. Now, Moragh threw the words back in his face, mocking him by saying it to his daughter.

He took a deep breath. He rubbed his temples, struggling to find the right words.

"My sister is mad at me," he admitted with a sigh.

"She's mad at everyone," Ari Ara muttered, rolling her eyes.

A fleeting smile lifted on Tahkan's face. He nodded in agreement then clarified.

"She's mad at me because I put her wife Sorrin in danger's path."

Ari Ara's gasp burst from her lips. She'd heard about Moragh's wife from Tala; the songholder had explained that, by desert tradition, marriages could be between two men, or two women, as much as between a man and woman. Tala had told her that Moragh's wife had died in the war, but she hadn't heard that her father had put her in danger.

"Moragh's wife was named Sorrin Mehta," Tahkan explained sadly. "She was Kirkan's sister. During the war, Sorrin wanted to fight alongside us. She had trained, of course, but she had only just passed her initiation test. In those days, many young people were rapidly passed through the warriors' test. We needed them. Many died."

Tahkan's eyes grew shadowed.

"Her brother, Kirkan Mehta, thought she was ready. Moragh did not," Tahkan answered slowly. "I supported Kirkan against Moragh's wishes."

To this day, they both rued that decision. Moragh's heart

broke at Sorrin's death. Her bitterness devoured her. Tahkan wished Ari Ara could have seen the older sister he once knew, before the war, before Sorrin's death. Moragh used to be brimming with laughter, bright and joyous, the life of any gathering, full of daring antics that drew people to her leadership like moths to flame. After Sorrin's death, she changed. For many years, she did not speak to her younger brother.

"But, Moragh was right. Sorrin was too inexperienced. On the battlefield, she faced Shulen and was killed."

"*Shulen* killed her?" Ari Ara gasped. "How could he?!"

Tahkan rubbed his hand across his face. The tight shock of adrenaline had fled his limbs, leaving him aching and wrung out.

"It was war, Ari Ara, not a match. Shulen did not realize who he struck down."

Not that it mattered on the battlefield. Tahkan quietly told his daughter the unvarnished truth of the brutality of the War of Retribution, the atrocities and the massacres, the reality of the war. The color drained from her face as he told of fighting ankle-deep in blood and gore. She swallowed hard at his description of how her Marianan aunt, Brinelle, had screamed when Tahkan had cut down her husband. She retched when he spoke of the women and children murdered by the Marianan army, pinned to the village gates with stakes.

"Shulen fought as we all fought," he told her, neither excusing nor condemning, "but he was - still is - a better fighter than most. He left fields of bodies in his wake, Ari Ara. There is a reason my people call him the Butcher."

Tahkan grimaced. He did not enjoy telling his daughter the awful truths about her beloved mentor. She knew Shulen was a warrior - the best, even better than Emir Miresh - and she knew, abstractly, what warriors did. But Ari Ara had never been to the front lines. She had never witnessed the madness of bloodlust, battle rage, or the terror-struck flailings for survival. He did not sing the ballads of those times for her. She did not need nightmares from seeing the song visions. His daughter was trembling enough already. When he spoke of how Shulen killed Moragh's wife, Ari Ara's eyes rolled back in her blood-drained face. Tahkan held her head, stroked her hair, and tried to ease the nausea his stories evoked. He had only seen this strong of a reaction once. Rhianne, the Fanten woman married to Shulen, had abhorred war with the vehemence shared by all her people. It made her physically sick.

If only we all reacted this way, he thought ruefully, *there would never be another war.*

Ari Ara straightened, shuddering.

"How-how can he live with himself?" she murmured, though on the same breath, the thought struck her that Shulen was haunted by nightmares and memories. She'd seen them in his eyes in broad daylight.

"Shulen is a warrior," Tahkan said with a slight shrug. "He only did what all warriors do. Even him. Even me. Even Emir will cut the life from people when he goes to war."

"Not if I can help it," she vowed fiercely. She would stop wars. All of them. None of her friends would kill or die on the battlefield. None of her relatives would ever again murder members of her family.

Tahkan smiled faintly. He reached out and roughed up her hair with his palm.

"I believe you. If anyone can do it, you can." He paused. His face turned grave and solemn. "But you can't stop wars if you become a sand lioness' dinner."

She sighed, anticipating a lecture, but Tahkan simply took a deep breath. He loved her more than life itself, this girl whom he had lost and found again. The honey-toned bronze of her skin, the sharp blue-grey of her riverlands eyes, the pointy little nose with its band of sun-darkened freckles, that stubborn chin: all of these were more precious to him than the jewels and silks of the whole world.

You can't protect someone who won't accept protection. His words to Moragh echoed in his heart along with a sorrow so profound, tears pooled in his eyes. Tahkan Shirar had lost his child. All those years of her smallness, her toddling, her newfound wonder at simple things, her first words, her first song; they were all gone. All that remained was this girl on the verge of womanhood, singing her Woman's Song already, set on an impossible druach to ensure that his country would hear her voice when she had grown into the young woman he could see striving to emerge from the protective shell of the girl. He could protect her no longer . . . he could only prepare her for the world that awaited, the beauties and sorrows, the dangers and possibilities.

"Come on," he urged his beloved daughter. "I won't tell you what to do . . . but I *would* like to show you how to avoid the desert's dangers so you can grow up to wage that peace you so boldly envision."

He offered his hand in the greeting of equals. Ari Ara smiled and took it. Then they set out to teach and to learn, and to search the dunes for her friend.

CHAPTER TWENTY

. . . . .

The Woman's Song

They traveled onward along the western range. Dry cracks opened in the earth then crumbled into powdery dust. The world baked like an oven. Ari Ara could never have imagined a heat so dry and unrelenting. Even the nights seethed with scorching edges. Ari Ara worried over Emir, imagining him collapsed in the dust, cracking into pieces. Their search through the dunes had turned up nothing. No footprints. No signs of campsites. No hints of a lone, wandering warrior. Ari Ara kept twisting over her shoulder for one last glance, hoping to see him, trying not to think of him swallowed up by collapsing sands or lionesses. She did not confess her fears. Words were powerful in the desert.

But as they journeyed from village to village with Mahteni and Tala, they began to hear tales of the River Dog Ghost. It was hard to tell what was real and what was only imagination running wild on dark nights. The stories contradicted one another. Some descriptions gave Emir a black pelt from head to toe, a long tail, and blood-dripping fangs. He vanished into thin air, frightened herds of goats, held swords to throats, and demanded first-born children. Ari Ara ignored these tales. Amidst the lurid and exaggerated horror stories were enough simple sightings of a ragged, sunburned, young warrior to maintain her hope. Ari Ara left messages with each village in case Emir passed back through. Tahkan urged them to make the youth welcome and send word to him. Under no circumstances were they to harm Emir - or his spirit, if that was the case, Tahkan patiently told them. Tala warned them it might set off an invasion of warrior-spirits through the Ancestor Wind. Ari Ara raised an eyebrow, but the songholder's face was a study of sincerity. Ari Ara decided to let the superstitions stand; if the Harraken thought he was a ghost then they might not try to kill him.

With a flash of illumination, she understood part of Throw-the-Bone's prophecy. Emir might not be hovering between life and death - the rumors and legends of the River Dog Ghost might have set the stone spinning. The wandering path of the stone across the tabletop map ran through her mind over and over; the trail of rumors roughly followed her memory of the prophecy. She pulled the lightning stone out of her pocket and stared at it in her palm. The seer said it was connected to Emir, so she squeezed it with a yearning prayer.

Stay alive; she urged her lost friend, whispering the message to the Ancestor Wind, *meet me in the Middle Pass, like the seer promised. Stay alive.*

They finished their journey through the crescent range of low mountains that rimmed the northwest corner of the desert. They turned south. Here, villages strung like gems along a winding river that shriveled with the heat, sometimes hiding underground. Spires of jutting rock ran like dragon ridges down the flank of a vast loneliness stretching to the west. The tenor of their listeners began to change. Relief gave way to suspicion.

Closed faces met the Outcry. Silence hung longer where the traditional offer of hospitality should have come. Fewer women came to the gates to hear them. The one that dared to greet the travelers reported that the other women were afraid to come. At one village, the young warriors stormed at them, shouting and heckling, breaking off their song with threats and insults. Ari Ara dove between a warrior and her companions, turning aside his angry attack with the Way Between.

"We are driving a wedge between the men," Tahkan remarked to Mahteni quietly that evening as they made camp under a canopy of stars.

"Yes," she agreed, "a necessary one. The Outcry draws a clean line in the sand: they either support the women and non-warriors' right to be heard . . . or they don't."

The following day, they approached a village of mud-plastered dwellings with tall, conical roof peaks of thatched grass. A wall of mud bricks surrounded the enclave, keeping goats in - and unwanted visitors out. They paused at a distance and shaded the midday sun from their eyes. The gates had been shut and barred. Tahkan and Mahteni conferred in hushed tones and decided that he should ride ahead to the village alone. Perhaps the Harrak-Mettahl could persuade them to open their closed gates - and minds - easing the way for the rest of them. Mahteni took the two youths to a nearby well where a windmill creaked and groaned, pulling up water into a wide trough. Herds of cattle and goats should have been plodding around the dusty region at this time of day. Their absence did not bode well for the travelers.

Ari Ara squinted up at the blue-white sky. Her messenger hawk circled overhead, a black speck wheeling in the winds. She called to him, but the bird was too high to hear. There was still no sign of Emir and she wanted to send an update to Shulen.

Rivera Sun

She threw her leg over Zyrh and slid off. With Tala and Mahteni, she approached the well to refill their waterskins.

A girl rose from behind the stone trough, stepping out from its meager shade. Her face was young, but aged with seriousness. She had waited hours for their arrival, tracking their progress from shimmering smudges on the horizon to these last few steps.

"Sarai," she stated, thumb to chest by way of introduction. She did not ask them their names. She knew. Her eyes inspected them hungrily as she passed around a shared cup of water in the ritual to welcome travelers.

"Why are the village gates barred?" Mahteni questioned her.

"They do not want to hear the Outcry," Sarai informed them, looking furtively over her shoulder. "The warriors ordered the gates to be closed."

Ari Ara kicked the sand in frustration. Lately, it seemed that the warriors rode one day ahead of them, turning the people against their cause.

"Oh?" Mahteni asked with a wry irony. "And your village listens to them even though the Tala-Rasa do not recognize their authority?"

"The men do . . . "

"And the women?" Mahteni pressed, noting the girl's careful phrasing.

Sarai shook her head vigorously.

"The women are furious, but they are afraid. Only I dared to try to meet you."

"They have to have courage," Mahteni urged, hands on hips. "Or they'll always live in fear. Do you want your daughters to be this afraid in the future?"

Sarai glanced sideways at her with a hopeful and shy look. She lifted her chin.

"No," the girl said boldly, "and neither do my mother and my aunts and my sisters. That's why I've come to ask a favor of Ari Ara Shirar."

She added the last with a bashful glance at the other girl.

"I have just begun my woman's blood," she announced in a formal tone. "I have come to invite you to my gathering this evening. I wish to include the Way Between in my Woman's Song and hope you will bear witness."

Mahteni's eyes lit up. A sunburst of a smile revealed the white gleam of her teeth. Less than a year ago, she had predicted that the Harraken girls would add Ari Ara and the Way Between to their songs as they crossed the threshold from girls to young women . . . and here was Sarai doing precisely that!

"It would be an honor," Ari Ara answered after a quick glance at Mahteni to make sure it was alright.

Sarai squealed with excitement, her formality and stiff maturity dropping away. She rattled out in a rapid-fire description of how to find the women's gathering place then spun away. After a few strides, she slapped her hand to her forehead and darted back, shooting a sheepish look at them. She lifted her water jug to her head and returned to the village.

"Clever," Mahteni chuckled, as they filled their waterskins. "We must remember this trick."

"What trick?" Ari Ara asked, drinking deeply of the cool, slightly iron-edged water.

"Meeting under the guise of a Woman's Song gathering," her aunt answered. "The ritual is held outside the village, under the stars. We will have all night to talk and the men will not bother us . . . they probably won't even know we attended."

Mahteni bolted upright and groaned with sudden realization.

"Call Nightfast down," she told Ari Ara as she dug into her travel pack. She pulled out a scrap of parchment, quill, and vial of ink. Mahteni squinted toward the village then wrote a swift, short line:

Hatching. Walking the Fire.

Tying the message to the black hawk's leg, she tossed the bird aloft to seek her brother in the village. It had taken him a while to convince the guards to let him in, but eventually, they relented . . . he was the Harrak-Mettahl, after all.

"I just realized that the warriors might be recruiting men to support their cause at the Hatching Songs," Mahteni explained. "Those are like the Woman's Songs, but for the boys when their voices crack. We call it *hatching out of the shell of the boy into the man*. They'll also be advocating for warriors-rule at initiations. All the men, even the non-warriors, attend the *Walking the Fire* ceremonies for the warriors."

Mahteni's lips drew into a thin, grim line at the thought. Then she clapped Ari Ara on the shoulder. They would turn that tactic around tonight and use it to their advantage.

When dusk fell, they made their way to the gathering place. Beyond the triple pinnacle Sarai had described in her directions, the eroding rock formations sheltered a horseshoe clearing. Firelight threw streaks of orange and gold onto the rising features of the high stones. The women's faces glowed. The pale silks of their outer robes gleamed.

Sarai stood amidst what looked like the entire female population of the village. The girl trembled with importance, her head lifting proudly to be the reason for such a significant gathering. She tossed her glossy, dark-brown hair behind her shoulder and boldly came to welcome the arrivals. She had the grace and confidence of a leader, despite her youth.

"Thank you for the honor of your presence," she told

Ari Ara, Mahteni, and Tala. "This is my mother, Sarra, daughter of Larli, daughter of Gushan."

Ari Ara turned to the older woman, a mirror of her daughter, and replied with a similar recitation of her matrilineal line.

"I am Ari Ara, daughter of Alinore, daughter of Elsinore, daughter of Eliane."

A consternated flurry of noise erupted as the names of their enemy's queens caught them by surprise. Mahteni cleared her throat.

"*And* the granddaughter of my mother, Dirrini," Mahteni added with a wry note, "daughter of Salma, daughter of many women all the way back to the first Shirar's mother who had the great misfortune to also give birth to Marin."

Laughter eased the tension. Horses were turned loose to sniff noses and tails. The women circled the guests with an equal mixture of suspicion and curiosity, welcome and caution, until all were accustomed to each other's presence. With a flick of tail, swish of skirt, and toss of mane or hair, everyone settled down to begin the ceremony.

Sarai sang out the verses praising the strengths of her female relatives; the inner steel endurance of her mother, the wisdom of her grandmother, the humor of her aunt, the grace of her older cousin. At each verse, the circle of women sang back the chorus:

May it be so,
may these gifts grow in you
may we tend them like seeds
in the garden of this young woman.

Ari Ara felt strange emotions twisting through her heart. She had not had that swell of voices when Mahteni taught her the Woman's Song last year. Then, she had been moved by the simple singing she and her aunt had done together, but now she saw how the strength of the community's support changed the music, imbuing it with tingling power. She understood, now, the longing and loneliness that had shadowed Mahteni's eyes. Her aunt had not even been able to tell her niece that she was her blood relative. They had sung as friends, but not as family. A twinge of envy ran through Ari Ara as she watched Sarai. The girl had walked her first steps under her mother's gaze and grown up alongside her cousins. She stood surrounded by her kinswomen and community at her Woman's Song. Ari Ara had had none of these experiences.

Then Sarai called out the verse with Ari Ara's name and the skills of the Way Between. Mahteni nudged her into motion, urging her to demonstrate the movements. When she finished, hands reached out and patted her shoulders and head. The chorus sang to an awed Sarai: *may it be so, may this gift grow in you, may we tend it like seeds, in the garden of this young woman.*

After the song, Sarai plopped down on the sand next to Ari Ara, regardless of the fine silk she wore, dark eyes glowing.

"You have to teach me the Way Between!"

"Hard to do that when we're not allowed in your village," Ari Ara pointed out.

Sarai pursed her lips into small salted plums, wrinkled with displeasure.

"*We* want you to come," Sarai insisted, gesturing to the women, "but the warriors won't listen to us."

"Couldn't you just sit down by the common fire and revive the village sing?" Ari Ara wondered.

"Mother tried. They hauled her away and locked her up in the pig shed for three days."

"But what if you all sat down together?" Ari Ara suggested. "They couldn't lock you all up, not forever, anyway. Who would take care of the children or cook or haul the water?"

"Or sew clothes, tend fields, and weave rugs," Sarai added with an exasperated sigh. She stared glumly at the older women conversing in low tones with Mahteni. "They'd be too scared to challenge the warriors."

"Why? Would they kill you? Beat you?" Ari Ara asked.

Sarai shrugged her narrow shoulders. It was hard to tell. They wouldn't kill their own mothers, daughters, sisters, and wives, but they might inflict other punishments: confinement, beatings, half-rations, extra labor, or even banishment from their home and children.

"It would be worth the risk, though," Sarai said decisively, pounding a curled fist into her open palm, "to stand as equals like our mothers and grandmothers and ancestors once did."

"You wanted to learn the Way Between," Ari Ara told her. "This is it. It's not just a bunch of fancy moves."

A quote from Shulen resurfaced in her memory. She hugged her arms to her chest, missing him fiercely.

Sometimes," she quoted, "the simplest actions have the greatest power in the Way Between . . . like daring to sing when your voice has been silenced."

"They won't listen to the Outcry," Sarai warned. "They're dead set against it."

"So, sing something else," Ari Ara sighed in exasperation. People often complained about what they *couldn't* do instead of figuring out what they *could* do.

Sarai gasped, an idea springing to mind. All at once, she leapt from the ground in a startling burst. By the time her feet touched the earth again, a song was on her lips. The women swiveled and conversations faltered.

Shirar wanted war,
the women sang peace,
Shirar wanted their sons
the women sang no,
Shirar wanted his way,
the women had theirs,
all by the strength of their song.

The melody swelled, old and haunting. Ari Ara recognized the ballad; Tala had sung it as they rode from one village to the next. It was the origin of the Outcry, the beginning of the lineage of women and the tradition of the protest song. Long ago, Alaren had organized a vast peace force trained in the Way Between. They had camped outside the gates of Shirar's ancient city and worked to stop the threat of war. The women from the desert had organized singing campaigns that melted hearts, crumbled walls, and opened the doors of the mind. They sang until the king relented.

Tala rose from a crouch and called out the counter harmony.

Shirar shut them out,
they sang their way in.
Shirar locked them up,
they sang the walls down,
all by the strength of their song.

"We cannot restore the balance simply by talking about it here," Sarai said as Tala held the melody of the song like a spell on the night air. "We must act. I say, when we go back to the village tomorrow, we go back singing, and we don't stop singing until this nonsense of warriors-rule is cast aside. Let's sing down the walls of their minds and crack open the stones of hardened hearts," Sarai urged, quoting the old ballad and gripping her mother's arm. "We can choose songs that remind everyone of times when unexpected voices spoke wisdom . . . like Timar the Lame, or the Wandering Woman, or Sechen's Tune."

Ari Ara didn't know those references, but the women did. Tala switched melodies and ran through a medley of one-liners at dizzying speed, rattling off other songs they could use. Voices leapt up in discussion; some for the idea; others against it.

Ari Ara chewed her lower lip, thinking. The Way Between could be used physically to interrupt fights and stop violence, but that was just the beginning. There were inner and outer practices. There were individual and collective ways to take action. With strikes and boycotts, protests and sit-ins, the Way Between organized people to neither fight nor flee from the conflict. It offered dozens of ways to remove support from a problem and build a solution, instead.

The Way Between required study and practice, but anyone could use it. Ari Ara had seen Shulen teaching people of all ages and experiences. The outer form provided insights into the inner form, and the other way around. Shulen taught people how to balance their usual tendencies. Some people rushed into fights. Others ran away from conflicts. Many froze, not knowing what to do. Everyone had their habits to work on. The Way Between challenged each person differently. Ari Ara could almost hear Shulen's voice calling out lessons, telling Emir to temper his warrior's impulses and stop attacking, ordering her cousin Korin to quit prancing and sidestepping like a noble, and stand firm. He challenged the noble girl Isa to do more than squeeze into a ball when she was confused or afraid. He taught the street urchin, Rill, how to keep others safe, not just herself.

Another memory surfaced, damp with trembling raindrops and dazzling with afternoon sunlight. In her mind, black-stoned mountain peaks rose overhead. Huge monsters of clouds devoured the sky. Spring had burst in the High Mountains, cool and moist. Her friend Minli walked beside her with his familiar step-swing rhythm as his crutch compensated for his missing leg. They were discussing how to remove support from a problem using the Way Between.

"It's like pulling away my crutch," he was saying.

"I couldn't do that to a one-legged - " she started to protest.

"Cripple?" he snapped, whirling so fast she nearly slammed into him. He glared at her. "If you go soft on me out of pity, I'll knock you off your feet with this crutch!"

It wasn't an idle threat; Minli often surprised her in practices. She was faster and stronger, but he was smarter. She stammered an apology. All at once, the fury cleared like a summer thunderstorm and Minli's gentle eyes laughed at her.

"What I mean," he explained, "is that the crutch is whatever holds up an injustice. You have to pull that away."

As usual, he was running mental circles around her. She stared blankly at him. Minli rolled his eyes. He loved his movement-loving friend, but she could be dense as wood and literal as a stone.

"It's a *metaphor*," he groaned. "If I was an injustice like . . . like war . . . if I was war, then you'd have to pull out the crutch to get me to topple over."

Metaphor had never been her strong suit. They had been studying epic war poems in Scholar Monk's class and even though she could read, thanks to Minli, she still got confused when the verses described the heroes as *roaring with a lion's breath* - that just sounded foul, not courageous. Hadn't any of those poets ever smelled a carnivore up close?

"Look," he clarified, "a war can't happen if no one shows up. If the soldiers don't go, or the nobles won't pay for the soldiers to go, or the smiths won't make weapons. *Those* are the crutches that hold up war."

Ari Ara's eyes snapped open to the present. The fire crackled and tossed sparks into the night. She could taste the desert's dryness, so different from her old home. The women clapped time as they memorized a song in a call-and-response with Tala. Ari Ara drew a bunch of stick-figure warriors in the sand to represent warriors-rule. That was the problem. She drew a crutch. What was the crutch?

People listened to the warriors, she acknowledged grumpily. That's what gave them power. The warriors gave orders. People obeyed them. She stared down at the sand drawing. Could it really be that simple?

"You have to stop obeying them," she blurted out.

The song quieted. Heads turned toward her.

"If the warriors tell you to marry off your daughters, will you do it?" she asked them. "Will you just sing sweetly and hope they listen?"

"No."

"Of course not."

"We can't."

The women answered with shaking heads and worried looks.

"Warriors-rule has no legitimacy," Ari Ara pointed out. "Not in times of peace. The Tala-Rasa refuse to support it. The Harrak-Mettahl condemns it. People in the north have rejected it. So why do you continue to obey it? You shouldn't support the warriors by doing what they say."

"Well, sometimes they have good ideas," one of the mothers said, trying to be fair. "Like replacing an old fence with a new one. Why wouldn't we do that?"

Ari Ara shook her head.

"If it's a good idea, you should hold a village sing, decide the same thing, and then go do it. But, if it's a bad idea, then don't do it. Don't obey them."

The circle of women burst into excited and nervous chatter. Mahteni watched them thoughtfully.

"Ari Ara is right," she agreed, rising to her feet. "We could sing until the stars fell from the sky, but if we still obey warriors-rule, why should the warriors bother to unblock their ears?"

Scowls grew around the circle.

"Sarai's idea about using songs to melt hearts and open minds is good," Mahteni added, easing their resistance, "but if we back up the songs with action, that's even stronger."

"It is not enough to sing about what we want," Sarai agreed. "We must *do* what we want, we must *be* the changes we need."

"We can use the Way Between like the water workers did in Mariana," Mahteni urged. "We can draw a line in the sand of our beautiful desert and refuse to take one more step in the direction the warriors are trying to lead us. None of us should support the journey down that dishonorable path, not by washing dishes or cooking meals, and not by obeying them. None of us should allow our children to walk in that direction, a direction in which their mothers and sisters are silenced. If the warriors try to cut our voices from the Harraken Song, none of us should lift a finger to help them!"

"What if they beat us?" someone called out.

A flurry of agitated debate rose up. The women muttered about floggings and banishments, fearful of the retaliations they might face for directly disobeying warriors-rule. Mahteni lifted her hands to request their attention. She pointed to Ari Ara, gesturing at the young girl sitting cross-legged on the sand.

"Her Way Between can help us," she told the women. "No one beats this girl. No one makes her marry where she will not. No one forces her to do all the work. They cannot touch her . . . and not because she will kill them, like Moragh's Black Ravens, but because her Way Between shows her a way between fight and flight."

Ari Ara heard the skeptical murmurings and spoke up, urging them to have courage.

"When the Marianans invade, don't you risk your lives to stop their army?"

Heads nodded.

"If the invaders are your own men," she argued, "if what they destroy is not your villages, but your customs, your traditions, the future of your daughters and children; wouldn't you be willing to take some risks to stop them?"

Shocked expressions crossed faces as they thought about this.

"The Way Between is not for cowards," Ari Ara said. "It took courage for me to stand against Shulen to free the water workers. To me, Shulen is like a father. He is my teacher, my friend. My heart broke to have to face him in that way, but he was on the wrong side of justice . . . just like your fathers, friends, and brothers are now."

"But you saved him," one of the women pointed out, her voice betraying her conflicting emotions. Even though she hated warriors-rule, she loved her husband. She did not want to hurt him.

"Yes," Ari Ara said, "and the Way Between can help us restore harrak for everyone. Violence would just cause more harm, pitting daughters against fathers, wives against husbands. The Way Between offers a path forward for all of us, not just the women. We . . . we can sing a new song."

She stumbled a bit over the phrase. When Mahteni spoke it, the words rang with meaning and power. Sensing her struggle with the language, Tala repeated the phrase with the full strength of Harrak-Tala.

"The Harraken Song is our past, present, and future," Tala reminded them. "It is all we have. To lose your place in it is the worst curse the Tala-Rasa can invoke. If the warriors have their way, all of you will be cut from the Harraken Song. As surely as if you lay dead from Marianan swords, you will be gone, no more than walking dead."

"And if this happens," Mahteni put in, "a time of horror will fall upon our desert, a dead time, a drought of voices. Who knows how long it will last?"

She shrugged then continued.

"It may take generations before our great-granddaughters lift their voices to demand their rightful place in the Harraken Song. Those young women will be exactly where we are today. They will shoulder the same burdens we face, and brave the same dangers to lift their songs. I will not wait for them. I will not let them take on such an impossible druach because of me. I will not let my name be remembered as the woman who let our songs go silent."

Will you?

Her unspoken question hung in the air as loudly as a sand lioness' roar. One by one, the women rose. One by one, they sang.

CHAPTER TWENTY-ONE

. . . . .

The Song and the Silencing

The sun perched high on the shoulder of the morning. Heat
waves shimmered on the horizon, blurring sky and land into a
pale white flickering blur. The sound of distant voices
murmured. A thunder of hoof beats underscored the melody.
Black figures winked in and out of the haze, mythical and
timeless.

Heads looked up from the village. Among the huddle of
conical roofed houses, men shaded their eyes. They peered
through the open gates, out beyond the windmill and the well.
The distant shapes shifted from blurs to horses. Riders' heads
emerged from dark-bodied centaurs. A clear-eyed child called
out a greeting to her mother. Recognizing the women returning
from the night ceremony, the men turned back to their tasks.
They grumbled over the late hour of return. The demands of
small children and double chores had frayed their tempers.
Relief and irritation warred in their faces.

The women rode into the village, past their children to the
center of the ring of houses. There, they dismounted and stood
in a solemn circle around the embers of the common fire.
Young Sarai fanned the flames awake and threw a handful of

sacred, purifying herbs onto the glow. A few young women led the horses to their pastures. The elder grandmothers crouched on their heels, eyes tired, but determined. Children ran to greet their mothers, clutching skirts and holding up arms to be lifted close.

The song they sang spoke of those children, and the importance of restoring the village sings. One by one, the men caught the words. Eyes widened. Then they narrowed. A husband grabbed his wife's arm.

"Enough of this," he demanded. "There's work to do."

"No," she answered, catching and holding his eye.

No work would be done in a world of warriors-rule. No woman in this village would lift a hand or take a step in that direction.

Sit down with us, the women sang.
When the balance is restored,
we will all walk forth together.

Resolve shimmered around them. Determination sounded in their voices; they would no longer obey warriors-rule. They sang down the walls of the heart. They cracked the stone barriers of the mind. The warriors commanded them to stop. They continued to lift their song. They sat down in the village center, and invited everyone to sit down at their sides.

By evening, all the men except for the sternest warriors had joined the village sing. By the end of the second day, all but two of those battle-scarred fighters switched their allegiance. By the third morning, one of the remaining warriors conceded. The other called to his horse and rode away. He sought his fellow warriors, to warn and complain of the rejection of warriors-rule in his village.

That was just the beginning. From one village to the next, the women closed their ears to warriors' orders and opened them to the village sings. It was a time of legends and magic, night-blooming cacti and voices calling across the winds. The songs of their ancestors kept tempo to the hoof beats of horses and footsteps of women. A spell hung on the days, a vision walking into the bright sunlight, carried by the voices and actions of the women.

Through the hottest parts of the summer, the women gathered at night under the auspices of a young girl's ceremony. The Way Between began to weave into a whole generation of Woman's Songs. Ari Ara trained all the women and girls in the basic techniques of how to thwart attacks, protect one another, stay out of harm's way, and remain steadfast in working for change. She showed them how the inner principles of the Way Between matched the outer, physical skills. Together, the women devised strategies for restoring the village sings. Then, they prepared to march back into their villages and sit-in at the common fires.

The women's ears turned deaf to the warriors meets. Village sings sprang up like in the old days before the war. The warriors tried to stop them, but it was like trying to stop the dust. The women simply refused to work until a village sing was held. The warriors could haul them away from the common fire . . . but they could not make the women work. The mothers, grandmothers, sisters, daughters, and wives simply refused to take another step in the direction of a world of warriors-rule. The warriors locked up the ringleaders without food; the other women smuggled them meals. A woman sentenced to flogging; the other women stood between her and the blows. The warriors threatened their children; the mothers spat on their lack of harrak. Shame-faced, the warriors backed down from those threats.

The three Shirars and Tala rode the long western horizon, tiny specks against the dragon ridge scales of the mountains. In the hot, pounding forge of high summer, tension snapped sharp as steel, but one by one, Mahteni's vision of blazing signal fires came true. One by one, the village sings returned. One by one, the women restored harrak.

Tahkan Shirar entreated the men to join the village sings. Wherever the women gathered, he slipped among the men and warriors to plead the case of restoring the village sings. He worked among his fellow men, reasoning, softening their resistance, encouraging them to listen. Without their deeper tones, he told them, the Harraken Song would not be complete. Every voice was needed in order to weave the harmonies of generations, from the high-pitched piping of children to young girls' sopranos to mothers' throaty contraltos to the quavering voices of elders.

The late summer rains came like giants, walking in long strides across the parched desert. Each afternoon, the vaulted clouds sank their blue bellies lower to the earth and growled. Lightning flashed like horse hooves striking sparks on stone. The wind picked up. The rain charged.

In seconds, tunics and hair flattened to skin and skull. Horses sank up to their ankles in mud. Dry streambeds roared to life, filling with hissing serpents of water. Tala sang greeting songs to all the rain beings. Shapes of clouds and types of winds were not merely objects or weather to the Harraken, but old friends who visited once a year in the end of the summer season. The people ran out into the rain and lifted their arms in welcome. Tala opened Ari Ara's eyes to the living, mystical dimensions of their desert world.

"Hear that?" Tala asked in the hot tension that built before the rain arrived. "That's the Trickster, sneaking around and shortening tempers. When the rain giants arrive, they drive the Trickster out and break the spell."

Ari Ara blew the sweat-dampened strands of hair off her forehead.

"Who is the Trickster?"

Tala chuckled.

"Anything and everything. Like the Tala-Rasa, the Trickster is neither male nor female. Ze is a shape shifter. Ze could be anywhere, hidden in anything. Ze is the Being that Is *and* Isn't; the Being that Was *and* Wasn't; the Being that Might *and* Might Not Be."

"We're not entirely sure that the Trickster exists," Mahteni added with a laugh. "Or what ze is without one of zirs thousands of disguises."

"The Trickster can take on an infinite number of shapes," Tala went on, reaching out to pat the blonde-white horse that Ari Ara rode, "perhaps including this one."

Ari Ara stared at the back of the horse's white mane and snorted, unsurprised. The creature had pulled a disappearing act on her this morning as she leapt to his back, reappearing several feet away, lips pulled back in a mocking horse-laugh.

"Look there," Tala said, pointing to where the horizon blurred in the heat. "That is called the Trickster's River . . . and out there," ze pointed to the west, "is the Trickster's Crossing. No one knows what lies beyond the furthest west."

The rain turned plains into mud holes and mud holes into marshes. Shallow lakes shimmered for miles and birds winged overhead in flocks so vast they blackened out the sun. They came to feast on tadpoles and marshworms and the teeming creatures that erupted out of dry season hibernation. As they rode, thundering swarms of birds darted skyward: iridescent green hummingbirds in startling blurs, orange-winged black birds, blazing yellow finches, blue birds that swarmed like patches of clear sky among the clouds of white warblers.

Villages sat on seasonal islands, some accessible only by secret underwater causeways or paths of lifted stepping-stones built over centuries. An occasional barge could be spotted, poling over the water. No boats . . . the Harraken had no word for ship or boat; they used the Old Tongue terms to describe "saddles on river dragons" from their tales of the Marianans.

One day, they approached a village that perched like a hat atop a marsh island. At dawn, the rising heat had yanked back the veils of fog, hissing and steaming. Now, the zenith sun smacked the water like the flat of a steel blade. Bright light glared off the ripples caused by the tremors of breeze. Schools of minnows darted away from the horses' splashing strides.

Tala walked ahead, humming and testing the ground with a long stick as the other horses and riders picked their way cautiously behind. Ari Ara rode at the back, wringing out the bottom edges of her tunic. Without Tala, the golden horse had amused himself all morning by tossing her off into the deeper pockets of water.

"You can't drown me, stupid," she grumbled to the stubborn horse. "I'm half-Marianan . . . you could sooner drown a fish."

Ahead, Tala halted abruptly, flinging up a hand of warning. Ari Ara saw her father's back stiffen. A flank of warriors strode out in front of the village gates, armed and scowling. They formed a defensive line on the narrow shelf of the island's hillside just outside the high wall encircling the houses. Slowly, Tala led the way closer. The travelers fanned out awkwardly in the shallows, horses ankle-deep in marsh water, keenly aware of the depths behind them and the submerged gullies and stones concealed under the murk churned up by the horses' hooves.

"You are not welcome here," the man with the stiffest stance called out.

"Has your harrak been washed away in all this rain?" Tala retorted with a proud toss of zirs copper-dusted black curls. "I am Tala-Rasa. No gates nor songs are barred to me."

"And I am your Harrak-Mettahl," Tahkan replied, keeping his tone light. "You have need of my presence if you squander harrak by denying hospitality."

"Not all who travel are friendly," the man answered sharply, fingering his sword hilt. "Three days ago, the River Dog Ghost attacked us."

"Emir!" Ari Ara cried.

Mahteni hushed her.

"Attacked, you say?" the woman asked, suspicious of the phrasing. "Is that what happened? Be careful with your words - one of the Tala-Rasa listens."

An uneasy shifting rippled through the men. No one wanted to stretch the truth in the presence of the songholder.

"There are only three reasons our enemies approach," the leader of the warriors finally said, "to kill, steal, or spy. We were justified in driving him away."

His shoulders shrugged to indicate that he cared little for the motivations of the lone warrior.

"You didn't kill him, did you?" Ari Ara cried out, hope and alarm coloring her tone.

"Unfortunately, no," the warrior confessed, leaning to the side and spitting. "He dove into the water and vanished in the marsh channel. Some thought he drowned, but I know better. The Marianan spirits live in the river. The River Dog Ghost simply escaped to attack again."

"Humph," Tahkan muttered under his breath. He spoke in an undertone to Ari Ara, reassuring her. "It's unlikely that he'd drown. He was probably swept downstream. The channel that drains the marsh flows rapidly near here."

His eyes flicked southward then back to the line of warriors.

"Give us shelter for the night and we will deal with the River Dog Ghost."

The man's lips twitched into a grimace.

"It is not just the Marianan ghost we guard against," he warned, "but the one he seeks."

His finger rose and pointed at Ari Ara. He tipped his chin and glared.

"She's the real problem. Look at her, river-serpent eyes, pale as our enemies. Good men died because of that girl . . . and now, she has turned our daughters and wives against us."

Ari Ara clenched her teeth over her hot sting of words. Just as her temper threatened to burst out, her father murmured one word, powerful and binding: *gitten,* silence. Her jaw fused. She threw daggers at him with her glare. She tried to nudge Zyrh forward, but the horse might have been stone for all he responded to her. Mahteni held up a hand - a warning to them all.

"You have spent many hours nursing those words," she said to the man. "You must have an Outcry . . . let us meet in the village center according to the old ways, and sing our cries. Then, everyone can weigh the two songs together and decide what to do."

Ari Ara blinked and looked at her aunt with new admiration. She had just maneuvered the man into the very place she wanted, using his anger as an invitation to restore fair practices.

"No," he barked. "You will not sing your witch song here . . . or your song will end here."

The refusal cut hard and was followed by the hiss of a

drawn sword. Gasps erupted, even from the warriors. Alarmed looks flashed across the men's faces. A shocked expression clung to Tala's features. Ze shifted to block the man's path - no one, no matter how furious, would kill a Tala-Rasa.

"Stop before you lose all honor," Tala warned him in a cold undertone. "If you spill Shirar blood over this, I will erase your name from the Ancestor Song."

"Times are changing, young Tala; the song is changing," the man declared gruffly. "You'd best choose the right side to stand on."

"A Tala does not choose sides, you know that," came the quick, scornful retort.

"Oh?" he countered. "Looks like you're standing on their side."

"Looks can be deceiving," Tala said, shifting zirs posture from that of a bristling young boy to a defiant girl back to zirs unique mystery to illustrate the point.

"Why do you turn us away?" Tahkan, cut in, challenging the man.

"We have a duty to protect our families - " he began to answer.

Behind the tall protective wall, a commotion broke out. Women's voices leapt into the air. The bellow of men drowned them out. A woman's shriek and scattered outbursts erupted. The sounds of a scuffle thudded. A pair of hands gripped the stones of the wall, followed by a head of dark hair. A set of familiar eyes emerged as the woman hoisted her body up on top of the wall.

"Orryn?" Ari Ara tried to call out, but Tahkan's spell still bound her.

The tall woman swung her foot up and pushed to standing, her arms flailing for balance.

"Shame on you!" she yelled at the warriors. "Curses on your harrak-less souls!"

Shouts flung at her from below. She glanced down. A pair of men's hands gripped the stones. He started to climb up the wall to catch her. She spun to leap down to the outside, but the warriors by the front gate stood below her. Wheeling, Orryn raced along the circular wall.

"The women of your village reject your so-called *protection*," she yelled. "You are not keeping us safe. You are crushing us under your thumbs!"

A second man leapt atop the wall on her other side, blocking her path. They closed on her like a pair of pinchers. The two men grappled with her for a moment, then pulled her down from view.

"You see?" the lead warrior shouted at Tahkan. "*This* is the poison that's been unleashed among us. A daughter-by-marriage should respect her new family's ways!"

Ari Ara choked. Daughter-by-marriage? Orryn wasn't married, was she? With a hot glare, she waved frantically to Mahteni. Her aunt's eyes widened, realizing the same thing. Her spine stiffened. Her hands clenched. She sat up tall on her horse.

"No one holds a desert woman against her will," she declared, eyes flashing. "Release the woman you pulled from the wall . . . and all the women who wish to leave with her."

Mahteni's words leapt out of her throat, loud and carrying. An Honor Cry lifted from behind the village walls then truncated abruptly. Tahkan frowned.

"Let it go, Mahteni," he urged quietly. "We will come back and convince them where harrak lies."

"The path of harrak lies right here, right now," she countered in a low hiss, glaring at him.

She nudged her horse forward a pace and drew a deep breath. Mahteni murmured a request to the Ancestor Wind to carry her words over the walls to the women who yearned to hear them.

"Tonight, I lift my song to the rising moon. She will reflect my call back to this village. All who wish to leave may seek sanctuary with Mahteni-Mirrin Shirar. The Ancestor Wind will tell you where to find me. These men have lost all honor, all harrak - "

"*Gitten,*" Tahkan commanded, cutting off her words.

Mahteni's hand flew to her throat. She swiveled around on her horse's back, eyes livid. Tahkan shook his head at her then turned to the warriors.

"There is conflict here; there are matters of harrak at stake," Tahkan remonstrated them. "Tomorrow, I will return, alone, to work this out. As your Harrak-Mettahl, I expect you to remember the courtesies and hospitalities due to my position."

"*You* are welcome here," the lead warrior stated, stressing the first word to indicate that Tahkan Shirar's female relatives were not.

Tahkan shook his head, but said nothing more, urging his mare around and gesturing for the others to follow him away. Tala sloshed across the shallows and hurtled onto Zyrh's back behind Ari Ara. The horse spun so fast that Ari Ara nearly fell off. Mahteni rode at their heels, gritting her teeth and following reluctantly. Tala sang out, guiding the horses' hooves along the submerged causeway. For a long stretch, they rode in tense quiet. Mahteni kicked her mare forward and drew even with her brother. She pounded his shoulder, glaring at him in bound silence. He grimaced and spoke the releasing word to his silencing command. Mahteni surged in front of Tahkan and wheeled her horse around to confront him.

"How dare you silence us!" she shouted.

The ripples of the horses' hoof beats spread over the marsh water. The light darted in bright lances from the lapping waves. On the horizon, the water and sky shimmered indistinctly, drowning them in blue. Tahkan's angular features turned hard and uncompromising.

"What were you thinking, Mahteni?" he barked sharply. "Those warriors would not simply allow the women to walk out to us!"

She lifted her chin. Her green eyes stung.

"They cannot stay in that village," she replied. "They must leave. And if the warriors had dared to stop them using violence, then it would show their poverty of harrak. No one holds a Harraken woman against her will!"

"Of course not," Tahkan answered, trying to soothe her, "and I'll set them right tomorrow - "

"It is not your place to silence a woman and solve all women's problems!" she retorted.

"I am the Harrak-Mettahl!" he roared. "Not you!"

"Keep silencing the women and you won't be for long!" she yelled.

"You are still young, Mirrin," he snapped, using her birth name to evoke earlier times.

"I am older than you were when you became Harrak-Mettahl," she answered stubbornly. "I have walked through the fire of my life, Tahkan. I am a woman, not a child. You had no right to silence me, no right to stop me from calling to my fellow women to use their ancestral rights. Your actions are without honor. Your harrak is less than those warriors. You, at least, should have known better."

"Mahteni, I was only trying to calm everyone down - "

"We do not need to be calm, Tahkan!" she shouted. Her

horse danced in place under her, alarmed by the explosion of her words. "The women of the desert should be outraged, loud, furious. Every one of us should be walking out of the villages. Every non-warrior, male or female, should be on strike. The women in that village should not stay one more night under the roofs of those warriors."

Her older brother - the one who had taught her to ride, watched over her, stood up to Moragh's temper for her; the one whom she had adored since she first opened her eyes, the man she respected beyond all others - stared at her like his beloved little sister was a stranger . . . and perhaps she was. She had lived in hiding during the long years of war then gone in disguise to Mariana for six years. When he followed, *she* had been the voice of caution, reining in his recklessness, making him slow down, urging carefulness, telling him to avoid discovery. Who was this roaring lioness sitting proud and tall on her horse, staring down the Harrak-Mettahl of her people and telling him that *he* was wrong, that *he* had lost his harrak.

"I do not know who you are any more," he murmured.

A surge of emotion threatened to overwhelm him: hurt, anger, sorrow, even a twinge of fear. Without another word, he kicked his mare past her and rode off along the causeway. Mahteni let him go, watching him shrink smaller and smaller until she could no longer see his figure. She did not want to speak to him further, not now with his wounded hurt blinding him to the truth of her words. He was in the wrong.

"He silenced me, too," Ari Ara muttered.

Mahteni blinked, remembering the presence of the two youths.

"Humph," she said, eyeing her niece. "I could read on your face that you were about to do something extremely unwise, whatever it was."

"I wanted to use Harrak-Tala to give that warrior a pig's snout to match his boorishness," she declared, "but I didn't know the words."

Tala laughed. Mahteni shot the youth an irritated look.

"Don't encourage her," she snapped.

Mahteni turned her horse alongside Zyrh.

"Ride with me," she said to Ari Ara.

"But - "

Her aunt's stern glare convinced her not to argue. She switched horses, letting Tala ride ahead.

"Your father never learned this lesson, but I wish he had," Mahteni sighed. "Words are powerful, Ari Ara, here in the desert more than anywhere else. When Tahkan loses his temper, he uses his words as power over others, commanding them to dance to his tune . . . sometimes literally. Worse, he uses his skill in Desert Speech to hurt those who anger him."

"Like calling down lightning from the sky?"

"Exactly." Mahteni's voice was sharp with disapproval. "There are some who hold him in awe because of this. I am not one of those people."

She nudged her niece in the back of the ribs.

"I want to tell you now that you face a choice. If you wield Harrak-Tala like a sword to hurt people, you may gain esteem in your father's eyes, perhaps even Moragh's . . . but you will lose it in mine."

A Shirar, Mahteni said solemnly, has a strength with words that few others have.

"We can use that strength to invite others to sing together . . . but we can also use that power to hurt others, to lash out in anger, and to drive people apart. With every breath, you must choose how you will use your words. You are a follower of the Way Between. I hope you will remember that when you speak."

Then Mahteni dropped into silence, letting her niece think over her remarks.

When they caught up, Tala had dismounted to find the path through a tangle of branching underwater roads. Grassy hillocks and marsh islands dotted the region. Swift channels of currents swept in unexpected rivers. The gullies between the shoulders of the submerged hills ran shallow in some places, deep in others. The unwary traveler could take a misstep, plunge in over their head, and be drowned in the undertows. Ari Ara climbed back on Zyrh and waited, watching Tala carefully sound the depths.

"How will the villagers find us?" Ari Ara asked.

"There is a little island chain to the southeast. Tonight, after the rains fall, the sweet wind will rise and blow toward the village. We will light a fire with the *minchi* herb and the scent will guide the women to us."

"Won't the warriors find us?"

Ahead of them, Tala chuckled.

"No," the slender youth replied. "It is a women's secret. The *minchi* herb is used as a tea for menstrual cramps. Once ingested, the scent of the smoke can be detected . . . but not if you've never tasted the tea."

Ari Ara's mouth dropped.

"And none of the men . . . ?"

Tala sniggered.

"It is well known that *minchi* causes impotence in men," Mahteni explained with a wry smile, "but, between you, me, and the Tala, that's just a tale made up to protect our secret."

"I thought you couldn't lie in Harrak-Tala," Ari Ara objected.

"You can't," Tala replied, "but it *is* a well-known story, even if it's not true."

Ari Ara laughed, seeing how they carefully circumvented the lie. Then they strode forward through the marshlands. They had a long way to travel before moonrise.

CHAPTER TWENTY-TWO

. . . . .

Marsh Island

The island was no larger than a tiny village, but it climbed steeply out of the marsh. Tahkan crouched on his heels on the far side, back to them, tension over the argument still quivering through his muscles. They had spotted him in the late afternoon, Tala whistled through zirs fingers to call to him. He rejoined them, but rode behind them at a distance, simmering and stewing. Mahteni ignored him, lips pursed. Ari Ara tiptoed around both of them as she gathered branches from the marsh island's dead trees to build a fire. Tala kindled the branches with damp grass - and a bit of word-magic, Ari Ara suspected, though the songholder denied it. They boiled water for tea and dropped a pinch of *minchi* into the brew. Moments later, Ari Ara sipped the dark umber drink and winced at the taste. Mahteni threw a smidgeon of the crushed herbs onto the fire. She sat back on her heels. Tala's eyes crinkled into crescent moons of mirth as ze watched Ari Ara and waited.

Suddenly, she gasped. A tingling rush flooded through her limbs. The *minchi* herb prickled her nose and stung her eyes wide open. The night came alive with scents. A wild and seductive aroma bloomed on the air, sweet like apricots, sharp like pine sap, bitter as lime skin, and musky as a goat. Ari Ara blinked as her eyes watered. Her mind opened like a trapdoor. Her soul poured out into the stars and darkness. The throbbing chant of the frogs surged in her ears. Her heartbeat slid into rhythm with the peeping chorus. Tala and Mahteni exchanged bemused glances and chuckled.

"Want some?" Ari Ara asked, offering the cup.

Tala raised a hand and refused with a wry smile and headshake. Ari Ara wondered for the thousandth time about Tala. The singer sensed her gaze and winked. In that moment, all her questions and confusion flew out into the sky and vanished. Tala was Tala, mysterious, indefinable ... and beautiful, Ari Ara realized with a strange lurch in her chest. She set the cup of tea down and rubbed her hot palms off on her tunic, hoping the minchi herb had no adverse side effects for those with Marianan blood running in their veins.

They sang and waited. The moon trekked across the eastern dome of night. The waters shone silver and sparkled with the motion of the breeze.

"It may take some time for them to come," Mahteni remarked, her eyes distant as she envisioned the challenges the women faced.

"Or they may never come," Tala countered with a slight shrug. "We may be wrong about the direction of the Harraken Song."

"No." Mahteni's voice was hard-edged. "We may fail today, and tomorrow, and for a hundred years, but we are not wrong about this. There is no harrak in cutting voices out of the Song, no honor in a situation in which a handful of our people tell the rest of us what to do."

And so, they waited. And sang. Just when Ari Ara had

given up hope of anyone coming, Tala leapt up. Chin tucked to chest, head tilted north, the youth held up a long-boned hand for quiet. Beneath the frogs' chorus and the lapping water, a song rose in a query of voices seeking the island. Tahkan came to stand silently beside Ari Ara. Together, Mahteni and Tala called back the response. The water carried the melody like a sleek-footed messenger. Hidden in the night, the travelers answered. Like that, back and forth, they called each other closer. At last, a thread of women rode into sight, splashing through the marsh on the backs of horses.

Ten, twelve, twenty . . . Ari Ara counted more than thirty as they reached the island's edge. Some had babies slung to chests; others rode double with elders. Young girls on the verge of womanhood slid off the backs of their horses and helped guide everyone to the flat crown of the island. Sleeping children roused gently as the rhythmic splash of hooves and water gave way to quieter treads across dry land. Zyrh whinnied a welcome. Orryn came to greet them. Ari Ara exclaimed in surprise - Nalia was with her!

"You came," Mahteni said, unable to hide her relief.

"It took some doing," Orryn confessed. "We meant to come on your heels, some of us, but we decided to wait for the others."

"Tell us everything," Mahteni urged.

The women looked to Orryn as they settled in a circle on the grass. Mahteni folded her legs under her and lowered to the ground. Ari Ara sat beside her. Tahkan, silent and pensive, sat on her other side. Orryn nodded and began her tale. After the Meet of Meets disbanded, Kirkan Mehta had sent a company of warriors to Moragh's Stronghold. They said they had been wrong to exclude the Black Ravens from the warriors meets. To demonstrate their sincerity, a warriors meet was held in the enclosure of the Stronghold. Moragh and her women joined the other warriors to hear the grievances of the women and children.

They promised retribution for the harm done. To uphold justice, they vowed to honor challenge the men on the women's behalf. It sounded reasonable, honorable. The warriors - men and women, both - had dispersed from the Stronghold in all directions, riding out to the villages to mete out justice for the women who had fled to Moragh's protection. Honor challenges clashed across the desert. Warriors won against herders and farmers. Whenever swords crossed, dust flew. With such powerful advocates taking up their causes, the villagers agreed to support warriors-rule.

"But, it was a trap," Orryn spat out bitterly.

Once they had solidified power, the warriors controlled all the decisions. Some were deemed wise by their people, others not. Orryn nudged her sister Nalia to speak up.

"Moragh Shirar herself heard my grievance against my forced marriage," Nalia shared, her eyes bright as the shining moon. "With three of her Black Ravens and half a dozen of the other warriors, she rode with me to confront my family. But, the men said the marriage was fair and when the time came to decide, Moragh and her women were outvoted. I spat in their faces, all of them."

"Why did Moragh allow this?" Mahteni asked, frowning. "Why did she not honor challenge the warriors on your behalf?"

"She had no choice," Orryn cut in to explain. "The men told her to abide by the decision or the women warriors would no longer have any place at the warriors meets."

"We were traded so the Black Ravens could have power," Nalia railed, lifting her fist to the impassive night sky. "It is wrong. I refused to accept the ruling."

Nalia had fought her marriage every step of the way. She said she would not leave her family, so the warriors decreed that Orryn would go with her and marry the brother of her husband-to-be. She and Orryn attempted to run away three times on the journey south. Their escorts tracked them down. They heard of Mahteni's ten-day fast at the Meet of Meets and launched their own hunger strike. The men shoved food down their throats, holding their noses to force them to swallow as they gasped for air. In the village, they sabotaged every aspect of the wedding preparations. They tore the silk robes during the fitting. They upended the tables at the welcoming feast. They refused the ceremonial gifts. They rolled in the dust each time they were sent through the purifying ritual. The outrage of the two sisters swayed sympathy from some of the village women. They started to help, even the family of the husbands-to-be. The mother of the grooms, not wanting these rabble-rousing women as daughters-by-marriage, refused to sing the ritual song-chants. The baker - an aunt of the men - destroyed the wedding cake four times, muttering about bad omens. The prized ancestor song-sashes that every man in this clan wore on his wedding day disappeared. The women were beaten. Orryn and Nalia were locked up.

"Then you showed up at our gates," Orryn recounted, "and one of the grandmothers let me out, hoping I could escape."

The choice to flee was the only option left for many of the women involved in the protest of the weddings. A dozen lashes was the penalty for violating the decrees of warriors-rule; not even the oldest women were exempt from this law. Orryn's voice quavered as she spoke. Nalia wrapped her wiry arms around her sister. Tears pooled in their eyes. Shadows haunted them.

"Let us sing," the young Tala urged with a sensitivity

beyond the count of years, reading fear and sorrow, and knowing the song-rituals to help.

As they began, lines of pain, despair, sorrow, and fury crossed the women's faces. Ari Ara sat, knees tucked to chest, clenching her arms around her legs as the waves of anger and outrage thundered through her. At one point, Mahteni leaned over and shook her shoulder gently.

"Sing with them," she urged. "They are your people, and your grief for them is part of the song."

Ari Ara joined the chorus quietly. The words to the chorus spoke of the witness of the Ancestor Wind and the turning of time. The refrain evoked the way green grass returns to scarred land when rain falls like tears across it. At the end of the song, a quiet space opened up. Into it, the women poured their thoughts and fears, one by one.

"We had to leave, all of us, together," one of the women said when her turn for speaking came, "or else the ones left behind would have been whipped by the anger of warriors who feel it is their right to have their way. We could not leave the elders and children in our absence. If we had left our youngest sons, they would have grown up in their father's shadows, and learned from their fathers to dismiss their mothers and wives. These choices ripped our hearts apart: who we had to leave behind, who we had to take with us, and what we all had to give up in order to save our harrak."

The woman's words were met by somber nods and choked gasps of sobs. For the first time, Ari Ara understood the sacrifice Mahteni had asked of these women. They had left not only the things they hated, but also the things they had loved.

Mahteni spoke then, rising to her feet with a power Ari Ara had seen only in Tahkan. The dark waters shimmered behind her. The moon glowed overhead. Tala hummed a quiet old tune, supporting Mahteni with the full weight of the Tala-Rasa's legacy, showing the hidden truths under the illogical seeming surface that ran like the roads beneath the marshlands' murky waters.

"Staying with the men would have kept us all on this dishonorable path," Mahteni told them firmly. "Leaving tonight, you have not abandoned the men; you have take a step toward saving all of us: ourselves, our children, our culture, and even them. Coming here tonight, you have walked away from a life without honor. Gathering together like this, we can sing our way forward through the dangers."

Tears were wiped away at her words. Lips trembled, but bit back the shaking sobs that had wracked them earlier.

"What says our Harrak-Mettahl?" a woman called out.

The question flung through the night with a bite of accusation. Tahkan had sat so still and silent, Ari Ara had thought Mahteni had bound his mouth shut. His lined face drooped with sadness. A fire of anger burned hot behind his eyes at everything he had heard. His hands spread wide in an entreating gesture to the women.

"Your Harrak-Mettahl cannot sing for sorrow," Tahkan confessed. "Your stories break my heart. How many injustices can our collective harrak bear? I say, not even one. When we lift our hands to hurt one another, we hurt ourselves doubly. We cannot endure this with our harrak intact."

His eyes blazed in the night.

"I wish to ride ahead of you, to prepare a path of sanctuary and healing for all my people. You have left your home . . . let your Harrak-Mettahl call upon the honor of our people to share their homes with you."

A cheer rose up. Tahkan's small smile flitted briefly across his features then subsided beneath shadows and sorrow. Even amidst their fleeting joy, troubles brewed all around them. The women sang long into the night as the silver moon graced them with her light. At dawn, Tahkan Shirar rose and stepped quietly up to his sister. Mahteni's skin glowed with spirit and exhaustion. She shone with the reverberations of the songs. The women looked to her for guidance, leadership, and strength. Tahkan had followed their eyes all night long.

"You were right," Tahkan said to her, touching his fingers to his heart and offering his apology for their earlier quarrel. "Watch over Ari Ara. Meet me at the Crossroads. I must go make right my wrongs."

CHAPTER TWENTY-THREE

· · · · ·

The Atta Song at the Crossroads

Voices twittered like birdsong under the arching boughs of the orchard. In the shade, rows of stalls and booths displayed crafters' goods and artisans' wares. Between the summer rains and autumn harvests, smiths and metal shapers, weavers and silk spinners, potters and stone carvers gathered at the Crossroads to barter and trade. Harraken journeyed from the distant corners of the desert to place orders and pick up promised goods. Messengers hawked a lively trade, delivering and returning.

Beyond the green of the trees, the blazing white of the Deep Sands Valley encircled the Crossroads. The dunes sparkled with stark beauty. Every year, the prevailing wind shoved the sand's edges closer to the eastern flank of the vast orchard. Each year, the crafters' apprentices shored up the massive retaining walls that held it back. For centuries, that had been the honor-bargain between orchardists and crafters: shade and water in exchange for cooperation in holding back the dunes. The aqueduct that carried the sluice of water from Turim through the Deep Sands Valley was a marvel of engineering. It carried and protected the lifeblood of the seasonal city of fruit and arts.

Along a spider web of footpaths, people gathered for games and meals, gossip and story. Low stools and spread rugs formed open air sitting rooms. A sense of repose and ease marked the banter, negotiations halted for songs. At night, laughter rose with a festive spirit.

Today, however, a buzz of rumors swarmed the market like the hives of bees that lined the orchard edges. A plume of dust rose along the northwest section of the Market Road. People claimed that an army of women approached, not the Black Ravens, but the unarmed women who rode from village to village reinitiating the village sings. Three days ago, the Harrak-Mettahl had ridden in and slept curled up in his cloak under the trees. Over breakfast, he'd told the potter next to him that he envied the strength of the potter's wares. Harrak, he had said, was easier to lose or break . . . and harder to repair.

"Whose harrak are you restoring today?" she'd asked him amiably.

"All of ours . . . starting with my own," he'd replied, looking so mournful that wild whispers of gossip speculated that he must have murdered someone.

All through the first day, Tahkan Shirar went from one person to the next, asking their views on warriors-rule versus village sings. The artisans tended to support the sings. They weren't warriors, after all, and what did warriors know of their trades? Last year, the warriors had levied a goods-tax on the Crossroads to support the fighters. The artisans resented it bitterly. In times of peace, why should they pay for warriors who rode around eating food and swinging swords and doing nothing?

On the second day, he gathered them together and made a

request that sparked roars of outrage and indignation. It took the Harrak-Mettahl hours to explain what he meant, why it mattered, what he'd learned from the women who rode with his sister toward the Crossroads, and why the artisans should honor his unusual request. He talked long into the evening, persuading and cajoling. At last, he struck a bargain, a daring wager to which they all agreed.

By morning, the buzz of tension, gossip, and excitement reached a fevered pitch. One by one, the haggling fell off. The hammering of horseshoes halted. People wandered toward the westbound Market Road to watch the growing plume of riders' dust.

Would he really do it, they wondered?

Bets were placed. Nails were bitten to the quick. Toes tapped nervously. When the company of riders reached the edge of the Crossroads, Tahkan Shirar walked out to meet them. Hundreds of crafters and artisans followed in his footsteps, curiosity burning like a fever in them.

He stood beyond the overhang of fruit trees, sleeves rolled to elbows, skin dark with summer sun. He looked thin, his usual wolf-leanness whittled down. A quietness clung to him, the stillness that comes from deep reflection. His face curved with smile-creases as he saw the riders. Ari Ara jumped down from Zyrh's back at a run, greeting him after the week of travel. Just as she threw her arms around him, she caught a glimpse of his sorrow darting behind his smile.

"What is it?" she asked.

"Nothing to worry about," he said, gently touching her cheek. He had missed her this week. It seemed she had grown taller since they last parted, and the speed of passing time struck him strongly. He'd lost her for most of her life and mourned every moment they had to spend apart.

As Mahteni dismounted and walked across the open space between riders and waiting crafters, swirls of dust chased her heels like tiny dogs. Tahkan stepped out to meet her. The first words of his song struck the space between them and she paused. Her face fell open like a book. Surprise and shock wrote volumes across the pages of her features. The Harrak-Mettahl was singing the Atta Song, the ritual chant of apology and forgiveness. He held out his hands in supplication, palms up. He dropped to one knee, then two, then sat back on his heels with his palms on his thighs and his head bent.

I am sorry, he sang,
for all the wrongs done,
for every slight and every silencing,
for every bruise and tear,
for the honor lost by men and warriors,
for all my faults and failures.

The Harrak-Mettahl had a responsibility to uphold the honor of his people. If they lost their way, he had failed his duties. Tahkan Shirar offered his apologies for his part in the problems and for the ways his actions had made the situation worse. It was wrong to silence anyone, he sang.

We are born equally of our mothers,
our feet rest equally on the sands,
the Ancestor Wind flows equally
through each person's song,
the rain bestows its blessing,
equally upon all our heads.

Ari Ara sensed the crafters behind him tightening like a

bowstring, as if the outcome of this moment decided their fates and futures. From the look of shock on their faces, Ari Ara guessed that the Harrak-Mettahl didn't often get down on his knees. She had once seen her father gather power like lightning to his chest and stride into a hall full of enemies like a tiger showering white sparks. He pulled that same power to him now; she felt it crackling in the air. His words sang of what it meant to be a man, a Harraken man. The Ancestor Wind stirred above them, bringing a sense of time and culture, antiquity and ancestors, to the ritual. Gestures of greeting fluttered from one Harraken to the next as the Ancestor Wind spiraled into a whirlwind, reaching down between the Shirar siblings, whipping their clothes and hair with its spinning winds.

If it is time for you, Tahkan sang to Mahteni-Mirrin,
to be our harrak-mettahl,
I release the wind to you.

The gasps of the Harraken made the wind spout waver, swaying on their in-drawn breaths.

Forgive me? Tahkan asked his sister.

Mahteni bent her head as if listening to the hushed whispers of the swirling wind that Tahkan held out like a flower on the palm of his hand. Ari Ara made herself breathe mechanically, frozen as the rest as her heart galloped madly in her chest.

At last, Mahteni spoke.

"Keep the Ancestor Wind, brother. We need you to call the spirits of the ancient grandfathers to speak to their grandsons and descendants."

She made a small gesture. The wind spout dropped to touch

the earth at their feet, stirring the dust. Everyone flinched and covered their eyes, waving the plumes away as they coughed. When the dust cleared, Mahteni clasped her brother's hands and lifted him to his feet, the reply of the Forgiveness Song on her lips.

Ari Ara joined in with the rest of the women, moved to tears. In the second refrain, she heard the men's voices joining from among the crafters. She thought she'd never heard anything so beautiful as the full spectrum of voices, low and high, honoring their honor keeper as his sister lifted him to his feet. When he rose, the heads of his people rose with him and the weight of shame and anger lifted from their backs. Tahkan Shirar, thin from fasting, trembling with power, stood both humble and proud, a man of his desert culture, a keeper of honor once more.

Ari Ara couldn't keep it back: the Honor Cry broke loose from her throat, high as a piercing hawk's scream, sharp and clear. It unlocked the throats of others and like a storm, the sound charged into the air. Tahkan's eyes shot to his daughter, and he nodded his thanks to her. When the cry quieted, Tahkan turned to the crafters still hidden in the shade of the trees.

"My part of the bargain has been met," he announced. "Now you must honor your end of our deal."

With that, Tahkan gestured and the crafters filed out from under the trees. The astonished women parted to let them pass, out of the market and into the dust of the road.

"There are as many Atta Songs to sing as there are people," he told Mahteni, "and we hope you will do us the kindness of hearing them. The Crossroads is yours. Each person must reconcile before entering again."

Ari Ara watched the crafters step out into the road with

resigned and determined looks. It was as if they had placed and lost a wager. Only later, when the moon rose high across the sky and the fire embers burned low, did she hear the whole story from her father.

"I did make a wager with them," he told her, practically translucent with the energy of the day's events shimmering in his exhausted body. "I wagered everything I had: my honor, integrity, dignity, even my position as harrak-mettahl."

"On what?" Ari Ara asked breathlessly.

Tahkan smiled wearily.

"I told them that if we offered these women a sincere apology for ignoring this situation too long, that if we apologized deeply and truly, and committed to being part of the solution, the women would forgive us."

When he said the word, *atta* - to forgive - it shivered in the air. Ari Ara sensed meanings beyond her Marianan translation. The Harrak-Tala word for forgiveness had no sense of forgetting to it, no returning to what was before, no action-less remorse. The Harrak-Tala word was inseparable from change, from doing differently, from repairing harm. It reverberated with the willingness to be a different person and to live a different way. And because it was Desert Speech, the word for forgiveness bound the giver and receiver like an oath.

"They were afraid - or resistant - to try," Tahkan confided, "so, I told them I would go first. It is my duty as Harrak-Mettahl, after all, to go first where others fear to walk . . . even into the Atta Song, which frightens men more than charging into battle."

If he was forgiven, he wagered, all of the crafters had to leave the Crossroads marketplace, giving it over to the women, and enter only after singing the Atta Song.

"But what if you were not forgiven?" Ari Ara asked in

awestruck horror at the stakes.

Tahkan shrugged, a wry smile on his face.

"Then I would not be fit to lead my people, anyway, and Mahteni would be a better harrak-mettahl for these times."

Tahkan had spent days listening to the Ancestor Wind, fasting, thinking. The women had just grievances. In the desert, everyone held up the Harraken Song. Everyone earned praise when things went right; everyone shared blame when things went wrong. If two brothers quarreled, the whole village took responsibility for their part in the argument. If a disagreement came to blows, everyone acknowledged how they either aggravated the dispute, or did nothing to try to help find a resolution. If they had turned one brother against the other, they admitted it. If they had ignored a chance to help the brothers reconcile, they acknowledged it. It was not just the person who flung a punch who was at fault for an injury, but those who cheered on a fight, or did not reach out to stop it.

Because of this, the Harrak-Mettahl needed to find a path forward that restored the harrak of all his people. No blood debts or honor challenges could solve this dispute. No act of violence could heal this rift. So, Tahkan sat and listened for a long time, staring out into the shimmering horizon. At last, the answer had come. In a flash of a memory, he saw his daughter practicing the Way Between. An old song about Alaren leapt to mind, reminding him of the root of the word, *atta*.

"Atta," Tahkan told Ari Ara, "is the word for reconciliation. It is not a Harraken word. It is a Fanten word from times long forgotten. Alaren brought it to our people in the days of healing from the pain of the first war."

Atta meant apology, forgiveness, and reconciliation. It was the same word backwards and forwards. The Atta Song was a call-and-response, a question seeking an answer, a cry awaiting its echo. So, the answer to Tahkan's question was the very question he had posed: atta for his people, starting with the man who must lead where others feared to go.

The Atta Song at the Crossroads went on for days. Tahkan had shown that anyone could sing it; that everyone played a role in letting the injustice fester, and everyone could help resolve it. Some had more to apologize for than others. A few sang the song but were not forgiven on their first try. These people – men and women both – had ignored complaints from relatives or supported the unjust decisions of warriors. Tahkan sat with them outside the gate and spoke with them. Mahteni sat with the women inside the market and talked with them. The Atta Song rose again, and sometimes a third time, until the people's willingness to change rang honest and clear in the notes.

There were some who refused to sing and rode off to other places. There were many who felt they had done no wrong. To them, Tahkan was firm and clear: if the Harrak-Mettahl could get down on his knees and sing Atta for his people, so could they.

"It will build your harrak," he pointed out, and no one could deny that Tahkan Shirar had shown great courage, walked through the fire of the Atta Song, and emerged stronger than ever before.

The season turned swiftly toward autumn. A touch of coolness hung on the night air. Soon, the Harraken would gather to bring in the crops. When all were reconciled at the Crossroads, the Harrak-Mettahl rode out again, this time toward Turim City to make the same request of those who dwelled within those walls. It was time to apologize, forgive, and change.

CHAPTER TWENTY-FOUR

. . . . .

The Cliffs of Turim

Turim City perched on the high cliffs, blazing red in the sunset. The rock face glared blood and burgundy. Proud, ancient, impenetrable, the sight of its sturdy stones sent a surge of joy through Ari Ara. She felt an odd sense of homecoming. It wasn't her home, but it was the first familiar place she'd arrived at in months. According to Throw-the-Bones' prophecy, it was also closer to where she'd find Emir . . . hopefully alive.

Ari Ara slid off Zyrh's back, yearning for a long soak in the city's hot pools of water. The heat of the summer had baked her into a hard, dark creature. She wore a patina of mud and dust and horse sweat. The sun had marked her cheeks and bleached gold streaks in her hair. As the season rolled into autumn, she looked forward to a change of pace. She was not alone in this longing. The women's company had swelled to nearly one hundred. Word had spread that Tahkan and Mahteni Shirar were going to re-establish the city sing of Turim City. Women rode from all over to join Mahteni's band of riders, eager to help. Thousands more had already gathered in Turim, coming to harvest the crops and support the women's cause.

Between the travel-weary women and the city, however, were warriors. Hundreds had camped at the base of the cliffs, blocking the stairs. As the women arrived, the warriors emerged from tents and gathered in a long line. Their faces glowered with resentment. Arms crossed over chests. Legs shifted into wide fighters' stances.

The women dismounted and unburdened the horses, eyeing the warriors. They murmured uneasily to each other as they combed the dust off the animals and rubbed the sweat of travel from their hides. One by one, they gathered in a wary cluster after kissing the horses' velvety noses and releasing them back to their roaming herds. Ari Ara tried to lay her forehead to Zyrh's, mimicking Mahteni's gesture of gratitude, but the annoying creature just chewed on her hair. She shoved him away with a groan. She stomped over to the huddle of women, slipping through the others to stand next to Mahteni.

The desert woman's bronze skin had deepened with ochre tones over the summer of sun and riding, heat and wind. The sunset poured its magenta onto her, giving her aunt an otherworldly glow. Her hard gaze was fixed on the warriors that stood between them and the stairs.

"Perhaps we should have gone around," she murmured with concern. There was another path up to the agricultural plain, though the detour would have taken days of extra travel.

"Ugh," Ari Ara groaned, "I'd rather march straight through them. What right do they have to block our way?"

Mahteni's mouth pulled sideways into a grimace. She shrugged, conceding the point.

"Are we worried about this?" Tala asked in an undertone, drawing close.

"We've come through so many obstacles," Ari Ara argued. "We shouldn't stop now."

Ari Ara recognized Gorlion's sturdy figure among the row of warriors, solidly planted in a wide stance, muscled arms crossed over his barrel of a chest. Ari Ara sized the youth up, wishing she could just honor challenge him for their passage. Beside her, Tala stiffened, head tilting north. A plume of dust heralded the approach of riders. In the golden light of sunset, black specks winged toward them in a raucous flock.

"Black Ravens," Tala and Ari Ara said at the same time, in the same ominous tone.

Mahteni sighed as she spotted Moragh's bright hair among the company of warrior women. The metal bits on their breastplates glinted. The dark oiled leather of their tunics caught beams of sunset and burned like dying embers. The ravens cawed and settled onto the riders' shoulders, fanning their wing feathers. When they arrived, Moragh's roan danced in a tight circle as she took stock of the scene.

"What is going on here?" she called out in her gravelly voice, sensing the tension between women and warriors.

"Nothing," Mahteni answered. "We are simply going to the city."

"And you?" Moragh barked at the warriors. "By whose order do you block these stairs? The entry to Turim City should stand open to all Harraken."

The warriors hesitated. Throats cleared. Elbows nudged the next person to speak. At last, Gorlion slouched forward. A surge of dislike rushed through Ari Ara. Her aunt's eyes narrowed.

"Kirkan Mehta told us to wait," he called back boldly. "He is conferring with your curse-of-a-brother about his latest assault upon our harrak."

"Watch your words carefully, young man," Moragh warned. "I tolerate no insults to my family."

Gorlion hid his flash of fear by pointing up at the cliffs behind him.

"Tahkan Shirar holds Turim City," Gorlion informed them, "and claims he will not let the warriors enter without singing the Atta Song."

Ari Ara grinned. No wonder the warriors were camped out in the horse field, sulking and furious, refusing to grovel - as they'd call it - to enter the city.

Mahteni took a step forward, lifting her hands to appease the two bristling warriors.

"As Harrak-Mettahl," Mahteni informed Gorlion coolly, "my brother has every right to demand such things. Now stand aside and let us pass."

"If we can't enter, neither can you," Gorlion declared.

"Perhaps you don't understand," Mahteni told him, gesturing to their company of women. "We don't have to sing Atta. We are not warriors."

Gorlion shook his head and spat to the side.

"Move aside, Gorlion," Moragh commanded testily. "Let us through."

Mahteni's eyes widened. She turned to her sister.

"Will the Black Ravens sing Atta, then?"

Moragh stiffened.

"We have done nothing to apologize for," she stated. "We did our best, but were overruled in the warriors meets."

"Hah." Mahteni spat bitterly at her sister's feet. "I had no vote, no standing according to warriors-rule, and yet, I did something. I maintained my harrak, sister. You lost yours."

She stepped back and cast a measuring eye over her scarred, ferocious older sibling.

"You have plenty to sing Atta about," Mahteni told her flatly.

Gorlion interrupted them impatiently.

"Enough quarrelling," he grumbled, pointing his thick finger at Ari Ara. "You! Climb the stairs and tell your father to stop this nonsense."

"You can't tell me what to do!" Ari Ara snapped back. "I obey no warrior."

"Oh, you'll do it of your own choice," Gorlion replied with a smug look, signaling to the other men.

He snapped his fingers and backed up to the line of warriors. Shocked gasps rose from the women as two warriors dragged a sagging figure forward by the arms. The head of bedraggled hair lifted.

"Sarai!" Ari Ara cried out. She hadn't seen the young girl since her Woman's Song, but her courage and dauntlessness hadn't changed. The girl's black eyes were fierce as ever, despite the bruises on her young face.

"Don't do it!" Sarai shouted. "I'd rather die than let this pack of beasts get their way."

She had courage, no denying that, but she could barely stand and her limbs looked thin as bird bones.

"What have you done to her?" Mahteni demanded in a stone-hard voice.

"Nothing," Gorlion stated with a shrug. "We rescued her from some men who disliked her song . . . but if you women don't want warriors' protection, then maybe we should return her to where we found her."

He smirked, knowing he had them trapped. In some parts of the desert, supporters of warriors-rule had been brutally squelching the growing dissent as their power weakened. If he returned Sarai to those who wanted to silence her, she could be flogged to set an example.

Ari Ara's fists clenched. She strode forward. An ominous

rumbling of anger rose in her chest like a thunderstorm.

"You harrak-less coward," she snarled. "Have you so little honor that you threaten a girl and claim it is protection?"

The words sparked from her, sharp and dangerous. She heard Mahteni shout a warning, but the cry meant nothing under the heat of her temper, melting into meaningless sounds.

"I ought to call lightning down on your pathetic head," she fumed.

Hands tightened on swords as she approached. Eyes jumped to the cloudless sky.

"I ought to honor challenge you and leave you in the dust like a spineless toad."

Gorlion scoffed. Ari Ara's temper fizzled and snapped.

"I ought to sing a spell that squeezes the Ancestor Wind from your lungs like an invisible snake," she threatened.

The air crackled with tension. The wind stirred. A drumming rose as the herd of uneasy horses stamped the earth with their hooves.

"I ought to call the horses to trample you all underfoot," she growled.

The warriors took a step back. They squinted as the sun dropped and turned her into a blaze of light.

"But I won't," she said.

"What will you do then?" Gorlion sneered at her, masking the pain of the sun's lances under his mocking expression.

"*This,*" Ari Ara answered.

As the light behind her blinded the warriors, she darted forward. She dropped and rolled under Gorlion's instinctive lunge. She leapt to her feet and dove for Sarai. Turning their attacks aside, she broke the warriors' hold on the girl and pulled her to her feet. Sarai staggered. Ari Ara wrapped an arm around her and hauled her to the stairs in the cliffs.

"Up . . . up! Go!" she urged Sarai.

A warrior tried to grip her ankle. She released the dark-haired girl to twist free of the man. Using the Way Between, she flung back the warriors as Sarai painfully limped up the steps, crawling and scrambling when her injured leg gave out.

Honor cries sounded like hawks screeching in hunting dives. Women's voices shouted, loud and distracting. Horse hooves thundered. A sudden commotion of moving bodies and stirring dust broke out. The Black Ravens charged to defend the women from the warriors' assault. The harsh clang of swords erupted. Battle cries screamed in the air. Above her, Ari Ara saw people rushing down the stairs. Someone leapt the flights of steps to help Sarai. On the ground, another woman made it through the chaos to the foot of the stairs. Ari Ara let her pass. Hands reached down the narrow passageway to help the woman climb. The other women were running in all directions, caught between the sparring factions. A horse charged up - Zyrh - and a woman dropped off his back. Ari Ara moved aside. The woman flung herself up the staircase. Ari Ara dove to turn a warrior away from the entry.

Count them, she thought as another woman arrived. She had to count them and stay until they all made it to safety. She registered about half of the company when she heard a song-chant above her ordering the warriors - men and women - to stop fighting.

She glanced up. Seven Tala-Rasa lined the first landing, outrage written on their faces. The warriors froze. The women ran for the steps.

Count them, Ari Ara reminded herself as they passed.

The young Tala stood beside her suddenly, staggering into view with an older woman who clutched her chest. One by one, they passed her. Ari Ara shaded the glaring sunset from her eyes and scanned the meadow for women. The men had regrouped and stood back at a distance; some glowering, others shame-faced. The Black Ravens gathered opposite them, wearing mirroring expressions. The sun turned them into dark silhouettes.

"Are they all here?" someone asked.

Ari Ara's breath caught in her chest. In the center of the trampled grasses, a figure lay on the ground, still as stone, still as death.

An anguished cry leapt up. A woman's unmistakable rasping voice, recognizable to all, screamed. A single word seared into every ear and pierced every heart.

"Sister!" Moragh Shirar cried.

CHAPTER TWENTY-FIVE

. . . . .

The Demands of Harrak

Ari Ara pressed her back to the wall as a cluster of healers rushed past. Dusk cast deep shadows on their grave faces. A basin of dark fluid sloshed as the healers swept by; a splatter of droplets hit the tiled floor. Ari Ara stared and swallowed hard, hoping it was not blood, remembering the trail Mahteni's injuries had left behind on the cliff stairs. Ari Ara had jogged after her aunts as Moragh carried Mahteni's limp body up the stairs to the healers in the city.

No one could say for certain what had happened. Accusations flew like arrows. The warriors blamed the Black Ravens' charging horses. The warrior women argued that the melee of colliding fighters knocked Mahteni down. The other women thought the free roaming horses could have accidentally trampled her. Ari Ara caught snatches of worried exchanges between the healers: crushed ribs, broken leg, dislocated shoulder, blood loss from a long gash, a possible concussion.

Fear shrouded everyone. Shock shivered in their limbs. The seven Tala-Rasa who had gathered on the viewing balcony were furious about the eruption of violence at the foot of the cliffs. Harraken should not war with Harraken. Disputes should be

253

settled one-on-one by honor challenges that ended with the first blood cut. The desert dwellers could not afford to kill their own people, not while the Marianans loomed as an ever-present threat.

The Tala-Rasa had descended to the horse pasture and separated the two fighting factions of male and female warriors. They sang of dishonor and shame, recounted tales of danger when Harraken in-fighting put everyone at risk. They made the warriors - male and female - set up camp beside the cliffs. They stood between the two groups to ensure peace. Undercurrents of resentment and remorse swept through all the warriors.

Under the eaves that ringed the garden courtyard, city residents comforted the shaken women of Mahteni's company. Sarai clung to Nalia as the older girl stroked her hair. Both wore shocked expressions. Orryn stood beside them, eyes distant. Ari Ara squinted into the fading light. A man's figure, barrel-chested and broad-shouldered walked from one woman to the next, speaking in a low tone. Ari Ara pushed off from the wall and circled closer under the eaves. The women's faces closed like flowers at dusk, snapping shut, tight and guarded. The man's shoulders slumped; his hands lifted palms up, entreating. Ari Ara rounded the corner and recognized the man's profile.

Kirkan Mehta.

She strode close enough to hear his words, skirting around people as the evening lamps were lit, flooding the courtyard with glowing light. Kirkan was vowing to sing the Atta Song for this, to make all the warriors apologize. He had ordered them to stay put at the base of the stairs; he had not meant for them to block the women's entry to the city. Ari Ara could hear the sincerity in his tone, the rumbling undercurrent of his shocked outrage at the action of the warriors.

"Harrak-less dog."

Kirkan whirled. Moragh charged out of the shadows. Her eyes gleamed gold-edged. Her mane of auburn hair flung out, wild and unruly. Her teeth bared in a snarl of hate. Kirkan dropped into an instinctive crouch, watching her warily. The huddle of women gasped and drew away from the pair.

"I will soak the sands with your blood," Moragh hissed. "Those spineless boars attacked on your orders. On your orders, my sister was harmed."

Kirkan protested, dodging away from her. She ignored his words, pursuing.

Ari Ara had heard the rumors of Moragh Shirar's battle magic. She had seen glimpses of it in the pine grove after rescuing Nalia. Now, she sensed it crackling in the night air, tensing through the shadows with a metallic whine, tightening like a taut-drawn bowstring. She saw real fear streak across Kirkan's features as Moragh crouched to spring.

"And, I neither forgive nor forget: on your orders, my beloved was sent into battle," she snarled. "On your orders, she died. I have had enough of you and your orders. I claim a blood debt for Mahteni's injuries. Here. Now. Tonight."

A woman screamed. Someone sprinted to find Tahkan. Kirkan's face grew stony. He opened his bare hands and stood facing her.

"Take it then," he said in a cracking voice. "My life, my blood. You know the debts I owe you for Sorrin's death."

"Fight, you coward," Moragh hissed back.

Kirkan shook his head.

"Fight!" she screamed, voice harsh as a drawn sword, commanding him to battle.

Ari Ara saw Kirkan's muscles tense. His jaw clenched as he gritted his teeth, resisting the power of her Harrak-Tala.

Where was Tahkan? Ari Ara thought wildly. Only he had

the strength to rein in Moragh in the grip of battle madness. The woman would tear Kirkan apart with her bare hands at this rate.

"Moragh," Kirkan entreated, sweat gleaming on his brow. "Don't do this. Sit with me. Sing with me. Let me offer Atta to you."

"Quiet!" she howled.

A shudder ran up his spine. His limbs jerked. His eyes squeezed shut then flung open. He gasped for air as he fought her command.

"Moragh," he pleaded. "Who have you become? Who is this creature of hate and fury? This is not you. This is not the sister-by-marriage I once knew. Come back to me."

"Gitten!" she screamed, flinging her hand out.

Sparks leapt from the ends of her fingers. Ari Ara's hand flew to her mouth in shock. Moragh drew her sword. Kirkan swallowed.

"Fight," she growled.

He shook his head.

"I would rather die," he said, voice tight with the tension of countering her magic.

"Then die you will," Moragh stated.

She lifted her sword and charged.

"No!"

Ari Ara burst forward. She erupted from the shadows into the glowing torchlight, running with all her strength. She leapt the last distance, sought the Way Between, and dove under her aunt's lunge. She clenched Moragh's wrist in her hands and twisted the sword from her grip. It skittered across the flagstones and clanged against a roof pillar. No one touched it.

Moragh spun on Ari Ara, eyes glaring. Her lips twitched in a curse.

"Stop!" Ari Ara shouted, diving to the side and scrambling out of reach. "Aunt Moragh, enough!"

"How dare you!" the mad-eyed woman accused. "This does not concern you. No one intervenes in the settling of a blood debt. Get out of my way."

The muscular woman spun back, charging for her sword. Ari Ara shoved off from the flagstones and tangled up her legs, tripping her. Moragh flung a blow at her, but she evaded it. Ari Ara leapt, low and long, to circle between her aunt and the sword.

"No, stop this," Ari Ara insisted. She stood firmly in the Way Between, ready to thwart her aunt, to turn her aside from the violence she sought.

Moragh lunged left. Ari Ara matched her. The warrior woman lunged right. The girl blocked her path. Moragh attacked her center. Ari Ara turned the blow aside and sent the larger woman rolling off in the other direction.

"*This* is the Way Between!" she shouted at her aunt. "And I can block you with it until the stars topple from the sky, I swear by Alaren's ancestor spirit!"

"You are meddling!" Moragh spat back. "You violate our laws by interfering."

"So?" Ari Ara retorted. "You and Kirkan don't need to fight each other. You need to talk to each other! You're both hurting. Why not help each other instead of kill each other? It won't make the pain go away."

"What do you care?" Moragh growled at her.

"I don't have enough family left to let my relatives keep killing one another," she said bluntly. "My mother is dead. My uncle on the Marianan side is dead. My grandparents. The remaining Shirars can fit on one hand with space for Kirkan Mehta. I don't want to lose either of you. Make peace."

"It is a matter of honor," Moragh said in a flat tone.

"Nonsense," Ari Ara retorted. "It's a matter of pig-headed pride. I ought to know the difference by now."

At her rueful expression, a smattering of laughter broke out from the onlookers.

"There are other ways to restore harrak," Ari Ara urged. "Please. Don't do this. Death solves nothing."

"What does a river dog know of harrak?" Moragh grumbled, scowling at her amber skin and river-water eyes. "Since you came to our desert, there has been nothing but turmoil and fighting. You talk of peace, but your actions cause chaos. We had peace before you came."

"Hah!" The sound burst out of her before she could stop it. *Don't mistake ease for peace,* Shulen had told her once. "You had silence, not peace. You had fear. You had women squashed under warriors' thumbs. That's not peace."

"You know nothing about us," Moragh said dismissively.

"I know about the Way Between," Ari Ara countered.

"Then take your Way Between," Moragh snapped at her, "and go back to Shulen the Butcher. We did not ask for you to come here. We did not ask for your help."

Ari Ara staggered back a step, stung by the animosity in her aunt's tone. She blinked back a sudden shock of tears. Ari Ara cast a quick glance around the courtyard, but every face was somber and guarded. Orryn gazed at her with pity and made no move to defend her. Nalia's eyes were wide and frightened. Sarai's mouth hung open.

A small commotion ruffled the silence. The cluster of onlookers shrank back, opening a path for Tahkan Shirar as he sprinted forward. He skidded to a halt, looking from his sister to his brother-by-marriage to the ring of fearful faces. His gaze fell at last on Ari Ara. She read bewilderment in his eyes.

"Oh, my daughter, what have you done now?"

CHAPTER TWENTY-SIX

· · · · ·

The Exile

Ari Ara couldn't believe it. She was being thrown out of yet another country.

"I'm being exiled from exile?" Ari Ara exclaimed when Tahkan told her the ruling of the city sing.

"No, you're not," Tahkan countered in a firm tone that suggested she was trying his patience. "You're just being sent away for a little while."

"But I saved Kirkan's life!" she protested.

"You broke the Harraken law by interfering in our ancient custom of blood debts," Tahkan repeated, rubbing his temples. "You're fortunate this is all they're calling for; the usual punishment is much harsher."

"Aunt Moragh would have killed her brother-by-marriage," Ari Ara pointed out. "Where's the harrak in that?"

"You don't get to invent the rules of harrak, Ari Ara. Not even the Harrak-Mettahl can do that."

"Well, it's a stupid custom," Ari Ara muttered, kicking the wall in frustration.

Tahkan privately agreed, but his daughter had been riding across the desert all summer calling upon harrak, invoking desert traditions, singing ancient ballads. When she broke the law to stop Moragh and Kirkan, she kicked open the ants' nest of the warriors' resentments. They had pushed the city sing to expel her for meddling. The warriors were quick to point fingers at her for flaunting their laws. Certain factions blamed her for the conflicts of the summer. Her intervention in a blood feud gave them an excuse to get rid of her. To some, it was not a moment too soon. Mahteni's injuries had brought the conflict to a head. The Tala-Rasa, shocked at the violence that had broken out at the cliffs, had called for a full Harraken Sing at the Dark Moon on Winter Solstice. Every Harraken able to travel would gather in the south. The matter of warriors-rule versus village sings would be decided upon once and for all.

"But they feel it is best if you are not there," Tahkan stated to his daughter, a look of inexpressible sadness on his face.

The words fell coldly on her ears, hard and cruel. Ari Ara's heart split in two.

"How can they send me away?" Ari Ara wailed, throwing her limbs onto the narrow cot and burying her face in the pillow.

Tahkan gingerly sat down next to her, clasping his hands between his knees. He owed her an explanation, at least. After giving her testimony around the common fire, she'd been sent to this room at the back of the common building. The words of the city sing rose and fell in muffled waves, sharp with anger, loud with indignation, and bitter with hard truths. People disagreed about all other points, but everyone agreed on one thing: Ari Ara Shirar en Marin was not an ordinary Harraken girl. Her burst of action using the Way Between had shocked many; they'd seen her in trainings, of course, but besides the former water workers, no one realized that the Way Between truly could disarm the desert's greatest warriors. From shock grew fear. If no warrior could stand against the girl, then how could justice be kept? If no one could beat her in an honor challenge, she could take control of the Harraken. She's a foreigner, people argued, a Marianan. She doesn't belong here.

"But I don't belong there, either!" Ari Ara cried as Tahkan slowly explained the fears and concerns of the people. "I can't go back."

"I know. That's why I offered a compromise," Tahkan sighed. "You will go to Shulen in the Border Mountains until after Winter Solstice."

"How could you agree to that? That's months from now!" she objected, feeling betrayed by him. "What about Mahteni? What about the women and the village sings? I can't just leave."

She shoved off the bed and hurled her limbs across the room, hardly listening as her father spoke.

"My daughter," he said gently, letting her hear his pain at the decision. "You don't mean to cause trouble, but you do. Everyone is on edge. The warriors threaten to rebel. The Black Ravens are on the verge of fighting back. The Tala-Rasa and I can barely hold our people together. You are too much like me: fiery, tempestuous. I look at you and I see the fire of the Shirars, but you are a wild spark that flies high. Though you shine brightly against the dark night, when you land . . ."

He paused.

"This is not the wet riverlands. This is a dry desert, ready to go up in flames. If you set off a brush fire right now, we may not be able to stop it from consuming us all."

His eyes begged her to understand. She refused to look at him.

"You do not know our ways well enough yet. Many do not see you as one of us. Many object to your . . . ah . . . meddling, as they call it."

"But it's *your* traditions that they're ignoring!" Ari Ara shouted, whirling.

Tahkan stared steadily back.

"And if it wasn't?" he challenged her. "If the Harraken had no tradition of village sings? If we had only warriors-rule, if women were not held as equals in this society? What would you have done?"

Ari Ara's mouth fell open. Her mind scrambled for a response. Tahkan watched his daughter come to the understanding he had long seen: if Harraken culture forced her to be a warrior or obey their orders, she would change the culture. It was not in her nature to do otherwise.

"I would stand against war and for equality, no matter what," Ari Ara admitted quietly.

"And everyone knows that," Tahkan answered. "Some admire you for it. Some fear you. That's why they want you to leave. You push them to change when they don't want to."

Her misery poured down like a Marianan rainstorm, thick and impenetrable. She slumped down on the edge of the bed, holding her face in her hands. Her skin flushed and her lips trembled, threatening tears.

"Ah, *betta*," Tahkan sighed, using a desert term of endearment. "It's not forever. It's just - "

She slapped his arm away. Tears spilled over the rims of her eyes.

"When?" she demanded in a cracking voice. "When do I have to go?"

Tahkan's heart broke at the wail in her voice, hidden under the heat of anger. He saw the small child Shulen encountered in the High Mountains, half-wild, running the ridges, alone - always alone. Ari Ara meant *not this, not that*. She stood outside every home she'd ever found. Someday,

Tahkan suspected this would be her strength and saving grace. Today, it only caused her sorrow.

"We can stay a few days. I'll travel to the pass with you - "

"Why wait?" she flung back, quivering with barely held hurt. "If you're so eager to be rid of me, let's leave at once."

She stalked across the room, hurtled her limbs into a chair, and turned her back to him. Tahkan sighed. He hoped she would forgive him someday.

CHAPTER TWENTY-SEVEN

· · · · ·

Only One Daughter

Every step east into the Border Mountains wrenched her heart. She felt betrayed and abandoned, hurt and excluded. They rode in silence. Zyrh trod placidly behind her father's black mare. It annoyed Ari Ara to see the beast so calm and docile for once; it meant even the horse agreed with sending her away. Behind them, she could hear the fading strains of song rising from the roofs of Turim City. The whole populace sang for Mahteni-Mirrin Shirar as she recovered, lining the rooftops and lifting their voices to the sky. They sang to the Ancestor Wind, thanking the spirits for letting Mahteni live, for returning her wandering spirit to her body, for building a song-bridge over which her spirit came back home to the battered limbs lying in a bed. The women's voices rose in the ancient melody, haunting and reverent. Male voices, low as thunder, rumbled under the women's higher tones. Even the warriors sang for Mahteni. Ari Ara's eyes swept back to the rooftops as the music swelled. Ari Ara mouthed the chords of the refrain, but no sound emerged. Her throat clenched tight over emotion. She hugged her arms to her chest. Tahkan's anguished words after her testimony at the city sing echoed in her ears. He'd brought her to the small room and told her to stay put, pausing in the doorway with a rueful look.

"For ancestors' sake," he had moaned, "why can't you look before leaping into things?"

The heavy thud of the door shutting slammed a finality onto the end of his answerless question.

Ari Ara rode in a stew of misery and outrage. *Everything she did put someone in danger,* she thought savagely, frightened and furious. *Every step she took led to disaster.* Her tears refused to fall. Anger built up in her chest, hot and heavy. She was nothing but trouble to both her families . . . she and her Way Between.

Nightfast had been sent ahead with a message and Shulen waited for them by the road. To the side of the trail to the Way Station, Shulen had built a small, one-room dwelling with stone walls and a thatched roof. Ari Ara stared silently at the house. It made her irrationally annoyed that he'd managed to build a home while she'd just messed everything up. Tahkan could not stay long - his people teetered on a knife's edge and he keenly felt the error of staying away from them too long - but he spent the night conversing with Shulen by the fire as the stars spun slowly overhead. Shulen was not happy with him, nor with the events of the summer: Emir lost, Ari Ara outcast. The stern old warrior's face was lined with disapproval. He had held his temper in check through the afternoon, but once Ari Ara fell asleep, he spoke his mind to his old friend.

"How can you abandon her like this?" Shulen snarled at Tahkan, furious.

"I'm not abandoning her," Tahkan protested.

Shulen's silence stung with rebuke. The fire crackled. The shadows danced. The glow of light heaved and bucked.

"I had no choice," Tahkan confessed. "It was the one demand of the warriors. They agreed to the Harraken Sing, but not if she was there."

Shulen grunted.

"You traded her for politics," he accused.

"I didn't - "

"You're her *father*," Shulen told his old friend. "She needs someone to stand by her no matter what. That's what fathers do."

"You have no idea how hard she makes it," Tahkan protested. "She is not at all like an ordinary desert girl."

"Why would you want her to be one?" Shulen asked bluntly.

"If she's going to be the next harrak-mettahl - "

Shulen cut him off.

"Tahkan, you only get one daughter . . . and you do not get to choose who she will be. You either love the daughter you have, or you don't. That's it. There are no other options."

The old warrior's words kept him tossing and turning all night long. In the morning, with an aching heart, he bid his daughter farewell. He studied her anxious face, her wild blue eyes and wind-teased copper hair. Her yearning for acceptance was written like a song across her features.

"Please?" she begged, not bothering to explain. He knew what she wanted.

"No. Stay here."

"You're just like the warriors, telling me what to do," she accused in a sulky tone. "You're as bad as Nalia's father telling her to get married."

It was a low blow; they both knew it.

"There is a difference between you and Nalia," Tahkan stated in a tight tone.

"My mother's blood?" Ari Ara guessed in a resentful mutter.

"Your age. You are still a child - "

"I've sung my Woman's Song!" Ari Ara retorted fiercely.

"Have you completed your druach?" he shot back.

She stared at the ground.

"Until then, you are still subject to your parents' rules."

He did not have to remind her that he was the only parent she had.

"I hate you," she spat at him, turning her back.

"Ari Ara Shirar en Marin!" Shulen called out, overhearing her outburst. "Apologize to your father and stop acting like the sullen child you say you're not."

Hot tears pricked her eyes. She scuffed the ground with her toe.

"It's alright," Tahkan told Shulen in a pained voice, turning away and starting down the path.

"Ari Ara of the High Mountains," Shulen told her in a hard tone, "if you were my daughter, I'd be ashamed of you."

"If I were your daughter, you wouldn't be sending me away!" Ari Ara snapped back.

"You only have one father," he warned her. "Don't part in a quarrel."

Then he walked back into the house to leave her to make her own choice. The sudden silence snapped her out of her temper. She bolted down the trail, catching up to Tahkan as he reached his horse.

"I'm sorry," she blurted out.

He turned toward her.

"I am, too," he said. He met and held her eyes. "I promise that, when this is all over, I will come and get you. You'll see; it won't be long."

She nodded mutely, every fiber in her being wanting to go with him back to the desert.

"Please tell Tala I'm sorry I didn't say goodbye," she said at last.

"Tala will understand."

"Tell Mahteni I miss her already."

"She will be glad to hear that," he answered.

"And . . ." she paused.

Tahkan waited patiently. Ari Ara ran forward a few steps and threw her arms around him.

"I'll miss you, too," he said, answering the words she could not say.

CHAPTER TWENTY-EIGHT

· · · · ·

Shulen's Advice

Shulen put her back in training that morning, drilling her in the Way Between on the flat sandy stretch in the middle of the Way Station ruins. She was sloppy and distracted. She botched the simplest exercises. She dragged her feet when he sped up the pace. She gave up in matches, letting him win without half trying. Shulen scowled. Who was this creature? It was as if the desert had stolen the Ari Ara he knew and replaced her with a lanky changeling. Why was she resisting the Way Between, the one thing she loved beyond all else?

He quickened the tempo, trying to startle her out of her slump. She faltered, tripped over her own feet, and sprawled in the dust.

"You're not trying!" he barked at her, annoyed.

"Yes, I am," she protested, getting up.

She started the drill again. He flipped her to her back.

"You're failing on purpose," he grumbled. "Get up."

A spark of her old fire lit in her eyes. He let her rise. She leapt at him. He flung her aside, easily, languorously, with an offhandedness he hadn't been able to use in trainings with her since her early days in the High Mountains.

"What's wrong with you?" Shulen asked, scrutinizing her for signs of illness.

"Nothing," she muttered. "Maybe I'm just not as good as you think."

Shulen's eyes narrowed. He shook his head.

"You're better than even I know, but this is not your best," he sighed. This wasn't working. Switching tactics, he pointed to a boulder as tall as his chest.

"Up," he said, slapping the stone with his palm.

The surface felt cool under the bare skin of her calloused feet. The flat section was just over a hand's width; one foot fit, not two. She balanced comfortably, tucking her other sole up against her thigh just above the knee. Light spilled over the high shoulders of the rocky peaks. Autumn's chill lifted in small ghosts of mist. The birds called out wary greetings before winging southward. Shulen lifted his hands, palms out, fingers touching to greet the sun. Then he folded them at his waist and waited. He had mastered stillness this summer as he waited for word of his two young apprentices. He had spent hours meditating like one of the patient stones tumbled from the time-eroded slopes. He studied the girl as she balanced on the rock. Ari Ara had grown. Once again, her wrists and ankles extended beyond the cuffs of her clothes. The shadows of growing pains haunted her eyes.

"Tell me," he said simply, and the story of the summer spilled out of her.

He had heard the main events - both she and Tahkan had flown the wings off Nightfast, sending messages - but he needed to hear her voice, bold and lively, annoyed and embarrassed, unrepentant and chagrined. He questioned her along the way, noticing when she avoided looking at him, when she railed up at the sky, when she groaned in exasperation, and when she tensed from head to toe over a memory.

Ari Ara wobbled on the stone as she related the events at the cliffs of Turim City. Her voice cracked with emotion and her lip trembled as she told him about leaping between Moragh and Kirkan's fight.

Why did this upset her so? Shulen wondered. Compared to the turmoil she had catalyzed across the desert, this was nothing.

"And then . . . I was sent away," she finished, brushing hot tears from the edges of her eyes. "As always. I'm Ari Ara, *not this, not that,* the girl who belongs nowhere."

She flailed, losing her balance completely. Shulen's arm shot out to steady her.

"I can't even stand on a stupid stone anymore!" she wailed, hopping down.

"You're distracted," Shulen replied evenly, finally seeing what bothered her so deeply.

He narrowed his eyes.

"It won't work, you know," he told her.

She frowned.

"What won't work?" she asked.

"Failing at the Way Between so the Harraken will accept you."

When she flinched at his words, he knew he had hit the problem spot-on.

"I'll never be one of them!" she cried, face flushing red with pent-up emotion. "I can't sing like a true Shirar. I can't make the song-visions. Everyone looks at me like I'm a monster, a river-dragon. Even Sarai and Nalia! The other youths made fun of my accent, my skin, my eyes. They teased me for not being able to ride that stupid horse."

"That doesn't matter - " Shulen tried to interject.

"Yes, it does!" she shouted, spinning to face him in a wide stance, eyes wild, fists clenched at her sides. "It does matter. You don't understand! It's a matter of harrak - only babies and lazy people ride like the Marianans. I have to ride like a real Harraken!"

Her voice shook. She crossed her arms over her chest, shoulders hunched in tight anger.

"He hates me," Ari Ara blurted out, blue-grey eyes anxious. "He's disappointed in me. He probably wishes he never met me, that I'd never been found."

Shulen didn't need to ask who she meant - only Tahkan could evoke that intensity of reaction. She kicked the side of the boulder, stubbing her toe in the process.

"Are you done?" Shulen asked wryly as she hopped around with her toe clenched in her hands. She nodded sullenly. "Tahkan does not hate you. He loves you. He's proud of you, proud beyond words. He's just . . . stretched between his duties as a father and his duties to his people."

"All I wanted was to be a good daughter," Ari Ara sighed.

"You have been," Shulen told her, laying a hand on her shoulder. "You've done exactly what a daughter of the desert should do, exactly what the daughter of a harrak-mettahl must do to protect the harrak of her people."

"But they don't see it that way," Ari Ara protested. "They said I was a meddling outsider for using the Way Between."

Shulen grew still.

"Can you not belong to them all? Alaren of the Way Between, Marin of the Riverlands, and Shirar of the Desert were all sons of the same mother. Can you not be Alaren's daughter in spirit, and Marin and Shirar's by blood?"

The Way Between was her home, her culture, her tradition; Shulen knew this beyond a shred of doubt. She took to the Way

Between like a fish to water. The motions sprang to life in her limbs as if they had simply lain dormant inside her. She could not turn her back on the Way Between. It was welded to the fiber of her being.

"You'll have to choose, Ari Ara," he told her gently, "whether your name means that you don't belong anywhere, or whether it means that you belong everywhere; whether you belong to no one, or to everyone."

He pointed to the stone and gestured for her to climb back up. She needed time and stillness to think about that. No one could answer that question but her.

The days turned chill and the nights colder still. Ari Ara warmed her limbs by racing up and down the steep slopes of the mountain pass. She threw herself heart and soul into the drills and trainings. After a handful of sleepless nights, rehashing the events of the summer in her mind, Ari Ara decided that - right or wrong, traditional or not - she wouldn't have been able to live with herself if she had just stood aside and let Moragh kill Kirkan. She was a follower of the Way Between.

The shrubs blazed scarlet and orange. The leaves burst into gold and tumbled from the trees. As the days stretched into weeks, Tahkan sent Nightfast back and forth with messages. The harvest was gathered from the fields surrounding Turim City, abundant and fruitful thanks to the water Ari Ara had helped to return to the desert. Mahteni was recovering; everyone hoped she would be able to ride in a month's time. Tahkan had even managed to broker an uneasy truce between Moragh and Kirkan, convincing her that the bear-like man was not to blame for the violence at the cliffs. Everyone held their breath until the Dark Moon, counting down the days until the Harraken Sing. The inhabitants of Turim City worked at a frenzied pace, preparing for the gathering. Long caravans of food, tents, and supplies departed south to the gathering place. Tahkan's letter included a rough-sketched map to show her the distance. She traced the route with her finger, wishing she could go.

Every day, Ari Ara gritted her teeth and tried to ride Zyrh. The horse sidled and reared, bolted and froze. She landed in the dust so many times that Shulen forbade her from leaving the wide, dusty road for fear she'd strike a boulder as she fell. She came no closer to riding the trickster horse like a true Harraken.

On the night of her thirteenth birthday, the dark sky shone with cold stars. A breath of frost settled on the pass, decorating the bare branches with intricate white patterns. On the highest peaks, a touch of snow clung to the cliffs. It was a night of loss and hauntings. She lit the candles for her mother's spirit, and for Shulen's wife and child. Ancestor spirits hissed and howled in the wind. Ghosts of the past stirred uneasily in the shushing of dry leaves. They sat in somber silence for a time, staring at the flickering flames. Twice, the old warrior and the young girl startled at the tread of footsteps beyond the stone walls of the house. Shulen rose once to peer out the door, but nothing lurked in the darkness. Nothing that could be seen, anyway.

Ari Ara didn't dare ask if the ruins were haunted. She didn't want to hear ghost stories on a night like this. The veil between realms stretched thin in autumn. She had danced with the ancestor spirits in the Fanten traditions, but who knew what souls haunted these mountains?

She spent the evening reading the bundle of birthday greetings her father had sent by way of Nightfast. There were messages from Sarai, Orryn, and Nalia. Mahteni sent her a long and loving letter, telling her how proud she was of her niece, how she disagreed with the decision of the city sing, and how she was glad Ari Ara had interrupted the blood feud. Mahteni concluded with a fierce line to her niece:

Remember, no matter what anyone else says, there is no right or wrong way to be a desert woman. That song is made by those who sing it . . . including you. All of the women make this song, together.

Ari Ara smiled at those words and hugged the letter to her chest. Mahteni's faith in her never wavered. Her aunt had always been fair and honest with her, speaking up when she was wrong, defending her when she was right. Ari Ara was grateful for that.

There was also a thick roll of parchment from Tala. The songholder missed her with a vengeance. *It's dull without you,* Tala wrote, c*ome back.* Ari Ara snorted. Half the trouble she got in was Tala's doing! The next lines of Tala's letter confirmed her view.

I'm sending you something that will probably get me in a lot of trouble. But I had to! Gorlion and bunch of other idiots - Ari Ara paused to bite back a laugh at the description - *keep saying you're not really a Harraken. I hollered at them all and sang all the old songs, the ones they're too young and stupid to know, about the Women of the Outcry. You're just like them, and our culture has been shaped more by the women who raised their voices than the ones who behaved and stayed silent!*

Ari Ara blinked at that idea. Tala was right. The Women of the Outcry had changed the course of Harraken history over and over. They had defined harrak. They had established the village sings. They had ensured that women stood equal to men. Where would the Harraken Song be without them?

So, this is for them, Tala wrote, *and for you.*

Ari Ara squinted at the spidery lines of Tala's handwriting. It was hard to decipher, especially when ze was excited, but it looked like Tala had sent the verses of a poem. She worked out what appeared to be a title: *Daughter of the Desert.* She gasped.

This wasn't a poem! It was a song . . . Tala's new song, the one ze was not supposed to sing.

This is a song
born in a dream
in visions not yet seen
of possibilities shining
on horizon's edge
and whispers on the breath
of the wind.

Ari Ara smiled, hearing the melody perfectly - after countless hours of Tala's humming this summer, how could she not? She blushed a little at the next lines. She had known the song was partly about her, but it was still strange to read lyrics about her life.

This is a song
of a girl who came
over mountains from a foreign land.
Daughter of water,
daughter of fire,
child of light and dark,
heat and cold,
desert and rivers,
not yours, not mine,
but ours.

Ari Ara felt her heart constrict over the words. A prickle of tears blurred the writing. She brushed them away with the back of her hand.

Tala's song was a ballad that told the summer's story and the problems between warriors and women. Ari Ara's breath caught at the beauty of the song. Tala had captured the constant motion of the past months, the yearning, the struggling, the journeying. The chorus hummed in her throat. The rhythm hammered in her heartbeat. The story reverberated in her bones.

Oh, can you hear
on wind and wing
on hoof beat, breath and drum?
A new song rising
in the heartbeats and thunder,
in the drum rolls of changing times.

In the next section, Tala had scrawled a nearly illegible note, saying that this part went to the melody of the Outcry. Ari Ara could imagine it: harsh, bracing, uncanny, unsettling. The verses chanted the invocation of the women's names . . . if done right, the ancestors should appear in song-visions. Ari Ara smiled. She could imagine her aunt and father pulling off a stunt like that.

Oh, Daughter of the Desert,
how could you forget,
the strength of Karinne,
the courage of Shireen and Mirka,
the love of Farrah,
the honor of Annoush,
the vision of Tala-Oon.

Oh, Daughter of the Desert,
sing soft, sing loud,
sing harsh, sing bold
sing true.
This is a song
born from your voice
and without your voice,
there's no Song.

Ari Ara nodded. The last word referenced the Harraken Song; without every person's voice, it was not complete. Tala's lyrics went on, speaking of the Way Between and its role in restoring the village sings. The last verse spoke about harrak returning like the water, the people, and the green. It wove the connections between a song of all voices and the possibility of a lasting peace. In the end, Tala repeated the opening lines in a wistful refrain that reminded the listeners that the song was a vision yet to come. At the bottom, Tala's spidery scrawl ended with a final note:

The song is done. All it needs is a singer.

Ari Ara sank back in the chair, overwhelmed by the gift. It was beautiful! She couldn't wait to hear Tala sing it, or Mahteni or Tahkan. She spent the evening memorizing it, humming it under her breath. The rhythm caught in her heart. The words echoed in her mind. The Women of the Outcry rose in her imagination, real enough to touch. She wished she could make them appear in song-visions, but no matter how hard she tried, nothing happened.

She was so absorbed in the music that she almost didn't notice her father's note lying unopened. She broke the seal and scanned it. She gasped in delight!

Her father's letter contained the best gift she could hope for: news of Emir.

A patrol of riders had spotted him near Turim City. He approached, sunburned and dusty, with hands raised, unarmed. He asked if Ari Ara Marin en Shirar was in the city; he'd heard rumors that the Harrak-Mettahl was in residence. The patrol told him the gossip that was on everyone's lips: the red-haired girl had been banished from her banishment, exiled from exile, and sent to Shulen the Butcher in the Border Mountains.

"Your loss, then," Emir Miresh had told them, shrugging and starting to back away.

The warriors tried to take him captive - and nearly succeeded - but Emir broke free.

"No one holds a follower of the Way Between against his will," he said with a laugh. "Tell Turim that the River Dog Ghost sends his regards."

Then he vanished. Or so they said. Tahkan believed the encounter had been real, but he suspected the tale of the vanishing ghost had been invented to cover up lost harrak.

Now he knows where you are, Tahkan wrote to his daughter, *so be on the lookout for him.*

Ari Ara burned with a hundred unanswered questions: when had the patrol seen him? Was he hurt at all? How long would it take him to walk to the Way Station? She begged Shulen to let her go and look for Emir.

"No," the old warrior said flatly. "He will make his way here. Wait."

She'd never been good at waiting.

As the dying embers popped and hissed, Shulen watched her eyelids sag and leap as excitement and exhaustion vied. He poked the coals and pulled his cloak tighter about his shoulders, preparing for a long sleepless night of vigil.

"Come back," he murmured to Emir Miresh, wherever he was, certain that the young man was still alive and headed this way. "We're waiting for you."

Ari Ara slept fitfully. Her limbs twitched with dreamed motion. Her eyelids shivered with slumbering visions. She muttered unintelligible words. Once, she threw her arm out as if whirling to face some unknown danger. Shulen rose and tucked her back under the warmth of her blanket.

Then he sat and waited.

CHAPTER TWENTY-NINE

. . . . .

Dreamwalking

In her dreams, the women rose. They leapt skyward, birds in flight, dark and light against the eternal blue of the sky. She stood on the ground, one yearning arm stretched after the women as they dwindled into high-soaring specks. Then they dove and sang for the sheer joy of flight. Laughter rippled through her; their joy was her joy. The dream hung, timeless, a moment, a year, a second, a century.

Then the warriors came with nets weighted with rocks. They tossed the netting high. It spun like a sinister spider web in front of the sun's orb. Then it caught the women in a shrieking tangle. Screaming in horror, they fell.

Ari Ara woke from the dream with a gasp of fright. Her throat burned raw. The dream rattled in her limbs. She shoved back the blanket and scrubbed her face with her palms. Shulen sat in shadow, his expression hidden in darkness.

"I need some air," Ari Ara muttered, blinking, trying to wipe away the sensation of invisible cobwebs clinging to her skin.

He made no objections - he didn't even seem to hear her -

so Ari Ara rose to her feet and reached for the door latch. She stepped into the pooling darkness without a backwards glance. Had she looked over her shoulder, she would have startled at the sight of her sleeping form still curled under the blanket. As it was, she slipped out the door in her dreambody without noticing that the latch had not lifted, the door had not opened, and Shulen had not seen her go. The moon had risen, casting a silvery blanket of light over the soaring mountains and deep ravine. Above her, the stone foundations of the ruins of Alaren's Way Station gleamed like polished bone. She could walk for miles by this light, she thought, and even though she knew Shulen would disapprove, she began to hike, picking her way slowly over boulder and stone, scree and shrub. The hulking shapes of the mountains loomed like watchful giants.

Ari Ara walked with a strange floating sensation. She crested the ridgeline and stood overlooking the fall of the foothills. From here, the pinpricks of Turim City's lights winked like fishermen's lamps bobbing on a vast lake of silver and midnight blue. The wind shushed against the slopes. She shivered, though it was not the cold that bothered her. The sheer size of the desert broke her heart. Somewhere, Emir was making his way through the distances toward her.

"Oh Emir," she sighed, her breath forming a white cloud on the cold air, "I'm so sorry."

Her head dropped. The Atta Song leapt to mind. She thought of her father standing at the Crossroads, singing for his people, kneeling to his sister, apologizing for his part in the problem. As the moonlight poured down on her and the foothills shivered in the wind, Ari Ara felt the melody rise in her chest and burst out through her lips. She sang her apology to Emir Miresh for throwing the waterskin, quarreling with him, losing him. She apologized to his spirit, living or dead, for leaving him on the forest floor back in Moragh's territory. Ari Ara sang in Marianan without meaning to: the language of her remorse took the shape of her native tongue, following pattern of her churning thoughts over the past months. The sound fell small and lonely as a reed pipe against the wide slopes of the mountains. The immense sky swallowed the melody. Still, she sang. The moonlight pooled around her slight frame as she stood, dwarfed and tiny in the dark lake of night.

When she finished, the silence hurt with its emptiness. There was no reply to her Atta Song, no answer, no forgiveness. Only the brutal silence . . . and its hard truth. Some wrongs cannot be made right. Some apologies came too late. A flash of wild fear shot through her: what if it *was* his ghost that had been sighted outside Turim? Throw-the-Bones had said he spun between the mortal and spirit realms; maybe he returned as a spirit.

The thought set her heart pounding in her chest. Tears sprang to her eyes. Then, unexpectedly, Ari Ara felt the tune of the return-to-life song rising in her, low and rumbling, the ritual chant that all of Turim City had sung to heal Mahteni. She didn't know the Harrak-Tala words, but the chant's melody was simple enough to sing with Marianan words. Shakily, she wove the languages together, blending her cultures to speak truth. She poured all the stories she knew about her missing friend into the verses, all the life he had yet to live; she sang of the people who loved him, of the sadness they would feel if he did not step back from the edge of the Ancestor River; she asked the ancestor spirits to bar his path and tell him he was too young to come to them. She sang of how much she missed him and asked him to stay connected to this life.

Then she rose and danced in the Fanten style, blending the gestures of the mysterious women who'd raised her with the language of her mother's people and the song of her father's people. Overhead, she sensed the spirits stilling, hovering in the darkness. She pounded out the rhythm of the return-to-life song with the footsteps of the Fanten's healing dance. She blended all three of her cultures in her song, dance, and prayer. For good measure, she added a touch of the Way Between, and asked Alaren for his help in carrying her song to Emir.

Ari Ara closed her eyes. She sensed a rushing motion speeding past like a spring-melt river. She heard the hush of ancestor spirits murmuring as they swept by. She felt her legs weaken. Like her father at the Crossroads, she fell to her knees, palms open and facing upwards on her thighs. She sat that way for an eternity until exhaustion pulled her to the side. She curled up in a ball. The silver moonlight gleamed. A warm glow softened its edges. The sense of golden firelight flooded the air around her. Her voice continued its song, murmuring the return-to-life chant, weaving in the refrain of the Atta Song, calling to the Ancestor Wind, the Ancestor River, all of the ancestors to return her friend to her.

With her eyelids closed, she did not see Shulen blink awake at the sound of her voice chanting in her sleep. She did not see his eyes widen as he recognized the shadow of her dream-body slipping back into the shell of her sleeping form. She did not hear Shulen's choking gasp of surprise, nor the unmistakable crunch of footsteps beyond the door.

Shulen rose shakily to shoulder the sticky latch into releasing. He took a step beyond the doorframe of the house. His shocked stare gazed out into the night. His mouth fell open. His eyes grew round and rounder still, and a tremble ran through him like a leaf in the wind.

Ari Ara opened her eyes just in time to see Emir Miresh's ghost glide to a stop just outside the open door.

CHAPTER THIRTY

· · · · ·

Emir's Return

Ari Ara scrambled to her feet and bounded toward Emir, freezing beside Shulen. She didn't dare reach out to his spirit . . . everyone knew you could get pulled into the Ancestor River and drowned that way. It took her a moment to realize he was speaking, then another to switch her ears from Harrak-Tala to Marianan, and then yet another moment to register what his voice was saying.

"How did you get here so quickly?" he was asking her. "I was right behind you, then you vanished."

Shulen ran to embrace the youth. They collided, solid and strong as all living men, pounding each other's backs and laughing.

"Emir?" Ari Ara asked tremulously. "Are you a ghost?"

"No, of course not," Emir answered, shaking his ink-dark hair. "I had to say that so they wouldn't kill me - a Marianan warrior can't just wander about the desert."

He sounded so exasperated to have to explain the obvious that his flesh-and-blood reality hit Ari Ara like a dose of cold water. She leapt the distance between them and flung her arms around his living, breathing, solid self so hard he staggered backward.

"You're really here!" she cried. "It worked! It worked! I sang you back to life."

"You can't sing me back to life," Emir protested. "I wasn't dead."

He had heard her, though, up on the ridge. It had kept him going even though he had wanted to stop for the night, he told them.

"What ridge?" Shulen asked, frowning. The girl had been sound asleep on the other side of the fire . . . unless she really had been dreamwalking like a Fanten.

Emir tried to explain, but gave up as Ari Ara hollered and laughed and cried and bounced up and down in delight. Only when she pinched him for the seventh time did he protest.

"Ouch! Quit it. I'm here. I'm real. And if you stop leaping around, I'll tell you where I've been."

That shut her up.

His story emerged in bits and pieces, interrupted by her questions. He'd been rescued by two Tala-Rasa and revived in their mountain cave above the Black Raven's Stronghold.

"Tala-Rasa! Why didn't Tala tell me?" Ari Ara cried.

"Is that the young Tala?" Emir asked. "I never met that one."

He'd heard of the young Tala, though; the elders complained about zir running off. Ze was spoken of with high praise, great affection, and sharp annoyance . . . not unlike a certain redhead he knew, Emir thought, hiding a smile from his friend.

The Tala-Rasa that had rescued him were old and strange, bone-thin creatures, eyes milky-white with visions and songs. Slumped against the rough bark of the old pine, he had drifted into the half-conscious state where hallucinations and reality blurred. Emir swore he had seen Ari Ara sprinting up the slope, hands cupped to her mouth, shouting for help. On the other hand, he also *knew* he'd seen her red hair dangling as the Black Ravens lifted her up and rode away. Clarity and confusion fogged over as he blacked out, waking later in the darkness of a cave with the two Tala-Rasa hovering over him and more gathered in the gloomy shadows.

"They claimed a Fanten dreamwalker threw her voice across the forest and guided them to me," Emir reported. He grinned at Ari Ara and nudged her shoulder with his. "Even in that form, you're apparently quite stubborn."

Tugged and pestered by the dreamwalker, the two Tala-Rasa turned their horses southward, discovering the collapsed Marianan warrior. They slipped water between the youth's cracked and bleeding lips. They listened to his delirious mumblings as they debated whether to help him further. They were reluctant to harbor an enemy warrior, but the young man hovered close to death. As he started to slip into the black Ancestor River, Alaren's spirit appeared and Emir called out him.

"And that's what saved my life," Emir told Shulen and Ari Ara.

The Tala-Rasa knew of Alaren from the ancient songs; a riverlands warrior murmuring the old rascal's name intrigued them. They brought Emir to their cave and nursed him back to health. As he recuperated, he answered the Tala-Rasa's barrage of questions, relating all he'd experienced in the desert and throwing in a handful of Alaren tales upon request. When he had fully recovered, they sent him on his way.

"They told me to follow a trail through the Border Mountains back to Shulen," Emir related, "but I ignored them."

He rubbed the back of his neck sheepishly. He'd hiked for a few hours down the trail they'd set him on, then circled back toward where he'd last seen Ari Ara.

"You were so close," Emir told Ari Ara, "or so I thought."

A rueful expression crossed his face. In hindsight, he had embarked on a fool's errand, on foot, through enemy territory. They'd passed each other like two night barges on the Mari River - not just once, but more times than he cared to admit in front of Shulen - turning north and south as he followed the rumors of her journey. As he told the story, Ari Ara grinned: at least she wasn't the only one who got into trouble by disobeying instructions!

Emir had made slow progress. Harraken warriors swarmed across the land. The summer heat blistered. Once the rains came, he floundered in the marshes. He was chased by the marsh islander warriors and dove into the channel to evade them. The current, stronger than it appeared, pulled him far downstream. Then rumors swept him even further off course. He tracked misinformation into the southern half of the desert, chasing false trails for months before he learned she wasn't there at all. He'd traveled so far south that he had glimpsed the salt ocean shining in the distance. As the summer turned to autumn, he trekked back north on foot, wishing he had a horse, or a messenger hawk, or at least a friend. At last, he made it to Turim City.

"When I heard you had been sent to Shulen," Emir reported, "I came straight here."

He turned to Ari Ara, who sat with her fingers laced together, spine bolting straight upward, hanging on every word of his tale with the white-lipped tension of someone who knew she was responsible for every danger and mishap. When he finished, she flung her arms around him and apologized for every word of argument, every pigheaded moment, and every idiotic thing she'd ever done.

"In your whole life or just since we reached the desert?" Emir teased.

In that teasing, she heard his forgiveness. Relief burst like sunshine over her face.

"I was so worried about you!" she exclaimed. "I thought you were dead."

"Don't be silly," Emir told her with an indulgent smile. "We who follow the Way Between are not so easily killed."

It took days to tell all the stories that had to be told . . . and longer when Shulen put both of his wayward and wandering apprentices back into training. He watched them with quiet pride. Emir had traversed hostile lands for months armed only with the Way Between, doing harm to none, persevering despite hardship. Ari Ara, thrust into one challenging situation after another, had chosen actions that - while lacking in maturity - at least compromised neither her honor nor her commitment to the Way Between. As the first snows dusted the ruins of the Way Station, Shulen lifted his silent thanks to Alaren's ancestor spirit for delivering them back to him.

The days rolled one into another. The spark of mischievous enthusiasm rekindled in Ari Ara's eyes. She pushed herself in trainings, laughing at the challenge of matches with Emir, surprising Shulen with unexpected moves inspired by the desert songs she'd heard about Alaren.

"I heard a great song about him, too," Emir started to say with a grin.

A screech overhead cut off his words.

"Nightfast!" Ari Ara called out, flinging up her arm for the messenger hawk to land. Her breath puffed on the air in cold clouds. She brought the bird inside to untie the frost-hardened leather lacings that held the tight-rolled scroll in place.

We leave for the Harraken Sing in the south today, Tahkan wrote. *I wish you could see the magnificent sight of our people riding out by the thousands! Mahteni sends her love. She has recovered, but is still angry with me. She says I should not have agreed to the warriors' demands to send you away. She says you are a true Daughter of the Desert, and that I should not have cut your voice from the Harraken Song.*

"Well, she's right," Ari Ara muttered, handing the letter to Shulen to read.

Shulen scanned the lines of Tahkan's handwriting. The desert man sounded conflicted. He wrote of regrets and wishes. He lamented the situation, but pointed out that, as Harrak-Mettahl, he was honor-bound to uphold his promise to the warriors.

"He wants you to come," Shulen stated bluntly, pointing to the final line.

I keep turning over my shoulder, Tahkan wrote, *half-expecting to see you riding up behind me. I wish you could.*

"Hah," she snorted. "Fat chance of that. I've learned my lesson. No more leaping into things for me."

All day long, then into the next, and the next, Shulen seemed pensive and distracted. He stared southwest for long periods of time. He cleared his throat as if to speak then fell silent. He lost track of his sentences. It was so unlike the sharp, clear-eyed, old warrior that Ari Ara finally cornered him at breakfast and told him to spit it out.

"I may regret saying this," Shulen sighed, "but . . . "

He trailed off.

"What? What is it?" Ari Ara pried.

"Are you sure you shouldn't go to the Harraken Sing?" he asked Ari Ara, startling her.

"No, it's better if I don't," she replied, shaking her head. For once in her life, she intended to behave. "It's not my song, not my people. It's their business, not mine."

"Is it?" Shulen wondered. "Alaren always said that the work of peace belonged to everyone."

"It's Harraken culture that's at stake, not war or peace," Ari Ara pointed out.

Shulen did not reply for a long time. When he spoke it was in a quiet voice made grave with long hours of contemplation.

"Do you know how many people wanted the War of Retribution?" he asked.

Ari Ara shrugged, glancing at Emir to see if he knew. The youth looked up from his porridge and shook his head.

"Very few," Shulen explained to them. "Most people felt waging war would be a betrayal of Alinore's work as a peacebuilder."

Shulen studied their faces. The wind scraped the rocky hillsides then stilled as if listening.

"Do you know how many people decided that thousands would fight and die in that war?"

"Thirteen," Ari Ara answered, referring to the Nobles Assembly that made all of the decisions in Mariana.

Shulen shook his head.

"One."

The word dropped like a stone into a pond. The Nobles Assembly had been split; six for war, six against, and the Great Lady Brinelle had turned to Shulen for advice. He did not cast a vote, but he bent his words toward war . . . and off to war the nation went in an unjust, bloody invasion of the desert.

"Ever since I first heard of the tension over the warriors meets and the village sings," Shulen remarked, "I have wondered if Mariana would have gone to war if the mothers and fathers, elders and children, had all been asked instead of me. If the Great Lady had turned to her people for counsel, instead of turning to a grieving warrior, the course of history may have been very different."

He paused and gazed at Ari Ara.

"As this summer passed, I often wished I could tell you this story, or share it with Tahkan. But it is not the sort of tale you write in a messenger hawk's scroll. What would I say? *Greetings, I told my country to invade yours. How's the weather?*"

The self-loathing and scorn in his voice made Ari Ara wince.

"And perhaps, I was too much of a coward to speak this truth," he admitted, "even to myself. But now, it seems like the Harraken face a choice to revive the tradition of their many voices . . . or go in a direction of fewer voices that decide for everyone."

Shulen's eyes slid southwest as if searching for the thousands of riders headed toward the distant desert gathering point of the Harraken Sing.

"At first, it seems like a matter only for the Harraken," he said, "but warriors see everything as a battle to be fought and won. With them in charge, war is inevitable. In that case, the choice to between warriors-rule and village sings concerns everyone."

He turned back to Ari Ara.

"I cannot enter the desert to tell this story," he said to her, "but you can."

He asked her to carry his tale to the Harraken Sing.

"No," she refused. "I promised I wouldn't go leaping into trouble any more."

"It's not the leaping that's the problem," Shulen mentioned in a gentle, thoughtful tone. "It's not looking before you leap that's dangerous. You ran across the High Mountains as a child, you know what I mean. You wouldn't hurtle off a cliff without knowing how far down the drop fell, right? It's the same with this. Take a look. Consider the risks. Weigh the possibilities. Then leap."

Ari Ara's eyes widened. Her heart lifted. All this time, she had wrestled with her impulsiveness, feeling like caution ran against her character, like a stream flowing uphill.

But, it's fine to leap, she repeated silently, *just so long as you take a careful look to know what you're leaping into!*

Her face turned toward the desert. Her muscles yearned to take action, but she forced herself to wait and think, to consider the consequences, the unknowns, the possibilities. She mulled on the choice for days. Three nights later, as Emir and Shulen sat by the hearth conversing in low, companionable tones, the youth laughed over something, ducking his head. His blue-black hair caught the firelight and gleamed. A flash of a memory shot through Ari Ara. She dove across the small house, startling the others with her sudden urgency. Her fingers scrabbled in the bottom of her traveling sack. She hauled it into the light, searching for the lightning stone from Throw-the-Bones. She brought it out and rolled it in her palm, feeling its age and smoothness.

When the young warrior returns, Throw-the-Bones had said, *the old warrior will ask for your help. You will give it.*

That was the payment the seer had demanded in trade for her prophecy about Emir. It hadn't made sense at the time, but here was Emir, the young warrior returned, and Shulen was an old warrior, asking for her help. Someone had to carry his story where he could not go.

"I'll do it," she said suddenly, clenching the lightning stone in her fist. "I'll go to the Harraken Sing."

Shulen burst into a smile. Emir lifted both eyebrows and hid his laugh. For days, Shulen had been telling him to just wait . . . the girl would decide to go.

"It's a long journey," Shulen told her, rising and beginning to collect traveling gear. "You'll have to leave at first light to get there before the Dark Moon."

Ari Ara suddenly groaned in a horrified tone. She smacked her forehead and paced across the tight confines of the house.

"Oh no," Ari Ara moaned. "It's so stupid, but I'll never make it in time."

"Why not?" Emir asked, his dark eyebrows drawing together in a frown.

"I have to go on foot," she muttered.

He shook his head, confused.

"Why wouldn't you ride?" he wondered, gesturing over his shoulder toward the small pasture and half-shed they'd built for Zyrh. "Isn't that a horse out there, getting fat and glossy, doing nothing but standing around eating all day?"

"No," she answered flatly, "that is a Trickster Being disguised as a horse; a trickster that dumps me off his back whenever he gets the chance."

Emir burst out laughing.

"It's not funny!" she objected.

"It is if you know what I know," he smirked.

"What's that?" she bristled.

His eyes crinkled with mirth. He gestured for her to join him by the fire.

"The tale of how Alaren tricked the Trickster," he answered.

CHAPTER THIRTY-ONE

. . . . .

Tricking the Trickster

The song began in a cadence of hoof beats, the rhythm of wanderers and travels. Once, in a time lost to memory, the Trickster whipped up mischief like the towering dust beings that spiraled in giant strides across the sands. Ze stung children into squabbles and women into fights and men into duels unto death. And because the Trickster's boredom was as vast as zirs infinite life, the Trickster delighted in setting off wars.

Emir told her the whole story by the evening fire. His voice rang out, deep and even, steady as his nature, fluid as the laughing waters of a stream. He had learned the tune from the Tala-Rasa and memorized it to bring back to Shulen. It had kept him company on lonely nights of wandering and given him strength when all seemed lost.

"Now, the song travels with you," he told Ari Ara as she bid farewell to the two warriors.

The dawn broke, fresh and clear, over the mountain peaks. Zyrh's flank shivered in the frost. Ari Ara leapt to his back. He reared in protest. She held on.

"You can't trick me anymore," she told him with a laugh. "Not with the song I know."

299

Ari Ara sang the words to the ballad as she raced the golden horse down through the ravine, past the empty city of Turim, onto the wide plains. She shot across the sands, chanting the song-story like an incantation to get her to the Harraken Sing in time.

Alaren told the Trickster
let's make a wager, you and I
if I lose, you can keep your tricks,
but if I win, you'll stop causing war.

Ari Ara smiled to herself as the winter sun arced overhead. The red, frost-stung northern grasses gave way to the lower elevations' warmth as she led the horse down one plateau onto another, heading south day after day. She sang the song each night and it wound into her dreams.

The Trickster Being lived for a clever wager, the old ballad explained, so ze asked Alaren his terms.

"You turn into a wild horse," Alaren said calmly, "and I'll see how long I can stay on your back. Then we'll switch. You transform into a man and climb up on my back. Whoever holds on the longest, wins."

The Trickster eyed old Alaren, white-bearded, rangy and lean, knobble-kneed, and wrinkled. The ancient being examined the exact wording of the wager. A wicked chuckle rumbled like thunder.

"Agreed," the Trickster answered and changed into a horse.

When the Tala-Rasa sang this story for Emir, they had paused to debate about the color of the horse. One Tala claimed it was red like fire. Another said it was black as night. A third insisted that the horse was silver like moonlight. A fourth shrugged and suggested that maybe the Trickster-as-a-Horse changed color with each breath, shifting to match the description of everyone's most troublesome steed. As Emir sang the ballad for Ari Ara, she imagined the Trickster-as-a-Horse looking exactly like the trouble-making Zyrh. As she rode southward through the shortest days of the year, Zyrh's pale hide shifted color with the light, turning lavender grey before dawn, then gleaming pink-orange in the sunrise's rosy hues, then shining gold in the full burst of the rising sun. In her mind, Zyrh shape-shifted just like the Trickster in the song.

In the song, when Alaren hopped on, the Trickster gave him a wild ride, bucking and charging, leaping and shaking. But, no matter what the shape-shifter tried, old Alaren clung like burr.

"You can't shake me, Trickster," Alaren declared with a bold laugh, "I'm a follower of the Way Between."

The Trickster rumbled with wicked laughter and all at once began to change form. Ze might have agreed to turn into a horse ... but ze hadn't promised to *stay* in that form. The shape-shifter turned into a bear and rose up on two legs, roaring. Ze turned into a mountain and danced in avalanches and earthquakes. Ze became a river and tossed Alaren between the currents. Ze became a hawk to soar the heights and plummet down in dives. But, wherever ze went, whatever ze did, Alaren found and followed the Way Between. The Trickster couldn't shake him, not even as a wind, a giant serpent, a swarm of hornets, a howling blizzard, a forest fire, or a spiraling tower of dust.

Later, as Ari Ara rode the long and winding road south, she thought of these stories. When a winter snowstorm nearly froze her, she remembered Alaren and kept going. When exhaustion tried to pull her off, she thought of Alaren and held on. When the wind slammed her to the side, she found the Way Between.

When Zyrh sidestepped out from under her, she followed the horse's dance like Alaren on the Trickster's back.

The last verses of the old ballad had taught her the most important lesson of all.

After hours of shape-shifting, the Trickster had called a halt. Alaren hopped off and they switched roles, the Trickster climbing onto the old man's back. The mischievous being was tired from all that changing, but ze still plotted new transformations. After all, according to the wording of the wager, nothing prevented ze from shape-shifting on Alaren's back!

Would ze become a snarling bear? No, no, the Trickster discarded the idea. Alaren was clever, he'd simply change into a spindly tree and slip zir off. Maybe a boulder to crush the old man? No, no, Alaren would become water and trickle out from under zir. Perhaps ze should become despair, self-doubt, and sorrow; the greatest weights in the world - how could the old man possibly shake those?

The Trickster clung to Alaren's knobby spine, waiting for the man to begin. Nothing happened. Alaren didn't even turn into a horse. The wind ruffled the boughs overhead. Somewhere, a cow lowed. The flies buzzed around their heads. Still, nothing happened. After another minute, the Trickster lost patience and jumped off.

"What's the matter, old man?" ze cried in exasperation. "Why won't you turn into a horse?"

Alaren looked up with a smile creasing his eyes.

"I never said I would," Alaren answered evenly, "and you just lost the bet."

The Trickster's jaw fell open. Ze spluttered. Ze made a choking sound. Ze gasped. It was true. Alaren had won the wager. By standing still and having patience where the Trickster had none, Alaren had tricked the Trickster into jumping off his back after only a couple of minutes.

"So, you're saying I need to have patience?" Ari Ara had grumbled when Emir had finished singing the last strains of the song.

"It wouldn't hurt," Emir told her, rolling his eyes.

"But how's that supposed to help me ride Zyrh like a true desert rider?"

"It's not," he retorted. "Ari Ara, you're not Harraken. You're not Marianan. You're Ari Ara, *not this, not that.* You have to ride in your own style . . . like a true follower of the Way Between."

Ari Ara's mouth fell open. She blinked. Shulen's words came back to her: you have to decide for yourself what Ari Ara means - the girl who belongs nowhere? Or the girl who belongs everyone, to everywhere? She couldn't ride like a desert rider because she wasn't one . . . but maybe Alaren gave her another way to ride . . . *a Way Between.*

"Think it will work?" she wondered.

"You'll never know until you try."

She rode over plateaus and through canyons, down descending staircases of giant cliffs. She found the Way Between in the gait and rhythm of the racing desert horse . . . and not just any horse, but a trickster horse. For every trick Zyrh tried, Ari Ara discovered a way to counter him. The horse moved and she moved with him. He bucked and she held on. He veered off course, she steered him back.

"You can't trick me anymore," she told him.

She patted his neck and urged him forward.

They rode with the Way Between.

CHAPTER THIRTY-TWO

. . . . .

The Harraken Sing

She halted on the edge of the ridge, a small figure under an immense sky. The wind tossed her red hair into a torch of blazing copper. The golden horse lowered his head and sniffed the scents of wood smoke and people rising up from the valley basin. His ears flicked, listening to the rumble of thousands of voices: men's tones, low and sonorous; babies wailing and laughing; mothers soothing and chatting; grandmothers quavering and cackling; the toothless mumbles of great-grandfathers; the blustering of young men; the giggles of flirting girls. A river of sound poured like an invisible, inverted waterfall up from the gathered Harraken into the swallowing expanse of sky.

Ari Ara studied the teeming city. The mass of tents and horses, humans and wagons made the Meet of Meets seem paltry by comparison. This far south, down from the higher altitudes of the north, the chill of winter lifted and the air was temperate and pleasant. The Harraken were well prepared; they were wanderers at heart, herders and riders. They dwelled in their villages, but crisscrossed their country, departing for

305

plantings and harvests in Turim City, trading at the Crossroads, driving goats and cattle to pastures, and journeying to visit extended family clans.

Built for a whole season of gatherings, the encampment would stand for the entire winter from solstice to just before equinox. The massive city spread out in organized efficiency. Tents were arranged in concentric rings with spokes of roads leading to a central gathering place. A wide river curved in a long, slowly ambling half-moon on the western edge, providing water for all. To the east, horses grazed in lush pastures watered by irrigation ditches from the mountains. At the base of the plateau, a row of stone houses provided shelter for the healers' hall and storage sheds for the common kitchen. In the middle of the city, at the place where all roads converged, lay an amphitheater carved of stone. Tiers of benches ringed a circular bowl. A small open space in the bottom sat like a stage in a round theater.

Above the bowl, the Old Ones towered.

Sculpted by time and wind, seven pillars of stone formed a ring of sentinels. Tall as hills, their tops brushed the hard blue of the sky. Erosion shaped them into figures and revealed their ancient geology. Mineral layers robed them in tones of ochre, umber, fawn, rust, sand, and slate. Their slowly rotating shadows marked the day's time like an enormous sundial.

It was said that the Harraken gathered in the shadows of the stone pillars because the Old Ones bore witness to time and justice. Beneath their gaze, wrongs would be made right. Tyrants would topple. Tricksters would get their comeuppance. During the Harraken Sing, the people deliberated in a circle, sitting in a vast amphitheater that had been carved by generations of stoneworkers. In this way, each person saw the next, and the Old Ones towered behind them all. No one could forget that choices made in the present had reckonings long into the future.

Ari Ara's gaze ran across the wide, shallow basin to where the horizon line shimmered in the distance, unearthly and mysterious. The Trickster's River, it was called, the place where sky and earth blended and all possibilities emerged. Zyrh danced beneath her, eager. Ari Ara patted his flank.

"Come on," she said, urging him to turn east to where the ridge met the foothills and the land poured down onto the valley like water from a pitcher.

By late afternoon, she had circled through the hills, snaking down the winding switchback trail into the valley basin. She turned Zyrh loose among the other horses, shouldered her packs, and thanked the dusty horse. It was a measure of how far they'd come that, when she bent her forehead in gratitude, he pressed his forelock to her brow. Ari Ara nearly squealed in delight - then he swiped her face with his slobbery tongue.

"Ugh. Gross. I should have known," she muttered, stalking away.

She may have found a way to ride him, but he was still the trickster horse.

The sun streamed from the west, casting long shadows and blinding shards of light through the rows of tents. The city seemed deserted as she entered; all the bustle of midday had vanished. The tent flaps billowed in the sweeps of wind. Curls of banked fires wafted through the slanting light.

Ari Ara tread silently toward the Old Ones, shivering as she stepped into their shadows. As she approached, she heard the murmur of many voices rising from the amphitheater. She slipped up to the shoulder of a stone pillar and peered beyond.

The tiers were packed with people. A ring of white-robed Tala-Rasa stood near the center. Tahkan, Mahteni, and

Moragh sat just behind them, side by side. Kirkan and a pack of warriors lined the opposite slope of the basin. Ari Ara couldn't read the expressions at this distance, but she caught undercurrents of both satisfaction and worry in the clamor of voices. People spoke in loud bursts of pent-up noise. Their arms flung out, gesticulating wildly. Ari Ara heard snatches of words: *warriors, decision, compromise, fairness, makes sense.*

Her dusty, travel-worn tunic and trousers would stand out. The desert dwellers wore robes as dazzling as peacock plumage: scarlet and gold skirts, chartreuse and burgundy vests, tangerine and cerulean embroidered cuffs, boots appliqued with strips of shimmering silks, headdresses and hats with designs stitched into the bands. Ari Ara gaped at the Harraken of the South with their shaved heads and tattooed cheeks. Some of these clans came from as far away as the legendary ocean that tasted of salt. She spotted hill tribe clans from the southeastern spire of the Border Mountains, families related by blood and traditions to the Riderlands Peoples of Mariana. She saw the fierce and rugged western clans who lived on air and song in the empty sands beyond the dragon-ridge mountain range.

Ari Ara was just about to slide into the back rows when Tala sprinted around the other side of the Old One. The songholder nearly bowled her over with a leaping embrace. The youth wore a simple tunic of pure, white silk. A grin exploded across zirs dark-skinned features.

"I knew it!" Tala hissed in an excited undertone. "The other Tala-Rasa said I was crazy, but I knew the wind was whispering about you!"

"What's going on down there?" Ari Ara murmured to Tala, gesturing into the amphitheater.

"Trouble," Tala stated in a worried undertone. "Trouble disguised as compromise."

The warriors had made their case for warriors-rule that very afternoon. Kirkan Mehta led them, promising to uphold harrak and rein in the abuses. He offered a place at the meets for all who trained as warriors, and called for another Harraken Sing to reassess the situation in one year.

"He's the voice of reason," Tala groaned, "and people were swayed by his suggestion. They see Kirkan's Compromise, as they're calling it, as a way to stay protected from the Marianans while avoiding the pitfalls of bad decisions."

"But that's not the same as restoring the village sings!" Ari Ara protested.

"Exactly," Tala answered grimly. "People are even saying that it's a Way Between."

Ari Ara groaned. This wasn't the Way Between. This was settling for an easy option rather than doing what was right.

"So, that's it?" Ari Ara asked. "Is it all decided?"

"It seemed so," Tala admitted, "but a handful of young women refused to agree. They sat down in the speaking circle and won't leave."

They leaned around the shoulder of the Old One. Tala's fingers darted out to touch the stone with a whisper of prayer. Ari Ara followed suit, feeling how the stone had been worn smooth by countless fingers. A flight of stone stairs led through the tiers of benches down to a flat, open space in the center. A group of young women stood in a cluster with crossed arms and determined looks. A ring of white-robed Tala-Rasa sat on the first benches. Behind them to the west, rows of warriors shouted at the women.

"Give up the floor!"

"No!" they protested.

"You've been outvoted!" Gorlion bellowed, cupping his hands to his mouth.

"That is *not* the Harraken Way!" Sarai shouted back. "That is *not* the tradition of the Harraken Sing. Either we all agree or there is no agreement! With the Tala-Rasa as our witness, we refuse to accept this!"

"Be reasonable. Everyone else agrees."

"That does not make it right!" Nalia cried, linking arms with Sarai.

"It's just one year," a warrior argued.

"Anything can happen in a year," Orryn stated bluntly, tall and strong beside the shorter women. "My sister and I were to be married against our will in just a matter of weeks."

"Give up the floor!" a warrior shouted again.

"No!"

"Then we'll drag you out by your hair!"

Ari Ara erupted into action, bursting into a run, leaping the steps three at a time, Tala sprinting at her heels.

"Don't you dare!" she shouted.

She skidded to a halt between the young women and the warriors, glaring back at them, fierce as a small sand lioness. Astonished gasps leapt up throughout the amphitheater at the unexpected arrival of the daughter of the Harrak-Mettahl. Ari Ara tossed her hair out of her eyes.

"No one hurts my friends," she declared boldly. "Not without facing me."

She stared down the warriors one by one, matching their surprised looks with ferocious determination. She didn't care how many Harraken traditions she was breaking - no one was going to drag Sarai or Nalia anywhere, not by the hair, not by the arm, not by anything. She would honor challenge every last warrior if she had to.

"What's she doing here?" someone cried out.

"She doesn't belong here!" a warrior thundered.

Ari Ara stood firm.

"I am a follower of the Way Between," she stated boldly, hands on her hips, ready to thwart their attacks. "We stop violence and end wars. I belong wherever there is danger of either. I belong wherever the Way Between is needed."

A burst of booing and hissing erupted from the warriors, but one of the Tala-Rasa rose suddenly, lifting a hand. Silence fell instantly. The Tala was old, thin as a bone and wrinkled as a newborn. Ze leaned on the young Tala's shoulder as ze slowly stepped around to face Ari Ara. The people held their breath. The silence was absolute, unbroken by even the smallest children.

"And what," the Old Tala asked in a voice as rasping and timeless as the wind, "makes you think the Way Between is needed here?"

Once, Ari Ara would have dropped her eyes from the piercing scrutiny of the elder's gaze. Once, she might have shuffled her feet. Once, she might have sought out her father's support. Not now. Not about this. She stood rooted in her own path, not Harraken, not Marianan, but something else entirely. She was Ari Ara, a girl who was neither this nor that, but everything possible in between.

"The decisions you make today will affect my future, not only as a half-Harraken, but also as a half-Marianan. Warriors make war," she pointed out. With them in charge, warriors-rule made war inevitable. "What will I do on that day? I cannot tear myself in two and fight against myself."

She shook her head.

"I have to work for peace. Then, now, forever. The Way Between is always needed, everywhere, anywhere, but *here and now* more than anywhere else."

She took a deep breath.

"And that's why I've come. I know I wasn't supposed to, but I made a promise and had to keep it. I have a message to deliver."

"Don't listen to her, she's a foreigner!" a warrior shouted.

"Throw her off the speaking circle," another demanded. "She doesn't even have standing!"

"That's true," a third voice called out. It was Gorlion leaping to his feet and pointing at her with a look of dislike. "She's breaking the law!"

His chin jutted out. He glared expectantly at the Tala-Rasa, waiting for them to intervene. Mutters rose up from the others.

"That's right."

"Can't speak until you've sung."

"He has a point."

Ari Ara shifted closer to Tala.

"What are they talking about?" she murmured.

Her friend shot her a concerned look.

"Technically, you're supposed to have sung for the whole assembly of Harraken before you can speak," Tala explained in a worried tone. "It's a rite of passage. All the kids do it, either in solos or with their friends. It's call the Finding Ceremony, where the young find their voices and show the elders they're ready to speak to their people."

The other Tala-Rasa leaned into clusters, heads close together, voices low and hushed, conferring. Ripples of conversation ran around the mass of people lining the tiers of benches. Ari Ara grimaced. She's broken yet another law without meaning to. She could see her father whispering urgently to the Tala-Rasa, his face troubled. They waved him aside with stern looks. Ari Ara heard one speak.

"The law is the law, Tahkan. She must sing before she speaks."

Her stomach flip-flopped as he groaned and buried his face in his hands briefly. When he glanced back up, she saw a familiar look on his face. A steeled expression settled on his features, masking his disappointment in his daughter. She had seen it often in those ill-fated singing lessons he'd tried to give her. Tahkan set his jaw, preparing to weather the shame of listening to his daughter's weak voice in front of the entire Harraken Sing.

Ari Ara pulled her eyes away, unable to bear his disappointment. She saw Moragh, arms crossed over chest, eyes hard, lips drawn into a thin line. A twitch of a smile hung in the corner of her mouth, as if she looked forward to watching Ari Ara fail.

She expects me to make a fool of myself! Ari Ara realized furiously. A surge of defiance flared up in her heart. She wasn't *that* bad of a singer! She'd sung on her own all autumn after they exiled her. She'd heard her voice sounding against the steep sides of the pass, bouncing around the old ruins, humming under her breath in Shulen's stone cottage. Sure, it wasn't as good as Tala's or Mahteni's, but it wasn't the mewing kitten her father had mocked over the summer!

A hot flame of indignation burned in her chest. She spun to the Tala-Rasa.

"I'll sing," she declared. "Here. Now. And then you'll hear my message, right?"

She stared at them, one by one, ignoring her father's strangled gasp and the whispers that whipped around the bowl. The Old Tala met her bold gaze.

"Yes," ze answered, and a gleam of interest shone in zirs eye.

Ari Ara remembered what her father had once said about the Tala-Rasa: they loved seeing history in the making. They couldn't resist a scene that could later be made into a song.

Oh, I'll give them a song alright, she thought, *a new song.*

"Tala," she requested, drawing near to her friend, "clap the rhythm to the *Daughter of the Desert* song."

The youth tossed her a startled look.

"Are you sure?" ze squealed, excited and terrified at once. "What about the invocation - "

"Don't worry about it," Ari Ara retorted quickly, though a wave of anxiety shot through her. It was true, she'd never managed to sing that part of the Outcry right. The invocation required ferocious strength, lungs like a roaring sand lioness, and a touch of that rare magic that made the song-visions dance in the air.

Ari Ara's eyes darted to Mahteni. Her aunt gazed steadily back at her, a faint, knowing smile on her lips. *You can do this,* her green eyes assured her niece. Her birthday message returned to Ari Ara: *There is no right or wrong way to be a Harraken woman. That song is made by those who sing it.*

A jeering catcall sounded from the stands. Someone else hollered at the person to show some harrak. A third individual cupped their hands to their mouth and shouted at her to hurry up. A grandmother snapped at them all to be quiet. A clamor of yells and shouts erupted, flinging back and forth across the bowl.

Under the cacophony, Ari Ara took a deep breath. She reached for the Ancestor Wind the way her father had tried to teach her. She pulled the air into her living lungs, filling her heart with the knowledge of the past, bringing that wisdom to bear on the problems of the present. Then, releasing her breath into the first note of the song, she sent out an answer to the question of the future.

This is a song
born in a dream
in visions not yet seen
of possibilities shining
on horizon's edge
and whispers on the breath
of the wind.

No one heard her at first. The noise of the arguments boomed and crashed like a flashflood exploding down a slot canyon, but her voice held steady. The notes rang true and clear. She carried the chords without wavering. The hours spent singing alone at the Way Station had strengthened her. Exiled from exile, the silence gave her a chance to hear her own voice. Day after day, humming to herself, singing her favorite melodies, letting Shireen's song burst out of her heart and echo across the steep mountainsides, she'd found the space to make mistakes and learn from them. Away from her father's impatient pressures, she'd been able to fail and try again. Without Tala at her elbow, she'd taught herself the new song, making it her own, learning it her own way, braiding its melodies into her own intonations.

When she sang, it was her voice: bold, defiant, hopeful, and sincere. Ari Ara sang with passion more than perfection, but her spirit shone in the notes. Her honesty brimmed in the chords. This was the voice that had sung Atta to her missing friend, the voice that had blended all of her cultures into the return-to-life chant that guided Emir back to her, the voice that sang the Trickster's Song as she rode southward. She'd come a long way with this voice . . . and now, the sound leapt out of her into the ears of the waiting Harraken.

She saw Tahkan's eyes widen, hearing her despite the commotion. His mouth stretched from a surprised oval into a broad grin. He jumped up out of his seat and spun to the crowd, flapping his arms to get them to be quiet. As Tala clapped the tempo, Sarai joined in. Their hands flew, drumming the rhythm of hoof beats and pounding hearts, the pattern of movement and change. Nalia noticed and took it up, then Orryn and the others picked up the clapping. The crowd slowly quieted. Eyes turned toward them, sharp and expectant. Tala nudged Ari Ara into the very center of the speaking floor, where the sound leapt like magic and the Old Ones amplified her song.

History circles in the Old Ones' shadows,
the past runs into the present,
the future unfolds in the footsteps of now,
descendants and ancestors live inside us.
Old stories revive
in times when they're needed,
legends return to life.
The Women of the Outcry,
rise from forgetting,
and rising,
they answer our call.

The clapping intensified. The sense of anticipation built, taut and tense. This was the part where the song called down the ancestors, invoking the presence of legends. Ari Ara swallowed and took a deep breath. This was it. Either she could call the wind . . . or not. Either the ancestors would listen to her and acknowledge her cry . . . or not. Either she was her father's daughter . . . or not.

Then, suddenly, absolutely, Ari Ara knew that she couldn't do it. She couldn't invoke the song-visions. She wasn't strong enough. Her heart skipped a beat then crashed into the rumbling hoof-beat rhythm. Ari Ara's gaze leapt wildly from one woman to the next. Sarai, Nalia, and Orryn all watched her with trusting eyes; they relied on her to do this, to help them, to be the heroine they needed. Ari Ara's chest constricted in panic. She couldn't do it. She wasn't strong enough on her own . . . she looked away and found Tala's eyes.

Then again, she thought, a memory returning to her, *a desert heroine isn't strong on her own.*

Harraken heroes were people who inspired others to do the right thing, together.

Ari Ara whirled to Nalia.

"Sing the invocation of the ancestors in the Outcry, the part that calls Farrah down from the wind. Ask her to come stand by your side."

Nalia startled, but nodded. Her clear young voice cracked through the stadium, chanting the invocation of an ancestress who, like her, refused to be sold into marriage against her will.

"Orryn!" Ari Ara said, darting between the huddle of clapping girls to the tall, dark-skinned woman. "Call upon Annoush!"

Orryn's strong alto leapt to the Ancestor Wind, crying out to the woman who had so bravely flung herself in front of blows meant for another.

"Sarai!" Ari Ara called, spinning to the small, defiant girl's side. "Call Shireen to us."

The feisty youth jumped to the task, singing out to the spirit of the ancestress who started the village sings.

One by one, Ari Ara asked the women to join their voices together in the weaving harmonies that invoked the presence of the women who had come before. Complex, startling, eerie and haunting, the song wove and dove. The sound swooped like a flock of birds, rising and falling, calling out to the ancestors that rode in the wind.

Only one more part was needed.

Ari Ara closed her eyes. In a breath of prayer, under the voices of the others, she found the Way Between them all, adding the thread of subtle power that made visions dance on the air. She heard startled murmurs rising from the listening Harraken. Gasps of breath swept the bowl. People stirred, shifting in their seats as they turned to look around. Ari Ara didn't dare take a glimpse. She remained focused on the song, pulling the silvery threads of possibility out of the complex harmonies of the other women.

"Open your eyes," Tala whispered in her ear. "Look what you have done."

Fearing the worst, Ari Ara's eyes flew open. For a second, the song faltered in her throat. She scrambled to pick it up again. She glanced at Mahteni. Her aunt's mouth was closed, though a smile stretched wide on her lips. She looked at her father: Tahkan's face was equally still. His eyes were fixed, like everyone else's, on something hovering above the stands of people.

Ari Ara's eyes swept up to the gold-infused sky. She swiveled in an astonished circle. Bold as rainbows, shining with light and radiance, larger than anything she'd ever seen, song-visions of the Women of the Outcry hung in the air over the Harraken. Towering, tremendous, rippling with ancient power, the women were woven out of sunset and horizon lines, dust and song, hopes and longings, truth, myths, and legends. Farrah, Shireen, Mirka, Karrine, Annoush, and Tala-Oon. They rose as tall as the Old Ones behind them, bestowing their blessing on the young, red-haired singer, declaring with their presence that the women in the speaking circle followed in their footsteps.

We are true Daughters of the Desert, their towering figures proclaimed, *and so are the women who called us.*

Ari Ara's throat tightened over awe and emotion. Her hand pressed tight to her madly beating heart. A ripple of laughter and wonder rumbled through her song. Alone, she could never have called the song-visions. Alone, she did not have enough strength to lift the invocation of the Outcry. But, with the other women pouring their hearts and voices into the song together, she did not have to be loud. She did not have to be fierce. She did not have to be strong all on her own. She was enough. Her voice was enough. In true desert style, her strength was enough when combined with others'. Ari Ara lifted her head proudly. She sang to the ancestors shining in the light. She sang to the young women standing boldly beside her. She sang to the Tala-Rasa and the thousands of Harraken. She sang to her aunts and her father and the wind. She sang with harrak and she sang from her heart. She had found her place in the Song.

CHAPTER THIRTY-THREE

· · · · ·

Walking the Fire

An astonished quiet hung in the air as the last strains of the song settled. The golden hues of evening poured in beams of light between the Old Ones. No one dared to speak. No one wanted to break the spell. Ari Ara was the first to talk, and she spoke gently, the way a mother wakes her child from a deep sleep.

"I came to the Harraken Sing to honor a promise. I came to deliver a message."

She paused and looked to the Tala-Rasa for permission to continue. The Old Tala eyed her thoughtfully, and then nodded for her to go on.

"Shulen, whom you call the Butcher, says to tell you," she had to pause to wait as the Tala-Rasa quieted the gasps at the sound of their enemy's name, "that the Marianans have much to learn from the wisdom of the Harraken."

A flurry of intrigued murmurs rose up at the words.

"In Mariana, thirteen people make the decisions for everyone else. Sometimes, even fewer. And, because the Marianans silence so many voices from their song," she emphasized the ritual phrase, even though it did not translate to riverlands customs, "great harm has come to their people and to yours."

She told them about Shulen's role in launching the War of Retribution. She related how his one voice had tipped the scales in favor of war. She spoke of how that decision haunted him still. Then she paused to let the message sink in. The Harraken nodded gravely; they understood the cost of that choice. Rivers of blood had spilled. Their people had been unjustly attacked. Thousands of lives had been lost. She looked around at all the faces, the young, the old, the mothers and fathers, the herders and riders, the crafters and warriors.

"The Harraken have a powerful tradition in the village sings - one that the Marianans could learn a lot from - but this tradition is in danger of being lost. Please," she urged, "don't abandon the village sings. The Marianans have already followed the path that you are considering walking down. The voices lost from their song led to the deaths of your people and theirs."

She pivoted to face the young Tala.

"Tala once told me that everyone's voice strengthens the Harraken Song, from a baby's first wail to an elder's last exhale. It's not just warriors, and not just women that make the Harraken Song strong. It is everyone."

Ari Ara gestured to the young women standing behind her.

"All summer long, my friends have stood up, over and over, to remind you of this truth. They have been willing to give up everything except harrak: their villages, families, children, marriages, safety, even their lives. And they've done so without striking the ones they love, without causing harm to any Harraken, without even fighting in honor challenges."

Ari Ara turned to the Old Tala.

"You asked me why I thought the Way Between was

needed here . . . but perhaps you should ask these women. It is they who have used it with courage and love to try to restore the honor of their people, and to remind you that the Harraken Song is not complete without everyone's voices."

A quiet met her words. For a long moment, it hung, thick and heavy. Then, into the silence, the Honor Cry leapt, startling everyone with its ferocious sound. Heads swiveled as it wheeled around the circle like a soaring bird. Shock fell across faces as they realized its source: Moragh Shirar. The warrior woman lifted the Honor Cry for her niece. Emotion strained the face of the toughened warrior. No one could believe their eyes when Moragh Shirar's gloved hand brushed aside the tears brimming in her eyes.

"From the mouth of this girl comes a truth I have long felt and had no words to say. My wife died for the silence of women's voices, for the silencing of my own when Sorrin's brother and mine let her go into battle. Now, I hear that many of us died because of the silencing of the Marianan mothers and fathers when the nobles chose to wage war."

Moragh's harsh voice cracked painfully over grief. To admit these words was hard for her. She could strike their enemies with word and sword. She battled for her people with equal ferocity to anyone, male or female. She feared no man and would fight anyone to defend her harrak. But, to publically admit her weaknesses and heartaches pressed her to the limits of her courage.

"Courage is a strange thing," she confessed. "I dared to stand up to our own warriors with my sword; I was willing to kill you all before I let my sisters be ground under your heels." Moragh paused. Her eyes turned to the cluster of young women who had refused to accept warriors-rule. "But I did not have the courage to *fight* like these young women, to put aside weapons and stand before you again and again, unarmed and vulnerable, with truth and love, with open arms and an offer to restore honor. These women's respect for their people never once wavered, not even when they were mocked and beaten and driven away."

Moragh turned to her Black Ravens who listened with bated breaths.

"A song without their voices is not a song I am willing to fight for. It is not a song I am willing to let our sons and daughters die for. I withdraw my support for Kirkan's Compromise and join my sisters in calling for the restoration of the village sings. The Harraken Song must be made whole."

A thousand gasps alighted like a flock of birds. Moragh stepped beyond the Tala-Rasa and stood next to Ari Ara. She held out her hand, palm up.

"I owe you an apology, perhaps," she said to her niece in a quiet voice. "I set a druach for you, thinking you would fail. I did not think you would find the strength to uplift the strength of others. But you did. I was wrong. And, I offer the apology I owe you."

Ari Ara slid her hand over Moragh's.

"You owe me nothing not owed in return," she answered, choking up a bit on the words.

Ari Ara's speech shifted the direction of the Harraken Sing. Moragh's unexpected declaration turned the tide from bitter arguments to honest discussions. As the sunset burst across the sky, a Black Raven rose to claim the speaking spot, lifting a lament for the lives lost in war and appealing to the warriors, one and all, to recognize that sometimes the best way of protecting one's people was letting other voices be heard alongside one's own. A mother spoke next, staring her husband in the eyes to remind the men that it was a shared song, an equal song, which was being sought. There was room for the men's and warriors' voices in this Song. A man from the Crossroads told his tale of crossing through the Atta Song like a gate, and the healing that he had found on the other side. A young warrior swore he would not grovel with the Atta Song when he'd done nothing wrong. Mahteni spoke, suggesting that perhaps the Atta Song was not necessary for everyone. One of the young women shouted down that she'd never speak to her father again if he didn't sing Atta. Just as the discussion began to fall apart into arguments, the Old Tala rose and held up zirs hands.

"The Atta Song is traditionally a song of healing, sung between those who wish to reconcile. I recommend that it remain a song of voluntary reconciliation, but no one may enter a home where an unsung Atta Song has been requested but not yet sung."

Approval met the elder's words and the Tala-Rasa steered the conversation back towards the subject of village sings and warriors meets. Dusk surrendered to darkness. Tall braziers were lit, throwing gleams of orange and gold firelight upon the faces of the Old Ones. The shadows carved the people into sculptures of myth and legend. The night swirled overhead, thick with stars. The Harraken Sing continued, back and forth like waves, listening and speaking. Ari Ara found herself turning the stone Throw-the-Bones had given her over and over in her hands.

"That's what we're doing here," Moragh murmured to her, pointing to the stone in her hand, "turning the matter over and over, examining it from all angles."

Ari Ara blinked and looked up at her ferocious aunt. Moragh smiled briefly then turned her attention back to the speaker. A small smile grew on Ari Ara's face as she sensed who her aunt could be as a friend, not just a force of nature.

The discussion spun around and around the circle, one person standing after another, adding their piece of the truth. At last, the thirteen Tala-Rasa rose. The oldest spoke.

"We have heard what the day has brought. Are we ready to sing together?"

A quiet fell. Eyes darted from one face to the next, trying to sense if there was agreement among the people. Tahkan scanned the warriors' faces, noticing the closed and wary expressions and tight jaws. He lifted his hand to request a moment's time to speak. The Tala-Rasa nodded.

Tahkan Shirar stepped forward. His voice spoke, slow and measured, weighted by all that he had heard today. He addressed the warriors.

"All of you are my brothers, and none more so than Kirkan Mehta, my brother by friendship and my brother-by-marriage. I do not think we can sing together - "

A murmur of consternation swept the circle.

" - unless one more thing is said," Tahkan stated, holding his hands up to still the reactions. "There are some - my sister included - who have said he is without harrak."

An uneasy quiet stirred at those words. Kirkan's face was unreadable, as motionless as carved stone.

"But," Tahkan went on, "I say Kirkan Mehta's harrak is equal to any of ours, and greater than many I know."

Kirkan's head snapped up at those words. The hush deepened.

"Kirkan is a man of great honor. He did not push for warriors-rule for petty reasons, but for reasons of protection and concern. I know him as a Harraken rich in harrak, a true leader of warriors, a protector who loves his people deeply. He is willing to stare down dangers without flinching, to charge into death's reach without hesitating, to do difficult tasks without faltering."

Tahkan's eyes caught and held Kirkan's.

"He is a man who will walk through fire to protect his people. That is why I know he has the strength to be the first to change, and the first to lead the warriors through this conflict.

"I ask you, Kirkan, to help your Harrak-Mettahl restore our people's harrak, our warriors' harrak, our children and women's harrak by helping us restore the village sings. We cannot do it properly without you and the warriors. It takes all of us, together, singing in one voice, a voice made of every Harraken, a voice with no one missing . . . not one woman, not one warrior. Until this happens, we are all beggars of harrak, impoverished in our honor. And the poorest among us is me, your friend, brother, and Harrak-Mettahl, for I will have failed at my duty to my people."

Tahkan Shirar, a man who could roar down a sand lioness, stood gentle as a desert hare before his friend. He who could blaze brighter than the sun, showed his human frailty before his people. He released his pride and held out his dignity. His weathered hands stretched out to Kirkan.

"I am asking for your help," Tahkan said quietly. "We need someone, a man, a warrior, who is strong enough to walk through the fire of this moment, strong enough to be the first to change. I believe that man is you, Kirkan Mehta."

Ari Ara could hardly breathe. Her hands clenched together, white-knuckled. Moragh's fingers gripped her arm hard. Mahteni stilled, taut and tense, on her other side. The moment stretched long and uncertain. Kirkan stood like a statue. Tala's head shook. Tahkan's shoulders slumped.

Suddenly, Moragh rose, her voice growling and hissing over the words of a song.

Walk the fire, Kirkan,
walk the fire of warriors-making,
walk the fire that makes men, men,
and the fire of honor-making.

Her voice quavered and softened, and all at once, Ari Ara saw the pair as the friends they must once have been. She saw the echoes of their younger selves, their courage and undaunted hope. In the scars of time and lines of age, the core of their hearts still reached toward each other. Moragh's face shone with grief and beauty as she sang to him.

Walk the fire to me, my friend,
walk the fire through what we've lost,
walk the fire to me, my brother,
walk the fire to what might come.

Kirkan shivered and his stony stillness cracked. He shifted. No one breathed. He moved from his seat. No one dared to blink. He stepped down from the tiers. The torches in the braziers gleamed behind him. He walked in a river of rippling shadows and flooding gold. One hand reached out to Tahkan. The other stretched to Moragh. The two Shirar's lurched forward . . .

. . . and the circle erupted into song.

People leapt from their seats, laughing and hugging and crying. Only the sheer number of voices held the Harraken Song aloft over the choked up throats and surging emotions.

Walk the fire, they sang for Kirkan, for Moragh, for the men and women, for all of them.

Walk the fire, they sang to each other, a people made only of honor.

Walk the fire, they sang together, for the children, the elders, the couples and families, and for the future they had won.

EPILOGUE

. . . . .

The Ancestor Wind strode across the sky, kicking the tops of clouds and trailing its fingers along the ridges of the desert lands. It whistled a jaunty tune through its wintery teeth. Spring was on its way. The scent of snowmelt clung to the air. The days steadily lengthened. The Harraken Sing had ended. The wind had come to bless the people's departure.

The Ancestor Wind spiraled slowly above the Old Ones, telling them stories of distant places and listening to their secrets. It eddied and ambled, examining the changes since its last visit. Many unusual conversations had taken place beneath the Old Ones' broad shadows this winter. The strength of the thousands of voices singing had sent pebbles showering from their sides. The wind sniffed the stones like a curious dog inspecting old friends. The scent of wood smoke and people clung to the crumbling rocks. The Old Ones held memories of speeches and song. For months, the vast bowl of the circle had cradled the people through change and truth-telling, tears and laughter, arguments and reconciliation. They were a different people than the bitterly divided thousands who had come at the Dark Moon.

The wind pounced down from the Old Ones, prowling among the stone benches collecting hints of stories: the salty traces of brushed away tears, sweaty palm prints, the scents of warriors' leather, the brush of fine silks. There'd been weddings and separation songs sung; Atta Songs issued and received, complaints settled before the Tala-Rasa, babies named, and elders mourned. The voices - young and old; male, female, and neither; warriors and non-warriors - had lifted up in all their beautiful complexity. They sang in different keys, different harmonies and different words, but the song they sent out to all directions was a shared song. Soon, the Old Ones would settle into long months of silence and stillness as the Harraken Sing dispersed . . . but never truly ended.

Like seeds flung to the wind, the decisions of the Harraken Sing would land in villages and strongholds, herders' encampments and crafters' markets. They would take root in hearts and minds, actions and deeds, until the people all returned to the Old Ones the following year, grown and changed . . . ready to grow and change again.

The last time it had visited the Old Ones, the Ancestor Wind had come to hear a specific song, a long-awaited song, a song the ancestors had wanted to hear since time immemorial. Just after solstice, in the watery light of the returning sun, the Harraken people had spent long hours discussing the case of Shulen the Butcher. The Ancestor Wind had heard it all, listening as it slowly circled above the Old Ones, stilling and idling, lingering from curiosity. The wind had work to do, snowcaps to fling into the sky, messenger hawks to tickle and harry, storm clouds to herd across the plains, ancestor spirits to collect from tired old bodies, advice to whisper in descendants' ears . . . but the story of Shulen the Butcher interested the wind, and the ancestors it carried who had been lost in the war.

Moragh Shirar claimed Shulen owed her blood debt. Her sister and brother, however, claimed his help ending the Water Exchange cancelled out what was owed. Moragh Shirar and Kirkan Mehta objected; Sorrin's life could not be traded for any other. Harsh words and bitter truths had been flung back and forth across the circle; everyone had an opinion. The Marianan warrior's fate was weighed on the many-sided scales of Harraken judgment, but no decision could be reached. Then the red-haired girl had whispered in her warrior-aunt's ear. The two murmured, mulling on her suggestion like a stone turned in the palm of their hands. Moragh spoke to her brother-by-marriage. They whispered, forehead to forehead. Kirkan's hand wiped his eyes. His lips trembled. He nodded.

Moragh Shirar straightened and astonished everyone.

"We will release the demand for a blood duel if Shulen the Butcher will sing the Atta Song for my wife."

The Ancestor Wind sped the black messenger hawk on its way to deliver the summons to Alaren's Way Station. When the two Marianan warriors - the young one and the old - rode south, it blew at their backs the whole way. It wanted to hear Shulen sing the Atta Song, the first warrior - Marianan or Harraken - ever to do so for an enemy's death. The Ancestor Wind had crouched down in the emptied bowl; the Harraken had been sent away from this first meeting, but the ancestor spirits gathered to bear witness.

Moragh and Kirkan sat on one side of the circle. Mahteni and Tahkan sat next to them. Emir and Shulen sat on the other side. Ari Ara completed the ring. Before Atta could be sung, truths had to be spoken. The conversation was hard. There were wounds that never healed fully, scars that gripped the soul like twisted skin, clenched patterns of sorrow that refused to release. Two Tala-Rasa, the oldest and youngest, guided the discussion as deep-held pain rose to the surface and broke loose: the rage at losing a loved one, the shame carried by the killer, the blame in many directions, the agony of loss, the wracking grief that haunted all those involved. But, Shulen listened with humility. Moragh gripped her fury under tight control. Mahteni stood ready to counter her battle madness if it broke loose. Emir and Ari Ara were prepared to intervene if tempers turned into attacks.

Moragh spoke long and low, calling Sorrin's spirit down from the Ancestor Wind. She hovered in the center of the circle, a young woman built like her brother, stocky, strong, and brave. Her story was told again from childhood until the day she died. Tahkan and Kirkan apologized to Moragh for ignoring her concerns, and for sending her beloved to her death.

Then Moragh Shirar's red-rimmed eyes gripped Shulen's. It was the old warrior's turn to speak. Shulen began quietly, haltingly, in a Harrak-Tala that rang with truth. He had known the young woman. In times of peace, when he and the Shirars were young, he had offered trainings to Moragh's wife. He had encouraged her to follow the warrior's path, never considering the day they would meet on the battlefield. War had slammed them together at full charge. At the end of a day that bled red from dawn until dusk, when terror and battle rage blinded them both, the deathblow was struck before their eyes ever met.

Everyone wept, even Shulen, and the sight of those tears on the stern warrior's face did more to ease Moragh's grief than any of his words. The woman's death still haunted him in nightmares.

"But, there are no excuses," Shulen said harshly, "and there is no way to make this right."

But Moragh disagreed.

"I have heard," she said in a voice that rasped like stone

against stone, as if she dragged the words out of an unfathomable buried depth, "that you have considered renouncing the Warrior's Way in favor of the Way Between."

She studied him, her head thrown back, and her eyes flashing green. She had spent many long nights contemplating this moment. She knew what she wished to say.

"You cannot bring my beloved back, but you can end the cycle of your violence."

Ari Ara heard the wind billow in surprise. The ancestors of a thousand generations stirred and stilled, listening. The spirits of warriors killed in battle held their breaths.

"Renounce the ways of violence and swear by the Way Between," Moragh demanded, her eyes hot and bright, "and I will count my blood debt paid in the lives you spare from this day forth."

At that, Shulen's stony face cracked like a boulder split by the pressures of an underground spring. A great weight lifted off him. Relief swept through him. He wept openly. Moragh offered him an unexpected healing. She demanded that he travel the path he had long yearned to walk. She gave him a way to leave the ways of warriors behind. He agreed.

Kirkan made a second demand.

"I want Atta for our people," he said in a choked voice. "I want you to sing the Atta Song for your part in launching the War of Retribution, and for the deaths of our people under your sword."

So the small family's circle around Shulen's blood debt triggered a larger reaction. Exiled as he was, Shulen could not issue an official apology on behalf of the Marianans, but he could sing Atta personally. That evening, in the amphitheater of the Harraken Sing, Shulen stood in the center of the circle, surrounded by narrowed eyes and suspicious faces. He sang Atta for the Shirars and for all the Harraken. He sang without expectation of being answered. He walked through the fire of that moment, voicing hard truths and sincere sorrows about the war. He acknowledged his parts in that vast tragedy. Then Shulen the Butcher renounced the Warrior's Way, once and for all, forever and for always. He unbuckled his sword and laid it at the feet of Moragh Shirar. He stood unguarded and unarmed in the midst of his former enemies.

Ari Ara felt the shivers of the ancestors. She heard their excited whispering in the wind. She sensed Alaren's spirit watching them through the expanse of time. Shulen had come full circle, putting his weapons aside to follow only the Way Between. He was one man surrounded by thousands, many of them warriors bearing arms, but he looked at the youths, Emir Miresh, the young Tala, and Ari Ara most of all. He saw the shine in their eyes, the wild hope and impossible daring. After centuries of violence and war, one by one, person after person, peace was being forged.

One song ran into the next. Dark nights gave way to bright dawns. The time came to depart and disperse. One by one, the tents of the Harraken Sing came down. The wagons packed up. The horses were called in from the fields. The people made ready to ride. Thousands headed to Turim City to prepare for spring planting. Others departed for distant corners of the desert to carry out the decisions of the Harraken Sing. Everywhere they went, the village sings would rise up around the night fires like stars shining across the dark sky. Kirkan led the warriors in a great effort, one that would enshrine his name in the Ancestor Song: the effort to restore lost honor among the people, to right the wrongs, to sing Atta with courage until the wounds healed. Moragh and the Black Ravens rode with them. Their task was to ensure that the messages of the Harraken

Sing became lived realities in the villages, that the Atta Song was sung where needed, and that the promised changes came true.

The Ancestor Wind searched the crowds, winding through legs like a cat, knocking caps off heads, pulling blankets off horses' backs, searching for one rider in particular. It wound around the shoulders of Shulen and Emir. It whistled in the ears of Tahkan and Mahteni. It flipped Moragh's hat off her head, but allowed Kirkan to catch it and hand it back to her. The Ancestor Wind tried to knock the young Tala off zirs feet, but the old Tala chided the wind for its bad manners.

At last, the Ancestor Wind found the girl perched on top of a white-gold horse. Zyrh pawed the dust near the long winding road leading north. The creature paced and pranced, as eager to gallop and ride as the girl waiting on his back. Ari Ara had grown long of limb and stout of heart, balanced in caution and courage. She had won her druach against all odds and restored the women's voices to the Harraken Song. The scent of the dry heat and desert dust clung to her. The sun had baked into her skin. Her copper hair shone with gold streaks. She sat easily on top of the horse. The Ancestor Wind rippled with delight: she had grown into the desert at last.

The wind swept up to scour the faces of the Harraken riders. They laughed and waved, calling out to Ari Ara as they passed. She was one of them, this girl named *not this, not that, but everything possible in between.* The wind chuckled to itself and tousled her hair, pleased with the changes it sensed.

Ari Ara hummed a jaunty, bold little tune. It was the song the times had been singing, humming under its breath all year. The words had been emerging from the summer, autumn, winter . . . and this spring it would burst into bloom. It was the song of people who didn't fit into the world they were given . . .

so they set out to change the whole world, together. It was a song that once lived only in dreams and imaginings. It was a song born in the hearts of many. It was a song that grew into reality as the people lived the story into existence, together.

As Ari Ara sang, the Ancestor Wind carried the breath of the past into her lungs and wove her heartbeat into the story of the times. The red-haired girl sat straight and proud on the golden horse. She sang out her answer to the question of the future. The wind pealed with laughter and swept up to the heights. She felt the touch of its blessing and smiled.

Then she turned and rode with the wind.

The End

AUTHOR'S NOTE

At its heart, *Desert Song* is a story about finding your voice. It's a story about finding the courage to speak when others try to silence you. It's a story about who is listened to in our societies, and who is ignored. It's about what happens to our cultures when a few people make all the decisions for everyone else.

Desert Song is about a culture at a tipping point. As Ari Ara heads into the desert, political tensions and cultural shifts have dislodged the traditional equality between men and women. Military rule is spreading from one region to the next. Our real world is full of cultures (including our own) that are only just emerging from centuries of patriarchy. In *Desert Song*, I wanted to explore how women could stop the slide into a patriarchal society. What are the moments where we sense that we are standing at a precipice or at a crossroads? How do we step back from a dangerous path? How do we assert, at the very moment that counts, that everyone has a right to exist and shape our society on equal footing?

The tension between war cultures, gender equality, and how decisions are made plays out in hundreds of different ways, not just in human history, but also currently all over the world. There are places where equal access to military service offers a certain kind of empowerment. There are other places where decades of military rule and war have eroded women's rights and freedoms. In the end, a novel like *Desert Song* offers questions instead of solid answers. These questions help us think critically about our society. Is there a connection between war and women's rights? What is it? How does the power of the military affect how our decisions are made? Whose voices are listened to in our society? Who gets ignored and why?

It seems to me that these questions - and questions of how to ensure equality, justice, peace, and democracy - are some of the most important questions humanity has yet to answer. That's why I explored them in *Desert Song*.

The inspiration for this book came from archaeology. Once upon a time, according to the studies, there was a time before violence and war. Doesn't that sound like a fairy tale? (A Disney version, not a Grimm's fairy tale.) It's true, however. Archaeological digs show that ancient societies across Europe had no signs of blunt trauma wounds and no weapons of war. Around 4,000 BCE, an invasion of sun-worshipping, horse-riding warriors took over, and everything changed. They brought violence. They brought male domination and patriarchy. They brought inequality and the notion that some people would be rich, while others would be poor. These are all things archaeologists suspect from their examination of the burial sites and buried ruins of these cultures.

I found it interesting that violence, patriarchy, and inequality all literally "rode in on the same horse". Flash-forward six thousand years and people today are still struggling with these very same entwined issues. Few of us see the ways these three issues are tangled together throughout human history - it's certainly not taught in schools - and as we emerge from the wreckage of patriarchy, it's important to be aware of our history so we don't wind up repeating it with a "women's empowerment" variation.

Women warriors and teen girl assassins are in vogue right now. But we have to ask: is it really an achievement for women to succeed in the structures and systems built by patriarchy, domination, racism, classism, and exploitation? Some say yes. Others say no; it's the dismantlement of these systems (and their replacement with fair and just practices and policies) that represent the incorporation of equality - gender or otherwise - into our world.

I am always interested in the stories a culture tells - myths, fables, urban legends, movies, bestselling novels, folk tales - and the reasons we tell them. Right now, the warrior woman archetype seems to be everywhere. Wonder Woman, the new Captain Marvel movie, Xena the Warrior Princess, Catniss Everdeen in the *Hunger Games*, Rey in the new Star Wars movies, Alita Battle Angel, Tris Prior in the *Divergent* series ... I could go on. Everywhere I look, movies and books are churning out yet another teen girl assassin or woman soldier. Many people find these stories empowering. I find myself questioning *why* we're telling so many of these stories right now.

In the United States, there is a concerted effort to get more women involved in the military. The Pentagon is trying to figure out how to expand the military draft to women. Recent articles have celebrated the rise of women to the top positions in the military-industrial complex. The RAND corporation has spent a lot of time trying to figure out how to train teenage girls to become war commanders. (It's a lot like the scene in *The Lost Heir*, where the Marianan nobles, including the girls, train to wage war through the War Game.) Is it any coincidence that popular movies increasingly feature women warriors, teenage girl assassins and fighters, and women in the military?

These movies claim to be about female empowerment, but we have to challenge the notion that anyone's power can be found through violence and war. In epic stories and movies, the warrior is always on the side of justice. In real life, that's rarely the case. War is complicated. There are few clear-cut good guys and bad guys. Too often, evil is defined as "the person trying to kill us" without any analysis of the fact that they're trying to kill us because we're trying to kill them. We are their definition of "evil" and vice versa. If we're not careful, finding our empowerment through violence or the military will turn us into the oppressors of others.

The woman warrior archetype is a powerful one. I love her, honestly. I grew up running around the backyard swinging a stick as a sword. The warrior woman archetype has much to offer us in our world. She teaches us courage, ferocity, a sense of taking action for justice, power, strength, and skill. What we need to question is if violence is the only - or best - tool for us as we "fight" for what's right. My friend Sherri Mitchell - Weh'na Ha'mu' Kwasset says that in her Penobscot Indigenous culture the warrior is not defined by violence. The warrior is someone who is willing to stand between a danger and their loved ones. Can a warrior be someone who is nonviolent? Mohandas K. Gandhi and Dr. Martin Luther King, Jr. thought so. Badshah Khan, a friend of Gandhi's who built an 80,000-person nonviolent peace army thought so.

It is my belief that the violent warrior archetype did not *define* courage and ferocity for humanity, he/she/they *borrowed* those qualities from other sources. (Perhaps starting in 4,000 BCE when war cultures took over Europe through conquest.) Now, it's time to reclaim courage and ferocity from war and violence. The warrior archetype can be someone in our society who dares to challenge and transform a danger. They can be "armed" with nonviolent action, peacebuilding, restorative justice, and conflict transformation skills.

Desert Song is a novel that takes risks. It explores complex ideas. Like its characters Tala and Ari Ara, it is neither this nor that. It doesn't fit into neat little boxes or black-and-white frameworks. It doesn't offer easy answers. Instead, it makes us ask important questions. It helps us see our world in new ways. It helps us think about our lives differently. To me, this is exactly what a good novel should do. I hope you enjoy the adventure - both on and off the page!

Thank you for reading,
Rivera Sun

ACKNOWLEDGEMENTS

A novel is shaped by many hands. I would like to honor a few who have gifted this book with their wisdom, strength, sensitivity, and care.

To my team of beta-readers: thank you. Jenny Bird, Cindy Reinhardt, and Nancy Troeger, you have kept this novel from fatal missteps and awkward moments. Your wisdom and compassion can be felt on every page.

My gratitude also goes out to the numerous musicians and singers who have inspired me to hear the songs in this book. Special thanks to Ysaye M. Barnwell for teaching me, years ago, that beyond rockstars, communities use song to shape culture and resistance, change and endurance.

This novel would not have been possible without the work of archaeologist Marija Gimbutas. Her research made me think about the dynamics between war cultures and women's rights, democracies and military rule. Thank you to the Taos Public Library for including her books in their collection. In a similar vein, I wish to thank the many feminists - of all genders - who strive for gender equality, past, present, and future. The women who organized and invited me to participate in the Entrepreneurial Feminist Forum have had a deep impact on me, particularly Lex Schroeder, Petra Kassun-Mutch, and C.V. Harquail. The work and writings of Starhark have given me language and courage to weave these themes into novels. The list of feminists is too long to name here, but my appreciation goes out to them all.

Special thanks to everyone who is working at the intersection of peace and women's rights, particularly Medea Benjamin, Jodie Evans, and Code Pink. In a time when the violent women warrior archetype is being used to prop up the war machine, it takes courage to challenge that form of female empowerment.

I wish to also thank my gender non-conforming and transgender friends. You have taught me to think outside the boxes and craft characters who also do so. To the young ones defying labels, my respect goes out to you. You are the ones who inspired Tala's character - you know who you are.

This novel is dedicated to my mother, a strong woman who showed me what it looks like to stand tall in our beauty and power. Without her living example, I would not be who I am today. Thank you, Mama.

Deep thanks goes to my partner, Dariel Garner, who walks along this writing path with me, each step of the way. The list of everything he does to help my novels come into existence would fill its own book. Thank you!

Lastly, this novel would not have existed without the high desert of New Mexico. This vast being, truly a network of ecosystems, has taught me that deserts are more than sand and dust. It has my deep respect.

To all the people, young and old, of all genders, who read this book: thank you for your curiosity and questions, for your open minds and wild hearts. May you find your voice . . . and may we all listen to your song.

With gratitude,
Rivera Sun

ABOUT THE AUTHOR

Rivera Sun is the author of *The Way Between, The Lost Heir, The Dandelion Insurrection* and other novels, as well as theatrical plays, a study guide to nonviolent action, three volumes of poetry, and numerous articles. She has red hair, a twin sister, and a fondness for esoteric mystics. She went to Bennington College to study writing as a Harcourt Scholar and graduated with a degree in dance. She lives in an earthship house in New Mexico, where she writes essays and novels. She is a trainer in strategy for nonviolent movements and an activist. Rivera has been an aerial dancer, a bike messenger, and a gung-fu style tea server. Everything else about her - except her writing - is perfectly ordinary.

Rivera Sun also loves hearing from her readers:
Email: info@riverasun.com
Facebook: Rivera Sun
Twitter: @RiveraSunAuthor
Website: www.riverasun.com

Read all of Ari Ara's adventures! Each novel stands on its own and can be read in order or separately.

Praise for *The Way Between*
Book One of the Ari Ara Series
by Rivera Sun

Between flight and fight lies a mysterious third path called *The Way Between,* and young shepherdess and orphan Ari Ara must master it ... before war destroys everything she loves! She begins training as the apprentice of the great warrior Shulen, and enters a world of warriors and secrets, swords and magic, friendship and mystery. She uncovers forbidden prophecies, searches for the lost heir to two thrones, and chases the elusive forest-dwelling Fanten to unravel their hidden knowledge. Full of twists and turns and surprises, *The Way Between* is bound to carve out a niche on your bookshelves and a place in your heart!

"This novel should be read aloud to everyone, by everyone, from childhood onward. Rivera Sun writes in a style as magical as Tolkien and as authentic as Twain."
- Tom Hastings, Director of PeaceVoice

"Rivera Sun has, once again, used her passion for nonviolence and her talent for putting thoughts into powerful words."
-Robin Wildman, Fifth Grade Teacher, Nonviolent Schools Movement, and Nonviolence Trainer

Praise for *The Lost Heir*
Book Two of the Ari Ara Series
by Rivera Sun

Going beyond dragon-slayers and sword-swingers, *The Lost Heir* blends fantasy and adventure with social justice issues in an unstoppable story that will make you cheer! Mariana Capital is in an uproar. Ari Ari, a half-wild orphan, has been discovered to be the long-lost daughter of the King of the Desert and the Queen of Mariana. As the heir to two thrones, Ari Ara is thrust into a world of nobles and street urchins, warriors and merchants, high fashion and dangerous plots. The splendor dazzles her until the day she sneaks out to explore the city and makes a shocking discovery . . . the luxury of the nobles is built by the forced labor of her father's people.

"Ms. Sun has created a world filled with all the adventure and fun of mystics, martial arts, and magic contained in *The Hobbit*, *The Ring Trilogy*, and the *Harry Potter* series but with deeper messages. There are not enough superlatives to describe this series!" - Brenda Duffy, Retired Teacher

"During times when so many of us, especially the young, are still figuring out how to make this planet more just and livable, this book couldn't have come at a better time."
- Patrick Hiller, War Prevention Initiative

"A wonderful book! It's so rare to find exciting fiction for young people and adults that shows creative solutions to conflict."
- Heart Phoenix, River Phoenix Center for Peacebuilding

351

Praise for *The Adventures of Alaren*
by Rivera Sun

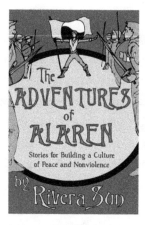

In a series of clever and creative escapades, the legendary folkhero Alaren rallies thousands of people to take bold and courageous action for peace. Weaving new epic tales from real-life inspirations, author Rivera Sun brings a new kind of hero to life.

Get ready to be inspired . . . and to share the joy with others!

The Adventures of Alaren offers perfect stories to teach peace at home, conflict resolution in the classroom, and nonviolence in faith and peace centers. Each fictional folktale includes a footnote on the real-life inspiration and discussion questions for classrooms and small groups. For readers of all ages, *The Adventures of Alaren* warms hearts, opens minds, and gives us ideas for waging peace!

Kids, parents, and teachers will love the adventures and escapades of this creative and clever peacebuilder! Add *The Adventures of Alaren* **to your library today!**

"Rivera Sun deserves an international audience and I hope she gets it." – Amber French, Editorial Advisor, International Center on Nonviolent Conflict

"Rivera Sun's creativity, wisdom, insight and joyful nonviolent activism for all ages fills me with awe and hope. If we were all to read her books the way we have read Harry Potter's, we would be well on our way to sending a different message to our children." – Veronica Pelicaric, Pace e Bene/Campaign Nonviolence

Praise for Rivera Sun's
The Dandelion Insurrection

A rare gem of a book, a must read, it charts the way forward in this time of turmoil and transformation." - Velcrow Ripper, director Occupy Love, Genie Award Winner

"When fear is used to control us, love is how we rebel!" Under a  gathering storm of tyranny, Zadie Byrd Gray whirls into the life of Charlie Rider and asks him to become the voice of the Dandelion Insurrection. With the rallying cry of life, liberty, and love, Zadie and Charlie fly across America leaving a wake of revolution in their path. Passion erupts. Danger abounds. The lives of millions hang by a thin thread of courage, but in the midst of the madness, the golden soul of humanity blossoms . . . and miracles start to unfold!

"This novel will not only make you want to change the world, it will remind you that you can." - Gayle Brandeis, author of *The Book of Dead Birds*, winner of the Bellwether Prize for Socially Engaged Fiction

"Close your eyes and imagine the force of the people and the power of love overcoming the force of greed and the love of power. Then read *The Dandelion Insurrection*. In a world where despair has deep roots, *The Dandelion Insurrection* bursts forth with joyful abandon." - Medea Benjamin, Co-founder of CodePink

"THE handbook for the coming revolution!" - Lo Daniels, Editor of Dandelion Salad

"The Dandelion Insurrection is an updated, more accurate, less fantastical *Brave New World* or *1984*." - David Swanson, author, peace and democracy activist

". . . a beautifully written book just like the dandelion plant itself, punching holes through the concept of corporate terror and inviting all to join in the insurrection." - Keith McHenry, Co-founder of the Food Not Bombs Movement

"Rivera Sun's *The Dandelion Insurrection* takes place in a dystopia just a hop, skip and jump away from today's society. A fundamentally political book with vivid characters and heart stopping action. It's a must and a great read." - Judy Rebick, activist and author of *Occupy This!*

Also Available!
The Dandelion Insurrection Study Guide
to Making Change Through Nonviolent Action

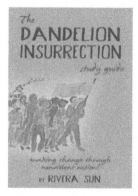

You'll love this lively, engaging journey into the heart of The Dandelion Insurrection's story of nonviolent action! Taking lessons off the page and into our lives, author Rivera Sun guides us through the skills and strategies that created the thrilling adventure of The Dandelion Insurrection. Using your favorite scenes from the book and also drawing on historical examples of nonviolent struggles, this study guide brings the story to life in an exciting way.

Praise for *The Roots of Resistance*

You're in for an exciting ride as incendiary writer Charlie Rider and the unforgettable Zadie Byrd Gray rise to meet the political challenges flung at them from all sides. Freedom and equality loom just out of reach as the outraged corporate oligarchy scrambles to take back power after the Dandelion Insurrection's successful nonviolent revolution. Everyone from schoolteachers to whistleblowers leaps into action to help them confront the forces of corrupt politics. But the struggle turns volatile when an armed group called the Roots shows up. They claim to be protecting the movement . . . but who do they really serve?

"If you loved Starhawk's *Fifth Sacred Thing*, if you loved recently-departed Ursula K. LeGuin's *The Dispossessed*, if you admire the spirit of the Standing Rock Water Protectors, you will drink in this must-read page-turner . . . an epic story that will move your spirit, bringing tears to your eyes and healing to your soul." – Rosa Zubizarreta, Author of *From Conflict to Creative Collaboration*

"Rivera Sun always gifts us with usefully creative fiction. Her *Roots of Resistance* – the second novel of her Dandelion Trilogy – offers an inspiring story to help guide love-based strategic change efforts . . . . It takes a storyteller like Rivera Sun who inspires us to rise to the challenge as her characters do, because her stories tell us how."
– Tom Atlee, Co-Intelligence Institute.

Reader Praise for Rivera Sun's
Steam Drills, Treadmills, and Shooting Stars

Steam Drills, Treadmills, and Shooting Stars is a story about people just like you, filled with the audacity of hope and fueled by the passion of unstoppable love. The ghost of folk hero John Henry haunts Jack Dalton, a corporate lawyer for Standard Coal as Henrietta Owens, activist and mother, wakes up the nation with some tough-loving truth about the environment, the economy, justice, and hope. Pressures mount as John Henry challenges Jack to stand up to the steam drills of contemporary America . . . before it's too late.

"This book is a gem and I'm going to put it in my jewelry box!"

"It 'dips your head in a bucket of truth'."

"This is not a page turner . . . it stops you in your tracks and makes you revel in the beauty of the written word."

"Epic, mythic . . .it's like going to church and praying for the salvation of yourself and your people and your country."

"Controversial, political, and so full of love."

"Partway through reading, I realized I was participating in a historical event. This book has changed me and will change everyone who reads it."

"I am sixty-two years old, and I cried for myself, my neighbors, our country and the earth. I cried and am so much better for it. I would recommend this book to everyone."

Praise for Rivera Sun's *Billionaire Buddha*

BILLIONAIRE BUDDHA

A NOVEL BY
RIVERA SUN

From fabulous wealth to unlimited blessings, the price of enlightenment may bankrupt billionaire Dave Grant. Emotionally destitute in the prime of his career, he searches for love and collides with Joan Hathaway. The encounter rattles his soul and unravels his world. Capitalism, property, wealth, mansions: his notions of success crumble into dust. From toasting champagne on top of the world to swigging whiskey with bums in the gutter, Dave Grant's journey is an unforgettable ride that leaves you cheering!

".. . inspirational and transformational! An enjoyable read for one's heart and soul."
-Chuck Collins, senior scholar, Institute for Policy Studies; co-author with Bill Gates Sr. of 'Wealth and Our Commonwealth'

". . . inspiring a skeptic is no easy task and Rivera Sun manages to do so, gracefully, convincingly, and admirably."
- Casey Dorman, Editor-in-Chief, Lost Coast Review

"People, if you haven't gotten your copy of *Billionaire Buddha* yet, you are letting a rare opportunity slip through your fingers. It's that good."
- Burt Kempner, screenwriter, producer and author of children's books

"This is the kind of book that hits you in the gut and makes you stop and think about what you just read."
- Rob Garvey, reader

"A clear and conscious look at our times and the dire need for a real change to heart based living."
- Carol Ranellone, reader